Screaming at the Window

The True Story of Blanche Monnier's
25 Years of Imprisonment by her Family

by R J Dent

KERNPUNKT PRESS

Editor: Patrick Parks

Cover art: Edvard Munch, Symbolic Study (1893)

ISBN-13 979-8-9865233-9-2

KERNPUNKT Press
Hamilton, New York 13346

Contents

Preface

In one way, this book is not an original piece of work; it is a reconstruction and a retelling of a true case of imprisonment that occurred at the end of the nineteenth century. In another way, it is the arrangement of the materials and information, along with the translation of the original French newspaper reports and trial transcripts which imbues this story with any originality it might have. It may also be the first time a full-length non-fiction account of Blanche Monnier's imprisonment has been told to English readers.

Based on details and information reported in contemporaneous newspaper reports, in a handful of books, and on several websites and blogs, Screaming at the Window is the true and tragic story of Blanche Monnier, the young woman who became known throughout France as 'The Prisoner of Poitiers' (La Séquestrée de Poitiers').

Just before her twenty-fifth birthday, Blanche was imprisoned in an upstairs room by her mother and her brother for twenty-five years.

In May 1901, an anonymous letter alerted the police to the fact that Blanche Monnier, the daughter of Louise, an aristocratic mother, and Émile, a former dean of the faculty of letters, was imprisoned in a completely dark room with padlocked shutters.

According to the letter, Blanche had been confined by her parents and her brother for twenty-five years. When the police found Blanche, she was half-starved, sedated and naked.

The victim's mother and brother were arrested and charged with kidnapping with violence, and criminal confinement with aggravating circumstances.

This is Blanche Monnier's story.

Part One:
Liberty

An Anonymous Letter
(May 1901)

22nd May, 1901 (morning)

On May 22nd, 1901, Léon Bulot, the Attorney General of Paris, received an anonymous letter, dated May 19th:

> Dear Monsieur Prosecutor,
>
> I am writing to you on behalf of a wrongfully-imprisoned person, in order to make a very serious accusation. There is a house, 21 Rue de la Visitation, Poitiers, which is owned by an old, widowed lady named Madame Monnier. She lives with her daughter whom she has imprisoned for 25 years. The window of the daughter's room is shuttered and padlocked and only one person, an old maid, has permission to enter that room.
>
> The imprisoned woman is deliberately kept naked, sedated, starved and in a state of repulsive uncleanliness.
>
> In the name of humanity, I ask you to use your legal powers to free this woman. If you refuse, I will go to the Department of Justice so that that old criminal can go and rot in prison as she should.
>
> A loyal, but angry citizen.

On receipt of the anonymous letter, which had arrived with the morning mail, Attorney General Bulot began to collect and collate information about the Monnier woman living at 21 Rue de la Visitation. The letter specifically mentioned a crime, possibly several crimes. Therefore, in accordance with French law, Monsieur Bulot had to have the reported crime investigated. By late afternoon he had the following information:

- 21 Rue de la Visitation was a very large three-storey, twenty-room house owned by Madame Louise Léonide Monnier, nee Demarconnay, born on November 28th, 1825, which made her 75 years old.

• Madame Monnier was descended from royalty. Her father, Louis Demarconnay was the son of Louise's grandmother, Therese Demayne, the daughter of Louise's great-grandmother, Magdeleine Girardin de La Rousseliere, and Magdeleine's father, Louise's great-great grandfather, was Henri Girardin de La Fond, the son of Philippe II of France.

• Madame Monnier was a widow; she had been married to Émile Monnier, Professor of Rhetoric at the Faculty of Letters and Dean of the Lycée de Poitiers. Émile Monnier had died in April 1882.

• Émile and Louise Monnier had had two children, Marcel, born in February 1848, and Blanche, born in March 1849, both of whom were now adults. Marcel was a Doctor of Law and had been the sub-prefect of Puget Théniers. He was currently unemployed and lived on a pension his mother paid him. He was married and lived with his wife (Angèle) and daughter (Dolores) in a house opposite his mother's house in Rue de la Visitation. The house he lived in rent-free with his family was owned by his mother.

• With regards to Blanche, there were several different accounts as to what had happened to her and where she was. According to the various reports the Attorney General was able to collate, Blanche Monnier had either gone to a boarding school in England or Scotland and had decided to stay there; or she had gone to a boarding school in England or Scotland and while there had contacted tuberculosis (consumption) and died; or she had begun a clandestine relationship with an older man, had become pregnant, had the pregnancy terminated and had died during the process; or she had survived the pregnancy, had given birth to a healthy child and was living with distant relatives somewhere in the French countryside; or she had survived the pregnancy, had given birth to a stillborn child and was living with distant relatives in the French countryside; or that she had eloped with the older man and was living anonymously somewhere in France or Belgium; or she had gone mad after her grandmother

6

and then her father had died and she had been confined in an attic room for the safety of herself and for others; or she had started posing naked at her bedroom window flaunting her body and making obscene gestures to any passer-by, especially the soldiers queuing outside the Cabaret Rivaud on the opposite side of Rue de la Visitation.

23rd May, 1901 (8.30am)

The following morning, Attorney General Bulot contacted Commissioner Bucheton, the Central Commissioner of Police of Poitiers, and gave the Commissioner a series of orders, along with some very careful instructions. He ordered the police commissioner to initiate an immediate investigation.

23rd May, 1901 (2.30pm)

It was two-thirty in the afternoon on 23rd May, 1901, when Commissioner Bucheton, accompanied by a police sergeant from the Poitiers police force, rang the doorbell of 21 Rue de la Visitation.

One of the two maids, whom Madame Monnier employed, Juliette Dupuis, answered the bell.

Bucheton: *Madame Louise Monnier?*

Dupuis: *Madame does not receive visitors, Monsieur. She is bedridden.*

Bucheton: *Please tell Madame Monnier that I am Commissioner Bucheton, the Central Commissioner of Poitiers police force and that I wish to speak to her immediately.*

The maid then went upstairs. She returned a few moments later.

Dupuis: *Monsieur, Madame says to please address your request to her son, Monsieur Marcel Monnier, who lives in the house opposite.*

The Commissioner then knocked on the door of the house opposite, the home of Marcel Monnier. After a while, a maid answered.

Bucheton: *May I speak to Monsieur Marcel Monnier?*

Maid: *I'm sorry, Monsieur, but Monsieur Monnier is unwell and is unable to receive visitors.*

Bucheton: *It's a very strange coincidence that everyone seems unwell in these two houses. Tell Monsieur Monnier that*

I am the Central Commissioner, and that I must speak to him immediately regarding a very serious matter.

The maid showed the Commissioner into the house. He was announced to Marcel Monnier.

Monnier: *Yes?*

Bucheton: *I have received a letter which accuses your mother, Madame Louise Monnier, of having confined your sister Blanche, for twenty-five years, on a bed in the middle of an upstairs room that is full of rubbish, rotting food and general filth. The letter states that Mademoiselle Blanche is deliberately kept naked, unwashed and uncared for, and that the room window is shuttered and padlocked. Indeed, when I arrived at the house, I did notice, on the second floor, a window whose shutters are closed and secured from the outside with a chain and padlock. So, would you now take me to your sister?*

Monnier: *Who are you?*

Bucheton: *I am Commissioner Bucheton, the Central Commissioner of Poitier's Police Force. You are fully aware of who I am, because your maid just announced me.*

Monnier: *Then let me say this: whatever you have been told is a terrible slander. I find the fact that you're taking this far-fetched accusation seriously to be very peculiar. Besides, my mother and my sister live together in a house other than mine. Respectful of my mother's wishes, who is very much the mistress of her own home, I do not interfere in any way with her affairs.*

Bucheton: *That may be so, but whatever the case may be, I would like to see your sister for myself first-hand. The best way to prove your lack of involvement and your innocence in this matter, Monsieur, is to let me see your sister, so that I may talk to her and ascertain the truth.*

Monnier: *I cannot let you see her without first calling the family doctor. My sister has been suffering from a pernicious fever for more than ten years and she is not supposed to receive any visitors. Only the doctor will be able to determine if you can enter her room without upsetting or distressing her.*

Bucheton: *Could I have your name and your age, Monsieur?*

Monnier: *I am Marcel Monnier. I'm fifty-three years old. And let me inform you of something else: I'm a Doctor of Law and a former sub-prefect.*

The policeman accompanying the Commissioner made a few notes.

Bucheton: *And your sister?*

Monnier: *My sister Blanche is fifty-two years old. She has not been imprisoned nor has she been neglected. I go to see her myself several times a day. There have been quite a few occasions on which I've seen her two or three times in one day. That's not unusual. Therefore, I protest very strongly at this denunciation of my mother and I shall be referring your accusations to the Public Prosecutor.*

Bucheton: *Monsieur Monnier, I can assure you that the simplest way to negate any of these 'accusations' is to take me to Mademoiselle Monnier's room without further delay.*

Monnier: *I don't see how that will do anything to negate such vile accusations.*

Bucheton: *As I said, when I stood outside your mother's house, I happened to observe that the shutters of a room on the second floor were held closed by a chain which is padlocked. From the outside! Such a precaution is highly unusual and obviously, it gives some plausibility to the accusations made in the letter.*

Monnier: *Very well, I will take you to see my sister. But first, I have to obtain my mother's permission, as she, naturally, decides everything in her own home.*

Accompanied by the Commissioner and the police sergeant, Marcel Monnier went into his mother's house. He went into her room and spoke to her. He informed her of everything the Commissioner had said. Madame Monnier hesitated for a long time, and then, at the Commissioner's insistence, finally acquiesced.

Monsieur Marcel Monnier led the two policemen to a door on a second floor of the house. The door was closed. Marcel Monnier tried the handle and the door was locked. He looked at the Commissioner and the Sergeant in turn, and then made a gesture of helplessness.

Bucheton: *You have a key to this door, so please open it. Unless, of course, you would prefer us to break it down.*

After a few moments of hesitation, Marcel Monnier took a key from his jacket pocket and put it in the lock. He turned the key and pushed the door open.

Émile and Louise Monnier

Émile Monnier

The father of the imprisoned woman, Blanche Monnier, was Charles Émile Monnier, or Émile, as he preferred to be known, He was born in Amiens on March 12th, 1820 to Charles-Estelle Monnier, a hairdresser, a native of Petit-Andelys (Eure), and Hippolyte-Firmine-Sophie Lavallard, the daughter of a wig maker. The family lived at 7 Rue des Sergents in Amiens, where the hairdressing salon was also located, in the old quarter, between the cathedral, the town hall and the courthouse. Although the family's background was humble, the Monnier parents had ambitions for their son.

At the Royal College of Amiens, Émile proved himself to be a bright and able student. He passed his baccalaureate, on 18th August, 1840 which enabled him, as a scholarship student, to attend the École Normale Supérieure, located in the former Collège du Plessis, Rue Saint-Jacques in Paris.

In September of 1843, after graduating from the École Normale Supérieure and obtaining a degree in literature from the Sorbonne, Émile Monnier was appointed associate professor at the Collège Royal de La Rochelle, where he taught several second-year classes.

The following year he was given a teaching job at the Royal College of Poitiers. Émile Monnier was twenty-four years old when he arrived in Poitiers. He lived on Rue des Trois-Piliers, which was one street away from the college.

In 1845, he met Mademoiselle Louise Demarconnay, and in 1847, he was made a full professor.

The inspector of the academy who observed Émile Monnier in 1849 described him as 'a young, reasonably capable teacher. He has a methodical mind, his lectures are clear, and have precision. He holds the attention of his class and has authority over his students. His criticism is sufficiently constructive. The students work hard and he gets good results.'

Several of Émile Monnier's students went on to distinguish themselves in brilliant careers. Edmond Ernoul became a lawyer, and then the legitimist deputy of the

Vienne and Keeper of the Seals in the ministry of Broglie in 1873. Amable Ricard became a lawyer, a prefect, then the republican deputy of Deux-Sèvres, and then the Minister of the Interior in 1876. François Allain-Targé went on to become the Republican deputy of the Seine. Émile Faguet became a literary critic and member of the Académie française. Arthur Ranc became the deputy and then the Republican senator of the Seine.

Louise Monnier

When Mademoiselle Louise Léonide Demarconnay met Émile Monnier in 1845, she was five years his junior, and was immediately attracted to the quiet, reserved and studious young man. Louise Demarconnay was small in stature and rather stout. In France, she would have been described as 'boulotte'. She was also the only daughter of a city stockbroker, which was no small advantage for a young college teacher, especially one with no useful contacts or associates in the city – and with very little in the way of savings.

Louise Demarconnay's grandfather, Charles Demarconnay, was a judicial officer in Rue des Basses-Treilles, Poitiers. On 15th November 1796, he had married Thérèse-Rosalie Demayré, daughter of a notary of Jaulnay, and three children had been born of the marriage. The eldest son, Victor, worked in the same profession as his father in Vouillé, a large rural village of which he had become mayor. Louis, the youngest, had first been a lawyer and then had risen in the social hierarchy by buying a stockbroker's office. On February 7th, 1825, Louis Demarconnay had married Louise Pauline Kleiber, the daughter of a music teacher.

According to the few testimonies that have been collected about her, the young Madame Louise Demarconnay, nee Kleiber, who would later become Blanche's beloved grandmother, was a pious, charitable, and benevolent woman, indifferent to her tenuous noble ancestry and kind to her servants, a fact which did not mean she was weak; she ran her household efficiently and properly. She had also inherited from her father a passionate love for music and she played the piano with some ability. The two spouses therefore were very different, but they complemented each other perfectly. They lived for a while in a small house with a large garden, located at 11, Rue de la Celle.

On November 28th, 1825, in that unremarkable household, their daughter, Louise, the woman who would later marry Émile Monnier, was born. Her parents named her Louise Léonide Demarconnay, which was her mother's name.

Her parents were upper-middle class and they made sure she was well-educated. She was taught by several very good private tutors. Nothing else is known about her childhood or her teenage years. At the age of twenty, the woman who would become Louise Monnier was a forceful young woman lacking any obvious charm or grace. She did, however, have delusions of grandeur due to a number of her ancestors' fortuitous marriages which tenuously linked the Demarconnay family to the Demayres, who in turn were linked by marriage to the Girardins, who were the French royal family. This link to royalty by marriage went to Louise Monnier's head and she firmly believed that she herself was an aristocrat.

As she had a strong personality and an iron will, she was able to impose that will on her parents and marry the man she chose. For his part, Émile Monnier readily accepted that his wife was, according to all accounts, authoritarian, strong-willed and stern in demeanour.

Arthur Ranc's parents were in the same social circle as the Demarconnay family and Ranc's mother told her son at the time of the marriage: 'I pity your poor teacher, for he has married a little shrike'.

Her words were prophetic, for in the years that followed, Madame Monnier dominated her husband in the same way she seemed to dominate everyone who entered her sphere of influence.

On the eve of the wedding of Émile Monnier and Louise Demarconnay, on July 7th, 1846, the marriage contract was signed in the home of the bride's parents, in front of the notary, Maitre Henri-Antoine Bert, of Rue des Grandes-Écoles in Poitiers. The Demarconnay family was present in its entirety, but, on Émile Monnier's side, only his father had made the trip; his mother, who had remained in Amiens, had given power of attorney to her husband. Émile's brother, Charles-Éric Monnier, was also absent. He was unable to attend as he was the director of a small theatre abroad.

Émile's father sold his hairdressing salon on Rue des Sergents, in Amiens and moved into a beautiful house in the Porte de Beauvais district, south of the episcopal and administrative centre of the city. In the notarial deed, the former hairdresser declared himself 'businessman/owner', but he was a working-class man who had managed to rise to a higher social status without having acquired the relevant manners or savoir-vivre.

On the occasion of the marriage of their offspring, it was a habit for parents to make donations to help the newly-weds during their first years together. From his parents, Émile Monnier received a dowry of twenty thousand francs, paid over five years, with interest of five percent per year. For their part, Louise's parents gave their daughter a dowry of forty thousand francs, half of which was paid in cash and the remainder to be paid six months after the future spouses had ceased to live with the donors. Louis Demarconnay and his wife undertook to house, feed, heat and light the couple's household for a year after the day of the marriage.

The young college teacher had married an heiress. The signing of the notarial deed was followed, as was customary, by the contract dinner. The next morning, the exchange of contracts took place at the town hall in the presence of Doctor Arsène Orillard, first deputy mayor. This was followed by the religious wedding ceremony, which was celebrated at St. Peter's Cathedral, one hour after the civil wedding. The witnesses for Émile Monnier were the rector of the Delalleau Academy and Thomas Bréard, a professor at the college. The witnesses for Louise Monnier were Jean-François Grilliet, the former Presiding Judge of the commercial court, and her grandfather, Charles Demarconnay.

The general consensus was that all of the family's money came from the Demarconnays. This was not entirely accurate, since Émile Monnier had received twenty thousand francs as a dowry from his parents. He also had his teacher's salary, which was added to the household's income that was generated from the properties the Demarconnays rented out. There was a significant difference in the husband and wife's attitude to money; it was a difference that everyone around them noticed. Ultimately, it was a difference that would go on to ruin several lives.

For Louise Monnier, it was money and its acquisition that was her motivation in all things. It was money that caused the initial issues between the newly-married husband and wife, just as it would later cause serious problems between Madame Monnier and her son, as well as having tragic consequences for her daughter Blanche.

The 'shrike' was also a despotic and greedy woman with an indomitable will. Not only did she make herself the sole authority for all household responsibilities, but she also had an intractable character. Several witnesses portrayed her as one of those domestic tyrants before whom everyone and everything had to bend and yield. And in the Monnier household, everyone bent and yielded to Louise Monnier's will. Louise Monnier no doubt grew accustomed to being obeyed.

It would be another fifteen years before someone challenged, flouted, ridiculed, and disobeyed Louise Monnier's authority. Once that happened, Louise Monnier responded with calm, cunningly-planned and calculated brutality.

Marcel Monnier (1)

The Monniers' son, Marie Louis Charles Monnier was born on February 27th, 1848, and he was christened in the local church the day after his birth. His godparents were his maternal grandfather Louis Demarconnay and his maternal great-aunt, Marie-Rosalie Malherbe. His family immediately started to refer to him as Marcel, the name he used throughout his life.

Until he reached school age, little is known about Marcel Monnier's first few years. Under the Second Empire, the children from upper-middle class families were raised and educated at home. It was from their parents or tutors that they learned the first rudiments of reading, writing and mathematics.

At the age of nine, Marcel Monnier began to attend the Imperial High School, where he studied Latin, because it was believed to elevate thought and demonstrate a nobility of style worthy of being imitated. The young Monnier was a diligent student; by the end of the 1858-1859 school year he had won first prize in Latin, second prize in history, and third prize in French grammar and classical recitation.

Marcel Monnier suffered from profound shyness, due to the fact that he was small in size and short-sighted. In the playground, he did not know how to defend himself and quickly became the butt of aggressive pranks played on him by some of the more belligerent pupils. Several of his peers also complained that he habitually neglected his personal hygiene, which caused him to smell and many stayed away from him because of that, which reinforced his loneliness.

In the autumn of 1861, Marcel Monnier entered the fourth grade of the Imperial Lycee. His school work earned him a second prize for excellence: he distinguished himself in Latin verse, for which he won the first prize. Four years later he was a student in his father's rhetoric class, and he received a fifth award for excellence. Paternal influence may have played a role in this, but the results he obtained are comparable to those he collected the previous year and the following year in the philosophy class. Marcel Monnier was of average intelligence, with the same understanding of literary culture that anyone with a reasonably good memory could acquire through reading diligently. However, he generally seemed to lack initiative and ambition and had no real skills, nor any vocational drive. The impression he gave was of being very naïve and having poor judgement.

In 1866 he passed the baccalaureate and at the beginning of the academic year was enrolled as a student at the Poitiers Faculty of Law.

Blanche Monnier (1)

Marie Léonide Pauline Monnier was born on March 1st, 1849, and was christened on the 3rd of March in the same church her brother had been christened in. Her godfather was her paternal grandfather Charles Monnier, who due to his infirmity had stayed at home and was represented by Charles-Jean Malherbe, Blanche's maternal great-uncle. Her godmother was her maternal grandmother, Louise Pauline Demarconnay.

Marie Léonide Pauline Monnier would be known as Blanche Monnier for the rest of her life.

Apart from a few testimonies by maids, very little is known about Blanche's early years, or her education. Unlike the records pertaining to Marcel Monnier's childhood, there are no school records for Blanche. The main reason for this is that girls from affluent backgrounds were not sent to primary schools where they might meet working class children. Consequently, Blanche was educated within the family home, being privately tutored from the age of five until the age of twelve. Her lessons included reading, writing, mathematics and geography. She also had piano lessons with a local music teacher, Mademoiselle Gilbert.

Due to the way Louise Monnier controlled and ruled over her household, Blanche's girlhood was subject to strict maternal vigilance; she was expected to obey a whole host of very rigid and precise rules pertaining to conduct and comportment, and any contravention of those rules resulted in swift retribution and severe punishment.

Fortunately for Blanche, her mother's simultaneous emotional aridity and the alacrity and harshness with which she punished the slightest breach of her rules was tempered by the kindness and indulgence of her grandmother, who provided some of the maternal love that Louise Monnier was emotionally unable to provide.

Marie Fazy

The Demarconnays had several servants, so they allocated a maid, Marie Fazy, to the Monnier household. Marie Fazy, nee Poinet, the wife of Pierre-Ange Fazy and the sister of Modeste Bourliaud, entered the service of the Demarconnay family after the marriage of Émile and Louise Monnier.

Marie Anne Pauline Poinet was born on October 15th, 1834 in Courtiou, an isolated farm located in the town of Rouillé, a large rural village about thirty kilometres south-west of Poitiers. She was the fourth child in a large family of Protestant farmers and like many rural girls, Marie had never been to school and remained illiterate all her life. At the age of seventeen, she found a position working for the Demarconnay family, where one of her sisters, Modeste Poinet, soon joined her.

By the time they moved to 21 Rue de la Visitation, the Monnier family employed three domestic staff: two house-maids and a cook, a number that was not unusual in affluent upper-middle class households.

One maid was employed to care for Louis Demarconnay until his death in 1883.

The relationship between the Demarconnays, the Monniers and the Fazys was an unusual one; Louis Demarconnay, Émile Monnier and his two children, Marcel and Blanche were witnesses at Marie Fazy's wedding and signed the parish register in Saint-Porchaire when Marie had married a domestic named Pierre-Ange Fazy on July 2nd, 1860.

When Marie Fazy's sister, Modeste Poinet, married François Bourliaud in Saint-Porchaire church on 23rd October 1871, Madame Monnier and Blanche, then twenty-two years old, were invited to the wedding and signed the parish register as witnesses. It was Émile Monnier who arranged for Bourliaud to have a few days leave from the Orléans Railway Company.

Émile Monnier and his wife clearly held the Poinet sisters in high regard and trusted them implicitly. This goes some way to explaining why they appointed Marie Fazy to be Blanche's maid. It is also easier to understand why

Madame Monnier, after the death of her husband, preferred to entrust the care of her Le Pilet estate to François Bourliaud and Pierre Picherault, the husbands of the Poinet sisters.

Marie Poinet had first been hired as a housemaid, then she had become a cook. When she was twenty-six, she married Pierre-Ange Fazy. Once she was married, her life did not change in any noticeable way. She remained in the service of the Demarconnays and Monniers, and her husband continued to work for Amirault, a wine and liquor merchant at 41 Rue des Trois-Piliers, until he left there in order to work for a grocer, Moreau-Chabot. Pierre-Ange slept every night in the maid's room that the couple occupied, on the third floor of the house on Rue de la Visitation. As time passed, the Fazy couple began to see very little of each other, especially during the summer months when the Monniers holidayed at Le Pilet. If Pierre-Ange Fazy wanted to spend any time with his wife, then he had to travel to Le Pilet on Sundays and public holidays. This may go some way to explaining why the couple did not have children. When Pierre-Ange died on 13th April 1887, Marie Fazy had long since become a surrogate mother to Blanche Monnier.

Modeste Poinet took a different employment route to her sister. She left maid's service to work in the same household as her husband, François Bourliaud. The couple settled first in Bordeaux, then in Luxé, in the Charente, and then returned to Poitiers to live in a small house on route de Biard in the suburb of Montmidi. This was an area in which many railway employees lived because of how close it was to the locomotive depot.

Whenever she visited her sister, Modeste Bourliaud always took care to politely greet her former employer, or to ask about her if Madame Monnier did not want to receive visitors.

It was not long before Marie Fazy became an important and integral part of the Monnier household. The robust and energetic country girl inspired confidence in her employers. Although she was very outspoken, as some cooks are, she was also well-respected because she was very good at her job and seemed able to produce a whole variety of delicious dishes at short notice, despite working on a very tight budget. Unlike a lot of cooks who are temperamental or have volatile personalities, she always remained calm and worked efficiently. She always seemed to know how to pre-pare any of the dishes she was asked to create.

The Monnier children and the cook had a close rela-tionship based on affinity and tenderness. Marie Fazy spoiled both of them by preparing French toast, cakes and berlingots.

Later, when Blanche was in her twenties and initially confined to her room, Marie Fazy made sure a maid took up at least one meal a day for her.

21 Rue de la Visitation

On 21st January 1859, Émile Monnier and his wife, using money from their respective dowries, jointly purchased 21 Rue de la Visitation. This was the building at the corner of Rue de la Visitation (today Rue Arthur Ranc) and Rue des Basses-Treilles (today Rue de la Marne), adjacent to the house owned by Louis Demarconnay.

Together, the buildings were imposing. At right angles to each other on the corner of the two streets, the two main buildings formed one enormous structure that was three storeys in height; as there were no windows in the walls that faced the public road, the structure had the appearance of a fortress.

The other side of the Monnier's house was lower and built into a recess, and it was separated from Rue de la Visitation by a courtyard and a boundary wall surmounted with an iron railing. There was another entrance via a discreet but solid gate in the wall in Rue des Basses-Treilles.

As much as the facades dominating the two streets were austere, the rooms opening onto the garden through French windows were pleasant. The ground floor included a large living room overlooking a large vestibule, a smoking room, a dining room and two kitchens, both with pantries.

Below ground each house had a cellar, a scullery and store rooms.

Both upper floors were occupied by six bedrooms, four of which had adjoining closets and bathrooms, and two of which had adjoining offices. In addition, there were attic rooms and maids' quarters under both roofs.

There was comfort and luxury everywhere; the rooms were furnished according to the taste of the Second Empire, with mahogany furniture, heavy drapes and dark wallpaper.

Outside, surrounded on all sides by a high wall and out of sight of the house due to screening shrubs and trees, the pleasure garden was both secluded and attractive. It was well maintained, with gravel walkways, shrubberies, boxwood borders surrounding flower beds, a stable which was being used as a lumber room, a laundry room, a hayloft, a cistern, greenhouses and sunrooms and arbours and bowers in the gardens.

By marrying the daughter of a stockbroker who was descended by marriage from royalty, Émile Monnier had risen socially. From humble beginnings, he had reached a point where he was well-respected and highly regarded in the city, especially since he had been appointed faculty dean. With his wife, his children, and his Demarconnay in-laws, to whom he owed much of his success, Émile Monnier led a simple and conventional life in the large, imposing-looking house on Rue de la Visitation.

Le Pilet

Eight kilometres north-west from Poitiers was a property that Blanche and Marcel's grandfather, Louis Demarconnay had bought. It was named 'Le Pilet', and the whole family loved spending time there. It was a particularly beautiful property and had been built on a large piece of land.

The building was rectangular and plain-looking. Access to it was through an arched carriage gateway into a walled courtyard. The only ornamentation was a virgin vine that climbed the building's facade and framed the windows. There was an ornate pleasure garden behind the house, which was very well-maintained.

On the right side, separated from the main building, was an outbuilding with a furnace in its attic that could only be accessed by a ladder. On the left was a small cottage inhabited by Auguste Joubert and his wife, Rosalie, sharecroppers employed by the Monniers and the Demarconnays as resident caretakers, responsible for the maintenance of the property, the grounds, the vines and the fruit trees.

The buildings were located in the middle of a seven-acre piece of land enclosed within tall stone walls, and included arable land, two small woods, fruit trees, meadows, an arbour and a pond. Outside this vast walled enclosure, there was a small hillside meadow planted with poplar trees. From the top of the hill there was a view of Auxances.

Every Saturday and at the beginning of every holiday, a cab – the first of which had just been introduced to Poitiers – carrying the Monnier and Demarconnay families, arrived in Migné, then trundled slowly up the narrow road that led to Le Pilet, where it entered the courtyard through the carriage entrance and stopped in front of the house. The two children immediately scrambled out the carriage and ran off to play, while the rest of the Demarconnay and Monnier families alighted from the carriage in a more dignified manner.

To the children, Le Pilet was a vast space for them to enjoy unsupervised games. It was an enclave that offered them all they could imagine in their wildest dreams as they explored every corner of the vast property.

Alone, together, or sometimes in the company of the

sharecropper's children, Marcel and Blanche played hide and seek in the barns, attics and stables. They would pick strawberries, raspberries or currants from the vegetable garden, or they would pick cherries, plums, and grapes and eat them until they made themselves sick.

Blanche loved animals. There was a cat in the Poitiers house and when Blanche was at Le Pilet, she never tired of watching the farmyard poultry, the rabbits in their hutches, or the goat that was tethered to a stake by a long rope. She enjoyed clambering up onto the sharecropper's mule and taking a donkey ride around the grounds. She had other ways of amusing herself, some of which were supervised: hopscotch, taking turns on the swing that hung from a thick branch of a tree, the building of huts and 'dens', dressing up and putting on disguises, fishing with nets on the banks of the Auxance. The children sometimes climbed over fences and went on adventures in the woods.

In the countryside, during the holidays, Émile Monnier was able to be a little closer to his children. Free from faculty duties and responsibilities, he took Marcel and Blanche for walks through the woods and along by the river. He answered their questions and was always ready to listen to their comments on the flora and fauna they observed. The children played in the meadows and, in the evening, brought back to the house bouquets of flowers from the fields. The flowers Blanche picked were pompom roses, carnations and larks' feet.

At the bottom of the Le Pilet garden, hidden amongst the thick foliage of a copse of large trees, there was a small chapel built with a wrought iron frame and frosted plate-glass walls. Inside was an altar on which were arranged two statues in plaster painted in bright colours, in the Sulpician style, one representing Saint Joseph carrying the baby Jesus in his arms, the other the Blessed Virgin, her arms by her sides, her hands open, in the same attitude as on the Miraculous Medal. Vases of blue opaline and white porcelain with gold leaf festoons held bouquets of flowers.

In front of the altar, there was a wooden prayer-desk to kneel at to make devotions. The chapel had been built at the request of Madame Demarconnay, who was very devout. She often meditated there and did not fail to take her grandchildren there to recite a dozen rosaries. Although the

Le Pilet chapel had not been built inside a cave or a natural shelter, as was usual for family chapels, the Monnier family referred to it as a cave out of reverence to the Lourdes grotto.

Le Pilet was a place of immense happiness and idyllic wonders for Blanche and for Marcel Monnier. Years later, when all of the Monnier properties were auctioned, Marcel Monnier bought Le Pilet and used it as his holiday residence for the rest of his life.

Marcel Monnier (2)

In 1868, Marcel Monnier, then twenty-year-old, went before the military selection board, as did all the young men of his class from Poitiers. Marcel Monnier was one metre sixty-two tall; despite his small size he could have been declared 'fit for active service' because only young men less than one meter fifty-five in height were exempt from military service according to the law pertaining to conscription. He immediately informed the board of his myopia, which was duly noted by the military doctor. The board, after a short discussion, took the decision to reject him for active service based on 'weakness of eyesight'.

Marcel Monnier continued his studies at the Faculty of Law. He obtained his licentiate degree in 1869 and immediately took the Oath of Attorney before the Court of Appeal. Although he regularly mentioned that he was an 'advocate of the court', the title was purely honorary and had no responsibilities, powers or salary attached to it.

Marcel Monnier decided against taking any legal training; consequently, he was never registered on the Tableau de l'Ordre, which alone confers the rights and prerogatives attached to the profession of lawyer. The young student, however, had a penchant for criminal law.

On 29th November 1872, at three o'clock in the afternoon, in the faculty's public record room, Marcel Monnier defended his doctoral thesis. Its title was: *Complicity in Roman Law and French Law*. The examiners included Dean Alphonse Lepetit, professor of commercial law, who was the chair, Pervinquière, professor of Roman law, Arnault de la Ménardière and Guiron Lecourtois, professors of civil code, and Jean-Hugues Normand, an associate professor.

With legal precision and meticulous attention to detail, the candidate addressed the question of complicity in Roman law, in old French law, in the penal code of 1791, and in the penal code of 1810. He carefully drew a distinction between the offender, the co-perpetrators and the accomplice, so as to identify the facts that constituted complicity. He also explicated its application to specific cases of criminal association, including concealment, and crime against the internal and external security of the State. The great merit of his thesis was to oppose the articles of the penal code that equated the penalty of the accomplice with that of the main instigator. Instead, he advocated new theories that envisaged imposing on the accomplice a different and inferior penalty.

'The criminologists are divided into two very distinct camps, the supporters of the doctrine of assimilation and the supporters of the doctrine of distinction: the former are the religious observers of tradition [...], and they scrupulously follow the constant principles of our ancient law; the second are innovative, bolder, rejecting those respectable but out-dated remnants of ideas that have fallen from a social state that has disappeared, listening only to the voice of reason and the cry of humanity. This group founded the rational science of criminal law and showed the path that every wise and civilized nation must follow today. In the face of these two opposing theories, we cannot therefore hesitate for a moment in the choice that should be made; it is the system of distinction that must obviously prevail, because it alone is rational, it alone is fair... The requirements of public order, we must never forget, have a limit that cannot be exceeded: the just; beyond that, the right to punish ceased to exist.'

Marcel Monnier obtained his law doctorate and had his thesis copied and bound by a printer in Poitiers. His education was complete. He now had to decide on what he was going to do with his life.

Blanche Monnier (2)

Blanche Monnier took her first communion at the age of twelve. All of the Poitiers newspapers covered the event, so the first record regarding Blanche is from local newspaper reports of the communion service which took place on Sunday, May 26th, 1861, the day of the Holy Trinity, in the church of Saint-Porchaire in Poitiers.

Marcel and Blanche Monnier both took their first communion on that day. Marcel Monnier was thirteen years old. It was usual for children to take their first communion when they reached the age of twelve, but Madame Monnier, obsessively frugal, had forced her son to wait until Blanche was twelve so that the costs of the ceremony and the accompanying family meal would be reduced. The siblings had attended catechism classes twice a week for six months under the guidance of Canon Rouland, the parish priest, and his two vicars. After a week of prayer and the confession of sins, the day of the ceremony arrived.

Marcel Monnier was wearing a suit consisting of trousers, a waistcoat and a jacket in black serge. Around his left arm he wore an armband from which two strips of white silk ribbon hung.

Blanche wore a very simple, plain dress, a hat with a veil of white chiffon, with a wide belt, as recommended so as not to inspire vanity, but also, for the Monnier parents, in order to avoid unnecessary expense.

The Monnier siblings joined twenty-one boys and twenty girls who were also taking their first communion at Saint-Porchaire. The communicants' parents were from a variety of professions: masons, roofers, house painters, carpenters, blacksmiths, chefs, launderers, seamstresses. There were also the children of two faculty colleagues of Émile Monnier's: a mathematics teacher and a chemistry teacher. Families and friends of the communicants, all in their Sunday best, filled the church's two naves.

Red oriflammes with orange fringes and golden tassels hung between the church's central stone columns and the side walls. The religious service began and the ceremony was performed. After leaving Mass, Marcel and Blanche returned home with their parents and relatives. Lunch was served in the house on Rue de la Visitation and Marcel and Blanche were each given a gold watch as a communion gift.

Education for girls in France in the second half of the nineteenth century unfortunately became a battleground on which both state and church fought political battles for women's minds. The result was that both church and state became preoccupied with denying the other's place in schooling rather than advancing education for all girls.

The Marquis de Condorcet, a revolutionary philosopher, suggested in 1791 that instruction should be the same for women and men. More commonly, the champions of education for girls in this period envisioned the development of separate girls' schools, and a wide range of girls' schools emerged in the early nineteenth century in order to help young women assume these tasks more effectively within the private sphere.

In France, most middle-class institutions for girls were relatively small, privately run ventures where, for a fee, girls were given lessons in a relatively wide range of subjects: literature, history, geography, some natural sciences, foreign languages (but generally not Latin and Greek), and religion, as well as the indispensable female accomplishments: sewing, embroidery, painting, music, etc. Prior to state involvement, these institutions were run by religious orders, resulting in separate elementary girls' schools which were very successful, less as a result of state involvement than of religious initiatives.

The 1850 French Falloux Law required communes with a population of eight-hundred to open a separate school for girls, but even in the public sector religious teachers far outnumbered lay teachers: in 1863, seventy percent of the teachers in public elementary schools were nuns.

After her communion Blanche joined the Christian Union on Rue de la Psalette-Sainte-Radegonde (currently Rue Arthur de la Mauvinière). Founded in Lyon in 1630 by Madame de Pollalion, the Christian Union of Saint-Chaumond had been transferred to Paris, under the direction of Saint Vincent de Paul. Nuns of the Christian Union arrived in Poitiers in 1802 in Poitiers and the community was reconstituted in 1804 to teach the young girls from upper-middle class families. As in other educational institutions, the nuns of the Christian Union were primarily concerned with developing spirituality and piety. They also sought to prepare the young women for their role as wives, mothers, and mistresses of the house, with the hope that some of them would in turn have the religious vocation. The discipline was severe. In the different classes, the girls learned to maintain a conversation, to write beautiful letters and to keep accounts, which required sufficient knowledge of spelling, grammar and arithmetic. In addition, there were courses in history, geography, physics, natural sciences and an introduction to English. An important place in education was given to needlework and some of the arts. Students had to learn singing, piano and line drawing.

Blanche Monnier remained at the Christian Union for three years. She started the school year at the beginning of autumn in 1861, aged twelve, and left in June, 1864, aged fifteen. When she left, Blanche Monnier was, according to one witness, 'a charming, distinguished, intelligent teenager, endowed with real musical talent.'

Her father, keen to complete her education, wanted to give her a comprehensive understanding of literature and even undertook to teach her Greek. She continued to take piano lessons under the guidance of a music teacher, Mademoiselle Gilbert, and she seemed to have inherited a certain ability to play the instrument from her grandmother. Despite the unhappiness she felt due to her mother's authoritarian severity, Blanche began to lead a quiet life in the house on Rue de la Visitation.

Her parents expected little from her and their lack of interference in her life suited her personality, for she bridled at any form of restriction. During that time, from the age of sixteen and up to her twentieth year, Blanche grew very close to her grandmother and the two women took walks through the nearby park and alongside the River Clain.

Louise Demarconnay enjoyed attending trials and she often sat in the courtroom's public gallery and listened to the cut and thrust of legal battles in criminal cases. Once she considered Blanche to be old enough she took her with her. Including Blanche in her courtroom visits was a simple gesture made by a kind and thoughtful grandmother, but it was to change the course of Blanche Monnier's life forever.

A Battle of Wills

Louise Monnier, nee Demarconnay, was, as previously mentioned, authoritarian, strong-willed and stern in demeanour. She dominated everyone who entered her sphere of influence. She gave herself sole authority for all of the household responsibilities, and she had an intractable character. Several witnesses portrayed her as one of those iron-willed domestic tyrants before whom everyone and everything had to bend and yield.

With regards to her attitude to her children, Louise Monnier did not express any love for either of them, nor did she show them any tenderness. Blanche only ever saw her mother's harsh, stern demeanour. As each year passed, it became obvious that Louise Monnier actively despised her children, and that she felt nothing but contempt for both of them. She knew nothing of Blanche's personality, and made no effort to get to know her daughter.

Consequently, Blanche transferred her filial love to her grandmother, Louise Demarconnay.

As a twelve year-old, Blanche was civil and good-natured with her father and her brother, but she had begun to be offhand or curt with her mother. Before long, she began to openly challenge her mother's authority.

Louise Monnier intensely disliked the way Blanche comported herself. This was another cause of contention. Instead of playing with dolls, Blanche preferred ball games and leapfrog. When the family stayed at Le Pilet, she went butterfly hunting with a net. Blanche's adventurous and inventive nature amused her friends and acquaintances, but did not suit her mother at all.

Part of Louise Monnier's disapproval of Blanche's behaviour, which she felt should be more 'lady-like', stemmed from the supreme importance that Louise Monnier attached to her family's ancestry and its tenuous links to the royal family. This fortuitous lineage had given her an inflated sense of her own importance. It caused her to have delusions of grandeur. She was not royalty, nor was she acknowledged by royalty. She had no relatives nor friends at court. In reality, Louise Monnier was the wife of a moderately successful small-town academic who worked at the local faculty of arts. By the time Blanche reached her teens, their mother-daughter relationship was turbulent, with both women prone to frequent outbursts of anger.

Short in stature, like the rest of the Monnier family, Blanche was slender, lively and energetic, with large, luminous eyes and beautiful jet-black hair that she had inherited from her maternal grandmother.

In order to control and restrict what she considered to be her daughter's wayward tendencies, to suppress her natural exuberance, and to force her to obey, Madame Monnier was very severe. Blanche was often punished by being banished to her room or by being deprived of meals. Her outright refusals to follow instructions, or her outbreaks of anger were punished, always by her mother, by being sent to her room and given dry bread and water as a substitute for the family meal.

Louise Monnier most likely believed that the punishments she inflicted on her daughter would make her see the error of her ways and teach her to follow the house rules, which were essentially Louise Monnier's rules.

Repeated punishment did not teach Blanche to respect or obey her mother; on the contrary, it diminished any remaining filial respect she may have had and it strengthened her resolve to pay no heed to other people's rules at all; to do whatever she wished whenever she wished, and to be nothing like her mother.

The nickname Blanche had for her mother was Bounine, which was a shortened version of bout de naine (dwarf woman) and Blanche began to use it more frequently, calling her mother by it to her face, especially when they argued.

Blanche often felt anger at her mother's lack of maternal warmth. She found she could not rely on her father's love or support as he was often absent from home because of his work, and because of his subjugated personality and his lack of authority when he was at home. Blanche found her mother to be narrow-minded and dull.

One of Madame Demarconnay's former maids, Modeste Poinet, Marie Fazy's sister, and later the wife of François Bourliaud, a railway employee, provided information about Blanche's early life.

Modeste Poinet/Bourliaud: *I knew Mademoiselle Blanche as a very young girl; she kindly offered to be a bridesmaid at our wedding and gave me a beautiful gift. When she was twenty-one years old, she was very beautiful, a good musician, very cultured, a free spirit, gentle and generous, and very charitable, but always hiding what she did from her mother. Blanche suffered a great deal because of the authoritarian character of her mother, who took pleasure in upsetting her. Blanche had a rather adventurous, fun-loving nature, and when she was a teenager, she wanted to go out like young girls her age, have fun, enjoy life and go to parties, but her mother, who never went out herself, who hated social events and gatherings, refused to let Blanche go to parties or balls. She did this on purpose, to upset Blanche. Her father sometimes agreed to take her to the ball, and then, when Blanche was dressed, ready to leave with him, the old girl would say many cruel and cutting things about her daughter's appearance, until Blanche abandoned her plans to go out and ran to her room crying.*

Madame Monnier also hated it when her daughter sometimes played the piano. Violent quarrels often broke out between the two women whenever Blanche sat down and played a tune she liked. Sometimes Blanche would stop playing, slam the piano lid down and go up to her room, and other times, she would confront her mother. It was during those confrontations – which grew more frequent as Blanche learned that her mother's authority was a chimera; nothing more than a hollow pose – that Louise Monnier learned just how strong-willed her daughter was.

When they argued, Blanche's father would sometimes come out of his study to try and appease them and Blanche, in deference to her father, would go up to her room. The young woman, who had shown clear signs of possessing a strong personality during her childhood, was now openly defiant, but only with her mother.

Despite her efforts, and despite her strong will and her indomitable character, Louise Monnier was increasingly unable to exert any control over Blanche. Maids reported screaming arguments between the two women. Blanche had developed her own incredibly strong will, and it was a far stronger will than her mother would have ever wanted her to have.

Whenever Louise Monnier and Blanche quarrelled,

Blanche became very angry very quickly. And unlike when she had been a child, there was no question of punishing Blanche by making her go without a meal or by sending her to her room. Louise Monnier tried to do that once and very quickly regretted it.

Modeste Poinet/Bourliaud mentioned one particular incident in her testimony. It concerned Louise Monnier attempting to stop Blanche from playing the piano.

Modeste Poinet/Bourliaud: *My sister (Marie Fazy), who was in charge of Madame Monnier's maids, told me about an incident in which Madame Monnier tried to stop Mademoiselle Blanche from playing the piano. 'It's too loud,' she said. 'It's too loud.' Mademoiselle Blanche stood up at the piano and stared at her mother. She took a step forward and stood directly in front of Madame Monnier. 'Say "It's too loud" one more time and see what happens', she said. My sister said she could hear the anger and the threat in Mademoiselle Blanche's voice. Then Mademoiselle Blanche said in a calm and pleasant voice: 'Go away, mother. Go away right now and do something useful – if you know how.' Then Mademoiselle Blanche sat back down at the piano and played a jaunty tune she liked. Madame Monnier looked at her for a few seconds, then turned and left the room. My sister said no one saw Madame Monnier for three days after that incident. She took her meals in her room. My sister took them to her.*

Modeste Poinet's testimony also made a reference to other ways in which Blanche would stand up to her mother and demonstrate her own iron will.

Modeste Poinet/Bourliaud: *My sister (Marie Fazy) told me that Mademoiselle Blanche had a far stronger will than her mother. That's why Madame Monnier didn't like or get on with Mademoiselle Blanche. She [Fazy] said that Madame Monnier had one time ordered her [Blanche] to go to her room, and Mademoiselle had laughed in her mother's face and then said: 'The way you keep confusing me with Marcel is very amusing, mother, but if it ever stops being amusing, then I shall put a very definite stop to it. Now get out of my sight.' My sister said that Madame Monnier had no idea how to react to her daughter's words and just walked away and didn't speak to anyone for several days, except to give Marie [Fazy] orders about the running of the house.*

Several maids testified that there were frequent

screaming arguments between the two women. It was quite clear that Louise Monnier was unable to control her daughter in the way she was able to control others: her parents, her husband, her son, her servants – in fact everyone who entered her sphere of influence.

Théodore Touchard, a plaster worker and a neighbour of the Monniers who lived in Rue de la Visitation, was acquainted with 'Mademoiselle Blanche', as he explained when he was interviewed by journalists in 1901 after the discovery of Blanche's imprisonment.

Touchard: *She was so vibrant, so lively. I saw her grow up. I think she was about ten years old when she first came to visit us. She would call out to Madame Demarconnay: 'Grandma, I am going to Monsieur Touchard's house.' And she would come in and talk to my wife for a while and then she would run off to play with a ball, or to chase other children. She played games in the street like all children of her age.*

Although Blanche was always civil and polite to her father and her brother, the opposite was the case with her mother; Blanche and Louise Monnier seemed to clash whenever they came into contact with each other. This no doubt stemmed from them both being very strong-willed women. Unfortunately for Louise Monnier (although unfortunately for Blanche ultimately) Madame Monnier was unable to exert any influence over Blanche at all. She could not control her, not intimidate her, threats were useless and orders were pointless, no matter how curtly they were given, as Blanche would simply laugh at her mother and continue doing as she liked.

After innumerable instances of Blanche either flouting, ridiculing or undermining her authority, Madame Monnier was presented with an opportunity to rectify the matter.

Part Two:
Sequestration

Victor Calmeil

When Blanche was twenty-years old, Madame Demarconnay started taking her grand-daughter to the local courts to sit in the public gallery and watch the legal proceedings. Blanche enjoyed her first trial very much and thereafter, the two women attended court sessions regularly. One trial which Blanche and her grandmother attended was a case defended by a Poitiers lawyer, Victor Calmeil, who worked for his father, Jacob Calmeil.

In 1870, a rumour started to circulate that Blanche Monnier was in a clandestine relationship with Victor Calmeil. According to some, the relationship was not approved of by Blanche's parents, mainly due to the fact that Calmeil was a Protestant and a Republican, was nearly fifteen years older than Blanche and, as a provincial lawyer, did not have, nor would ever have a way of accruing, a personal fortune.

At Marcel Monnier's trial, Théodore Touchard, a local plasterer testified that Blanche, accompanied by her maid, Marie Fazy, would often go Victor Calmeil's house in Rue des Écossais, a cul-de-sac just off Rue de la Visitation.

It was around this time that one of Louise Monnier's maids reported to her employer that she had seen Blanche standing naked at her bedroom window, so that anyone passing by in the street below could have seen her.

After interrogating the maid, Louise Monnier finally got to hear about Blanche's relationship with Victor Calmeil. She instructed the maid to say nothing to anyone else, especially not to her husband or her son, but to discreetly report back to her if she saw Blanche doing the same again. The maid dutifully reported back to her employer two days later, stating that once again she had seen Blanche standing naked at her bedroom window. Both incidents had taken place at about the same time.

Louise Monnier surmised that her daughter was exposing her naked body to an admirer, probably the lawyer, Calmeil.

Over the next few days Louise Monnier had her daughter watched very closely by that one particular maid. Everything Blanche did was reported back to Madame Monnier by her maid.

According to the maid, at two on the afternoon, every other day, Blanche would undress and stand naked at her bedroom window. The maid had gone to Louis Demarconnay's room and looked out of the window and seen Victor Calmeil standing in the street, looking up at Blanche.

On one of those afternoons, the maid saw Blanche write a note, put it in an envelope and drop it out of the window into the courtyard below. The maid swore she saw Victor Calmeil retrieve it, open the envelope and read the note. She also said she had seen Blanche perform a naked dance for the lawyer, after which she had dressed and he had gone back to his house.

Théodore Touchard, one of the Monniers' neighbours was interviewed and had the following to say:

Théodore Touchard: *As a neighbour of the Demarconnay and the Monnier families, I saw a lot of the Monnier children and their parents. If memory serves, it must have been about 1871, when Mademoiselle Blanche was around twenty-two or twenty-three years old, my attention, and that of the neighbours, was drawn to the manoeuvres of the young Mademoiselle Blanche, who would often go with Madame Fazy, her maid, to a house on Rue des Écossais, a nearby cul-de-sac that was just off Rue de la Visitation. It was where a lawyer named Victor Calmeil lived. He was quite a few years older than Mademoiselle Blanche. A while later, I heard a rumour that Mademoiselle Monnier was going to marry Victor Calmeil, which surprised me and the neighbours, because there was quite an age difference between them.*

Several months then went by without any marriage taking place, and after that Mademoiselle Monnier stopped leaving her home and being seen; I heard that Madame Monnier hadn't wanted her daughter to marry Victor Calmeil – because she thought he was too old and too poor for Mademoiselle Blanche. As I said, I never saw Mademoiselle Blanche again after that. It was one of those rumours that seemed likely, but of course it was only a rumour; obviously I know absolutely nothing about any decisions that the Monnier family might have made regarding Blanche.

I don't know a lot about Mademoiselle Blanche's condition before 1880. Marie Fazy, who worked for a long time as a servant for Madame Monnier, told us that at first, Made-

moiselle Monnier wanted to be married; later, when that was forbidden because of her poor choice of husband, she considered taking her vows and joining a convent, but her mother was apparently against her doing that too.

My wife said that it was as though Madame Monnier wanted to have total control over every aspect of her daughter's life.

Because Louise Monnier attached a great deal of importance and significance to her distant royal ancestry, and was avowedly Royalist and Catholic, she would have objected to any type of relationship between her daughter and Victor Calmeil, a republican protestant with very little by way of a personal fortune.

Extremely repressed and prudish by nature, Louise Monnier would have found the idea of Blanche showing her naked body to an admirer abhorrent.

Louise Monnier consulted the family doctor, Doctor Guérineau, the director of the medical school. After a very long meeting with the forceful Madame Monnier, the doctor came to understand that Blanche's mind was deeply troubled. According to Madame Monnier, her daughter often stood naked at her bedroom window, making lewd gestures and posing provocatively for every passer-by, to such an extent that Madame Monnier's husband was seriously considering fitting shutters to his daughter's bedroom window in order to make it impossible for men to gather in the street below her window – as they currently did on a daily basis – to watch the young woman making an obscene spectacle of herself.

The doctor's diagnosis was that Blanche was suffering from some sort of 'pernicious fever', which, in her case, was manifesting itself as excessive sexual excitement or lust mania, for which he immediately prescribed a daily dose of potassium bromide, a 'tonic' that was known to calm nerves and which was frequently used to combat epileptic seizures or hysteria. He tactfully mentioned that it dampened down fevered libidos, and he also suggested that Blanche be given twice-weekly ice baths to cool her 'hot blood'.

When Louise Monnier mentioned that her husband was considering having shutters fitted to Blanche's room window, purely as a way of preserving his daughter's modesty, Doctor Guérineau concluded that such a preventative measure might be beneficial for everyone concerned.

Letters and Notes

Like many educated young women, Blanche Monnier was accustomed to writing down her thoughts in a journal. She was also a dedicated letter writer and constantly asked for paper and pencil in order to write every day, which the maids obtained for her.

Long before her confinement, Blanche had written love notes to Victor Calmeil; each day she sealed her note in an envelope and dropped it from her room window into the courtyard below. She had watched him retrieve it and then cross the road until he was standing opposite her room window. He would then open the envelope and read her words of love.

As he had read her note, Blanche would dance erotically for him, slowly removing her clothes until she stood naked at her window, posing provocatively, her arms flung wide so that Victor Calmeil could enjoy the sight of her young, naked body. If anyone came along the street during her dance, she would move out of sight until they had gone; Victor Calmeil would stand and reread the letter. Then Blanche would stand at the window again, letting the afternoon sun shine on her smooth skin and light up her charms for her lover.

Once her confinement began, the young woman took the opportunity to write letters to people she knew. After putting it into an envelope, she would slide the sealed letter through the slats of the shutters on her window and let it fall into the courtyard below, hoping that one of the maids or someone passing would see it, pick it up and put it in the mail.

One day, Madame Monnier noticed an envelope falling into the courtyard and asked a maid to retrieve it. Realising what her daughter was doing, Louise Monnier instructed the maid to pretend she was going to the shops to buy items needed for the day and therefore leave the house noisily, but actually to quietly pick up the letter, return silently to the house and hand the unopened letter directly to Madame Minnier.

The maid did as instructed and after silently dismissing the maid, Madame Monnier opened the envelope and read the contents.

Later that day, Madame Monnier called a meeting with her maids and told them very clearly that if her daughter dropped other letters into the courtyard, it was their job, without Blanche knowing, to collect the letters and bring them, without opening them, immediately to her.

She explained that this was because there was nothing of any consequence in her daughter's letters. They were mostly incoherent and filled with meaningless phrases and jumbled words.

Virginie Magault, nee Neveux, who testified at Marcel Monnier's trial, went into detail about Blanche Monnier's letter writing.

Virginie Magault: *For some time, Mademoiselle Blanche asked every day for paper and pencil in order to write. Her mother had us take them to her. Mademoiselle Blanche would write a letter and place it in an envelope. She addressed her letters to many different people – I can't remember any of the names though. She would then push the envelope between the thin gaps in the shutters covering her window, so that the letter fell and landed in the courtyard. She would then instruct Marie Fazy, the cook, to have it taken to the post office. I was often instructed by Madame Monnier to go out by the servants' door, collect the letter and go quietly back in through the main door, and then pretend that I was taking Mademoiselle Blanche's letter to the post office, and do it in such a convincing way that Mademoiselle Monnier would really believe I was posting it for her. Once back inside the house, I would hand the letter to Madame Monnier, who told me that when her daughter dropped letters, they should always be retrieved immediately and given straight to her. She insisted that the letters should never be opened as they contained nothing of any importance.*

The young lady never wanted to see or to have anything to do with her mother, whom she called Booneen. In one single week, Mademoiselle threw six chamber pots at her mother, and they all broke on the stairway. Madame Monnier said she wouldn't provide her daughter with any more of them and she would leave her in her filth, to which her daughter replied that she was already in it.

When she was plunged into the freezing water of an ice bath, Blanche would scream. When that happened, Louise

Monnier threatened her. She told Blanche that if she continued to scream, she would send for the police commissioner who would come and arrest her. Although this ruse silenced Blanche for a while, it did not take long for Blanche to realise how her mother was deceiving her. Thereafter, the threat proved ineffective, so Louise Monnier decided it would be best to keep all the windows of the house closed, even during the summer.

It was during that last half of the year that passers-by heard frequently heard someone in distress screaming at the window of an upstairs room of the imposing house on the corner of Rue de la Visitation.

The house, with its locked doors, its high walls, its permanently-closed shutters, and from which screams of terror could be sometimes heard, quickly became the source of gossip, some of it wild and speculative, which gave the imposing house a mysterious and forbidding air.

Some of the neighbours were becoming concerned.

Sedated (1)

The 'tonic' that the Monnier's family doctor, Doctor Guéri-neau, prescribed for Blanche, which would be administered by Madame Monnier, was potassium bromide. Potassium bromide (KBr) is a salt that was widely used as an anticonvulsant and a sedative in the late 19th and early 20th centuries. The anticonvulsant properties of potassium bromide were first noted by Charles Locock in 1857. Bromide is generally regarded as the first effective medication for epilepsy. At the time, it was commonly believed that epilepsy was caused by masturbation. Potassium bromide calmed sexual excitement and was used successfully to treat seizures. In the latter half of the 19th century, potassium bromide was used for the calming of seizures and nervous disorders on an enormous scale, with the dose for a given person being a few grams per day.

When taken as a drink, single doses of fifty milligrams (the equivalent of one sixteenth of a teaspoon) of potassium bromide dissolved in water significantly hampered memory formation. Furthermore, long term administration of potassium bromide at the dose of fifty milligrams a day for twenty-eight days led to severe cognitive impairment. The memory impairment induced by the solution included bouts of confusion, semi-coma, anxiety attacks, neurosis, and paranoia.

Prolonged use of potassium bromide causes a number of central nervous system reactions. These include: depression, lethargy, somnolence (from daytime sleepiness to coma), loss of appetite, cachexia, nausea, loss of body fluid, loss of reflexes or pathologic reflexes, clonic seizures, tremors, ataxia, loss of neural sensitivity, paresis, cerebral edema with associated headaches and papilledema of the eyes, delirium, including confusion, abnormal speech, loss of concentration and memory, aggressiveness and psychosis.

Dermatitis and other forms of skin disease often occur, as well as mucous hypersecretion in the lungs. Asthma and rhinitis often worsen. Often, tongue disorders, aphthous stomatitis, bad breath, and constipation occur.

The doctor informed Louise Monnier that she would

have to give Blanche a daily dose of potassium bromide, with a few drops of it dissolved in a drink of sugar water. This would help to keep her calm. The doctor suggested that, for the sake of staff discretion, Madame Monnier should refer to it as 'a tonic' at all times. He also suggested that it might be best for everyone concerned if Blanche was unaware that she was being treated – just in case she refused the treatment.

Madame Monnier said she could surreptitiously put a few drops of the 'tonic' in Blanche's morning drink; one of the maids would make sure Blanche drank it. The doctor agreed that such a strategy was not only necessary, but would probably work.

The 'tonic' was mentioned by Virginie Neveux, one of the maids who worked for Louise Monnier's for two years from 1871, and who testified at Marcel Monnier's trial. She stated that Blanche sometimes refused to drink the morning bromide-laced beverage, so her mother simply had the maid transfer the contents into another drinking vessel and offer it to Blanche again later, whereupon she would drink it.

Virginie Neveux: *Blanche Monnier ate the same food as her mother, but Madame Monnier only allowed Blanche to drink sugar water in which she had dissolved a tonic. If it happened, as it sometimes did, that Blanche refused to drink it, then her mother had instructed us to take the drink out of the room and then offer it to Blanche throughout the day, until Blanche drank it, which she always did.*

The deception worked and without realising it, Blanche began her days of potassium bromide-induced lethargy. By early 1872, the potassium bromide had begun to have an effect. Blanche Monnier had begun to suffer from nervous tics; she would laugh aloud at nothing, or talk to the air in front of her as though there were someone standing there listening to her, and she would suddenly utter inarticulate screams that could be heard in the street outside 21 Rue de la Visitation.

Rumours

One of the most persistent rumours going around Poitiers about the Monniers was that because the family was royalist and Catholic, Louise Monnier had forbidden a union between Blanche and the protestant republican lawyer, Victor Calmeil. Heart-broken, due to being unable to marry the man she had set her heart on, Blanche Monnier had gone 'a little crazy' and started exposing herself to strangers, so her parents had had no choice but to follow the family doctor's advice and 'sequester' their daughter in an upstairs shuttered room until she recovered her wits and gave up any idea of marrying Calmeil.

Le Journal de la Vienne reported Blanche Monnier's affair with Victor Calmeil, who had died in 1885. The relationship was considered to be the original catalyst for Blanche's imprisonment. *Le Journal* added further detail by recycling the rumour that Blanche had been imprisoned because her relationship with the lawyer had resulted in an illegitimate child, which had either been born and then killed, or else had been aborted. That particular rumour was so powerful that searches were undertaken by the police in the garden of 21 Rue de la Visitation to find the corpse of a new-born baby, although no search of the grounds of Le Pilet was ever ordered, even though Auguste Joubert, who lived in the sharecropper's cottage in the grounds of Le Pilet in Migné, testified that the Madame Monnier, on becoming a widow, had forbidden her son to ever visit her property in Le Pilet.

Auguste Joubert: *After she became a widow, Madame Monnier refused to allow her son to visit her property in Le Pilet. She also ordered her gardeners, Bourliaud and Picherault, to continue to care for and maintain the property's grounds.*

In his testimony, Doctor Léger, the director of the bacteriology laboratory at the medical school mentioned the conclusions of his examination of the bones that the police had found in the garden of 21 Rue de la Visitation.

Dr. Léger: *I had been asked to examine various bones uncovered by a search of the garden. The question was whether these were not the bones of a new-born child. I have not found any trace of such bones. The bones I examined were a cat skele-*

ton, some chicken vertebrae and a few sheep bones.

The speculation in the press was that the birth of an illegitimate child would have been the cause of Blanche's imprisonment. Following the family's refusal to consent to the marriage, followed by the birth of a child, the young woman was reportedly deprived of her liberty and given a sedative to become quiet and docile – drugs which ultimately caused her to become mentally unbalanced.

Within a very short space of time, the young woman's behaviour became strange, bizarre, and eccentric. Servants gossiped; it was rumoured that Blanche Monnier had lost her wits. Because of her mother's contempt of Blanche and Calmeil's relationship, and through her brother's indifference to her imprisonment, the unfortunate woman had then fallen into the pitiful state in which the Commissioner had found her.

Following Louise Monnier's refusal to consent to any form of relationship, let alone marriage between Blanche and Victor Calmeil, neighbours spoke of a lot of shouting and screaming over the following few weeks.

Madame Monnier's categorical refusal to allow Blanche to be a friend with, to be in a relationship with, or to marry Victor Calmeil, was inevitable. Victor Calmeil was a successful lawyer and a partner in his father's firm, Jacob Calmeil and Son. The Calmeil family was known and respected throughout Poitiers. Jacob Calmeil had been elected Chief Advocate four times between 1831 and 1865.

Louise Monnier would have been against such a match for several reasons. Firstly, Victor Calmeil was a staunch republican, and Louise Monnier, with her tenuous noble ancestry was an avowed royalist. Secondly, the Monniers were devout Catholics and the Calmeils were non-practising Protestants. Thirdly, under the Napoleonic Code, in the event of marriage, everything that belonged to Blanche would legally half-belong to her husband. Fourthly, Louise Monnier would also need to provide Blanche with a suitable dowry, half of which would immediately be Victor Calmeil's. Fifthly, as Blanche's husband, Calmeil would have access to every legal document pertaining to his wife and also to any money or property she inherited; as a lawyer, he would scrutinise every document carefully in order to safeguard his wife's (and therefore his own) property and fortune. Sixthly, there was an age gap of nearly fifteen years between Blanche and Victor; she was approaching twenty-five, he was thirty-eight. The age difference Louise Monnier allegedly invoked to prevent their marriage was therefore the most insignificant part of her argument, but she made it appear that it was the prime reason for her refusal to give her permission or her blessing.

In 1873, Blanche was on the cusp of her twenty-fifth year and it was not uncommon amongst the upper-middle classes for an older man to marry a younger woman. Finally, Louise Monnier took pleasure in exercising her power in ways that thwarted her daughter's plans, and she would probably not have missed this particular opportunity to do so.

Louise Demarconnay's Death
1873

Blanche was profoundly shocked when her grandmother died.

On 9th March 1873, Louise Demarconnay died in her sleep. Blanche was devastated by the death of her beloved grandmother; her godmother; the woman who meant the most to her and the one member of the family with whom she had more than a passing resemblance.

Louise Demarconnay's death took away from the young woman the only person who had been able to give her the strength and courage to stand up to her mother's authoritarianism. Blanche had a deep love and respect for her grandmother, as well as admiration and tenderness. Louise Demarconnay was Blanche's surrogate mother. For Blanche Monnier, the loss of that incredibly significant woman in her life was unbearable.

A careful examination of Louise Demarconnay's legal documents soon revealed that Madame Demarconnay's love for Blanche was equal to Blanche's love for her; in her Will, Louise Demarconnay had bequeathed half of her properties and half of her fortune to her husband, Louis Demarconnay. The other halves of each she had bequeathed to Blanche. No one else was named a beneficiary of anything in the Will.

This was a huge blow for Louise Monnier, as she felt she should have been the rightful beneficiary of all of her mother's properties and fortune. Once she had taken stock of the situation, she took one day to decide on the strategy she would use to rectify what she perceived to be the glaring omission in her mother's Will.

For Louise Monnier, the death of her mother was simply another pretext to continue isolating and sedating Blanche.

On noticing Blanche's profound grief and deep melancholy, Louise Monnier again consulted the family doctor, Doctor Guérineau. After another very long meeting with Louise Monnier, the doctor came to understand that Blanche was 'hysterical with grief' over the death of her beloved grandmother, and her grief was manifesting itself in a number of ways. Blanche often refused to leave her room; she refused to wear clothes, and when she did leave her room, she walked around the house naked; she flew into violent rages very quickly, often for no obvious reason, and she had recently started throwing objects: plates, cutlery, candlesticks, anything she could lay her hands on, at anyone who was anywhere near her.

Doctor Guérineau, again without making any attempt to either see or examine Blanche, advised Madame Monnier to continue to give Blanche the daily doses of potassium bromide, also to continue with the ice baths, and to perhaps consider locking the room door if Blanche's angry outbursts became violent and threatening.

Louise Monnier also informed the doctor that Blanche was considering taking her vows and entering a convent. Doctor Guérineau objected to this on 'medical grounds'.

Madame Monnier conveyed the doctor's diagnosis to Blanche, who protested and accused her mother of interfering in her life. Louise Monnier immediately arranged for two sisters from the Holy Cross convent to visit Blanche and make an assessment of her suitability for convent life. Shortly after the meeting with the nuns Blanche abandoned her religious ambitions.

Louise Monnier's systematic thwarting of her daughter's plans was carried out under the guise of caring. To any casual observer, the young woman's mother appeared to be acting in a way that was guided by her awareness of the requirements of her maternal duty. The general consensus of those who knew Madame Monnier agreed that although it was true that she avoided displays of affection and although she was reluctant to have physical contact with her daughter, she had provided her with a luxurious home, a good education and many enjoyable holidays.

As for Blanche's father, he was often absent from home; his duties kept him at the faculty. His paternal role, reduced by Louise Monnier's dominant personality, was almost non-existent. Diminished as a husband and as a father by his wife, Émile Monnier remained silent, submissive and ultimately forgotten.

Meanwhile, Louise Monnier continued with her project to gradually bring about her daughter's mental deterioration; a project which appears to have begun in earnest around Blanche's twenty-third year.

In May, 1872, Blanche Monnier's regular church attendance ceased abruptly. Her absence was immediately noticed by the Abbé de Montbron, the parish priest.

When he politely enquired after Blanche, Louise Monnier told him, just as she was soon telling anyone who would listen, that the family doctor's diagnosis was that Blanche had been stricken with a 'pernicious fever' that was so serious that it had left her in a very weakened and exhausted state. Unfortunately, the distraught mother added, the fever had affected the poor girl's mind so much that she had become violent and unpredictable. The family doctor was closely monitoring Blanche and was providing her with long-term treatment which included keeping her medicated and confined to her room as much as possible.

From that moment on, no one saw Blanche Monnier (or Louise Monnier) outside 21 Rue de la Visitation again until 1901.

The Prefecture Councillor
1873

Marcel Monnier was attempting to find a position that related to his qualifications. The recently-qualified doctor of law had considered entering the judiciary, but when Edmond Ernoul, deputy of Vienne in the National Assembly, became Keeper of the Seals, on 24th May 1873, in the ministry of Broglie, Émile Monnier wrote to his former student of rhetoric to recommend his son for a clerical position.

The minister immediately responded by offering Marcel Monnier a job as a prefecture councillor in the Landes department. His main function would be to rule, as an administrative tribunal, on the claims of individuals vis-à-vis the administration, in various fields: applications for public works contracts, main secondary road disputes, public health issues. The prefecture councillor was also at the disposal of the Prefect to assist him with administrative tasks.

Marcel Monnier commenced his duties at the Prefecture of Landes on 17th October 1873. He was twenty-five years old and he was starting a new life.

The society of Mont-de-Marsan, although traditionalist and closed, was less so than that in Poitiers. The young councillor settled in a house on The Allée Delamarre facing the terraces of the Midou, but which was just outside the affluent district of the Madeleine. Nevertheless, he was immediately welcomed in many of the salons.

He had not been there for long; no more than three months, when he noticed Maria de los Angèles Francisca Paula Calista Conget. She was a young woman from a Spanish noble family and she had Francized her name to Angèle. His friends noticed his interest in her and sent her a bouquet, pretending that it was from Monnier. They then told their friend that by sending the young woman flowers and thereby declaring his love for her, he had compromised her and now had no option but to marry her.

The young lady, born in Bilbao in 1852, was the grand-daughter of a former governor of the Basque province. Her late father was a doctor and one of her uncles, a Colonel in the artillery, had been killed during the recent Spanish civil war. As a result of those events, Madame Rosario Ariana de Conget had taken refuge in France with her daughter, and the two women had settled in Mont-de-Marsan, where they were held in high regard. They were acquaintances of the famous virtuoso pianist Francis Planté, who gave concerts throughout Europe. On his tour intervals, he liked to rest and relax in the city of Mons.

Marcel Monnier and Angèle de Conget made plans to marry. The young civil servant wrote to his parents asking for their consent. While the age of civil majority was set at twenty-one years, the parents' permission to marry their children was required up to twenty-five years for boys and twenty-one years for girls. Such provisions were intended to prevent misalliance by forcing the son or daughter to reflect on the consequences of his or her marriage.

Madame Monnier wanted to oppose the union, which she considered to have happened too hastily. Admittedly, the young woman was from Spanish nobility, but she was a foreigner, moreover a refugee, and the information about her mother was hardly favourable. Madame de Conget was mysterious; a spendthrift and burdened with debts despite her fortune. She frequented the salons and eagerly attended the parties given in good society, it was said, in order to find a suitable husband for her daughter.

On the other hand, Marcel Monnier could not remain single indefinitely. To succeed in his chosen career, he needed to strengthen his position in the city and be recognized as someone of importance – he also needed to marry as soon as possible.

Émile Monnier understood his son's social aspirations and he gave his consent to the marriage; for once, his wife had to resign herself to his decision. Although he was most often absorbed in his studies, the professor of letters was concerned about his son's future and happiness; the father knew his son very well.

This can be seen in a letter dated 12th March 1874, from Émile Monnier to the Prefect of Landes, thanking him for giving his son the clerical job. In the letter, Émile Monnier praised Marcel's qualities without trying to gloss over his son's defects and shortcomings:

'You have judged him well, Monsieur le Prefect. He was

raised in a somewhat austere environment so as to help him avoid luxury and ostentation. He has proven reliable in his occupations. He has only the usual infirmities (a possible reference to Marcel Monnier's myopia) and is maybe a little solitary, although he does have a few long-lasting friendships, some from his school days, and some from law school. My son is able to apply himself to most things and has a natural aptitude despite having learned more from books than from life. He is a first-rate young man whose imagination and heart often lead his head. He will only ever agree with whatever is confirmed, but has an honesty that abhors bad deeds and bad judgments and has a mind that does not bother with the inconsequential. This is the point he is at in his life and I bless his good intentions in wanting the person who employs him (to whom he will be utterly loyal) to be worthy of his research and our esteem.'

Everything was going well. But there was a delicate and embarrassing point that the father of the Monnier family could not and did not try to hide as the wedding approached, and that was Blanche's strange, almost lethargic and distracted behaviour. In the same letter, Émile Monnier was realistic about his daughter's condition:

'My daughter is not cured of her affliction, nor will she be for a very long time, I fear, but she is quite out of danger. Languor, a desperate languor that is her usual state of health, has now replaced the initial crisis. My wife and I were infinitely touched, Monsieur Prefect, by the part you deigned to take regarding our concerns.'

It is possible that Émile Monnier knew nothing about Blanche's daily dose of potassium bromide; he was probably unaware that it was measured into a cup or a glass by Louise Monnier, after which one of the maids, probably Marie Fazy, then filled the drinking vessel with the sugared water drink that Blanche liked so much. And even if he had been aware of it, it is unlikely that he would have questioned it; after all, it was the 'tonic' prescribed by the family doctor as a 'cure' for whatever mental anxieties afflicted his daughter.

His words reveal his great sadness. For Émile Monnier, his daughter's 'pernicious fever' was an incurable condition. Although it was possible that Blanche might experience lulls of lucidity between her lethargy, her full recovery, which meant the recovery and restoration of her mental faculties, was impossible.

Marcel Monnier's Wedding
June 17th, 1874

The date for Marcel Monnier's wedding to Maria de los Angèles Francisca Paula Calista Conget was set for June 17th, 1874. The Monnier family had to wait until the year of mourning for Louise Demarconnay had been observed (on March 9th, 1873) before they could begin to make wedding arrangements. The custom then was that there could be no bridal blessing during the month of May, as the month was dedicated to the Blessed Virgin. Once the June date was agreed by all parties, the other details were decided upon. The wedding ceremony would take place in Mont-de-Marsan and the groom's parents had decided to go there the day before with their daughter in the hope that she would not cause them any embarrassment with her behaviour, which was becoming more bizarre with each day that passed.

Madame Monnier ordered two dresses for Blanche from a Poitiers seamstress. She had to have them made without taking any measurements and without a proper fitting, because Madame Monnier did not want anyone going into her daughter's room and witnessing the way Blanche was being treated in her home environment.

The day before the wedding the signing of the marriage contract took place in the presence of Maitre Lacroix, the notary. The future spouses declared that they could be married without impediments and a clause in their marriage contract provided that they would receive an annuity of five thousand francs per year.

This pension would be paid for half by Marcel Monnier's father and mother and for the other half by his grandfather, Louis Demarconnay, with the important point that it was to end on the death of each of the donors in the proportion for which he had contributed to it. This meant that on the death of Louis Demarconnay, the pension would be reduced to two thousand five hundred francs per year.

In addition, the overall annual pension was to be reduced to three thousand francs, under the same conditions, as soon as the events in Spain enabled Madame de Conget's widow to provide the spouses with an annuity of two thousand francs per year. In the immediate future, the bride's mother could not access her income or her capital because of the war in Spain, but she undertook to satisfy the needs of the household in the proportion of two-fifths; however, a clause provided that Madame de Conget was the sole payee at the time she was to begin paying that pension. Despite her promise, this meant that she would never pay it.

Émile and Louise Monnier, Blanche, Marie Fazy and Marie Pinaud left for Mont-de-Marsan two days before the wedding. Louis Demarconnay had refused to attend the wedding, stating that he did not want to leave his home.

The next day, after the civil marriage at the town hall, the parish priest of the Madeleine church received the exchange of consents. Next to the signatures of all of the members of the Conget family, was that of Émile Monnier, but not the signature of his wife, an omission which clearly marked her disapproval of the match. For entirely different reasons, Blanche's signature was also not on the document.

On the day of the wedding, several guests thought that Blanche Monnier was acting in a very eccentric manner. After she had been led to a chair on which she remained seated for most of the reception, she made a number of sudden, strange gestures: she spoke to the air and even tried catching flies with her hand. She had an absent gaze, her movements were sudden and spasmodic, and every so often, tears ran down her face which she wiped away quickly. She had arrived at Mont-de-Marsan with a large braid combed to one side which accentuated how thin she had become.

As Louise Monnier no doubt intended, the guests could not help but notice the groom's sister, the sad-looking young woman who, due to the effects of a 'pernicious fever', could barely stand upright; who turned down the very few dance invitations she received and whose official chaperone was so bored that he ended up leaving her alone amongst a sea of curious faces as soon as he understood that he was not really needed.

It was a beautiful, sunny day, the guests lavished presents on the young couple, and the food was abundant. There were Spanish dances to honour the bride and country dances for the groom.

Inevitably, Blanche made an impression on many of the guests.

Madame Coste, one of the invitees, noticed the sickly state and the singular looks of the young woman.

Madame Coste: *It was obvious that she [Blanche] was not voluntarily attending the wedding ceremony. She had clearly been forced to attend by her family.*

The musician, Francis Planté also noticed the shadow that Blanche's presence cast over the event.

Francis Planté: *There was a kind of shadow over the wedding reception, created by the presence of the groom's sister, who was far more than just ordinary in physical and moral terms, because she gave the impression of being someone who was null, bizarre, and sick, so that no one in Mont-de-Marsan was in any way surprised to learn shortly afterwards that the mental state of that young woman had deteriorated significantly.*

Louise Monnier had insisted that Blanche attend her brother's wedding because she wanted to keep up appearances, but she also needed to have witnesses to Blanche's 'pernicious fever'; the tightly-controlled wedding ceremony and reception provided her with the perfect way of having Blanche's 'fever' seen publicly, so Blanche was there, as in everything else, against her will. There was obviously no question that Louise Monnier would have let her daughter remain alone at Rue de la Visitation; even with servants. For a month, Blanche had not left her bed and the following month she had also been bedridden, telling the various servants repeatedly that she felt ill; that she felt weak, devoid of strength; that she did not feel her usual self; that she felt that she was going to die.

After the wedding, any reference to Marcel Monnier's marriage caused Blanche to burst into tears.

Also, importantly, Blanche, who had always taken great care over her appearance, had suffered the indignity of having her mother, not someone known for her sartorial elegance, choose the clothes she wore for her brother's wedding.

Madame Monnier was a short, round woman who generally gave no thought to how she dressed. The clothes she wore at home were generally plain and old-fashioned. In France, her type of physique was referred to as 'boulotte'. Her daughter, who also was not tall – she was barely one metre fifty-five (five feet, one inch) tall – was determined to take care over what she ate and what she wore in order to avoid looking like her mother in any way.

Despite her attitude to the clothes she wore in her own home, Louise Monnier knew the importance of 'looking right' at social occasions. As she had a very specific agenda regarding Blanche's public outing, she ensured that Blanche was dressed correctly for the event and for her purpose. She had decided on an outfit that would emphasise the sickly pallor of her daughter's face; the pink and grey dress she had chosen for Blanche to wear to the wedding emphasised the dark circles around her eyes and her pale complexion.

Marcel Monnier's wedding day was the day on which Louise Monnier achieved most of what she had set out to achieve. She had a son who honoured her because the whole city of Poitiers knew who he was – she had sent announcements to all of the notable citizens of Poitiers – and she had a daughter who, despite having been physical and mentally ill for some time, had made a supreme effort to attend her brother's wedding.

The bride's parents and grandparents were there in their ranks, well-dressed, handsome and majestic. Marcel Monnier had what he wanted: a wife, a good job, and the respect of several notable and influential citizens. Like his mother, he was fulfilled, now he was going to be able to leave everything he owned to the children he and his wife would have.

His wife, Maria, now known as Angèle, was a young woman who looked like a little like Marcel Monnier's sister. Like Blanche, Angèle Monnier was petite and had long black hair. But whereas Blanche was pale, introverted, and refused to make eye contact, Angèle had sparking eyes and the olive skin of a woman who spent a lot of time in the fresh air. She radiated good health and drew many compliments, whereas Blanche, pale and withdrawn, provoked only sympathetic whispers.

Blanche barely ate. She sat on the same chair for most of the day, hardly speaking. She had enough mental awareness to realise that her mother was exhibiting her, although it is unlikely that she, along with anyone else present, grasped the reason.

Another guest, Doctor Despaignets, stated (under oath) that 'the mother and daughter both seemed quite unbalanced.' The next night, one of the guests came to find him and explained how many of the guests were made uncomfortable by the way Blanche Monnier had been behaving. The Monnier family with the imperious mother and the strangely-behaved daughter was a blemish on the good society of Mont-de-Marsan.

Marcel Monnier was no doubt relieved when his parents and his sister took the train back to Poitiers. Blanche returned from her brother's marriage more introverted, withdrawn and taciturn than ever.

The newlyweds honeymooned in Paris.

On April 1st, 1875, Marcel and Angèle Monnier's daughter was born. They named her Marie-Dolorès which was, perhaps inevitably, shortened to 'Lola'. The couple settled on Place de la Tenaille, east of the Madeleine district.

Escape
1875

Meanwhile, on the other side of Poitiers, the repeated ice baths that Blanche Monnier was being forced to take were very quickly becoming a form of negative reinforcement, so much so that Blanche simply stopped bothering with her personal hygiene, possibly in the hope that the ice baths would stop, which they very soon did once Blanche escaped from 21 Rue de la Visitation.

It happened in June, 1875.

By that time, Madame Monnier had ordered her maids to remove every item of clothing from Blanche's room. She had also given orders for the drawers in Blanche's dressing table to be removed. She also insisted that all of the bedclothes were to be taken out of Blanche's room. The maids carried out her orders, leaving Blanche with one folded sheet spread over her rotting mattress. They also left her a very dirty and very holey scarf, which she used to cover her face whenever anyone entered her room.

One warm June evening, when one of Louise Monnier's less-than-conscientious maids had left Blanche's room door unlocked, Blanche took the opportunity to escape from 21 Rue de la Visitation. She did not go anywhere specific, so it is possible that her escape was a gesture of defiance and a way of her asserting herself.

On finding her room door unlocked, she managed to make her way into the room next to hers. Unable to find clothes, she quietly climbed out of the window, naked, and then used the window railing as a climbing frame to lower herself as far as she could, before dropping the last two metres into the garden. After waiting for a few minutes to be sure she was undetected, Blanche went out through the gate and into the street. Keeping to the shadows, she made her way to Rue des Halles. It was a ten-minute walk from Rue de la Visitation; a walk which no doubt took Blanche, with her bare feet, a little longer.

She made her way along Rue Victor Hugo, where one or two people saw her. Someone called out, but Blanche ignored whoever was calling out and quickly turned the corner into Rue Charles Gide, and then into Rue des Halles. She kept walking until she reached Place du Maréchal-Leclerc, the large boulevard at the end of Rue des Halles. She walked around the boulevard, pretending to look in the darkened shop windows. Then she sat on the stone steps of the municipal building next to the Hotel de Poitiers. Someone from the hotel must have notified the police that a naked woman was outside their establishment, for the police arrived within a few minutes. They spoke quietly to Blanche and she got into their carriage willingly enough. One of the policemen gave her a blanket, which she wrapped around herself like a cloak. When one of the policemen asked where she lived, she provided him with the Rue de la Visitation address. They took her home and handed her over to her parents.

Blanche went to her room still wrapped in the blanket the policeman had given her.

Émile Monnier thanked the policemen and retired to his study, saddened.

Louise Monnier thanked the policemen and closed the door.

Once the police had gone, Louise Monnier instructed Marie Fazy to remove the blanket from Blanche's room at the first opportunity.

The next day Louise Monnier informed her husband that, just before they had left, the policemen had told her that Blanche had been making lewd poses and crude gestures in Place du Maréchal-Leclerc in the boulevard at the end of Rue des Halles.

Sedated (2)
1882

When Doctor Guérineau died in 1882, Doctor Chédevergne succeeded him as director of the medical school and became the Monnier's family doctor. Just like his predecessor, he did not prescribe the appropriate treatment for Blanche. He had his first meeting with Louise Monnier, who informed him of Blanche's 'madness', her 'escape' and her penchant for exhibitionism, obscene poses and lewd gestures. She carefully outlined the treatment that Doctor Guérineau had prescribed.

Without bothering to examine Blanche, Doctor Chédevergne accepted Madame Monnier's description of her daughter's mental state and simply increased the dosage of potassium bromide in order to keep her calm during moments of nervous crisis. He ended up, as he said at Marcel Monnier's trial, content to visit Madame Monnier 'from time to time', although, as it transpired, he never made any effort to actually see Blanche, let alone examine her, preferring instead to take a detailed description of Blanche's symptoms from Louise Monnier.

The daily doses of potassium bromide had gradually wreaked their inevitable damage on Blanche's mind and body. The drug was an appetite suppressant so she was less hungry than she had once been and therefore ate very little. Consequently, she was a lot thinner than she had once been. Her eyes had sunk into their sockets and her cheekbones had become more pronounced.

The drug-induced lethargy meant that she lay on her bed for most of the time, which caused her muscles to atrophy. There were also hormonal disorders and the cessation of her menstrual cycle. The young woman found she could no longer control her sphincter, and she involuntarily fouled her bed with faeces and urine.

When this happened, which it frequently did, Louise Monnier would order the maids to give Blanche an ice bath, as the doctor had prescribed. The maids would prepare the bath and then drag Blanche into it. Blanche would scream and struggle, but in her much-weakened state she was no match for two strong women. Once back on her bed, Blanche would shiver and tremble and sob uncontrollably. Sometimes Blanche would call for her mother, but Louise Monnier would ignore her daughter's calls. After getting no response, Blanche would scream and yell loudly. These may have been the screams that the neighbours heard. Blanche's mental and physical health continued to decline steadily, but Louise Monnier, who was only interested in having her plan succeed and was therefore very carefully monitoring her daughter's deterioration, gave the impression of having absolutely no interest in her daughter's health or well-being at all. The impression she gave was the opposite of what she actually felt, for in reality she had a huge amount of interest in the exact state of her daughter's mental and physical health and well-being.

Émile Monnier's Death

Émile Monnier died on April 9th, 1882, aged sixty-two. His body was kept for two days in the mortuary chamber. The Duc de Landry was just one of the many notable public figures to come and pay his respects.

Louise Monnier had given her son the responsibility of writing the funeral announcements and invitations. Following her advice, he invited all the royalist families of Poitiers and of the surrounding areas to attend his father's funeral service. The invitations were printed by the best printing house in the city. Responding to Marcel Monnier's invitations, more than a thousand people attended. One after another, the wreaths were put in place. There were hundreds of them.

Émile Monnier's funeral took place on a freezing April morning. A small flurry of snowflakes fell.

Louis Demarconnay refused to attend his son-in-law's funeral. He told his daughter that he felt ill, but he had never forgiven his son-in-law for going along with Louise Monnier's opposition to the romance and possible marriage of Blanche to Victor Calmeil. As for the padlocked shutters, he could not bear the thought of them; but he felt powerless to help Blanche. He knew that she was still suffering from the loss of his wife, her dear grandmother. This made the old man very unhappy. He suspected that, with Émile gone, his daughter would grow stricter and Blanche's situation would worsen.

The future would prove him right.

And so, Louis Demarconnay refused to attend the funeral. To him, his daughter and her husband were a monstrous couple; thirsty for money, greedy with ambition. He had learned to do without them. He would not even make the effort to go to the mortuary chamber.

Émile Monnier's service was in the cathedral. Paul Duillaume, the Bishop, gave the homily which lasted more than two hours. When the death bell rang, the hearse set off towards the cemetery, with everyone walking behind it.

Louise Monnier had arranged things perfectly. A meal was waiting for all the guests in a large room hired for the event. The room contained four hundred seats, but many of the guests had to stay outside. There were people every-where. The people standing together spoke as much about the deceased as they did about politics.

It was, according to all of the newspapers, a beautiful funeral.

Émile Monnier's Will

When Émile Monnier died, his wife and his two children were his heirs. However, according to his Will, which he had signed on April 7th, 1877 and deposited with Maitre Louis Bodin, the Poitiers notary who was the Monnier family's lawyer, the deceased had bequeathed to his wife the minimum available portion recognized by the civil code between spouses, which was a quarter of his property in ownership and a quarter in usufruct.

The buildings composing the estate included two houses in Amiens and half of the house bought jointly in 1859 by the two spouses, located at the corner of Rue de la Visitation and Rue des Basses-Treilles, adjacent to the one owned by Louis Demarconnay. The other three-quarters of Émile Monnier's properties and his money was to be divided between his son and his daughter, which meant they would be the legal majority owners of 21 Rue de la Visitation. Blanche was twenty-six years old.

Once she was aware of the implications of the legal technicalities of the Will, Madame Monnier used every means at her disposal, including offering to pay the notary generously, to ensure that she remained the owner of all properties without being accountable to anyone else.

This reveals Louise Monnier's pathological state of mind, as Blanche was the rightful heir to half of her grandmother's property and half of her fortune, as well as having joint ownership (with her brother) of three-quarters of her father's property and fortune. This arrangement was not, for the avaricious Louise Monnier, a suitable arrangement and she began to find ways to relieve her children of their inheritances. Louise Monnier had only one thing on her mind, and that was, as always, money. She convinced herself that her children risked making her destitute if they claimed their legal share of their inheritance.

Legally, Marcel and Blanche Monnier were entitled to ask for an inventory of their father's assets, and to demand their share of it. If necessary, they could force their mother to sell their father's property in order to receive what their father had left them. Louise Monnier was determined she was not going to let that happen. She once again made an appointment with the family lawyer, Maitre Louis Bodin, and had a long conversation with him. The following day, she received him at 21 Rue de la Visitation in the presence of her son.

The notary informed Marcel Monnier that he was due to inherit a part of his father's assets, but that an inventory of the assets would be needed to ascertain their value. He advised Marcel Monnier that inventories were very expensive and time-consuming, and that it might be better to leave the assets as they were and receive a substantial monthly life pension from the estate, rather than liquidate the assets and receive one, possibly quite small, sum of money. The negotiations began, with Madame Monnier offering her son a pension of six hundred francs a month.

Marcel Monnier rejected that as too low a figure. He then rejected one thousand francs a month when his mother offered it. Finally, he demanded two thousand, five hundred francs a month, which he claimed would only just be enough with which to support his wife and daughter.

Madame Monnier protested, claiming such an amount would leave her destitute.

Marcel Monnier refused to accept less than his stipulated figure. He told his mother that if she refused to agree to the amount he had demanded, he would claim his share of the inheritance.

With a show of reluctance, Madame Monnier accepted this, whereupon her son informed her that he had no interest in a verbal agreement and wanted the agreement in writing. The notary agreed to this and offered to prepare the documents. Marcel Monnier then left.

After he had gone, Louise Monnier talked at length to Maitre Louis Bodin about her daughter, Blanche. She took her time, choosing her words carefully. Louise Monnier had a very specific question for her lawyer: because of poor Blanche's ongoing 'pernicious fever' and the dreadful and fragile mental state it had left her in, as well as her perpetual state of melancholy, would she, Louise Monnier, have to ask for Blanche to be subjected to a judicial interdiction, or could Blanche be 'encouraged' to sign a power of attorney in favour of her mother? The judicial interdiction process was a long and costly procedure. Was it really necessary to convene a family council and obtain a judgment from the tribunal who would inevitably have designated the mother as Blanche's guardian anyway?

The notary consulted Doctor Guérineau, the family doctor, and the latter, having been 'advised' on Blanche's state by Louise Monnier, confirmed that in Blanche's case the ban was not necessary. The young woman certainly did not have the full use of her mind, although she could still sign her name.

Maitre Louis Bodin prepared a formal power of attorney document and then, on 14th July 1882, he went to Madame Monnier's house, where he found Doctor Guérineau waiting for him. The notary wanted to enter Blanche's room, but the doctor refused to allow him to do so, telling him that he could not go in to the room and talk to Blanche because she was naked. At the request of the lawyer, Doctor Guérineau entered the room alone and immediately came out, and gave his advice.

Dr. Guérineau: *I advise you not to upset the poor woman any more with your continued insistence. She is very aware of what we want and she agrees to it. Give me the deed and I will have her sign it.*

Because he had a few doubts regarding the unusual nature of the proceedings, Maitre Bodin hesitated for a moment, as he later admitted.

Bodin: *I hesitated, as the situation was a little unorthodox. But then, having confidence in the doctor and knowing that the power of attorney would only be used for just things, I gave him the document he had already signed.*

The doctor went into Blanche's room and emerged a few moments later with the signed document.

By having the due legal process carried out in her home where she could control what transpired and how the transfer of ownership took place, Louise Monnier avoided a judicial interdiction, which was a legal requirement, and therefore preserved the secrecy surrounding matters of the inheritance. Perhaps more importantly, she had also avoided the publication and announcement of the prohibition judgment by means of notices in newspapers and public posters, a legal requirement that could be inconvenient for families wishing to keep their financial matters private.

Louise Monnier had, as always, achieved what she

set out to achieve. By legal means, questionable though they were, she had made her son financially reliant upon her – all she was now obligated to do was pay him a pittance twice a year for the rest of her life; an onerous obligation, but one which she would use to control her son over the following years. She had also managed to cheat her daughter out of two fortunes and several properties, and was keeping said daughter a prisoner in one of those properties. Everything belonging to and pertaining to the Monnier family was in her name and her name alone.

It was a significant moment of triumph for Louise Monnier, but there is no record of how or if she celebrated. In view of her personality, it is likely that she did not celebrate at all.

Louis Demarconnay's Death
and Marcel Monnier's Pension

When Louis Demarconnay died it altered Marcel Monnier's annual pension of five thousand francs that he received from his maternal grandfather and his parents. They had undertaken to pay Marcel Monnier according to the terms of his marriage contract, which stipulated that it was to be ended in part on the death of each of the contributors to the extent that the latter had participated in its constitution. As the Monnier parents had contributed together for half of the life annuity, the latter, on the death of Marcel Monnier's father, could have been cut by a quarter or one thousand two hundred and fifty francs less per year. Madame Monnier nevertheless continued to pay her husband's contribution to her son so that he continued to receive the agreed amount in full.

However, Louise Monnier had a completely different attitude when it came to the death of her own father, Louis Demarconnay, on 21st April 1883, for in his Will, she was named as the sole heiress of his estate.

Then, despite the repeated promises that Louis Demarconnay had made to his grandson, once her father had died, Louise Monnier categorically refused to pay her son the two thousand, five hundred francs of annuity that her father had paid annually towards her son's pension. She also decided she would no longer pay her husband's contribution, meaning that Marcel Monnier's annual pension was reduced to one thousand two hundred and fifty francs, which although it was the stipulated amount under the circumstances it was a sum that was only just about adequate for himself and his family to survive on.

Almost overnight, Marcel Monnier lost an important source of income; a source of income which was nowhere near compensated for by the receipt of rent from the tenants in the house in Amiens.

No matter how angrily he protested, no matter how forcefully he insisted on being given what his grandfather had promised him, and no matter how much he threatened his mother with legal repercussions, nothing made any difference. Louise Monnier was intractable because the wording of her son's marriage contract allowed her to be so.

Her attitude to money, particularly her reluctance (and often deliberate delays) in making the twice-yearly payments of her son's pension, would cause a huge rift between mother and son. In time, that rift would grow into an emotional wound that would never heal – for the simple reason that Louise Monnier did not want it to heal.

Imprisoned

After the Monniers had returned to Rue de la Visitation from Marcel Monnier's wedding, Louise Monnier set about consolidating her power and tightening her control over her children, particularly over Blanche. The next phase of Louise Monnier's plan was to make sure her daughter stayed locked inside her room. Blanche was going to be forced to make the transition from sedated 'patient' to drugged prisoner. Louise Monnier wanted this transition to take place gradually, without Blanche (or anyone else) being aware of the process as it occurred.

Louise Monnier spoke to her husband about Blanche. She had to choose her words carefully; too much emphasis on how the prescribed 'tonic' was not providing Blanche with the calm she required might force Émile Monnier to reconsider and have his daughter's treatment re-evaluated; too much praise for the medication's benefits would mean that Louise Monnier could no longer claim Blanche was a violent young woman who was a danger to them both. She negotiated a path that emphasised her role as an academic's wife concerned with potential scandal and damage to her husband's impeccable reputation, which she combined with her concern over their daughter's constant nudity, exhibitionism and inappropriate touching of herself, as well as her unwillingness to eat properly. She chose those aspects of Blanche's behaviour because she was aware that her husband would feel uncomfortable discussing them; that 'such matters' were not something a father should have to deal with.

When she had finished talking, Louise Monnier had managed to persuade her husband to maintain 'a semblance of normality' by having the shutters that had been placed on the windows of Blanche's room chained shut and padlocked. This had to be done on the outside of the shutters so that that they could always be kept closed and not pushed open from inside the room.

Blanche's health steadily deteriorated, but Louise Monnier paid no attention to her daughter's plight. In fact, Louise Monnier handed over all responsibility for Blanche to Marie Fazy.

74

The faithful servant, who diligently made sure Blanche drank her daily 'cure', was also able, to an extent, to manage and control Blanche. Blanche trusted Marie Fazy, and the former cook was able to exploit Blanche's affection for her and achieve a level of compliance from Blanche that no one else could. Consequently, when Blanche had spells when she was either confused or distraught, Marie Fazy was able to reason with her. The former cook was also able to keep Blanche clean, as Blanche would wash herself when directed to by the maid. Marie Fazy was also able to keep Blanche's room relatively clean. As Blanche often remained in bed, a sheet folded in four, intended to receive the faeces and the urine she evacuated was placed beneath her; the maids changed it daily; in the evening they replaced it with a clean one.

Blanche's room was five meters forty by three meters forty and it was cleaned every day. The walls were originally lined with a grey-blue paper that was almost green, with a beige and blue checked pattern. The wallpaper was starting to show signs of lack of care. It had faded in places.

Louise Monnier had the furnishings reduced to the essentials: to the right of the door there was a chest of drawers; on the right side, two white wooden shelves arranged on either side of a black marble fireplace; in front of the chest of drawers, an iron bed where Marie Fazy slept if she thought it necessary to sleep in Blanche's room; in front of the left shelf and facing the door was Blanche's wooden pallet bed. Against a wall there were six straw chairs in a row and on one of the chairs there was a box filled with old books. Madame Monnier had the maid remove the drawers from the chest of drawers and put them in an adjoining room. She told the maid that at no time was Blanche to be allowed any items of clothing. She qualified this order: No one was to take items of clothing of any kind into Blanche's room.

Louise Monnier: *She likes to be naked, so she can stay naked.*

Blanche's weight loss was accompanied by a regression of language and behaviour. The young woman muttered constantly, repeated some of her words and often her words were unintelligible. She also made a variety of sounds which no doubt indicated her current train of thought. Blanche also spoke quite clearly and at times sought to provoke her mother and shock those around her. She affected to speak patois and peppered her words with 'I was', 'I had' or 'I want'.

When she was angry, she would use the crudest words she knew and she would hurl insults at each maid. Included in her vocabulary of insults were: 'bitch', 'bitch's girl', 'fuckers', and 'buggers'. At other times, Blanche withdrew into herself and seemed unaware of her surroundings or indeed, of any external reality.

Doctor Lagrange was the chief physician of the departmental asylum for the insane in Vienne, and he examined Blanche in 1901 after her transfer to the Hôtel-Dieu.

Doctor Lagrange: *If Mademoiselle Blanche Monnier was intelligent in the past, as the information collected tends to indicate, she could have been afflicted, between the ages of about fifteen to twenty years, by a mental illness called hebephrenia or early dementia, and from that time on have remained in a state roughly identical to that in which she is now. I cannot affirm any of that, as that type of dementia does not make all of the faculties disappear.*

A locksmith reported that, having been called to make a repair to the door of her room, he found Blanche squatting naked on the floor in the middle of her room, her hair untied and hanging loose over her shoulders.

Locksmith: *When I pointed out to the young lady that she should not stay that way, she laughed at me and stayed in that same position, totally silent, the whole time I stayed in the room.*

Speaking to a journalist in 1901, a former maid (who asked the journalist to grant her anonymity) recounted in picturesque terms what she had observed when she was working at Rue de la Visitation.

Journalist: *I was told, Madame, that you knew the Monniers, and that you remained in their service for more than a year?*

Maid: *Sure I know them. I've a good memory! I saw some terrible scenes in that house.*

Journalist: *But wasn't the Monnier family considered to be respectable?*

Maid: *Yes, it's true enough that some of the family were respectable. The Grandfather, Monsieur Demarconnay was a very good man, and Blanche's father, Monsieur Monnier, not bad for two cents, for sure.*

Journalist: *You forgot Madame Monnier.*

Maid: *Oh! that old criminal. She was the cause of everything that went wrong in that house. She made life a misery for everyone she met!*

Journalist: *But what about the children, Monsieur Marcel Monnier and Mademoiselle Blanche?*

Maid: *Monsieur Marcel Monnier was not mean, just a little dull. As for Mademoiselle Blanche, that poor girl, she had moments of being crazy, crazy, and the gossip, oh! I could tell you a few things.*

Journalist: *How did her madness show itself?*

Maid: *First, Madame Monnier made her maid keep her daughter's body bare. When her maid, Marie Fazy, tried to give Blanche her clothes, that old woman grabbed what she could and made holes in it, and then she tore the rest to shreds. Blanche ended up with only a scarf on her head. She once went for a walk in the garden like that.*

Journalist: *You said that Marie Fazy tried to give her clean clothes; was a doctor treating her at that time?*

Maid: *Sure, Monsieur, she was being treated by the family doctor. Often, I went with Marie to Blanche's room. Sometimes she was taken down through the dining room and out into the garden; when Madame wouldn't let her come down, Marie carried her food up to her. She was given her cure in her drink when I was there, I tell you.*

Journalist: *What else did you observe?*

Maid: *Well, Mademoiselle Blanche was fine until she met her mother, Lord! Then she really changed.*

Journalist: *How did she change?*

Maid: *One time she applied make-up, put on a lovely dress and combed her hair. She was a very beautiful young lady. She stood at the top of the stairs and called her mother. When Madame came to the foot of the stairs, Mademoiselle Blanche said to her, 'Bunin, do you remember?' She then pulled the dress off and threw it at her mother. She was naked underneath and she stood there and grabbed cutlery, serving spoons, candlesticks, plates, and threw everything at her mother's head, screaming, 'Do you remember! Do you remember!' over and over again. Her mother was forced to go back into her room in order to save herself.*

Journalist: *What was Blanche's issue with her mother which caused her to become so angry when she was in her pres-*

ence?

Maid: *That, Monsieur, I never knew. But I can tell you that one day, if Marie [Fazy] and I hadn't intervened, Mademoiselle Blanche would have killed her mother. She was quite strong, Mademoiselle Blanche. After a scene like that, Madame Monnier would go up to her room, lie down and we wouldn't see her for two days.*

Doctor Chrétien, a professor at the school of medicine in Poitiers, recounted that his eminent colleague from the faculty of Paris, Professor Gilles de la Tourette, himself born in Poitiers, had told him, early in 1875, that Mademoiselle Blanche Monnier 'made unsuitable exhibitions of herself at her window.'

Georges Vacher de la Pouge, the librarian of the university, reported something similar in an interview: 'Between the years 1874 to 1878, there was much talk amongst the students about Mademoiselle Monnier and how that young lady was suffering from erotic excitement and that she could often be seen exhibiting herself naked at her bedroom window.'

Léon Marchand, the editorial secretary of *Le Journal de la Vienne*, also commented on this.

Marchand: *Around 1878, when I was a law student, it was common knowledge that Mademoiselle Monnier was suffering from some sort of hysteria and a dislike of clothing on her skin. Students would sometimes walk past her window to see if they could see her naked at her window. I never spoke to any student who had actually seen her at her window. It was probably malicious gossip, but many people believed it. The Dean, Émile Monnier could not have let the scandal continue, especially since his daughter's room was in front of a cabaret frequented by soldiers. For once in his life, he actually made a decision. He ordered shutters to be fitted to the windows, which were then closed and secured shut with a chain and a padlock on the outside, so as to prevent them from being opened from inside.*

Several people testified that Blanche's room door was not locked. These testimonies directly conflict with the Central Commissioner's report that stated quite clearly that Marcel Monnier unlocked Blanche Monnier's room door with a key that he took from his pocket.

One such witness was Madame Deshoulières, née

Brunet, who was in the service of Monsieur Demarconnay a little before his death.

Deshoulières: *The window of her [Blanche's] room was closed, but the door remained open.*

Another witness who said similar was Madame Dugué, a maid in the Monnier house for two and a half years, from 1879 to 1882.

Dugué: *Mademoiselle Blanche was well cared for... The door to her room was always wide open, only the shutters were secured closed.*

Madame Maingault, who was employed by Madame Monnier in 1883, also testified to this.

Maingault: *The shutters were closed, but Mademoiselle Blanche could open the window. She could also go down into the house. Her confinement was totally voluntary, and although Mademoiselle Blanche was deprived of any communication with the outside world, no one ever used any coercion to prevent her from leaving. When the mistress of the house recommended securing the door of her room so that it was carefully closed, it was because she feared that her daughter, a delicate young woman who was always naked, would get cold. These instructions were more important during the winter, naturally enough. The door was only opened, with Madame Monnier's consent when the smell of the room became too strong, which was usually during the summer.*

The neighbours soon suspected that the young woman was suffering from some type of obsessive neurosis. Several former maids and cooks testified that Blanche Monnier was mentally ill and that her behaviour made this obvious.

Manon Deshoulières (a maid): *Mademoiselle Blanche saw people who wanted to kill her. She would often shout at the murderer and not stop shouting until the murderer had gone.*

Madame Gaud (a cook): *Whenever Blanche came into the kitchen she was always naked, but she hid her face with a scarf. She often told me that ghosts were following her.*

Claire Maingault (a maid): *Mademoiselle Blanche screamed at night, and she was mostly agitated and upset by stormy weather.*

On his way home from work one evening, the plasterer, Théodore Touchard heard anguished screams coming from the Monnier house. It sounded as though Blanche Monnier was at one of the upstairs windows, screaming with all her strength. The screams were terrible. As he passed the small inn run by Madame Morillon, at the corner of the Rue des Ecossais, she spoke to him.

Morillon: *Monsieur Touchard, those screams are hurting my ears. What's going on at Madame Monnier's house?*

Touchard: *I don't know, but I'm sure that's Mademoiselle Blanche's voice.*

On another occasion, having heard screams again coming from the house, he approached the door of 21 Rue de la Visitation. A maid was standing in front of the front door.

Touchard: *Is there anything I can do to help?*

Maid: *No thank you, Monsieur.*

After a few moments, Madame Monnier came to the door.

Louise Monnier: *Monsieur Touchard, I am very upset because my daughter is crazy. The doctor is treating her, but her mind has gone.*

Touchard accepted that the young woman no longer had her reason. In an interview in 1901, he verified this.

Touchard: *I was no longer bothered by the screams and shouts that I heard.*

From the moment that Louise Monnier had informed the doctor of Blanche's 'madness', Blanche did not leave the house. The holidays at Le Pilet had gradually lessened until they came to an abrupt halt, which was unfortunate, as the peaceful pastoral setting would certainly have been beneficial for Blanche's mental and physical health.

The sharecropper Auguste Joubert, who had married Rosalie in 1874, admitted he had not seen Blanche Monnier at Le Pilet for many years.

Joubert: *When I went to Poitiers, to Madame Monnier's house, I heard about her daughter from a maid. I heard she was crazy and when I asked about her, I was told, 'She's not getting any better'.*

Joubert made no attempt to find out any more about his employer's daughter's mental state. Discretion and circumspection were important in such circumstances. No one went out of their way to discover the well-kept secret of the powerful and wealthy Monnier family with its rumoured links to royalty.

In the nineteenth century, domestic authority was undisputed and paternal power was sovereign. Every man was the master at home and no one had the right to, nor would have dared to, intervene. Children's errors were suppressed and more importantly, any form of mental illness or deformity was hushed up and treated within the family environment. Children were locked away if they proved to be an embarrassment to the family.

Parents were often reluctant to make their child's mental disability public. They preferred to keep afflicted children at home instead of sending them to a nursing home to receive proper care. Placement in a psychiatric institution was seen as abandonment and confinement to which families could only resolve at the last extreme, that is, when the mentally ill person became dangerous to themselves and to others.

Nineteenth century insane asylums housed a society that was deliberately and carefully kept separate from everyone else. Each asylum was a kind of prison, with bars and chains and restraints. These places resounded with screams and cries of anguish and pain. However, an asylum was not, technically, a prison, as it was meant to be therapeutic, not punitive. In reality, asylums were a type of hell at whose door it was necessary to leave all hope.

Émile Monnier, in agreement with his wife, had decided that his daughter would be cared for in the family home and not placed in an asylum.

One of the Monniers' maids, Victorine Kuenka, who testified at Marcel Monnier's trial, said that Émile Monnier had very definite ideas regarding his daughter's care.

Victorine Kuenka: *When I asked Monsieur Monnier about treatment for Mademoiselle Blanche, he said to me 'As long as I can have her treated by doctors, I will keep her here.'*

And so, Blanche became the patient of Doctor Guérineau, the Monnier family doctor and director of the medical school. Taking his cues from Louise Monnier, he did not bother to prescribe any special treatment. He was simply content to prescribe potassium bromide and authorise Louise Monnier to administer small doses of it daily. After all, potassium bromide was known to calm nerves and was frequently used to combat epileptic seizures or hysteria and to repress the libido.

As Arthur Ranc wrote: *The doctor who provided medical care to the presumed madwoman and who seems to me to have unfortunately indulged this dignified and well-regarded family [seems] to have made himself, more than was suitable, the auxiliary of the family's maternal authority.*

Later, when Blanche manifested psychic disorders, doctors were content to note the 'manic hysteria' without doing anything by way of treatment, as if it were inevitable. In the end, these complacent doctors considered that they should not meddle in what they regarded as a strictly family matter.

As Arthur Ranc suggested in *Le Radical*, there was collusion between the medical profession and Blanche Monnier's mother, but that collusion had a hidden aspect to it that no one but Louise Monnier and her staff were aware of. The effects that potassium bromide had on the central nervous system were not fully documented – as far as the family doctor was concerned, the prescription calmed the patient; as far as Louise Monnier was concerned, her daughter was reduced to a state of sedated lethargy and in that state, was unable to challenge her authority.

Émile Monnier, by allowing himself to be persuaded by his forceful wife to avoid therapeutic isolation for Blanche in a nursing home, was guilty of negligence and dereliction of paternal responsibility.

Louise Monnier's argument was that having Blanche treated in an institution would have been expensive, and the fact that Émile Monnier agreed to this shows exactly what their priorities as parents were. Monniers refused to consider such treatment indicates that the desire to keep the unfortunate young woman in the family environment was simply a rationalisation designed to camouflage her avarice. If Émile Monnier genuinely believed his daughter was mentally ill, which seems to be the case, then it is likely he felt an element of shame, perhaps also a sense of humiliation knowing that his colleagues at the faculty of arts were aware of Blanche's unpredictable behaviour. Ultimately, the wealthy Monniers' true nature was revealed the first moment they took the decision to refuse to spend any money on treatment for their daughter and basing that decision on their certainty that said treatment would prove useless.

Louise Monnier's Motives

Louise Monnier's motive was the acquisition of money. It was her driving force and her only interest; she cared for little else. She did not distinguish between acquiring money honestly and acquiring it dishonestly. In order to acquire money dishonestly, she understood the importance of taking slow, measured, and carefully calculated steps. In that respect she was a formidable tactician. Her strategy was one of incrementalism, whereby the first step, once taken, would, over a period of time, achieve something. This led inevitably to her taking a second step, which, when taken, would lead to a further achievement, followed by a third step being taken and so on.

Louise Monnier preferred strategies that looked as though they had been put in place by, or were carried out by, someone other than herself. She had suggested to her husband that, for the sake of propriety, shutters on Blanche's room windows would be beneficial and Émile Monnier had duly arranged to have shutters fitted. She had told the doctor about Blanche's 'exhibitionism' and the doctor had readily prescribed potassium bromide, the dosage of which Louise Monnier became responsible for administering. Although she was responsible for measuring out the 'tonic' into a glass, she had instructed her maids to make sure that Blanche drank her drink – or to continue offering it to her until she drank it. She had asked her legal advisor about a way to have Blanche's fortune transferred to her, and it was the notary and the doctor that eventually persuaded Blanche to sign the document that assigned all of her money and all of her properties to her mother.

Ideally, Louise Monnier preferred to use the type of strategy whereby those being exploited were unaware that any exploitation was taking place.

When Émile Monnier died, his wife and his two children were named as his heirs. According to his Will, which he had signed on April 7th, 1877 and deposited with Maitre Louis Bodin, the notary in Poitiers, the deceased had bequeathed to his wife the minimum available portion recognized by the civil code between spouses, which was a quarter of his property in ownership and a quarter in usufruct. The buildings composing the estate included two houses in Amiens and half of the house bought jointly in 1859 by the two spouses, located at the corner of Rue de la Visitation and Rue des Basses-Treilles, adjacent to the one owned by Louis Demarconnay. The other three-quarters of his properties and his money was to be divided between his son and his daughter, which meant his wife would become a minority part-owner of 21 Rue de la Visitation.

Once she was aware of the implications of the legal technicalities of her husband's Will, Madame Monnier used every means at her disposal, including bribing the notary, to ensure that she became the legal owner of all of the Monnier properties without being accountable to anyone else.

This reveals Louise Monnier's pathological state of mind, as Blanche was the rightful heir to half of her grandmother's property and half of her fortune, as well as having joint ownership (with her brother) of three-quarters of her father's property and fortune. This arrangement was not, for the avaricious Louise Monnier, a suitable arrangement and she began to search for ways to relieve her children of their inheritances.

Marie Fazy (2)

After the death of her grandmother, whom she loved very much, Blanche Monnier transferred all of her filial affection to Marie Fazy, who acted as a sort of surrogate mother. Louise Monnier, who was fully aware of her daughter's feelings of contempt and dislike for her, even though she was the young woman's mother, gladly accepted this turn of events. It was a useful development for Madame Monnier, as her daughter declining mental and physical health demanded the type of care which she was unwilling to provide.

Marie Fazy's biggest personality flaw was that she drank to excess. Constant hours of standing over stoves and ovens meant she had a permanent thirst which she sought to quench by drinking endless glasses of wine. Over time, she became an alcoholic, unable to go a day without having several drinks, which in turn resulted in her being known throughout the neighborhood as 'le Souluine' (the Drunkard).

Fully aware of her employee's weakness for alcohol, Louise Monnier, always on the lookout for a way to obtain an advantage over anyone, instructed the former cook to abandon her stoves and ovens in order to take care of Blanche permanently. To 'encourage' her employee to make the change from cook to personal maid, Louise Monnier had had several cases of expensive wine delivered to 21 Rue de la Visitation.

One of the 1883 monthly bills from the wine merchant, Maillard-Laurendeau was for twenty bottles of best-quality table wine at 0 francs 75 per bottle and ten bottles of fine Bordeaux wine at 2 francs 3 per bottle. Louise Monnier did not drink, nor did she entertain, so it is reasonable to assume that the wine was an incentive for Marie Fazy.

This particular decision by Louise Monnier is worth consideration, as it again shows the depths of callousness Blanche's mother actually had with regards to her daughter. After sedating Blanche into imbecility, and duping her out of her inheritances, Louise Monnier then promoted an alcoholic cook to the position of jailer, under the guise of being her daughter's personal maid – and gave that alcoholic jailer a constant supply of bottles of wine as part payment for that care.

The new arrangement meant that at night, Marie Fazy slept just outside Blanche's room, on an iron bed, so as to effectively monitor her charge. She was exactly the right maid for the situation. Everyone in the house found her presence just outside Blanche's room reassuring. Ironically, Marie Fazy was the one person in the house that Blanche seemed to trust. If Blanche became agitated of started screaming, it was Marie Fazy and no one else who was able to exert some control and calm Blanche in her moments of extreme emotional crisis.

As a result of these changes, the former cook's position within the household was strengthened as her authority increased. Marie Fazy became the woman in charge of running the household and watching over the other servants. Madame Monnier had put her in charge of her daughter, but she entrusted the former cook with many other tasks, especially after her husband's death in 1882. Marie Fazy took her orders directly from Louise Monnier and relayed those orders to the other maids. Marie Fazy actually ran the house. Even Blanche, with her diminished capabilities, understood this.

Marie Fazy watched over everything, received and signed for deliveries and made routine purchases. She was always very economical. She was also a formidable gatekeeper who knew how to deter unwelcome visitors.

21 Rue de la Visitation had become, over time, a house in which many of its rooms were filthy and should have been condemned. It was a house in which two women lived in seclusion, the mother, by choice, on the first floor and the daughter, as a prisoner, on the second. Maid service in the house was reduced to a minimum.

It was not long before Marie Fazy could no longer do the job she was being paid to do. She had varicose veins, grew tired very quickly, and the task of managing Blanche was soon beyond her declining strength. Also, Blanche's thinness had taken on frightening proportions.

Blanche Monnier's mental and physical faculties were deteriorating rapidly due to the continued administration of potassium bromide in her morning drink. Her rages and her silences were becoming more frequent. She soiled her sheets and mattress constantly, so much so that her mother reached a point where she simply refused to allow Marie Fazy to have the bed linen needed to change her.

Louise Monnier insisted that it was a waste of time trying to keep her daughter clean because she obviously enjoyed living in utter filth. Consequently, the poor woman often had to sleep in the midst of her own excrement. The overpowering smell in the room was difficult to bear, especially since the shutters were closed and sealed shut. The window could only be opened a crack, which was not enough to allow the stale air to be replaced with fresh air.

In her sedated state, which was akin to the drugged state of opium users, Blanche preferred to be left undisturbed. Consequently, the maids cleaned her room less and less, until they stopped bothering altogether. The 'dear little cave' had become a disgustingly filthy hovel. Marie Fazy tried her best to keep Blanche clean and respectable-looking in her prison, but even she had limits to her strength and determination.

Doctor Chédevergne, who called at 21 Rue de la Visitation in the early afternoon of every Saturday for his appointment with Madame Monnier, almost never went up to Blanche's room to check on her. In his opinion, Blanche was being treated using recognized and accepted methods, so there was nothing more he could do for her. Marie Fazy therefore received no medical advice from the doctor and was left to her own devices to provide Blanche with whatever sort of care she could manage. The maid was also aware that she would get no real support from Madame Monnier. It was this knowledge that caused the old maid to finally relinquish her responsibilities and take refuge in drink, to the point, it was said, of being drunk for most of the day, every day of the week.

In a frustrated rage, Blanche Monnier would sometimes break or damage things. If it became necessary to have something in the room repaired, Marie Fazy took care to get Blanche out of bed and move her into another room. A maid would then open the window to ventilate and clean the room. The workers noticed the torn paper, the rotten parquet and the broken furniture, but they blamed it all on the madness of the unfortunate woman.

In 1883, Téodore Touchard, a local plasterer, was called to 21 Rue de Visitation to repair a cracked fireplace in Blanche Monnier's room. Blanche was not in her room when he got there and although the room had been recently cleaned, it still smelled unpleasantly of faeces and urine. In an interview in 1901, Touchard said that as he completed the work he heard Blanche Monnier's voice.

Touchard: *I heard Mademoiselle Monnier's voice from another room. She said: 'My mother is no longer the mistress of this house; a servant is now in charge. She has told everyone that I'm a crazy woman. There's no justice.'*

Meanwhile, everyone who knew about Blanche's 'madness' praised her alcoholic jailer and her 'devotion' to poor Blanche.

On Sunday, May 26th, 1895, the faithful servant received the medal of honor of the Society for the Encouragement of Good. The society, founded in 1862 by the journalist and philanthropist Honoré Arnoul (1810-1893), aimed to spread the principles of religion and morality amongst the working class. It rewarded people who had distinguished themselves by acts of bravery, or who were employees who had stayed for a long time with a family or in a company. Marie Fazy received her medal and it was accompanied by a certificate that read:

Marie Fazy

Forty-five years of service in the same house.

Awarded for having shown, during those long years of service, great dedication and constant loyalty.

Marie Fazy undoubtedly deserved the distinction just as much as any other loyal and devoted servant deserved it. However, it is perhaps worth mentioning that Marcel Monnier was a friend of Prosper Puisay, the head of the military office at the town hall, and a close friend of Paul Druet, the former Chief Advocate, both of whom were members of the committee. It is therefore quite possible that, either on the recommendation of their friend or to please him, the medal was awarded to his mother's maid.

The Health Inspector

Early one spring morning in 1892, as Madame Monnier's former cook walked along Rue de la Visitation on the opposite side of the road to the Monnier house, she stopped to talk to Désiré Bricault, a café owner, who was busy hosing down the pavement in front of his café.

Fazy: *It's very good that you wash down the pavement in front of your café every morning. It's always very clean. But I must tell you, there are some very awful things happening at number twenty-one that keep me up at night.*

Bricault: *What is it? My God, what's going on there!*

Fazy: *In that house, the daughter is totally crazy. And the woman who is supposed to be taking care of her doesn't bother at all. She just leaves the poor woman in a locked room that's littered with excrement and rotten food. It's filthy. Come with me and I'll show you.*

Bricault: *No. It's none of my business. All I can do is inform the health inspector. I will do that.*

Désiré Bricault duly passed on the information to Monsieur Garnier, the public health inspector. Garnier decided to investigate. One morning, as he was passing through Rue de la Visitation, he decided stop at the Monnier house. He rang the doorbell and a young maid opened the door.

Garnier: *Mademoiselle, I am the public health inspector; in this capacity, I have the right to visit all apartments that are reported to me as not offering sufficient guarantees regarding public hygiene. I know that in this house there is a young woman locked in her room whose state of cleanliness leaves much to be desired. Would you please take me to her?*

Maid: *Oh! Sir. What you are asking for is impossible. No one ever enters this house.*

But Garnier refused to be deterred. He insisted and made such a decisive argument that the maid capitulated.

Maid: *All right then, go and see her if you want to!*

The maid pointed the way around the house and across the garden. The inspector walked around the side of the house and started to cross the garden. He was immediately seen by an inebriated Marie Fazy. At the sight of a stranger in the garden, she grew violently angry and began to shout at the interloper. She then ran out into the garden and charged at him, brandishing a walking stick.

Fazy: *Thief! Murderer!*

Alarmed by the shrieking and charging harpy brandishing the heavy-looking stick, Garnier hastily retreated to the gate, stepped out onto Rue de la Visitation and quickly pulled the gate shut behind him. He then walked briskly down Rue de la Visitation away from the Monnier house. The incident was not followed up.

When he was called as a witness at Marcel Monnier's trial, Désiré Bricault confirmed under oath the details of his conversation with Marie Fazy. He also explained that he had informed the public health inspector of what she'd told him. The health inspector, Monsieur Garnier was not called as a witness at Marcel Monnier's trial.

By 1892, Blanche Monnier had been locked away for over twenty years, and no one apart from Louise Monnier, her maids and Marie Fazy were aware of the terrible state that Blanche was in.

Outside the house on Rue de la Visitation, only a handful of people from Poitiers remembered that Madame Monnier had a daughter who had 'gone crazy' in about 1870 and since then had been locked away for her own good. No one knew how frighteningly emaciated she now was, nor could anyone have guessed the disgusting state of the filthy and rat-infested room she was locked inside. It had taken Louise Monnier just over twenty years to reduce her daughter to nothing more than a well-kept secret.

All of the maids who worked for Madame Monnier were sworn to absolute secrecy.

Marie Fazy made sure that there were no unexpected callers at the house; she also made sure that no one apart from those she authorized to do so entered Blanche's room.

Marie Fazy's Death

At the age of sixty, Marie Fazy was prematurely worn out. Her alcoholism had destroyed her health, and her once enviable strength and energy were no longer what they had been. She was physically deteriorating without any of her colleagues noticing the worsening of her condition.

She died on 16th May 1896, after three weeks of illness, in Blanche's room, where she slept on an iron bed.

Immediately, Louise Monnier had her maid's body moved without any fuss or fanfare into another room so that Blanche remained unaware of the former cook's demise.

Marie Fazy's funeral could have provided Louise Monnier with an opportunity to show her appreciation of all that her long-serving employee had done for her and her family. Instead, it revealed Madame Monnier's narrow-mindedness, her petty avarice and her absolute contempt for everyone, particularly those she felt were beneath her, which was everybody.

First of all, she promised the former cook's family that she would pay half of the funeral expenses. This was, she said, because Marie Fazy had been such a devoted and loyal servant.

The brothers and sisters of the deceased made an inventory of the furniture and personal effects their sister had left in her quarters in the house on Rue de la Visitation. Out of politeness and respect for the owner of the house, Louise Monnier was invited to attend. Louise Monnier had no intention of inconveniencing herself with something as mundane as the sorting out of the effects of a dead maid, so she asked her daughter-in-law to represent her.

In a chest of drawers belonging to Marie Fazy, her family found a box containing her savings. She had accumulated ten thousand francs. Marcel Monnier's wife immediately went to her mother-in-law and informed her of the discovery. Louise Monnier instructed her daughter-in-law to let Marie Fazy's family know that in light of their discovery she would no longer pay half of the funeral costs but would, instead, pay for a mortuary wreath big enough to cover the coffin.

When he heard that his mother had reneged on her promise, Marcel Monnier finally agreed to pay half of the costs of burying his sister's maid.

Marie Fazy was buried alongside her husband in Cimetière de Chilvert. Her grave was located right next to the Demarconnay and Monnier vault. And so, the former alcoholic cook remained linked with the family of her employer, even after death.

Other Maids
1897

After the death of Marie Fazy, a series of other maids succeeded her in the Monnier household. Although some of those maids were conscientious enough, they had neither Marie Fazy's experience nor, more importantly, her understanding of and her ability to manage Blanche.

The need to implicitly obey Madame Monnier; the long stretches of almost total idleness that had to be endured; the responsibility of caring for and guarding Blanche by sleeping outside her room door, or sometimes in her room if she grew agitated, was more than most domestic staff could tolerate, and the situation soon drove away those who were able to find positions in other houses.

In the early part of 1897, Madeleine Filleul entered the service of Madame Monnier, but she remained there only two days.

Madeleine Filleul: *Because of Mademoiselle Blanche, the position was intolerable.*

At the beginning of 1899, Victorine Mouroux was employed as a maid. On the evening she arrived at the Monnier house, she went up to Blanche's room to spend the night. She decided to look into the room to check on her charge. The stench of the room assailed her nose and she gagged. When Blanche saw Victorine Moyroux, she began to scream, which frightened the new maid. The maid immediately left the room and ran to the nearby pharmacy before it closed to buy the incense known as Papier d'Arménie in the hope it would dispel the noxious smells that permeated the room. Frightened by what she had seen and heard, she decided to return to the accursed house, collect her suitcase and leave, which she duly did.

Two other women showed up in the first months of 1899, one a maid, the other a cook. After seeing the filthy state in which Blanche was being forced to live, they too left the Monnier house in a hurry.

Madame Monnier was beginning to find it very difficult to find maids, even unqualified ones. In addition, by the end of the nineteenth century, there was a crisis of domesticity, due less to the decline in numbers than to the increase in demand from employers. The rise in the standard of living meant that a lot of working-class people suddenly found themselves in the middle class. Many felt that one of the quickest ways to distance themselves from their working-class roots was to employ servants, as many believed that to be served was a sign of class.

In 21 Rue de la Visitation, the cook was paid thirty francs a month, and the maid was paid twenty-two francs a month. These salaries corresponded to the average salary to female servants paid at that time in Poitiers. Additionally, and no doubt included by Louise Monnier as an inducement to stay, the maids were given food, a room and a uniform which was laundered weekly. Obviously, Louise Monnier, unable to resist displaying her usual contempt, made one of the maids responsible for the laundry, so in effect, one maid laundered her own uniform, as well as the uniforms of her colleagues. All of the domestic staff complained about the food, as Madame Monnier had the cook prepare a stew using very poor-quality cuts of meat. The maids referred to the stew as 'third-rate dog meat', which had only just enough nutrition to sustain them.

Whenever Louise Monnier heard any of her staff complaining, she would dismiss them on the spot, often without a reference, thereby making their chances of finding work more difficult than it needed to be. In the years after Marie Fazy died, Louise Monnier dismissed a lot of maids.

By 1898, there were only two domestic staff left in Louise Monnier's service: a cook and a maid. One of the cooks, Celine Quinqueneau, who was employed by Louise Monnier for six months between October 1898 and June 1899, was thoughtful and compassionate towards Blanche. Because of this, she was constantly confronted by Louise Monnier's acrimony and hostility.

Although Blanche seldom spoke any more, she did speak from time to time, especially if there was something that upset her or delighted her. She loved flowers very much. Celine Quinqueneau took a small bouquet into Blanche's room one morning and Blanche spent her entire morning looking at it and admiring it.

Celine Quinqueneau: *The following morning, Mademoiselle Blanche asked for another 'dear little bouquet', but her mother did not want her to have any more flowers in her room. She outright forbade it, saying to me, 'It will upset her, so I won't allow it.' Despite the old miser forbidding it, I sometimes picked some flowers and took them to Mademoiselle Blanche. She was very happy then.*

Celine Quinqueneau noticed that the mattress on which Blanche was lying was quite rotten, so she asked Louise Monnier if she could change her daughter's bedding.

Celine Quinqueneau: *I asked if I could change Mademoiselle Blanche's bedding. Madame Monnier replied dryly: 'Others have tried to do it, but they have not been successful, so don't bother trying.'*

One day, Celine Quinqueneau spoke to Louise Monnier, and perhaps in a moment of lapsed concentration, the old lady agreed that her cook could fetch a mattress from one of the bedrooms in the large main building. In that part of the house there were several unused but fully-furnished bedrooms. Celine Quinqueneau went to one of those rooms, took a mattress and carried it back towards Blanche's room. When Louise Monnier realized that it was going to be substituted for the rotten mattress, she forbade the change and ordered the cook to return the mattress to the room it had come from.

As for the sheets, it was the same thing: Blanche had only two sheets at her disposal, which were washed in turn. She was incontinent and soiled her sheets right through to the mattress. Although Louise Monnier's cupboards were filled with linen, she insisted that there was no point in having Blanche's bed linen changed as she would simply soil it over and over again. According to Louise Monnier, Blanche always ruined the linen by either soiling it or ripping it to shreds.

Blanche was always naked, and when she lay on her sheet, she covered her face with a scarf. The sheet was as rotten as the mattress, so the cook, despite fearing Louise Monnier's recrimination, fetched one of her own sheets for Blanche to use.

Also, Blanche had nothing in the way of support; neither pillows nor bolster; she spent most of her time leaning on her elbow. Celine Quinqueneau suggested placing a bolster and a pillow behind Blanche as support, but as they would have had to be replaced from time to time, Madame Monnier refused to allow it.

As a concession of sorts, but only after much hesitation and a great deal of reluctance, Celine Quinqueneau and a maid, Berthe Perroche, were given permission to make three small cushions filled with straw. One of the cushions was placed under Blanche's head and the other two were declared spares and put on one of the chairs in Blanche's room for later use.

The thrift, the greed, the avarice, the meanness, the miserliness, the malice, or whatever it was that was the reason (or reasons) Madame Monnier refused to provide sheets, pillows, blankets and a mattress for her daughter's bed, contrasted drastically with the money she spent on food for Blanche, both in quantity and quality.

Louise Monnier went out of her way to make sure that a range of specially-prepared dishes from the best hotels and restaurants in Poitiers were delivered to the house for her daughter. These were meals that she did not order for herself, as the last two servants engaged in 1899: Juliette Dupuis, the maid, and Eugénie Tabeau, the cook, both testified.

Adrien Roblin, owner of the Hôtel de France, confirmed that he was asked for dishes, often two or three times a week, and Ernest Vallée, of the Hôtel de l'Europe, also stated that he had provided a large number of sought-after dishes such as pâté foie gras. Blanche Monnier particularly loved oysters. Every day that oysters were in season, the maid went to buy some from the stall run by Madame Fort. Madame Monnier was a very demanding customer; she had instructed her maid to choose the freshest and the most beautiful oysters for her daughter.

At the butcher's shop, it was the same; maids had been instructed to buy only the best quality cuts of meat. Madame Monnier refused to pay for anything that was not a choice cut.

Any expenses or activities that were related to Blanche's cleanliness were not visible to the outside world, so for Louise Monnier they were utterly pointless. Appearances were everything to her. Therefore, ordering expensive meals from hotels and restaurants and having the meals delivered to the house regularly was a very visible activity. Louise Monnier could be seen to be doing something that would be interpreted as a caring act.

As Marie Fazy was no longer there to prepare the

meals that Blanche would have eaten, the old matriarch started ordering dishes from the best restaurants in the city. It was a very expensive way to feed Blanche, but such an expense that was, as everything Louise Monnier did, part of a much bigger strategy. It was one highly visible way for Louise Monnier to give the appearance of being a caring mother. And if anyone happened to think that she was simply doing it to redeem her inability to express her love and affection for her daughter in the usual maternal ways, then so much the better.

It is probable, bearing in mind Blanche Monnier's extreme emaciation, that she was never given any of the meals that her mother ordered for her.

As for what actually happened to those meals, while it is possible that Louise Monnier ate some of them, it is more likely that the maids who constantly complained about the meals they were given would have eaten them, thereby compensating themselves for the 'third-rate dog meat' stew provided by their employer. They would have eaten the meals whilst sitting outside Blanche's room, so that Louise Monnier would remain unaware that Blanche had not eaten again that day. A callous or calculating maid would only have needed to have left a plate containing a few scraps of the meal in Blanche's room for the deception to have been successful. However, Madame Monnier did not visit her daughter's room very often, so it is very likely that the maids made sure they benefited from the situation.

The maids sometimes took plates into Blanche's room and left them on the night-stand. Occasionally, they would make a show of collecting the plates in the morning; sometimes they would forget and dirty plates and scraps of food would accumulate in Blanche's room.

Neither maid liked oysters, so Blanche was given those, although the maids were too lazy to sweep up the empty shells that fell onto the floor, which inevitably attracted mice, rats, and cockroaches.

After Marie Fazy's death, Louise Monnier did not cancel her large wine order. The invoices presented by Maillard-Laurendeau, the wine merchant based at 4 Rue Rabelais, show that the same relatively large quantity of good quality table wine at seventy-five cents per bottle and a fine Bordeaux at two francs and three cents per bottle that was initially delivered monthly to 21 Rue de la Visitation for Marie Fazy's consumption, was still being delivered throughout 1899 and 1900. Bearing in mind Louise Monnier's habits of sobriety and extreme thrift, it is unlikely that she was spending money on wine for herself. She may have forgotten to cancel the order after Marie Fazy's death, or she may have used the wine to pay her staff, using alcohol as an inducement for them to continue working for her. A room in a big house, free food, free wine and a uniform, as well as twenty-one francs a month, in exchange for a small amount of housework and checking on Blanche would quite possibly have looked like a very good prospect for a young, unqualified maid.

The last two servants that were employed by Louise Monnier were Juliette Dupuis and Eugénie Tabeau. They were both quite young women from the country. Hired without references, they were neither conscientious nor dedicated. They neglected their responsibilities and were very quick to take advantage of Louise Monnier's declining health by ignoring her instructions.

Madame Monnier wrote a letter to her son, who was on holiday in Ciboure, complaining bitterly about her maids:

'I tell you this: as long as I have these two maids in my house, I will always be sick. These are the worst ones I've ever had here, you'll see. They are always standing by the door that leads out onto the street. On the day of the Assumption, there was a party at Madame Rivaud's house all day, with constant noise in the street. Well! Would you believe that these two maids who are supposed to be working in my house did not come back in through that door until after eight o'clock in the evening. It's shameful to have girls like that in one's home. Do you believe that when you are sick and surrounded by people like that, you have the means to recover properly? The bitches! I have to stay with the poor child; and when I ring, the maid paid to care for her does not go up; and where are they? They are stupid girls who have every fault going; I fear that one day they will inadvertently set fire to the house... If Angèle [Marcel Monnier's wife] knows of a reliable maid in Poitiers, I would take her with great pleasure, because there is no longer any way I can continue to live like this. Every night, *to get them to close the front door and hand over the key, I have to get angry with them. The bigger creature of the two is like a large sheep herder [Eugénie Tabeau] and she is more insolent than the other. I have never seen such a beast. She is the one who is paid to take care of Blanche and I am the one who is forced to take care of her even though I no longer have the strength.'*

The maids devised for themselves a routine that was purely social. Every evening, between seven o'clock and half past eight, and sometimes until ten o'clock, Juliette and Eugénie remained on the doorstep of the street door, doing their best to attract the soldiers who passed through the Rue de la Visitation to go to the cabaret.

Madame Monnier wrote to her son on 24th September 1900, explaining her frustration with her maids and the soldiers loitering around the Monnier house:

'The soldiers and young men make such an unbearable chatter, it's impossible to make them quiet. As long as there are soldiers at Madame Rivaud's house, they [the maids] stand outside the door to the street and the soldiers will not leave. If they [the maids] are told to return to their work, they are extraordinarily insolent. They are no better than each other.'

Live-in servants were not entitled to take time off for leisure activities apart from when their employers granted it. Talking in the street, during the day, to strangers, was deemed an unsuitable activity for young women; chatting to men at nightfall, on the doorstep and with soldiers, was an object of scandal that the puritanical Madame Monnier could not stand.

The old lady would have fired them, but how do you find two good new ones to replace them? It was necessary to have a strong constitution to be able sleep in Blanche's room and care for her, because of the state of physical and mental destitution she was in. The two maids, however, seemed to be able to bear the foul smell that emanated from Blanche's bed and from Blanche herself. Eugénie Tabeau slept in the poor woman's room and Juliette Dupuis slept just outside the locked door on the landing.

It is not that either maid was insensitive, but both of them were thoughtless young women lacking in discernment. Their main flaw was laziness. They neglected their household duties and dust accumulated on the furniture. They made no effort to clean Blanche's room, nor to clear away the accumulating food debris, mainly oyster shells, that now littered the floor around Blanche's bed. As a consequence, maggots and cockroaches teemed over the rotten food.

They were told that Blanche was unpredictable and spoiled and that was enough for them. They decided that they would make no effort to keep Blanche clean and her room tidy, especially as her own mother, after having forbidden either of them to ever take any clothes into Blanche's room, was content to let her daughter lie on a filthy, cockroach and rat-infested bed, totally naked except for a flimsy, filthy scarf she would sometimes use to cover her face.

During the day, most of their work was limited to taking delivery of the meal, then taking it up to Blanche at the agreed time. In the evening, between nine and nine-thirty, the two maids proceeded to carry out a routine that they called 'putting Mademoiselle Blanche to bed', the details of which were recounted by Juliette Dupuis at Marcel Monnier's trial.

Juliette Dupuis: *The daily task we called 'putting Mademoiselle Blanche to bed' consisted of the following: the young lady got up on all fours; the maid lifted up the sheet that the excrement from the last twenty-four hours was on; she folded it into quarters and removed it. She also removed a small straw-filled cushion that was absolutely filthy. The cushion was replaced with another, also filthy, and the sheet was replaced with one that had been rinsed out, but which was still very dirty, but not as dirty as the one that had just been removed. During this, Mademoiselle Blanche maintained her position on all fours. She kept her face covered even though she was facing away from us. I felt embarrassed for her. Once the bed was ready, she lowered herself back onto the bed and resumed her former position. Monsieur Marcel Monnier watched this scene more than once to my knowledge, so it would be very wrong of him to insist that he believed his sister was well taken care of. He couldn't have avoided seeing the state she was in.*

Madame Monnier, who was already afraid of being robbed by her son feared, even more, having any of her belongings stolen by her maids. She kept everything under lock and key and forbade them to clean the living room or her bedroom. From time to time, she asked Modeste Bourliaud, in whom she had complete confidence, to come two or three days in a row to ventilate rooms and to carry out major cleaning.

The old lady's mistrust was such that, when Marie Fazy's sister visited, she took the opportunity to give her twenty francs and begged her to go and buy a ball of thread, for she did not want to give her maids her money, fearing they would attempt to swindle her.

At his trial, Marcel Monnier claimed that when he was in Poitiers, he would visit his sister every afternoon. When he arrived in her room, he always said: 'Hello Gertrude, how are you, my sister?' Sometimes he would take her some sweets, then sit on a chair in her room and read *Le Journal de la Vienne*. He would usually leave after ten or fifteen minutes. Under oath, Marcel Monnier claimed that he did not notice or realize anything, neither the filth, nor the rotten food, nor the stench, nor the lamentable state of Blanche.

Exceptionally distracted and of poor judgment, sincerely believing in his mother's affection and devotion to his sister whom she preferred to him, he was disconcertingly ingenuous. Short-sighted and with no real sense of smell, he never noticed the repulsive and filthy state of the room, nor was he bothered by the horrible stench that reigned there.

When Marcel Monnier visited his sister, he always demanded that the door of the room remain closed and that he was not to be disturbed while he read his newspaper.

When they went out to do the shopping or stood on the doorstep in the evening, the two servants could not help but tell others about the life they led in the house, nor to give details of the pitiful state that Blanche Monnier was in.

They told a lot of people what they knew, including the neighbours, the delivery men, the people they met at the market and, of course, the soldiers who were courting them. Initially, they were not believed, as many of those they told simply refused to believe that such a respectable Poitiers family could treat a family member in such a way. So the two maids began to take strangers up to Blanche's room. They made sure to only take one person at a time to see her, and they were always very careful not to make any noise on the stairs, because Madame Monnier's room was immediately below her daughter's room. They soon found the best time for visits was early in the morning since Louise Monnier never got up until after ten o'clock.

In December 1900, Félicie Fritz, a milliner and a sewing machinist, who ran her business from a room at 60 Rue des Basses-Treilles, went to Madame Monnier's house to sell a hat to Juliette Dupuis. After Blanche Monnier's imprisonment was uncovered, she told a journalist from Le Courrier de la Vienne what she had seen.

Félicie Fritz: *It was between seven and seven-thirty in the morning, it was very cold and sharp and it was still more night than day. So I entered the kitchen where I handed the hat to the maid. Immediately, the maid said to me: 'Since you're here, Madame, you should go up to see Mademoiselle Blanche.' I went up behind her and entered the room where I stayed for only a few minutes.*

Journalist: *What was your impression when you entered the room?*

Félicie Fritz: *Well, I didn't notice anything abnormal at first. The room was swept and a good fire blazed in the fireplace, but it was impossible for me to see well, because I repeat to you, it was not yet daylight and, on the other hand, the maid held in her hand a small lamp with a bright glow.*

Journalist: *And Mademoiselle Blanche, what impression did she give you?*

Félicie Fritz: *Oh! A very sad one. However, I did not see her face, because she had the habit of hiding her head under her scarf. As for her bed, it was disgustingly dirty. On the nightstand, I saw bones, oyster shells and several other food scraps.*

Journalist: *There must have been a bad smell from the room?*

Félicie Fritz: *I have no recollection of that. Besides, there was a good fire in the room because it was cold.*

Journalist: *And did you talk to Mademoiselle Blanche?*

Félicie Fritz: *No, sir, she wasn't very happy that I had gone up to her room, since she said to the maid who accompanied me, 'You know I don't want you to bring any more visitors.' And so, I withdrew immediately.*

A young maid who declined to give her name also gave an account of what she had seen, during a conversation reported in L'Avenir de la Vienne on June 9th, 1901.

Maid: *I had often heard about Blanche Monnier, mostly from a maid employed by the Monnier family, a maid who is from the same part of the country as me, but I took everything I heard to be made up. Just stories. However, one day, yielding to my friend's requests, I decided to visit, just to see why everyone considered her a curiosity.*

Journalist: *When did you visit?*

Maid: *Last January.*

Journalist: *What were your impressions?*

Maid: *First of all, I could not really distinguish anything in the room because it was so dark. Also, there was such a repugnant smell that, as soon as I saw Mademoiselle Monnier, I ran away.*

Journalist: *What effect did Mademoiselle Blanche have on you?*

Maid: *She looked like a crazy woman and she scared me greatly.*

On June 10th, 1901, another young woman who wished to remain anonymous made the following statement to *Le Journal de la Vienne*:

Maid: *I was a child when, for the first time, I heard people speak of Mademoiselle Blanche Monnier and her madness. So, I was not surprised when, one fine morning, having gone to the home of Madame Monnier on business, I was invited by the maid, Tabeau, to go up to see the crazy woman. When the maid opened the door for me and I stepped forward to enter the fatal room, I stopped in my tracks, suffocated. A terrible smell had just struck my nose and my gorge rose in disgust. Finally, I overcame my repugnance and took a few steps into the filthy room. In a corner of the room, on a messy bed, I see, hiding under a blanket of rags, something formless; only two bare and emaciated arms, a leg reduced to the state of skeleton held my gaze. I left the room very moved, still pursued by that indescribable smell which had increased even more during my stay in the room because the maid who accompanied me had removed from the bed of the unfortunate a cloth wet with droppings. And going down the stairs, I said to her: 'I know you've told me many times that you often sleep in there, I don't believe you because it would be impossible – you would be sick or asphyxiated.'*

At least ten people reported that they had been invited by Juliette Dupuis and Eugénie Tabeau to go up to

Blanche's room, between the first days of December 1900 and May 23rd, 1901, the day Blanche was discovered by Commissioner Bucheton. All ten of them admitted that they had never seen such a sad and disgusting sight. The filthy, naked, emaciated, half-witted woman had become a kind of fairground freak, secretly (or, as it turned out, not so secretly) displayed to anyone who came to the house on Rue de la Visitation.

The two servants most likely acted out of sheer immature foolishness, but their actions may also have been a way of them attempting to relieve their conscience. It is possible that they were unaware that they were partly responsible for Blanche Monnier's pitiful situation, which they blamed fully on their employer. In their eyes, Madame Monnier was the real culprit because of her greed, her miserliness and her malevolent wickedness.

They also accused Marcel Monnier of having allowed, by his continued silence, such disgusting treatment of a human being to be perpetuated; but it was as much out of jealousy and resentment against him and especially against his wife, although she never again entered her sister-in-law's room after the death of the Marie Fazy.

Juliette Dupuis and Eugénie Tabeau criticised Angèle Monnier for being condescending towards them and for giving her mother-in-law what they considered to be malicious, but which were most likely, very fair and accurate reports about them.

The two servants, on reflection, became very frightened of the result of their negligence of Blanche, and so they started to do what they could to undo any damage they might have done by showing Blanche to as many people as possible, hoping that one of them would eventually decide to send a report either to the prosecutor's office or to the police. Neither of them dared to do it themselves, for fear of the consequences, for Madame Monnier, although a shadow of her former formidable self, would as their aristocratic employer, be able to make their lives very difficult. If they said too much, they both risked being dismissed immediately without a reference and no prospects of employment elsewhere.

At the beginning of April 1901, Madame Monnier, who was suffering from heart disease, fell seriously ill. She was cared for by her maids and Angèle Monnier, who put aside the many grievances she had with her mother-in-law and came to see her every day.

During this time, Blanche was left abandoned amongst the filth in her room. The two servants, left to their own devices, no longer bothered to care for her; they either forgot or could not be bothered to take her any food and they no longer changed her soiled sheet. The condition of the mentally-disturbed woman, already terrible, deteriorated further.

Blanche's mental health had deteriorated in successive stages without the family doctor examining her and intervening. Doctor Chiron, who had replaced Doctor Chédevergne in 1897, did not even make the effort to see her when he came to make his weekly visit to Madame Monnier.

Due to the long-term effects of the potassium bromide, which had been administered daily since 1870, Blanche had become psychotic, a state aggravated by her strong dislike and distrust of her mother. Blanche's unstable mental condition meant that those who had been employed to look after her were no longer able to provide her with the proper medical care she needed.

By the time of Madame Monnier's illness in April 1901, the two servants, after looking into Blanche's room one day, and becoming exceedingly frightened by what they saw but not knowing what to do about it, wanted to alert the police. Juliette Dupuis spoke to Marie Fazy's sister, Modeste Bourliaud, who, since the onset of Madame Monnier's illness, called at 21 Rue de la Visitation once or twice a week to check on her.

At first, Modeste Bourliaud tried to dissuade the maid from carrying out what she intended.

Modeste Bourliaud: *How would it benefit you? You're very well off here. You must know that? There are others who have felt as you do but have not said anything. You just have to be like them.*

Then, once Juliette Dupuis insisted, Modeste Bourliaud finally acquiesced.

Modeste Bourliaud: *Then you must do what you want. You know what state Blanche is being kept in and you are adult enough to know what your duty is.*

What happened on Sunday, May 19th, 1901, suggested that the inevitable outcome was near. That day, Marcel

Monnier, his wife and their daughter had gone shopping in La Cadoue, near the gates of Poitiers.

Angèle Monnier, late at night, went to her mother-in-law, who was still in pain and consequently very angry with everyone. Louise Monnier said that it was very late, far too late for anyone civilised to come calling. The visit from her son's wife had made her change her routine, which she did not like.

She had also just learned that, the day before, the two maids had brought the cook working at the Rivaud café-restaurant into Blanche's room. The maids had been taking strangers up to look at Blanche and although it had been going on for five months, Louise Monnier had never noticed. She had reprimanded Juliette Dupuis, who was on duty that evening. And now, late at night, she quarrelled with her daughter-in-law in particularly violent terms.

Louise Monnier: *It's not a convenient time to come and see me. I don't need you here. Marcel will pay for this. What will it take to sweep all of this away? Why won't everyone just leave me alone and stay at home as I stay at home?*

Angèle Monnier was about to leave the house when Juliette Dupuis joined her in the kitchen to tell her that there were cockroaches on Blanche's bed. Instead of going up to see what state her sister-in-law was in order to assess the situation, Angèle Monnier simply said that she would tell her husband. When she relayed to him what she had been told, he replied, 'I find that hard to believe, but I will tell my mother.'

It was quite clear to the maids that nothing was going to be done to help Blanche Monnier – not by Marcel Monnier and his wife, not by Modeste Bourliaud, not by the neighbours, not by the delivery men, and not by any of their acquaintances, for there were no servants of their acquaintance who could help them.

Juliette Dupuis and Eugénie Tabeau each found themselves alone with their conscience.

But one of the maids (there is no record of which one) had for several weeks been in a relationship with one of the soldiers; he was a trainee officer at the nearby barracks. The maid took him up to Blanche's squalid room and let him have a look at the wretched woman.

Although the identity of the author of the anonymous

letter that arrived on the Attorney General's desk on May 22nd, 1901 remains unknown to this day, it was probably that soldier, feeling a combination of immense pity for Blanche and anger at the lamentable state she was being kept in, who sat down on May 19th and wrote an anonymous letter (denouncing Louise Monnier, describing the terrible conditions Blanche Monnier was being kept in, and enclosing the full address of the Monnier house); an anonymous letter he then sent to Léon Bulot, the Attorney General of Paris, thereby instigating a process that brought an end to the imprisonment and the abuse of Blanche Monnier.

Part Three: Release

Discovery
1901

Monsieur Marcel Monnier led the two policemen to a door on a second floor of the house. The door was closed. Marcel Monnier tried the handle and the door was locked. He looked at the Commissioner and the Sergeant in turn, and then made a gesture of helplessness.

Bucheton: *You have a key to this door, so please open it. Unless, of course, you would prefer us to break it down.*

After a few moments of hesitation, Marcel Monnier took a key from his jacket pocket and put it in the lock. He turned the key and pushed the door.

No sooner had it opened than the Commissioner recoiled in horror; a pestilential smell forced him to turn and bend over the banister of the stairs and take deep breaths so as not to vomit.

Then, bracing himself, Commissioner Bucheton entered the pitch-black and foul-smelling room. He crossed to the window, where his observations regarding the room window were confirmed; daylight could not enter the room because the shutters were held closed from the outside by a heavy chain which was secured with a solid padlock. The gaps and spaces around the window and shutters were clogged with caulk that prevented air from passing in or out.

The Commissioner was surprised to see that Marcel Monnier did not seem to be bothered by the smell. Appearing very comfortable, he stood in the room and spoke to the Commissioner.

Monnier: *This arrangement with the curtains and the shutters is a precautionary measure to prevent my sister from throwing herself out of the window.*

Commissioner Bucheton, having become accustomed to the darkness, saw a mattress on which there was a shapeless mass in a corner of the room. The mattress was covered with rodent droppings, human excrement, both old and fresh, oyster shells, rotting meat and fish, mouldy vegetables and pieces of bread. Rotten food was strewn all over the floor. Over the disgusting pile of decomposing filth swarmed lice, fleas, bedbugs, cockroaches and other kinds of vermin. Making a concerted effort, the commissioner managed to knock a hole in the one of the shutters and let a shaft of afternoon light filter in.

It was then that a horrible spectacle was revealed to him. There was a woman on the bed! She was hiding her head beneath a filthy, holed scarf and screaming inarticulately. The unfortunate woman was completely naked and looked like a skeleton: her thighs were as thin as the wrist of an ordinary person, her arms were no thicker than the neck of a bottle, her fingers were like pencils and her nails were of inordinate length. The state of her head made him shudder even more: her hair, uncut and unbrushed for what may have been many years formed an indescribable mat, seeming to be more like entangled horsehair, and in that long swathe of hair fleas, mites, and maggots seethed.

Once his initial moment of disgust and indignation had passed, the Commissioner glared accusingly at Marcel Monnier.

Bucheton: *It is inhuman to leave a poor creature in such a pitiful state. There will certainly be significant legal consequences to this discovery, Monsieur.*

Having spoken, the Commissioner strode purposefully from the room. Marcel Monnier ran after him, protesting his innocence.

Monnier: *I am the victim of my filial piety. Whatever may have happened here is because I never wanted to go against the express wishes of my mother who wanted, as I've already said, to be the mistress of her own home.*

Hurrying to flee that appalling scene, the Commissioner, ignoring Marcel Monnier, made his way down to the street to breathe in some fresh air. The maid, Juliette Dupuis unlocked the door for him and the Commissioner left the house in Rue de la Visitation. Within half an hour, he had notified the public prosecutor of his discovery.

At five o'clock that afternoon, the public prosecutor, Maitre Férot, his deputy, Maitre Nicod, the investigating judge, Dollin du Fresnel, and a forensic doctor, Doctor Brossard, arrived at 21 Rue de la Visitation, where Marcel Monnier was already located. All of them went up to the second floor, but the lawyers all felt repulsed by the abominable stench that assailed them as soon as the door was opened.

The deputy, having a more delicate constitution than the others, hurried out of the room and vomited on the stairs. The prosecutor dictated his findings, which were noted by his deputy. He then began to interrogate Marcel Monnier, who repeated what he had said to the Commissioner.

Monnier: *My sister Blanche is suffering from a pernicious fever. She is very sick and her doctor has forbidden anyone to approach her. I myself have tried several times, including quite recently, to pull her out of her abominable state, but she has always refused in such a way that any insistence on my part was clearly useless. It is true, I was wrong not to go against the wishes of my mother and sister, but I am the victim of deeply-felt filial piety.*

The prosecutor concluded his interrogation by silencing Marcel Monnier's repeated protestations of innocence with a warning.

Prosecutor: *You are a criminal. Your place is not here but in front of a sentencing judge!*

The prosecutor then gave the order to open the windows and the shutters, and the men set to work. The operation, however, was not an easy one. The old curtains, which were made of mattress canvas, fell heavily, giving off considerable clouds of dust. The chain that was securing the shutters was rusty, as was the padlock; proof that for years the shutters had not been opened. In order to be opened, the shutters had to be taken out of their hinges. This took some time. Finally, daylight entered the room and the judges and lawyers were able to observe what the Central Commissioner had written about in his report regarding the appalling state of filth in which the unfortunate woman was being kept.

It was then that they noticed the inscriptions on the walls of the room, although many of them were covered by such a thick layer of dust and faeces that they could not read them distinctly. Despite the open window, the smell of the room was so foul that it was impossible for the men to stay any longer to make further observations.

The most urgent thing was to have the poor woman who was screaming in fear removed from there. She clung to her bed and begged to be left alone.

Blanche: *Please leave me alone. Just let me live in my dear little cave.*

Since the women entrusted with the task of taking her out of the room could not do it alone, they had to be assisted by commissionaires who were waiting on the street.

Blanche was lifted off the bed and the food scraps brushed off her. A witness later said that her body, which was as thin as a reed, was upsetting to look at, and her face, as sharp as a razor blade, was frighteningly pale. Her mass of jet black hair, covered in vermin, fell down her back.

Madame Monnier had insisted that Blanche should have no bed linen, nor any items of clothing in her room, so someone had to fetch a blanket from another room. Once the blanket was wrapped around Blanche, she was carefully carried from the room and down the stairs by a policeman, who gently placed her inside a small municipal ambulance carriage that was parked in the street outside the house, ready to transport her to the Hôtel-Dieu, the hospital near Notre-Dame in Paris.

The poor woman, frightened by the brightness of the sun, the kind of light that she had not seen for many years, began to scream again.

It was half past seven when she arrived at the Hôtel-Dieu. Once there she began to receive the medical care she needed.

After her departure, the public health inspector gave the order for the room to be disinfected. The arrival of the police and the judges during the afternoon, followed by the arrival of the municipal ambulance in the evening, had attracted a sizeable crowd on Rue de la Visitation.

The neighbours, standing on their doorstep, told reporters that they had heard the screams, but they had been told that from time-to-time Blanche would scream and they should think nothing of it. Some onlookers, believing themselves to be better informed, mentioned kidnapping, confinement, starvation and physical abuse. Others remembered the maids gossiping about how Blanche's room was in a state of despicable uncleanliness.

The next morning, Friday, May 24th, Marcel Monnier, completely distraught, went very early to Modeste Bourliaud's home and asked her to support him in his ordeal. As soon as he had entered her small house on the road to Biard, he explained what had happened.

Marcel Monnier: *A terrible thing has just occurred.*

114

Modeste Bourliaud: *Is your mother dead?*

Marcel Monnier: *No, it's my sister. She's been taken to the Hôtel-Dieu.*

Modeste Bourliaud: *That can only be a good thing. It's not a terrible thing at all.*

Marcel Monnier: *If you're asked, could say that you know that I did everything I could for my sister and that I cared for her very well?*

Modeste Bourliaud (frostily): *But I don't know anything about how you, or anyone else, cared for your sister.*

Marcel Monnier: *Then I am lost.*

Modeste Bourliaud: *But you know very well that I never went into your sister's room and I don't know what state she was in.*

Marcel Monnier: *Then I am lost, I am lost. Tonight I will be arrested.*

Marcel Monnier abruptly left Modeste Bourliaud's house in a panic. As a lawyer, he knew what he was risking by contacting Modeste Bourliaud. Already, the day before, the prosecutor had told him: 'You are a criminal. Your place is not here but in front of a sentencing judge!' And with a gesture the judge had indicated the nearby prison which was, by coincidence, at the far end of Rue de la Visitation.

Marcel Monnier was aware it would only be a matter of time before his arrest. On the afternoon of 24th May, he gathered some friends at his home, including Prosper Puizay, the former President of the Bar, Paul Druet and Captain de Lattre, to ask their advice on the best course of action to be taken.

At five o'clock, the Prosecutor, the investigating judge and the Central Commissioner returned to Blanche's room which, despite the still very strong smell, was now disinfected. They were there to make observations that the stench of the room had not allowed them to make on the first day. An inventory of the room's contents was immediately made.

Victor Merken, a local photographer whose studio was located at 5 Rue du Puygarreau, took several photographs. In particular, he photographed the many inscriptions written on the walls of the room, which included:

'It is terrible to be forced to live and die in a dungeon!'
'Some children are much more preferred than others.'

Monsieur Merkin photographed the padlocked shutters, which, once they had been removed, had been placed on the floor and leaned against the wall below the window. He also photographed the landing. Despite the light and the open window, his photographs couldn't help but suggest imprisonment, confinement, sequestration.

At six forty-five that evening, the prosecutor's office ordered the Central Commissioner to arrest Marcel Monnier and issued a warrant of committal. Pierre Bucheton immediately crossed the street and rang the bell. The door was opened by the maid.

Bucheton: *Monsieur Marcel Monnier?*

Maid: *He's here.*

The maid opened the door of the living room door and the Commissioner saw Marcel Monnier sitting in an armchair, talking with a small group of his friends who were obviously there to support him. Monnier, seeing the Commissioner standing in the doorway, beckoned him to approach. Commissioner Bucheton stood where he was and stared at Monnier.

Bucheton: *Monsieur Monnier, please take the trouble to come over here to me.*

Monnier got up and approached the Commissioner.

Bucheton: *Follow me, please, Monsieur Monnier; you will need to give a statement to the police.*

Commissioner Bucheton took Marcel Monnier to Louise Monnier's house and led him into a downstairs room where he handed him over to the custody of a police officer. The Commissioner wanted to avoid the curious crowd that had gathered outside, an ever-growing crowd that waited outside with feverish impatience. Every so often, someone in the crowd would shout out an insult or an accusation directed at either Louise or Marcel Monnier.

Two policemen took their prisoner out across the gardens and through the stable overlooking the street. When the more observant in the crowd noticed the ploy, they gave chase, but by the time they had gone around to the street on the other side of the property, the prison door had already closed on Marcel Monnier.

An hour later, on the order of the investigating judge,

Madame Louise Monnier was also arrested. The latter, after having been sick for two months, had risen that morning, as if she had had the feeling that something serious was going to take place. She was going about her business in her room when, at a quarter to eight, Commissioner Bucheton had her warned by her maid of the serious consequences of her actions. The news did not seem to upset her. She had a few words to say on the matter and then she was silent.

Louise Monnier: *Is it possible for such a fuss to be created over nothing?*

Louise Monnier's words indicate the full extent of her delusional state. At Marcel Monnier's wedding, Doctor Despaignet's observation had been that 'the mother and daughter both seemed quite unbalanced.' It is possible that the doctor recognised that Louise Monnier had a personality disorder, most likely, given her delusions of grandeur, a form of elitist narcissism. She had many of the recognised traits of that particular disorder; she felt privileged and empowered by virtue of her links through her ancestors' marriage to royalty; her entitled demeanour and aristocratic facade bore little relation to her reality – that she was a teacher's wife; she was ambitiously (although unsuccessfully) upwardly mobile and she had forced her quiet and studious husband to be the same; she cultivated advantages by association. Added to this was her iron will and her avoidance of the fact that had she achieved nothing in her life by her own efforts. She would have been unable to admit this, either to herself or to anyone else. Everything she had acquired, either honestly or dishonestly, had originally been created, bought or earned by someone else's efforts, whether that was her parents, her husband, or her children.

As the crowd waiting outside the house was still quite volatile, as was evident from their shouts and furious gestures, with some people waiting outside the door of the stable so as not to be deceived a second time, the Commissioner gave Juliette Dupuis very precise instructions.

Bucheton: *You are going to take Madame Monnier by the arm. You will leave the house through the staff door, and then, as though you were visitors, you will walk towards the prison.*

The prison the Commissioner referred to was the Prison de la Visitation, a former convent coincidentally located on the street in which the Monniers lived. As its name suggests, the former convent was run by nuns belonging to the Visitation Order, formally the Congregation of the Visitation of Holy Mary, a Roman Catholic order founded by St. Francis de Sales and St. Jane Frances de Chantal in Annecy, France, in 1610. The order was originally created to carry out charitable work, including visiting and caring for the sick and the poor in their homes, as well as providing prayer. Rue de la Visitation was the primary thoroughfare to the convent which, after the Revolution, was transformed into a prison and became the prison for the entire region.

As the two women set off, the ruse looked as though it would succeed. The furious crowd saw two women come out of a side gate onto the street and start to walk towards the far end of Rue de la Visitation. No one in the crowd attached any particular importance to them; it was probably staff finishing work. In fact, no one noticed the deception until the two women were almost at the prison door. Someone in the crowd asked who the women were, and the crowd immediately ran after them to find out.

Meanwhile, the Commissioner and several police officers rushed down the street to protect the two women, forming a protective circle around the them as the prison door was opened behind them. The two women stepped through the prison entrance, and the door was slammed shut once they were inside.

The angry, jostling crowd pushed against the prison door just as the guard inside pushed the bolts home.

The Commissioner and the policemen dispersed the crowd.

In the evening, large groups of angry people continued to stand outside the houses of mother and son, shouting curses, insults and calling for their execution.

Several of Marcel Monnier's friends, including the President of the Bar, Druet, and Captain de Lattre, went outside and told the crowd they were dissatisfied with the arrests, which they considered arbitrary. They had to retreat back inside the house when the hostile crowd started booing them.

It was ten o'clock at night before Rue de la Visitation reverted to its usual quiet and calm. During the night, anonymous chalk inscriptions were written on the doors of the two houses owned by the Monniers, including: 'Death! Execution! Murderers!

On Saturday and Sunday, the curious went again to Rue de la Visitation and stood in the street between the two buildings owned by the Monnier family.

On Saturday 25th, at around one-fifteen in the afternoon, the prosecutor, the investigating judge and the Commissioner returned to the scene one last time to seize the objects that were to be used as exhibits. Using a large white sheet to hold the objects they seized, they collected together: a mattress that was partly rotten; a rotting pillow that was stuck to the mattress, as well as various rags fused together by faeces and food debris, infested with various bugs and vermin. Also seized was a freshly washed rag; a small scarf with blue flowers on a once-white background; a large piece of mattress canvas hung at the window and used as a curtain; an old rag; a white cloth soiled with faeces; a bed sheet, folded in eight, which Blanche Monnier usually lay on.

Food debris that had fallen onto the floor was collected, wrapped in newspaper and placed in a crate. A partly rotten pallet bed was removed, which was wrapped in a piece of cloth, the two shutters, still connected by a chain and held by a padlock were seized. On a shelf was a trunk containing thirty-seven books, a satchel containing notebooks and a large quantity of notes written in pencil. These were all removed.

Also seized were two statuettes of the Blessed Virgin, a doll's head, a rosary, a ten-cent coin and five pieces of pencil found on and under Blanche's bed. The door of the victim's room as well as the doorframe and jamb were dismantled to be taken away. Care was also taken to peel off the pieces of faded green wallpaper on which were written the famous sentences that showed Blanche's cries for freedom.

Finally, some of the bugs found on the bed were placed in a jar by Monsieur Puy, a pharmacist-chemist, director of the Central Pharmacy, located at the corner of Place d'Armes (currently le Place du Maréchal-Leclerc) and Rue Victor-Hugo, to be analysed.

Doctor Maurice Léger, director of the laboratory of bacteriology at the Medical School of Poitiers, recognized two of the species. The longest, yellow in colour, were larvae of a beetle insect named tenebrion, larvae more commonly known as 'mealworms'. The others, shorter and black in colour, were the larvae of another grub, the dermeste, which, in environments that lack cleanliness, multiplies in decaying meat.

Once the items were removed, the room was sealed off and the staff instructed to stay away from any of the upstairs rooms.

What the Newspapers Said (1)

In Poitiers, all anyone wanted to talk about was the discovery of 'the prisoner of Poitiers' and her subsequent care at the Hôtel-Dieu, followed by the incarceration of Louise Monnier and her son in the Prison de la Visitation as they awaited trial.

For their part, the major Poitiers newspapers presented the sensational facts in calm, measured tones. They used the same tone to describe the poor creature who had been so horribly treated by a family that no one would have suspected of being capable of such an act.

'A sad affair', was the headline in *Le Courrier de la Vienne*.

'A very sad story,' was the headline of *Le Journal de la Vienne*.

Other newspapers and journals competed with each other by publishing countless sensational articles, photographs and drawings of the unfortunate woman. Some of them referred to her as the 'recluse.' Journalists focussed on the state of the room, the rotting mattress, the filth, the darkness, the rotting food, the stench. They described the maggots, the rats, and the cockroaches that swarmed around her. They dwelt on Blanche Monnier's immensely long and matted hair, on her disproportionately long nails, on her horrifying thinness which had reduced her to being little more than a living skeleton. The public, eager for all these macabre details, followed the case avidly.

The prisoner of Poitiers, or 'la sequestrée de Poitiers', which was the label Blanche became known by throughout France, was becoming a subject of interest to far more people than just the citizens of Poitiers. In Paris salons and in reading rooms across France, the Monnier case was the main topic of conversation and discussion.

The local newspapers sent daily reports to correspondents in Paris. Journalists from the capital came to Poitiers to interview witnesses and, if possible, to obtain information from the judges in charge of the investigation.

L'Illustration was able to provide its readers with a complete record of the case, with sensational photographs. On its front page, it published the famous photo taken of Blanche Monnier on her arrival at the Hôtel-Dieu which, because of its stark realism, made the whole of France react with horror.

In contrast, *Le Petit Journal*, which usually had drawings or cartoons in black and white or in colour representing bloody tragedies, atrocious crimes or exotic barbarities on the front page of its illustrated supplement, preferred to publish on its back page a peaceful image of 'the prisoner of Poitiers' on her hospital bed. In the drawing, she is seen surrounded by doctors, nuns in cornettes carrying bouquets of flowers, and the chaplain of the Hôtel-Dieu.

Subsequently, other newspapers began to change their tone; sensation gave way to indignation as the focus of newspaper stories shifted from Blanche Monnier to Madame Monnier and her son, who the newspapers started to portray as monsters who had committed a nightmarish crime.

In *La Fronde*, the first French feminist newspaper, J. Hellé (a pseudonym for Marguerite Dreyfus) wrote:

> 'The story of 'the Prisoner of Poitiers' seems to have been taken from pages that could only have been written by that strange genius, Edgar Allan Poe or some other master in terror [...]. This goes beyond any ordinary conception of measurable horror [...] A detailed study of this crime would not exhaust this chapter of contemporary mores which can nevertheless be told in two lines: a woman has been imprisoned for twenty-five years in a small dark room where she was found, skeleton-like, but alive, lying among her own excrement on a rotten mattress, amongst maggots, cockroaches and rats.
>
> 'Now try to accrue the sum of days added to days, nights added to nights, and try to imagine what this quarter of a century of a human life could have been... Imagine the corporal and moral isolation throughout every night, the endless torture of the mind and the nerves – the isolation of the flesh – without a helping drop of water or a blanket, or clothes, or any sort of covering – naked among the filth and the teeming 'creatures', physical torture, much more than

inhumane and inhuman...'

Newspaper articles after the Le Fronde piece started asking questions that focussed on Louise Monnier's maternal psychology: How could any mother be so unnatural that she could imprison her daughter and leave her wallowing in her own excrement, in a state of near starvation and deprivation?

Questions were asked of Marcel Monnier too: Why had the brother, a Doctor of Law and a former sub-prefect, and the son of a faculty Dean, not rescued his sister? How was it that he saw nothing, smelled nothing, noticed nothing, heard nothing or felt nothing, during his daily visits (sometimes three times a day) to Blanche's room? Why was there a conspiracy of silence in the household? What of the maids? What of the family doctor? What of the neighbours who claimed they were aware of Blanche Monnier's madness? What of those who later admitted to having heard screams and cries for freedom and rescue?

Some people quickly concluded that there was a criminal motive behind Madame Monnier's actions. Despite the fact that Louise Monnier had removed her son's name from her Will, some still felt that Madame Monnier's purpose for imprisoning Blanche was to rid herself of a troublesome daughter so that she could leave her considerable widow's fortune to her son, Marcel.

After Marcel Monnier's arrest and his pre-trial detention at the Prison de la Visitation, some of the newspapers started to examine the Monnier family's ancestry, and soon discovered the aristocratic lineage of the Demarconnays, the Demayres and the Girodins. The Republican press then used the family's ancestry to depict Louise Monnier as an example of the 'degenerate nobility' the Republic had been created to be rid of.

In other countries, some of the more astute newspapers realized the potential of the sensational story and started to print articles about the imprisonment of the young woman from Poitiers.

In Buenos Aires, on June 15th, 1901, the newspaper *Caras Y Caretas* ran a story ('*la secuestrada de Poitiers*') in which a journalist visited Blanche Monnier in hospital. He wrote:

The people present spontaneously had the ingenious idea of unravelling the artistic memories of the patient. It seems that Mademoiselle Monnier was a very good musician in her youth.

"With well-shaped fingers like yours," someone says, "you must be able to play the piano."

Mademoiselle Monnier says she plays, as there was such an instrument in her family home. Then she says with vivacity: "Still, when I get married, I will play again; yes, I will return to playing."

"We will come to hear you, Blanche," one of the nurses says, and it is difficult for us to disguise our emotions.

On 14th July, 1901, the *Chicago Tribune* dedicated a full page to the story. The headline was attention-grabbing in its sensationalism:

FRENCH WOMAN IMPRISONED FOR 25 YEARS, STARVED, NEGLECTED, AND DRIVEN ALMOST INSANE BY MOTHER.

In *The New York Times*, an article in their 9th July issue made one of the first references to the relationship between Blanche and Victor Calmeil:

SHE IMPRISONED DAUGHTER.; Girl Kept in a Dungeon Twenty-five Years Because She Was True to Her Sweetheart.
PARIS, June 8 – The death in prison of Mme. Monnier, a wealthy but miserly landowner in the neighborhood of Poitiers, forms the climax in a drama the pathos and horror of which has been the sensation of the week in Paris.

Inevitably, the foreign press started to depict Louise Monnier as a woman made monstrous by her greed and her lineage.

Marcel Monnier was accused of having been a barely-competent sub-prefect who had only appointed to a semi-important position because his father begged on his behalf.

To many, the former sub-prefect was a naïve dreamer who preferred to indulge in his favourite hobbies of reading poetry, walking and painting watercolours. The press accused him of giving parties in his house on Rue de la Visitation while, just opposite, his sister sobbed on a rotten mattress that was covered in her own filth.

Marcel Monnier sometimes received friends, but his income was not sufficient to allow him to host the ostentatious dinner parties he would have liked to have hosted.

In addition, some of the newspapers pointed out that, although Marcel Monnier claimed he sincerely loved his sister, he had done nothing to prevent her imprisonment and her abuse. Some believed he had been a perpetrator of the imprisonment and abuse of his sister.

Some newspapers pointed out that Marcel Monnier had always insisted on the room door being closed when he visited his naked sister in her darkened, secure room.

Nor did the critics spare Marcel Monnier's father, once it was recalled that Émile Monnier had been appointed dean of the faculty of letters.

Following the New York Times' lead, *Le Journal de la Vienne* reported Blanche Monnier's affair with the lawyer Victor Calmeil, who had died in 1885. The relationship was considered to be the original catalyst for Blanche's imprisonment. *Le Journal* added further detail by recycling a local rumour that Blanche had been imprisoned because her relationship with the lawyer had resulted in an illegitimate child.

The birth of a child would have been at the origin of the 'kidnapping'. Following the family's refusal to consent to the marriage, followed by the birth of a child, the young woman was reportedly deprived of her liberty, locked up in a dark room which ultimately left her mentally unbalanced. Because of her mother's relentless hatred of Blanche and Victor Calmeil's relationship, and through her brother's guilty indifference, the unfortunate woman had then fallen into the appalling state in which the Commissioner had found her.

Searches undertaken by the police to find the corpse of a new-born in the garden of the Rue de la Visitation only turned up a cat skeleton and other animal bones. However, no search was made of the gardens of Le Pilet.

The press was represented in Poitiers by two daily newspapers: *Le Journal de la Vienne*, a republican newspaper, and *Le Courrier de la Vienne*, a royalist newspaper. The first had the largest circulation in the region and it sought to keep its readers' interest by reporting new facts every day. The neighbours of the Rue de la Visitation and the country house of Le Pilet, the former domestic staff, the deliverymen and all those who had an opinion on the case were questioned.

Le Journal gave all the details, reported anecdotes and sometimes indulged in stories. For example, it circulated the news concerning Blanche Monnier's affair with the lawyer Victor Calmeil, a report which was picked up and repeated in the Republican press.

For his investigation, the editor-in-chief of *Le Journal* interviewed Arnault de la Ménardière, the President of the Bar Association and a professor at the Faculty of Law. According to the academic, the truth was that 'all of the people who lived in Rue de la Visitation knew that Blanche and her mother were crazy or half-crazy'. Blanche was suffering from 'manic hysteria.' Her mother had a taste for secrecy and kidnapping, she received no visitors and never went out. As for Marcel Monnier, he was a weak-minded man who 'did not concern himself about the lack of care being given to someone who was clearly sick... He was guilty of great weakness, but he is not responsible for the kidnapping, that is, if there ever was a kidnapping.'

This opinion expressed by someone of note who seemed to know the Monnier family well made quite an impression. Although he was a Doctor of Law and a former sub-prefect, Marcel Monnier was being presented as someone of little intelligence in order to minimize his responsibility. This, along with his claims of diminished senses (sight and smell), would be his defence strategy.

The photo of 'the prisoner of Poitiers', in which Blanche Monnier looked more like a skeleton than a living, breathing woman, was published in L'Illustration and shocked a huge number of French people, who began to consider the mother and brother of the victim to be monstrous.

The Monnier case became the first criminal case of the twentieth century to have immense cultural impact. Everyone waited eagerly for the dates of the trial, but there was even more interest in Blanche Monnier's recovery at the Hôtel-Dieu.

Marcel Monnier's Interview
Thursday, June 6th, 1901

On Thursday, June 6th, about ten days after his arrest, Marcel Monnier, in the presence of his lawyer, Maitre Dufour d'Astaffort, was interrogated by Judge Dollin du Fresnel. Marcel Monnier's appearance before the investigating judge was at three minutes to seven o'clock in the evening.

Judge Fresnel: *Why was your sister locked inside a filthy, dark, shuttered room for many years?*

Marcel Monnier: *In the year 1872, my sister Blanche experienced brain disorders as a result of a pernicious fever. At that time, she received medical care from Doctor Guérineau, the family doctor. My father, Émile Monnier, Dean of the Faculty of Letters, had to have shutters fitted to the window of Blanche's room in order to prevent her from jumping out of the window and ending her life.*

Judge Fresnel: *What were your mother's feelings regarding her daughter?*

Marcel Monnier: *My mother always had far more affection for Blanche than for me. Her affection for Blanche was so acute, that our mother avoided upsetting her too much. My mother was always striving as best she could to satisfy the whims of a sick child.*

Judge Fresnal: *You claimed you visited your sister three times a day. You were responsible, during your mother's illness for giving the servants orders to care for your sister. Why didn't you give the servants orders to feed and wash her? After you visited your sister, you would spend time talking to your mother. Why didn't you tell her the terrible state our sister was in?*

Marcel Monnier: *I did not go more than two or three times a day to my sister's room; often it was less or not at all. I did not feel it was my right, in my mother's home, to give my mother's servants any orders, but I did make one or two simple recommendations. If, after seeing my sister, I went to my mother's room, it was simply so that she would know that I had fulfilled my tasks.*

Judge Fresnel: *How is it that you were not inconvenienced by the terrible smell of that filthy and dark hovel when you visited Mademoiselle Blanche, as you did frequently?*

Marcel Monnier: *I never noticed anything abnormal. No doubt I realized, especially in the last few days, that my sister's room was not particularly clean, but it never occurred to me to look at the bed. I was amazed when I was told about the repulsively filthy state of the room my sister occupied.*

Judge Fresnel: *How did Blanche let you know she was aware of your presence?*

Marcel Monnier: *Blanche had the singular habit of covering her face with a scarf when I came near her; I never saw her face. She couldn't stand any cloth on her body.*

Judge Fresnel: *Were you never concerned for your sister's well-being?*

Marcel Monnier: *Of course, but I was not the master of the household; my sister lived in my mother's house. On many occasions, I tried to insist that my mother send Blanche to a nursing home, but my mother refused to listen to me and often got angry with me if I became too insistent. She threatened to disown and disinherit me if I persisted in mentioning putting Blanche in a care home. Aware of my mother's age and concerned by her weak heart, I finally stopped mentioning the subject to her. I was helpless. I deeply regret it.*

Judge Fresnal: *Please explain the locked shutters on your sister's room window. Locked from the outside.*

Marcel Monnier: *The confinement of my sister, if it is to be qualified as such, had been ordered by my father. As my sister insisted on constantly showing herself naked at her window, he found it necessary to resort to such measures for reasons of decency and my mother, as was her duty, simply bowed to her husband's will. When my father died, his widow continued to execute his decision in the matter.*

Judge Fresnal: *Do you think you should have challenged your mother's decision to keep your sister at home, when she should have been receiving proper medical care in a care home?*

Marcel Monnier: *As for myself, my filial piety has led me to become a respectful son who was, is, and always has been, purely and simply, deferential to all paternal and maternal authority.*

Judge Fresnal: *There are some very serious charges against you. Kidnapping is one of them.*

Marcel Monnier: *No one can accuse me of being guilty*

of kidnapping my sister Blanche, neither in law nor in fact, since many people have been to visit her and to see her in her room.

Judge Fresnal: *Why was your sister's room so filthy that the floor was covered in rotting food and excrement that had attracted rats and cockroaches?*

Marcel Monnier: *The room's state of uncleanliness that you observed does not date back very far, only to when our regular maid died. Other maids were not so conscientious.*

Judge Fresnal: *The other charge against you is regarding your disregard for your sister.*

Marcel Monnier: *Something to note is this: my sister has no wounds or traces of marks or sores on her skin, which would not have failed to occur if she had been lying naked on a filthy mattress for many years, as some have erroneously claimed.*

Judge Fresnal: *The hospital doctors say Mademoiselle Blanche is so thin it's a miracle that she survived. You say you visited her daily, sometime more than once. Why did you allow her to starve?*

Marcel Monnier: *With regards to my sister's weight loss, which I was totally unaware of until it was explained to me, it is now quite obvious that not all of the food sent up to her by our mother reached its destination.*

Louise Monnier's Interview
Thursday, June 6th, 1901

On Thursday, June 6th, about ten days after her arrest, Louise Monnier was interviewed by Judge Dollin du Fresnel, in the presence of her lawyer, Maitre Mérine.

A transcript of the full interview has not been preserved, but some elements of the interrogation were reported in *Le Journal de la Vienne*, which boasted of publishing fairly precise details regarding the questions asked and the answers made.

It was two minutes after nine o'clock in the evening when Judge Dollin du Fresnel proceeded to interrogate Louise Monnier. The old lady was in the prison infirmary, but she answered the judge's questions precisely, despite her old age and illness.

Judge Fresnal: *Do you understand the seriousness of the charges against you?*

Louise Monnier: *I don't understand what they want with me. What I do not understand especially is why my son Marcel has been arrested, as he has had nothing to do with me.*

Judge Fresnal: *What can you tell me about the way you treated your daughter?*

Louise Monnier: *My daughter! I adored her. I sacrificed myself for her by keeping her at home. If I had known all the trouble that my love for my child was going to cause me, and that all this would be the reward for my care, I would have acted like a stepmother, that is, I would have sent my daughter, my poor daughter, to a nursing home where she would have died long ago.*

Judge Fresnal: *Your daughter has been imprisoned by you for nearly twenty-five years. Why did you do such a terrible thing?*

Louise Monnier: *I never confined my daughter, who I love very much. Nor have I ever considered confining her. She has always been free to move around the house, but I must say that for the past twenty-five years, she has voluntarily stayed in her room. In fact, I believe it was in about 1876 that she decided she would stay in bed, rather than get up. Yes, she insisted on staying in bed, despite my efforts to get her up to go for walks* and get some fresh air. Even my husband, when he was alive, was unable to get her out of bed.

Judge Fresnal: *Some of your maids state that your daughter was healthy long ago, but her imprisonment has caused her health to deteriorate.*

Louise Monnier: *She always had very delicate health… but it never stopped her doing her school work. She loved the work that the school set for her to do, especially the reading.*

Judge Fresnal: *By locking her away, you have deprived her of a normal life, friends, a social life.*

Louise Monnier: *As a young girl, she rarely had any sort of social life. She preferred, above all, to visit churches. We all thought she had the vocation to become a nun.*

Judge Fresnal: *You have also put paid to any chance of her marrying and having a family.*

Louise Monnier: *She never discussed wanting to marry anyone with me. She never had any marriage plans. In fact, I'm convinced that she never wanted to marry, nor had any interest in marriage.*

Judge Fresnel: *What can you tell me about your daughter and a local lawyer named Calmeil?*

Louise Monnier: *I don't know anyone by the name of Calmeil. My daughter never mentioned anyone by that name to me.*

Judge Fresnal: *It seems that your daughter had a romantic interest in Victor Calmeil and he in her. It seems that they wished to marry. Did you forbid it?*

Louise Monnier: *I have never heard of Blanche having a romantic interest in anyone. My daughter has never mentioned a lawyer to me, nor has she ever informed me of any marriage plan.*

Judge Fresnal: *The doctors at the hospital say it is a miracle that your daughter survived. But she is very ill. And although she is calm, she will not, at present, speak to anyone.*

Louise Monnier: *I believe it was 1872 when my daughter was afflicted with a very serious pernicious fever that was life-threatening. The family doctor treated her for it, but her recovery was very slow. She never fully recovered from it. Since that time, she has never expressed any wish to see anyone, and she prefers her own company.*

Judge Fresnal: *Does the doctor still treat your daughter for her illness?*

Louise Monnier: *It's been several years since a doctor has been to see her because she hasn't been ill for some time.*

Judge Fresnal: *The doctors at the hospital say that Mademoiselle Blanche is very ill. On being admitted to the hospital, the doctors were shocked at how thin she was.*

Louise Monnier: *I ordered her a lot of beautifully-prepared meals from the best hotels, but she ate very little and over time she grew extremely thin.*

Judge Fresnal: *Why did you not attempt to determine the reason for your daughter's refusal to eat? Or to get your maids to clean the room and wash your daughter?*

Louise Monnier: *For the past three months I have been very ill myself and unable to visit my daughter in her room. Previously, I went to see her at least twice a day, and obviously I saw that the room was dirty and ordered my maids to clean it. Either they forgot, or Blanche made a huge fuss and refused to allow them to clean the room.*

Judge Fresnal: *Did the fever you mentioned affect your daughter's mind in any way?*

Louise Monnier: *No. She wasn't crazy at all, but she did have some odd ways of doing things.*

Judge Fresnal: *How would you describe the relationship between Mademoiselle Blanche and your son?*

Louise Monnier: *My daughter loved her brother very much. A few years ago, when he got married, she went to Mont-de-Marsan to attend his wedding. She did not enjoy going out in public, but she made the effort for him, although shortly after she returned to Poitiers, she shut herself away in her room again.*

Judge Fresnal: *Maids have stated that you insist on keeping your daughter naked. One of the maids states that you ordered all items of clothing and bed linen to be removed from Mademoiselle Blanche's room.*

Louise Monnier: *My daughter has a long history of refusing to put on any clothes. She used to stand at her bedroom window unclothed. My husband had shutters fitted to protect her modesty. She always used the pretext that she was too weak to put any items of clothing on. She also hates bedclothes, only wanting a single sheet on her bed. She refuses to wear a night-dress. She tears up clothes if she sees them.*

Judge Fresnal: *The maids have also said that they often asked you for permission to change Mademoiselle Blanche's mattress, which was rotten, and for clothes for her, and to wash your daughter, but you refused to allow it.*

Louise Monnier: *They are liars. They are two hussies.*

Judge Fresnal: *The doctors think that your daughter is very lucky to be alive. A few more months in the same terrible conditions and she would have died.*

Louise Monnier: *If I have made a mistake, it wasn't with the intention of killing my daughter. I have always sacrificed myself for her.*

Blanche Monnier at the Hôtel-Dieu

When she arrived at the Hôtel-Dieu on May 23rd, 1901, at half past seven in the evening, Blanche Monnier was appallingly filthy. Her face was as white as wax and she was dreadfully emaciated. Her skeletal body was covered with a thick layer of grime. Her long hair was compacted, tangled and matted with faeces and food debris. The foul-smelling stench of her hair filled the room to such an extent that the doctors quickly gave their permission for those present to smoke.

Blanche's hair was thick and long on the left side, but on the right side there were only a few individual hairs. Continuous friction had reduced and worn down the hair until there was nothing on that side but a few scattered hairs protruding from a bare scalp. This was a result of the position Blanche had stayed in for the entire time she had remained on her mattress, lying on her right side, curled up on herself.

Once she was admitted to the Hôtel-Dieu, Blanche was installed in a room that was well-lit and which overlooked the hospital gardens. From her bed, which was placed near the window, she could see the banks of a river and the poplars bordering the river.

Sister Saint-Wilfrid, the nurse appointed to care for Blanche, pointed out that, as soon as she arrived, Blanche wanted the windows to remain wide open, so that the light and the air filled the room.

Sister Saint-Wilfrid: *At first, I found that she wanted to hide her face under the covers. It's likely that the bright sunlight was tiring her eyes, because the following day she didn't try to cover her face entirely; she simply raised the sheet with her left hand to eye level. She still has that strange habit of covering her face, but now, quite often, and especially when she takes her meals, she leaves her face completely uncovered. Not once has she asked (and she knows very well how to ask for things that make her happy) for the window or the shutters to be closed.*

At the beginning of her stay in the hospital, Blanche often asked for 'her dear little scarf', by which she meant the filthy rag which she had covered her face with whenever someone had entered her room in the house on Rue de la Visitation.

The three forensic doctors who were treating Blanche, Doctors Chrétien, Doctor Lagrange and Doctor Brossard, gave instructions for Blanche's hair to be cropped short. Within the hour, her long matted mane had been cut off in one piece and preserved to be used as evidence. The matted length was one metre long and weighed two kilograms, five hundred grams.

Blanche herself weighed just over twenty-five kilograms (fifty-five pounds). She was so weak that the Abbé de Mondion, the chaplain of the Hôtel-Dieu, fearing her imminent death, administered the last rites.

The nurses washed Blanche from head to toe and trimmed her nails. Blanche struggled and tried to resist, but the nurses were used to dealing with recalcitrant patients and simply completed their task. Once Blanche was clean, she was put into a nightgown and given a cap to cover her close-cropped scalp. Then, for the first time in a very long time, Blanche slept between clean sheets.

It took her several days to adjust to this, for she was used to living among filth, faeces and rotten food. At night, nurses would hear her muttering 'my dear little cave' several times before she fell asleep.

For the first two days, Blanche refused to accept any of the food she was offered. Then, without a word of explanation, she started to eat whatever was given to her. Because of her weakened condition, Blanche could not initially be given solid food, so she was sustained with blackcurrant juice, biscuits, soup and vintage wine. When she began to get noticeably better and her weight started to increase, the doctors examined her carefully and found, incredibly, that her organs were perfectly healthy.

The doctors also directed that she be lifted twice a day and put in an armchair. She had to be supported, however, as she could neither stand up nor walk, as her leg muscles had atrophied due to her lack of movement over many years.

After eight days, she was given a bowl of strawberries, and she recognised the fruit immediately.

Blanche Monnier: *There's not enough here for everyone, but I won't eat them all myself.*

She ate some of the strawberries, clearly enjoying them. After swallowing each fruit, she closed her eyes and rubbed her stomach, like a child eating a delicacy. Then, having eaten what she wanted, she put the bowl on her night-stand.

Blanche Monnier: *I'll put them here so they're near me and I can take them whenever I want.*

The doctors then began measuring Blanche's ability to understand. One morning, they placed an envelope containing a letter in front of her eyes, and Blanche was able to see that the envelope was not addressed to her.

Blanche Monnier: *It's not for me.*

A few minutes later, someone brought another envelope, and this time it was plainly addressed to Mademoiselle Blanche Monnier. Blanche was delighted.

Blanche Monnier: *It's for me, Blanche.*

She eagerly pulled the letter out of the envelope and quickly read it. It was a letter created for the occasion. In it, one of Blanche's close relatives asked her how she was and if she had any news. After reading it, Blanche seemed quite emotional.

Blanche Monnier: *My dear little world.*

The doctors felt that this demonstrated that Blanche understood the contents of the letter. They briefed one of the nurses who was caring for Blanche.

Nurse: *Are you going to answer your letter, Blanche?*

Blanche Monnier: *No, not right now. Not right now.*

The doctors then checked that Blanche could distinguish gold from silver. They had one of the Hôtel-Dieu staff show her a silver watch. Blanche showed some interest in the time-piece because it looked similar to the one she'd been given as a communion gift.

Blanche Monnier: *It's silver. I have one just like it in gold.*

When she spoke, Blanche spoke French with simplified syntax, but she never asked any questions on any subject. She answered simple and precise questions simply and precisely although her answers were often quite childish. She was able to identify most of the objects that were presented to her, pencils, roses, glasses, food, and she always accompanied her naming of each item with the diminutive phrase: 'dear little', so a pencil was a 'dear little pencil', a rose was a 'dear little rose', and so on.

Sometimes. Blanche refused to communicate at all; at other times she uttered a string of obscenities and insults of the crudest kind.

The years of regular potassium bromide ingestion had taken their toll on Blanche's mental faculties. Unfortunately for Blanche, because the chemical cause of her mental state affected her central nervous system, it was either undetectable, ignored or overlooked, despite bromide's exceedingly long half-life in the body and its devastating side-effects. There were simply too many people in Poitiers who had accepted and then perpetuated Louise Monnier's initial claims that Blanche's mental crises had come about because of a combination of loss and grief, and that she had had a propensity for mental instability as a teenager and that her current mental state had therefore been inevitable. At no point during her hospital stay was the long-term administration of potassium bromide diagnosed as the principle cause of the destruction of Blanche's nervous system.

If Blanche decided that any of the demands being made on her were onerous, she would become angry and quickly go from a state of passive immobility to one of violent agitation. Fortunately for the nurses, her general weakness meant that they could usually prevent her from doing any damage or from causing harm to herself or to others. Once thwarted, Blanche would resort to hiding her face under her pillow and muttering angry words or phrases. Many of the words were unintelligible, but Blanche always interspersed them with several choice swear words.

After she had been at the Hôtel-Dieu for a few days, Blanche's doctors allowed her to have visitors. In fact, they actively encouraged this, believing that having visitors would help Blanche regulate her moods and maintain her calm. If she was in regular contact with people who spoke softly to her, then the poor woman could, despite it being unlikely that she would ever recover her mental faculties, at least have company and quiet conversation, two very simple-to-arrange things were integral aspects of a 'normal' life.

From then on, fellow doctors, aristocratic ladies, people who had once known her and a constant stream of journalists, all eager to report anything sensational, came to look at Blanche Monnier, just as they would have gone to contemplate a curious, unusual, or exotic creature in a freak show.

The interest in Blanche Monnier increased with the

news that members of the public were allowed to visit her. *L'Avenir de la Vienne* noted on June 20:

> 'This year, during the summer holidays, it will be a very simple matter to go and pay a visit to the prisoner of Poitiers. In any café in the city, all one has to do is express an interest in wanting to go and see her and immediately the manager will spring into action and say: 'Of course, sir. Would you like someone to take you to see her?' whereupon four or five 'guides' will happily offer to lead the way to the celebrity's bedside.'

The Mother Superior of the Hôtel-Dieu was eager to show the public her ward. She met the visitors and then guided them through the hospice corridors to Blanche's room. The Abbé de Mondion, the chaplain of the hospital, was always on hand to attend these visits, and both of them went to great lengths to emphasize the considerable progress Blanche was making.

A week after Blanche's arrival at the Hôtel-Dieu, one of the first medical experts to visit her was Doctor Lhuillier, from Montmorillon.

When Doctor Lhuillier called her by name, Blanche turned towards him. She looked at him for a few seconds, blinking and then closed her eyes against the light, which was very bright. At his request, she showed her tongue, then she gave him her hand so that he could take her pulse. He noted that her hand was warm and that her fingers were tapered.

With the doctor's permission, the duty intern offered Blanche a small bowl of orange segments that she ate with pleasure. Her pleasure increased when one of the sisters came into her room and presented her with a bouquet of flowers. She looked at the nun for a long time, then she held the flowers close to her nose and breathed in and holding in their scents for as long as she could, just as a child might have done, then she kissed the bouquet.

She finally spoke, and her words (which seemed to suggest that Blanche was remembering her childhood days at Le Pilet), although uttered very quickly, were clearly articulated.

Blanche Monnier: *Oh! how beautiful it would be if we*

had two bouquets like this, with a cave in the middle and a little Virgin in the cave. We'll have to do that another time.

After the clinical examination, the doctor granted *Le Journal de la Vienne* an interview during which he provided details about the 'celebrity' resident of the Hôtel-Dieu.

'Everything that has been said about the unfortunate woman falls far short of the reality. No description can give a sufficient account of the state in which she now finds herself; she is an absolute wreck of a human being, the most appalling example of a mere shell of a person. Blanche Monnier lies there on her stomach, her legs folded up, her face pressed against the bolster. Her right arm is folded under her, her left arm hangs out of bed and in her hand she holds (a pitiful sight) a small bouquet of roses very tightly. She seems to be sleeping. Her very calm breathing barely moves her chest. All over her body, her skin is a very distinctive white-yellow hue, veined with blue. Neither anaemia, chlorosis, nor any of the various cachexia would cause skin to turn precisely that colour: such a hue is the result of a malnourished being after a long, enforced stay in utter darkness. Her filthy mane of hair has gone. The hair, cut and clean, is still black; there are a few patches of scalp on one side. Was it perhaps to avoid the painful pulling of her hair (which must have weighed almost four and a half pounds) that the poor woman has become accustomed to resting in this way, on her stomach, her head strangely angled? For since she was admitted to the Hôtel-Dieu, she has not gone to bed any other way. And this position, certainly, has been maintained for much longer than any other, possibly for years. As a result, her face has undergone a significant change and become deformed, mainly around the nose.'

Doctor Lhuillier went on to give details of Blanche's mental state.

'It is my considered that Blanche Monnier is not a mad woman. She certainly gives the appearance of being an adult that has regressed to childhood, but it is only the temporary retreat of a tortured adult into a perfectly-remembered and pleasant childhood. Thanks to the

excellent care that is being provided by the hospital, and thanks to the new and rational studies that have been made of her mind and her senses, she has begun to regain sufficient individuality.'

After the doctor's vivid description, several journalists from *Le Journal de la Vienne* wanted to see for themselves the situation in which Blanche Monnier now found herself. On Friday, May 31st, one of them was invited to come and see her condition. When he entered the room where she was resting, Blanche hid under the blankets, revealing only the top of her head which was 'shaved like the head of a young conscript.' The chaplain called her name, 'Blanche! Mademoiselle Blanche! At the sound of his voice, which she knew well, the poor woman showed her face.

The journalist's subsequent article was published in *Le Journal de la Vienne* on Monday, June 3rd.

'We frankly admit to having had a dreadful shock when we saw this face illuminated by large black eyes, the brightness of which made the frightening pallor even more striking. The cheeks are hollow and the protruding cheekbones accentuate the features which, despite the suffering, have retained the purity of the lines of the face that only a very long nose spoils. The hospice chaplain, the Abbé de Mondion had a short conversation with the patient, who always replied appropriately. She even spoke with extreme volubility, but it was sometimes difficult to grasp the meaning of her words, as she expresses herself so powerfully. I wished to ask the patient a few questions, but my request was declined.'

Blanche, on seeing someone she did not know and on hearing an unfamiliar voice, became upset and hid her head beneath her bed covers.

Blanche Monnier: *Oh, no! I'm not going back to my room!*

The Abbé de Mondion saw that Blanche was growing upset and tried to distract her with a bouquet of flowers.

Abbé de Mondion: *Mademoiselle Blanche, see this pretty bouquet of roses?*

The poor woman, recognizing the priest's voice, looked up and then propped herself up on one elbow. She examined the bouquet of delphinium flowers (commonly called pied-d'alouette, or larkspur) for a moment and then tore off a petal and held it up, brandishing it at the Abbé.

Blanche Monnier: *This not a rose; it's a pied-d' alouette, a pied-d'alouette. It's just like the ones that grew in Migné, like the ones in Migné.*

A carnation from India was then put in her hand and Blanche was tested again.

Abbé de Mondion: *Isn't this a pretty rosebud?*

Blanche Monnier: *That is a carnation of India, like the ones in Migné, just like the ones in Migné.*

Blanche was able to recognize and name all the flowers, especially the ones that reminded her of the flowerbeds in the gardens of Le Pilet, which she had loved so much when she was a young girl. All her memories were attached to her childhood, perhaps because it was the only period of her life when she had been truly happy.

The Abbé de Mondion said to the journalist that he had one final question for Blanche, after which the interview needed to be brought to a close in order to avoid tiring the patient.

The Abbé de Mondion: *Tell me, Blanche, where are you?*

Blanche Monnier: *Oh! In my little bed, my dear little bed.*

At that point, suddenly very tired, Blanche put her head on the pillow, closed her eyes and almost instantly fell asleep. She was woken up a few minutes later to eat her evening meal which consisted of milk, eggs, strawberries and biscuits. As Blanche ate her supper, the journalist took the opportunity to leave.

The most touching visit was undoubtedly the one made by Rosalie Joubert and her husband, Auguste. They were sharecroppers at Le Pilet in Migné, and they decided to visit the daughter of their employer on Thursday, June 6th, accompanied by the same journalist from *Le Journal de la Vienne*.

'*Madame Rosalie Joubert had not seen her employer's daughter for over twenty-three years, and she was filled with apprehension. On the morning of the visit, she had picked a bouquet of flowers from the garden of Le Pilet and her husband had picked strawberries and put them in a wicker basket. In the courtyard of the Hôtel-Dieu, Madame Joubert could not control her emotions. She looked down at her bouquet of three roses and spoke to her husband: It upsets me very much when I think about how long it has been since I last saw her.'*

A few minutes later, the three visitors knocked on Blanche's room door. The nurse, a very old sister named Aurélie Raymond, opened the door immediately and the Joubert couple entered the room ahead of the journalist. After a slight moment of hesitation, Rosalie went straight to the bed where Blanche was resting. She stood at her bedside and, trembling, without saying a word, presented Blanche with her flowers. Blanche lifted herself up on her elbow, took the bouquet and removed a flower whose smell she breathed in. Her face cleared and she smiled, but she did not look at Rosalie; it was the flowers that had made her smile. When she was asked, she quickly gave the names of the flowers in the bouquet.

Suddenly, a small insect fell onto the bedclothes. Blanche shuddered and grimaced and quickly brushed it off the bed with an abrupt movement of her bony hand.

Rosalie Joubert took Blanche's hand and spoke softly to her.

Rosalie Joubert: *Mademoiselle Blanche! Mademoiselle Blanche! Do you recognize me?*

Blanche Monnier: *No! No!*

Rosalie Joubert: *Are you sure you don't recognize me? I'm your friend, Rosalie.*

Blanche Monnier: *Rosalie! Rosalie! Oh, yes, like Rosalie in Migné!*

Rosalie Joubert: *Yes. Rosalie in Migné. Do you remember, Mademoiselle Blanche, when you came to Le Pilet, during the holidays? I made you climb on the donkey; you put your arm around my neck!*

Although Blanche was now looking intently at the woman and was listening very carefully to what she was saying, it was quite obvious she did not recognize Rosalie. The two women had known each other as young girls and, since that time, the constant field work Rosalie (who was now fifty-eight years old) was engaged in had altered her features so that she now resembled the rough peasant she was. Her husband, Auguste, who until then had remained at the back of the room, had a little more success when he offered Blanche the strawberries from his basket. Blanche grabbed one and two, three, then four, then five; all disappeared with a speed that enchanted Rosalie.

Rosalie: *Mademoiselle Blanche! Would you like to return to Migné?*

Blanche Monnier: *Yes! Yes! but not now. Later, later!*

Rosalie, puzzled by Blanche's response, tried again.

Rosalie: *Come along, Mademoiselle Blanche. Are you coming?*

The poor woman stared at her former friend, for a moment before answering.

Blanche Monnier: *I am nothing, nothing at all in that house. Less than nothing, less than nothing!*

As Rosalie Joubert stood by Blanche's bed, no longer sure what to say to her childhood friend, Sister Saint-Wilfrid entered the room, so the journalist stopped her and engaged her in conversation.

Journalist: *I'm very pleased to see that your patient is returning to life. There seems to be progress.*

Sister Saint-Wilfrid: *Monsieur, I myself am surprised. Mademoiselle Blanche drinks regularly; she has quite an appetite and she eats well. Hold on, I have to ask her about her lunch menu.*

Approaching the bed, the nun spoke to her patient.

Sister Saint-Wilfrid: *Mademoiselle Blanche, do you want to tell me what you ate for lunch?*

Blanche Monnier: *A little chicken, a dear little chicken.*

Sister Saint-Wilfrid: *And what else?*

Blanche Monnier: *Truffle tart, truffle tart.*

Blanche answered all of the questions very quickly and perfectly correctly.

Once the sister had finished talking to Blanche, the journalist continued questioning Sister Saint-Wilfrid.

Journalist: *Does your patient maintain her calm when she is in her bed?*

Sister Saint-Wilfrid: *She is always perfectly behaved. Since Mademoiselle Blanche has been in this hospital, she has been an angel of sweetness. Also, she has never tried to take off her nightdress, nor remove her bedclothes. What's more, she no longer uses the rude words that came out of her mouth when she was first brought to us.*

Journalist: *Does your patient sometimes mention her mother?*

Sister Saint-Wilfrid seemed to find the question embarrassing and did not answer. After a few minutes, the journalist addressed Blanche directly.

Journalist: *Mademoiselle Blanche, would you like to see your mother?*

At these words, the unfortunate woman became agitated and started to shout.

Blanche Monnier: *Don't bring her here! Don't bring her here!*

Blanche gesticulated wildly; her face contorted with anger. Sister Saint-Wilfrid was only able to calm her down by offering her some of the Joubert's strawberries.

Faced with such fury, the journalist decided it would be best if he did not stay any longer. However, before leaving, he happened to glance at the table in the middle of the room. There he noticed a large number of letters and cards from all over the world, so he picked one up at random. It was an illustrated postcard from Neuchâtel in Switzerland. It depicted two small robins sheltering beneath a brightly-coloured umbrella. On the back he read:

To Mademoiselle Blanche Monnier
Care of the Sisters of the Hôtel-Dieu
France

A group of young girls who sympathize with you with all their heart send you their cordial greetings and all their wishes for your prompt and complete recovery.

Although Blanche's condition was improving daily, the many visits very quicky tired her out. The doctors who were treating her felt that this was detrimental to Blanche's full recovery. They informed the judges in charge of the investigation of their concerns. The judges were already very unhappy that every morning there was a story about Blanche in the newspapers; usually a story that included the interview of the previous day.

Alexis Fontant, Presiding Judge of the court and the

vice-president of the administrative hospices commission, took the decision to prohibit all visitors from Blanche Monnier's hospital room; the only people allowed to enter her room were the three forensic doctors, the Abbé de Mondion, the Mother Superior, Sister Saint-Wilfrid, Aurélie Raymond and a few carefully-chosen interns and day nurses.

In reality, the court order was ignored. The Abbé de Mondion continued to exhibit Blanche to any journalist who came to the Hôtel-Dieu to see her. He was convinced she was going to make a full recovery, so he thought it was necessary for the press to report any progress she was making.

One of the interns mentioned Blanche's fastidious eating habits to a journalist.

Intern: *She always asks if the plates and cutlery are clean. She still eats with her fingers, but with great delicacy. When she eats an orange, she always keeps the pips in the palm of her hand until she is able to dispose of them.*

Although Blanche always listened to what she was told and made efforts to understand, her answers were not always comprehensible. The Abbé de Mondion, Sister Saint-Wilfrid and Aurélie Raymond did all they could to help her express herself accurately. Aurélie Raymond, who was old and infirm and walked with a pronounced limp, seemed to have unlimited reserves of patience for Blanche. There was a close bond, almost a closeness between the two women, just as in the past there had been a similar relationship between Blanche and Marie Fazy. Aurélie brought Blanche her meals, groomed her, and somehow succeeded in making Blanche adopt habits of continence. After years of having emptied her bowels on her bed without being inconvenienced, Blanche was relearning the importance of personal hygiene. On 18th June, she asked for the chamber pot, knowing perfectly well how to hold back when the nurse was occupied. If, despite all of her efforts, an accident occurred, Blanche became very upset and would either hide her face, clearly embarrassed, or would become angry and resort to her old habits of swearing and shouting.

Blanche also no longer seemed to like staying in bed. She preferred sitting in an armchair, looking out of the window. On one occasion, when the nurses wanted to weigh Blanche and they proceeded to lift her up and put her on the scales. Blanche misunderstood and thought she was being put to bed. She waved her arms in protest and accidentally punched Aurélie Raymond on the nose. Shocked, Blanche burst into tears and clutched her nurse's hand by way of apology.

Blanche had also formed a close relationship with the Abbé de Mondion. She seemed to enjoy talking to him. This may have been due to the fact that the Abbé asked her lots of questions about her childhood. Blanche told the Abbé of the Hôtel-Dieu about her studies at the Christian Union and her holidays at Le Pilet. She also remembered the names of some of the companies and businesses that delivered goods to the family home. She specifically remembered that her parents did not buy desserts from Avenel, at 12 Rue de la Mairie, as they preferred Pasino's, the Italian patisserie, which was a little further along the same street.

The Abbé also asked Blanche about her travels, particularly about the places she had visited when she was a young girl. Blanche recalled the family excursions to Royat and Mont-Dore. She also remembered her trip to Paris and she explained what she had felt when she had visited the various famous landmarks and monuments in the capital. Unable to put his vocation aside, even for a moment, the Abbé asked Blanche if she remembered her first communion. Blanche told him that she did remember, and she was able to tell him the name of the priest who had officiated.

Visitors brought Blanche bouquets every day. Blanche was able to name every flower with ease; it become a kind of game that she won easily.

The woman who had been forced to lie naked and sedated amongst her own excrement now rested on a bed with freshly-laundered bedclothes on which were strewn rose petals. She often held the flowers in both hands and breathed in their scents. She looked at the petals that littered her bed and seemed happy to be in the midst of flowers that for so long had been denied to her.

Blanche was also delighted that she was able to see a river from her bed and liked to mention it.

Blanche Monnier: *Oh! how beautiful the dear little river is!*

When swallows flew past her window, she was delighted.

Blanche Monnier: *Oh! Look at the dear little swallows!*

Sister Saint-Wilfrid confirmed that not only had Blanche rediscovered the pleasure of being clean, but that she loved applying scent or cologne to her body. She was also very keen to wear a dress and she readily agreed to wear mules. When she was lifted out of bed to sit in her armchair, she would either wear a bathrobe over her nightdress or else she would put on one of several beautifully-patterned dresses. Once she was dressed, she would look at herself in a mirror and admire her reflection with obvious satisfaction.

One day when a group of well-meaning society ladies were visiting Blanche, they complimented her on her choice of dress. Blanche gave them a disdainful look, then told them in no uncertain terms what was wrong with the dress.

Blanche Monnier: *Cotton like this is only good for shepherdesses.*

The Abbé de Mondion often asked Blanche to talk about her childhood and teenage years. She was very happy to evoke these years, associating them with naïve descriptions of flowers, birds and the countryside. However, Blanche never spoke of (and the Abbé de Mondion deliberately never asked about) her years of imprisonment in her shuttered and locked room. No one mentioned the terrible state Blanche was in when she was discovered by the commissioner. Everyone who worked with Blanche seemed to consider that it was best not to ask Blanche about her years of imprisonment. Instead, the focus was on helping Blanche enjoy her new-found freedom as much as she could.

In general, everything light pleased her: not only daylight, sunlight, and lamp-light, but also light-coloured clothing and light-coloured or white objects. She hated darkness and dark colours. For example, she did not want to look at or touch any of the mourning letters that had been sent to her simply because their envelopes had the traditional black borders.

Blanche's dislike of her mother was intense and profound, and if anyone dared to mention her, Blanche would become very upset or incredibly angry.

Related subjects also drew Blanche's ire. When the Abbé de Mondion asked Blanche if she wanted to visit her old home in Rue de la Visitation. Blanche was dismissive and quickly closed down that particular line of questioning.

Blanche Monnier: *Let's not talk about that house. It*

forces everything to retreat, everything to retreat.

The Abbé de Mondion was a sympathetic man with a broad mind and a generous nature, and he was convinced that as a result of the care that Blanche was receiving at the Hôtel-Dieu, she would eventually recover her health and her reason possibly at the same time, after which she could gradually learn to live in society again.

The Abbé de Mondion's judgment about a possible cure for Blanche was based purely on his faith and his desire for his ward's recovery, and it was for those reasons that he failed to acknowledge that Blanche's ability to name flowers, birds, or food was not an indication that her reason was returning. Also, the Abbé was unaware of the irreparable damage to Blanche's mind and nervous system wreaked by the years of potassium bromide abuse, The result of that undetected assault on the patient's nervous system had resulted in her suffering from a regression of her personality to a very specific stage of childhood; the Le Pilet years, which manifested themselves in her attitudes, her interests and her language. She spoke and thought and acted like the young head-strong girl she had been. She was kind, interested in nature and single-minded.

She was also fifty-two years old.

Although Blanche was severely mentally impaired, it was not to the extent that it had caused her other faculties to become unreliable. Her eyesight, hearing, and other senses functioned perfectly, as did her memory. The main questions the doctors wanted answers to were: How badly damaged was Blanche Monnier's brain? Was the damage repairable or was it irreversible.

In the conclusion of their report, published on 19th June, the forensic doctors appointed by the investigating judge decided: Blanche Monnier would never recover her reason.

> *'From the mental point of view, we consider Mademoiselle Monnier to be an imbecile, minus habens, whose faculty for reason is far lower than normal. She must therefore be classified as insane because she is unable to take care of herself and direct her own life.'*

Malampia

There is an enigmatic aspect to this strange case that needs to be mentioned. It concerns some of the words and phrases that Blanche Monnier used once she was liberated.

Bearing in mind the amount of systematic damage done to Blanche's nervous system and to her brain as a result of her daily intake of potassium bromide, it could be that some of Blanche's utterances were meaning-free gibberish, or simply a recalling of some childish word game or code.

Specifically, this is an investigation into the ways that Blanche referred to her room in 21 Rue de la Visitation after her liberation.

The first reference she made to it was on 23rd May, when Commissioner Bucheton gave instructions for Blanche to be taken from her room and transported to the Hôtel-Dieu; Blanche lay on her filthy mattress, screaming.

Blanche: *S'il te plaît laisse moi seul. Laisse-moi juste vivre dans ma chère petite grotte.*

An English translation of these two sentences is: *Please leave me alone. Just let me live in my dear little cave.*

There is some ambiguity in the words due to the translation process; *chère petite grotte* translates as 'dear little cave', but it could just as easily be 'lovely tiny grotto' or 'darling little fissure'.

Another phrase Blanche used post-liberation was *mon cher grand fond*.

The phrase *mon cher grand fond* translates into English as 'my dear big bottom', or 'my much-loved great bottom', or 'my beloved large bottom', or 'my precious prodigious bottom', or 'my valuable ample bottom', or any permutation of those words.

Blanche used this particular phrase several times during her stay at the Hôtel-Dieu.

She mentioned *mon cher grand fond* twice in her interview with Judge de Fresnal; the first time was when he asked her about having pastries delivered to Rue de la Visitation.

Blanche Monnier: *We are quite rich enough at mon cher grand fond to buy pastries.*

The second time she used the phrase during the interview was when she was asked about her bed and her sheets.

Judge Fresnal: *At 21 Rue de la Visitation, did you sleep in a clean bed on clean sheets?*

Blanche Monnier: *What would one say at mon cher grand fond if one heard that?*

As mentioned in the previous chapter, Blanche studiously avoided mentioning her imprisonment directly; she used a number of phrases when answering any questions that related to her room, or to 21 Rue de la Visitation.

The other word Blanche used was 'Malampia'. There is no English translation for this word, as it is a neologism; an invented word. Even its spelling is uncertain because although it was uttered by Blanche, she never wrote it down. Instead, it was first mentioned by a journalist in an article published in *La Vie illustrée*. It is therefore a transcribed word, so its spelling may be inaccurate, but it was that journalist's spelling of that particular 'word' that became the standardised way of spelling Blanche Monnier's invented word. Of course, it may be two words: 'mal' and 'ampia', a mixture of the French 'mal' (sick, evil) and the Italian 'ampia' (broad, big, wide). Whatever its true meaning, in the article, the journalist capitalized the word, as though it was the name of a place. Consequently, the word garnered considerable attention, with some readers assuming that 'Malampia' was the name that Blanche gave to an imagined newer, cleaner, and unlocked version of her room in 21 Rue de la Visitation, a sort of sanitised and room-sized version of Utopia or Shangri-La.

Blanche first used it when she was trying on a dress one morning. After admiring the decorative lace that adorned it, she commented on the dress's opulence.

Blanche: *C'est beaucoup trop beau pour cette pièce. Il serait beaucoup mieux de porter cette robe à la belle, bien-aimée, grande maison de Malampia.*

In English, those words translate into: *It's far too beautiful for this room. It would be much better to wear this dress to the beautiful, beloved, big house of Malampia.*

Although Blanche Monnier occasionally mentioned her 'chère petite grotte' or her 'Cher Grand Fond' or 'Malampia', it is difficult to determine a precise meaning of each of these spoken phrases, as they are phrases that Blanche was either reluctant or unable to explain once she was liberated. They are not phrases found in the Poitiers patois of the time, neither are they colloquial French terms. They are phrases that are exclusive to Blanche Monnier. They may have been coined by Blanche herself. If not, then Blanche must have learned them during her captivity, so they might have originally been uttered by either Louise Monnier, Marcel Monnier, Marie Fazy, or one of the other maids.

Of all of Blanche Monnier's utterances, 'Malampia' is the most confusing of them all, as it bears no relation to anything that existed at the time Blanche was using it.

There is a small land mass named Malampaya Sound, which is located in the South China Sea on the north-western coast of Palawan Island in the western Philippines, although it is difficult to understand why Blanche would make a cryptic reference to this (if indeed she did) in relation to her room in 21 Rue de la Visitation.

Over one hundred and twenty years after she uttered them, Blanche Monnier's cryptic words and phrases remain mysterious and inexplicable.

Louise Monnier's Death

Louise and Marcel Monnier were held in the Prison de la Visitation on pre-trial detention and, like any detainee in their situation, they could, at their own expense, order their meals from outside. At noon and in the evening, Marcel Monnier's maid rang at the prison door with his meals.

Louise Monnier wanted her meals to be prepared by her servants, for which she offered to pay them ten francs a day. The maids refused, arguing that the payment she was offering was insufficient. From then on, Madame Monnier ordered her meals from the Hôtel de France. The meal she ordered most frequently was chicken with peas, washed down with vintage wine. When she found out that she could earn ten cents a day by doing the work the inmates did, which was shelling and bagging peanuts, she asked to be included in the work detail, as it allowed her to use the money paid to her by the prison to defray some of the cost of having her food brought in. For the money-obsessed widow, a cent was a cent and any opportunity to save money was to be fully utilised.

It is possible, due to her delusional state of mind, that Madame Monnier did not fully understand what was happening to her. She had been ill for several months, and it is most likely that she suffered an enormous shock following her arrest and incarceration, for she was very quickly moved into the infirmary. She appeared to be in a constant state of astonishment that she had been incarcerated 'for so little'.

Louise Monnier: *Everyone is free to do what they want in their own home. Since my daughter wanted to live that way; since she liked that way of life, and as she didn't want to see me, why would I have done anything contrary to upset her?*

Marcel Monnier remained calm, carefully and reasonably defending himself against the accusation of having cooperated in a kidnapping. A fellow inmate asked him why he was in prison.

Monnier: *I have no idea. I haven't done anything wrong. I don't know why they have got me here.*

The former sub-prefect made sure he stayed on good terms with the other prisoners. He helped several of them by writing letters to their families for them if they couldn't write.

After Madame Monnier's interrogation on the evening of 6th June, she began, for the first time, to understand the gravity of her situation; she was, she realised, being accused of threatening the life and the freedom of her daughter.

After the investigating judge had departed, her guards noticed that she had fallen into a mood of deep despondency. Madame Monnier was suffering from a heart condition and the intense shock and the heightened emotional state she was in took its toll on the weakened organ. She became very ill, very rapidly.

Doctor Jàblonski, the prison doctor, was called with some urgency. He examined Louise Monnier and found that she was failing fast. His diagnosis was correct: the old lady spent the entire day (June 7th) in a semi-comatose state and the following morning she slipped into a coma. The chief guard recalled Doctor Jablonski, who sat at the patient's bedside and made a few vain efforts to revive her. Realising his efforts were having no effect, the doctor sent for Canon Rosière, the chaplain of the prison.

When the chaplain failed to arrive, a guard was sent to ask Father Bertault, the parish priest of Saint-Porchaire, to come and administer the ritual. The priest was unable to get to the prison infirmary until nine-thirty in the morning, during which time, Louise Monnier had died of heart congestion. According to the testimony of Marie Foulon, a detained woman who worked as an infirmary nurse, Louise Monnier's last words had been about her daughter.

Marie Foulon: *At about five o'clock in the morning, she cried out: 'Oh! my poor Blanche!' After that, she didn't say anything further.*

The prison authorities decided they would not immediately inform Marcel Monnier of his mother's death. Instead, he was told that his mother was very ill that morning in his cell. Later during the day, he was told the news of her death. Marcel Monnier's wife, Angèle, and his daughter, Dolorès, were notified of Louise Monnier's death by her lawyer, Maitre Mérine. Accompanied by a friend, they took refuge in the convent of the Dames de l'Assomption in Rue du Pont-Neuf.

At the Hôtel-Dieu, the Mother Superior was away on convent business and no one else wanted the responsibility of telling Blanche that her mother was dead. The Mother Superior returned to the hospice on the morning of Sunday, June 9th, and she waited until lunch was being served before she went to Blanche's room to announce the death of her mother.

Mother Superior: *I have some sad news to tell you, Mademoiselle Blanche. Your mother is dead.*

Blanche started to dance a little unsteadily. Her former grace and agility were long gone.

Blanche Monnier: *I want a party! I want a party!*

Mother Superior: *Mademoiselle Blanche, listen to me carefully; when you return home you will no longer find your mother there.*

Blanche kept her eyes on the nurse who was getting her lunch table ready with a tablecloth and cutlery.

Blanche Monnier: *Pah! I just want to enjoy myself! To enjoy myself!*

Mother Superior: *Mademoiselle Blanche, I will help you dress in your best mourning clothes. And you must think of your poor bother, and the terrible grief he must be feeling.*

Blanche was not listening. She clearly had no interest in what the Mother Superior was saying about mourning clothes. It seemed that finally, her mother had become someone of absolutely no significance to her.

The death of Madame Louise Monnier was announced, with a headline, on the front page of most of the Poitiers newspapers and she was the subject of conversations and debates throughout Poitiers.

Some did not believe that she had died a natural death, claiming that the old lady had either committed suicide or else had been poisoned. Others thought that it was for those reasons that an autopsy had been ordered by the investigating judge. Although none of the various claims had any basis in fact, the prosecutor's office still asked for a report from Doctor Jablonski, who had cared for the deceased during her last hours.

Meanwhile, in Rue de la Visitation, groups of curious people gathered outside the Monnier house. Journalists arrived in search of a story and spoke to some of the people loitering in the street. Others, more intrepid, knocked on neighbours' door and interviewed or questioned them.

An officer of the 37th Artillery Regiment (which was

garrisoned at Bourges) rode his horse along Rue de la Visitation. On hearing the commotion, he asked someone why people were standing around outside number twenty-one. Several people told him.

Soldier: *Ah! So, the Monnier mother is dead. All that can be said of her is that instead of a heart, she had a Lourdes pebble.*

On Saturday morning, a journalist from *Le Journal de la Vienne* saw Juliette Dupuis and Eugénie Tabeau on the doorstep of their late employer's house. The two women were leaning against the wall, chatting with passers-by and laughing a lot.

Journalist: *You've heard the news then?*

The two women burst out laughing.

Eugénie Tabeau: *We've heard.*

Journalist: *Have you any thoughts?*

Juliette Dupuis: *The evil old woman died too soon; she should have gone to court and been tried!*

Journalist: *Don't you believe that one should respect the dead, or that death commands respect?*

Both women laughed derisively and the journalist walked away.

At about ten o'clock, an incident occurred in the street when the Abbé de Clisson, a neighbour of the Monniers, came out of the prison after praying over the body of the deceased. Several passers-by approached the priest.

Passer-by: *Oh! Is it true that the old woman is dead?*

Abbé: *Yes, and she died like the holy woman that she was! She was a martyr.*

Passer-by: *What? Do you really believe that the old woman was innocent?*

Abbé: *I believe the truth, not lies!*

On hearing those words, a few of the people present began to insult and then to attack the Abbé who, fearing the worst, backed away until he found he had his back against the prison wall. Two more people joined the angry mob, and closed in on the Abbé. It was at that moment that Maitre Mérine left the prison. He saw what was happening and without saying a word, dragged the Abbé away from the threatening mob which continued yelling threats and insults until he was out of sight.

The fact that there was such anger and simmering

violence on the public road outside the prison caused the authorities to think that it was likely that something similar would occur on the day of Louise Monnier's funeral, scheduled to take place on Monday, June 10th.

On Sunday, June 9th, the prefect, the public prosecutor and the central commissioner held a conference at the prefecture. After much discussion, it was decided, in agreement with Marcel Monnier's wife, Angèle, who was acting as the representative of the Monnier family, that Louise Monnier's burial would take place at one o'clock in the morning. Her body would be taken a few hours before the burial (under the cover of darkness) to the chapel in the Cimetière de Chilvert. The decision was kept secret. The prefecture officially informed the representatives of the press on Sunday night.

Despite the secrecy, by five o'clock in the morning, about fifty people were gathered outside the prison. The Central Commissioner, Pierre Bucheton, who had arrived early, took a small group of police officers into the room where Louise Monnier's body was being kept; an annexe located to one side of the prison entrance.

The captain of the gendarmerie paced up and down in the street outside, awaiting his orders. The gendarmes, grouped in the courtyard of the barracks near the Rue des Basses-Treilles, were ready to quell any acts of aggression.

At ten minutes past five, the hearse entered the inner courtyard of the prison, under the watchful eye of the central commissioner. Five minutes later a closed carriage arrived in the street that deposited Madame Marcel Monnier and her daughter, in mourning clothes and both wearing black veils.

Only immediate family and intimate friends were allowed to attend. The prefect issued them with cards to attend the service that would take place in the prison chapel officiated by Canon Rosière. The nine invited guests entered through the small door of the prison. They were: Paul Druet (Captain of the Bar), four lawyers: Maitre Mérine, Maitre de Poutier, Maitre Bodin, Maitre Molant, the Comte de Clisson and Monsieur Thenaisie (a neighbour of the Monniers), Madame Decharme (the wife of the director of the Bank of France), and the wife of Captain de Lattre (a friend of Madame Marcel Monnier). The investigating judge, Dollin du Fresnel arrived late and stayed for only a quarter of an hour.

Marcel Monnier was not allowed to enter the chapel. Two guards were assigned to keep him in a small room just off the prison chapel. He was allowed to hear the service and watch his mother's coffin being carried out to the hearse, but he was not allowed to meet or stand with his wife and daughter. When he was taken back to his cell after the prayers of absolution, he broke down and sobbed uncontrollably.

At six-thirty in the morning, the procession left the prison. Canon Rosière went ahead of the hearse in a funeral carriage. Despite the hour, there were about two hundred curious people gathered in Rue de la Visitation. A large contingent of them ran alongside or behind the hearse, shouting insults, for many of them believed that Louise Monnier was guilty of having imprisoned her daughter and kept her in the most appalling conditions and felt that the old lady had escaped justice by dying.

As a precautionary measure, the prefect had decided that Madame Marcel Monnier, her daughter and the other people who had attended the service would be driven directly to the Cimetière de Chilvert via the Boulevard de la Préfecture, Rue de Victor-Hugo, Rue de Carnot and Rue de la Tranchée. Meanwhile, the hearse would follow a different route; it would go along Rue de Basses-Treilles, Rue de Théophraste-Renaudot, Rue Saint-Hilaire, Rue le Cesve and Rue Jules-Ferry, along Faubourg de la Tranchée and then into the cemetery.

It was a wise precaution, for the supressed anger of the people was tangible as they followed the hearse or lined the streets to watch it pass. They reacted differently to how they usually would if a hearse passed them on its way to the cemetery. Due the intense anger that many felt towards Louise Monnier, the onlooking women did not bother to make the sign of the cross as they usually did, and the men who were wearing hats kept them firmly on their heads, instead of taking them off as a gesture of respect for the dead.

As the hearse made its way along Rue Jules-Ferry, many of the women who worked in the brothel, Le Tranchée, stood at their windows, either naked or scantily-dressed, yelling unflattering remarks about the deceased. In the doorway of the establishment, about sixty onlookers, mostly women, shouted insults and sang 'La Carmagnole' as a mark of their disapproval.

The police had given the order to keep the gates of Cimetière de Chilvert closed. Only family members and friends who had attended the prison chapel service, along with the representatives of the press were permitted to enter.

Inside the cemetery, a short distance from the boundary wall, the pallbearers, lifted the coffin out of the hearse and placed it on a stand at the edge of the plot where the body of Émile Monnier, the husband of the deceased, already rested.

Canon Rosière recited a burial prayer and then Madame Marcel Monnier, her daughter and their friends watched as the pallbearers lowered the coffin into the grave. The ceremony was coming to an end.

Meanwhile, a crowd of curious onlookers had gathered by the cemetery gates, waiting for the mourners to exit. As Madame Monnier and her friends climbed into their carriages, the excited crowd greeted them with jeers and insults.

Once the mourners were inside and the doors closed, the carriage drivers set off at a fast pace. As the carriages left the cemetery, the chapel clock rang to signal that it was seven o'clock in the morning.

Blanche Monnier's Interview
August 6th, 1901

Judge Dollin du Fresnel had tried several times to interview Blanche Monnier. The final interview was attempted on August 6th, 1901. A nurse was present.

Judge Fresnal: *Will you tell us your first and last names?*

Blanche Monnier (laughing): *Nothing at all. Nothing at all.*

Judge Fresnal: *Isn't your name Blanche Monnier?*

Blanche Monnier: *There are other women with that name.*

Judge Fresnal: *How old are you?*

Blanche Monnier: *I don't want to answer that.*

Judge Fresnal: *Where were you born?*

Blanche Monnier utters a few unintelligible sounds, possibly words. Finally, she speaks clearly.

Blanche Monnier: *But one can't stay here forever.*

Judge Fresnal: *Do you have a brother?*

Blanche Monnier: *Well, yes.*

Judge Fresnal: *Will you tell me his name?*

Blanche Monnier: *No.*

Judge Fresnal: *Is your brother married?*

Blanche Monnier makes some more unintelligible sounds.

Judge Fresnal: *Did you go to your brother's wedding in Mont-de-Marsan?*

Blanche Monnier: *Well, yes.*

Judge Fresnal: *And don't you have a niece? What's her name?*

Blanche Monnier: *Too bad for her.*

Judge Fresnal: *When you were young, did you have piano lessons with Mademoiselle Gilbert?*

Blanche Monnier: *I don't know her.*

Judge Fresnal: *What school did you go to?*

Blanche Monnier: *Fuck! I can't answer everything.*

Judge Fresnal: *Did your father take care of you and try to teach you Greek?*

Blanche Monnier: *No.*

Judge Fresnal: *Didn't you, for a long time, have a maid named Marie Fazy?*

Blanche Monnier*: Yes.*

Judge Fresnal: *What has become of her? Is she dead?*

Blanche Monnier: *I don't know.*

Judge Fresnal: *Where do you live in Poitiers?*

Blanche Monnier: *I don't want to say anything at all. It's not for me to talk.*

Judge Fresnal: *Didn't you live at 21 Rue de la Visitation?*

Blanche Monnier: *Yes, but it's 14, not 21.*

Judge Fresnal: *Was the garden nice there?*

Blanche Monnier: *Yes, and I'll climb over another wall if I go back there.*

Judge Fresnal: *Which floor was your room on?*

Blanche Monnier becomes agitated. She utters a string of unintelligible words.

Judge Fresnal: *Was your room prettier than this one?*

Blanche Monnier: *When we are at mon cher grand fond, it was better than here, but we have to wait a while before going there.*

Judge Fresnal: *Do you remember your father?*

Blanche Monnier: *Oh, yes.*

Judge Fresnal: *Is he dead?*

Blanche Monnier (laughing): *I don't know anything about that.*

Judge Fresnal: *Do you remember your mother?*

Blanche Monnier (angrily): *Enough talking.*

Judge Fresnal: *Would you like to see your mother?*

Blanche Monnier: *No. It's best if she stays where she is.*

Judge Fresnal: *Do you love your mother?*

Blanche Monnier: *Yes, but it's better she stays where she is.*

Judge Fresnal: *Has anyone told you that your mother is dead?*

Blanche Monnier (laughing): *She is still at mon cher grand fond.*

Judge Fresnal: *Did your brother come to see you often when you lived at 21 Rue de la Visitation?*

Blanche Monnier: *Yes, yes.*

Judge Fresnal: *Did he bring you sweets?*

Blanche Monnier: *We are quite rich enough at mon cher grand fond to buy pastries.*

Blanche Monnier laughs loudly.

Judge Fresnal: *At 21 Rue de la Visitation, did you sleep in a clean bed on clean sheets?*

Blanche Monnier: *What would one say at mon cher grand fond if one heard that?*

Judge Fresnal: *Why did you put a veil or a scarf over your face?*

Blanche Monnier utters a long string of words that are unintelligible.

Judge Fresnal: *Were you washed and did you have your hair washed at Rue de la Visitation?*

Blanche Monnier: *It wasn't me who had so much hair; that was someone else. There are others apart from me who have the same name.*

It was at this point that Judge de Fresnal realised that there was no point continuing the interview. He thanked Blanche for her time and left the room.

Louise Monnier's Will

Three days after the death of Louise Monnier, the investigating judge, Dollin du Fresnel, decided to search her home.

On Wednesday, June 13th, 1901, at five o'clock in the afternoon, the judge, accompanied by his assistant, Maitre Nicod and a clerk, Monsieur Pain, authorised the maid, Eugénie Tabeau, to open the room of the deceased.

During their search, the three men discovered a large wooden chest, which looked like a sea chest. It was obviously very full as it had a bulging lid.

Judge: *What's this?*

Tabeau: *What it is? It's in the old woman's trunk.*

The chest was locked and judges were looking for a way to open it when the maid intervened.

Tabeau: *Are you looking for the key? If so wait a minute.*

The maid left the room and returned almost instantly, triumphantly brandishing a key. The chest was duly opened and the judges then saw wads of bank notes and papers resting on neatly-piled stacks of louis. There were, in all, forty-two thousand francs, not to mention the bearer bonds and debt securities on individuals payable to Yves Agier, the stockbroker, for a sum amounting to ninety-eight thousand francs. Over the years, Louise Monnier had lent a lot of people a lot of money and her debtors belonged to both the nobility and the upper-middle class.

Louise Monnier's Will was also amongst the papers. The document was handed to Maitre Bodin for safe-keeping. The trunk, which the judges valued at approximately one hundred and forty thousand francs, was also entrusted to the care of Maitre Bodin, along with its key. It was subsequently handed over for safe-keeping to France's state-owned bank, Caisse des dépôts et consignations.

The Will, dated 5th January 1885, contained a number of important legacies:

> I bequeath fifteen thousand francs to Louise Poinet and her husband Pierre Picherault;

I bequeath twelve thousand francs to Modeste Poinet and her husband François Bourliaud;

I bequeath fifteen thousand francs to Madame Chardon, whose husband had been a teacher at the Lycée de Poitiers;

I bequeath thirty thousand francs to Alexandre Poinet, god-son of my poor daughter, café owner, and to his wife Olympe Pelletier, who were responsible for serving three hundred francs of annual and life annuity to their sister and sister-in-law Marie Fazy, on the condition that she was still in the service of the testator at the time of her death (Marie Fazy having died in 1896, the life annuity was null and void and the corresponding charge no longer existed);

To my daughter, I bequeath, by preciput and in full part, the usufruct (full use) and the enjoyment of three rooms on the second floor of my house, in addition to the one she already occupied.

I want my daughter to continue to remain, after my death, in the part of the house whose usufruct I have just bequeathed to her. She will receive the care of the woman Fazy, to whom she is accustomed, and, in addition, the company of one or two nuns of Bon-Secours whose convent is in Blois.

I decree that all of my daughter's income, as well as all that she will collect after my death, is devoted exclusively to the care she needs. As my daughter is unable to personally direct either her own person or her own property, I appoint to her as guardian and administrator Monsieur Paul Druet, a lawyer in Poitiers, and in his absence Monsieur Molant, solicitor in Poitiers, or Monsieur Faure, lawyer, of Rue du Moulin-à-Vent, in Poitiers, who will also be responsible for the full and complete execution of all my provisions and whom I appoint my executor.

I ask that if the gentlemen is willing to take on the arduous and delicate mission that I entrust to his loyalty, that he accept a sum of five thousand francs that I bequeath to him as recognition and as a very low remuneration for all the pain that will give him the functions of executor of the Will.

*I bequeath four thousand francs to the Little Sisters of the
Poor, two thousand francs to the charitable office of Poitiers,
and two thousand francs to the parish priest of Saint-Porchaire to distribute to the poor.*

*I bequeath fifteen thousand francs to the hospices of Poitiers
to maintain in perpetuity, in good condition of repair of
all kinds, my grave, that of my husband Émile and also
those of my parents who rest in the plot that I had built in
Cimetière de Chilvert and in which I want to be placed.
Upon her death, my daughter Blanche is to be buried there.*

*I do not want another plot, grave or vault to be established
on the land I bought and I charge the hospices of Poitiers
and my executor, hereinafter named, with this supervision,
and to exclude this land from my estate.*

The Will raised several issues and made several
obvious points.

The first was that Madame Monnier had made
substantial bequests to the members of the Poinet family.
L'Avenir de la Vienne called them 'lucky devils', but Louise
Monnier had simply rewarded Marie Fazy's sisters, brothers-
in-law, brother and step-sister for their dedication and the
many years of loyal service they had rendered to her.

Second, Mademoiselle Monnier's arrangements for
Blanche were a final twist of the knife from beyond the grave.
She had worded her Will in a way that would reinforce the
idea that Blanche was 'unable to personally direct either her
own person or her own property.' The wording suggested
that Blanche always had been, and always would be, 'unable'
to do this. The mother allocated the task of managing her
daughter's affairs to people she trusted. The Will also specified that all of Blanche's income, derived from the property
received by inheritance from her father and mother, would
be devoted to her ongoing care. Only after death did Louise
Monnier allow her daughter to benefit from the income of
properties that she had conned Blanche out of all those years
ago.

As she no doubt intended, the very careful wording of the Will pertaining to Blanche and Blanche's welfare

made Louise Monnier look thoughtful, considerate, caring and generous, despite the fact that she still did not plan, nor had never planned, to place her daughter in a nursing home where she would have received the proper medical care her poor health required. Instead, Madame Monnier reserved for Blanche the very same room that Blanche had been imprisoned in on the second floor of the house in Rue de la Visitation, along with the use of a couple of other rooms on the same floor. She also stipulated that Blanche's care was to be provided by one or two nuns that Blanche would not know, as, since the Will had been written, Marie Fazy had died and Louise Monnier had not had it updated, despite the fact that Louise Monnier's lawyers had been present in her home on several occasions after Marie Fazy's death. Louise Monnier's refusal to update her Will, her choice to leave the document worded as it was, was therefore deliberate and malicious.

Obviously, some of the newspapers saw the macabre side of what Louise Monnier had put in place for her daughter. After all, the Will stated quite categorically that Blanche Monnier was to remain permanently in her room. The legal document was nothing more than a written version of Louise Monnier's interdict that Blanche's imprisonment in her room was to continue until her (Blanche's) death.

Finally, the Will did not mention Marcel Monnier, or his wife, or his daughter at all. It was as though they did not exist, which, as far as Louise Monnier was concerned, they did not.

According to Article 913 of the Civil Code, a son is the lawful heir of at least one third of the estate when the disposing party has left two children. However, as Louise Monnier no doubt planned, the numerous legacies and the money reserved for the benefit of Blanche's care made considerable inroads into her son's share of the inheritance.

Having left her son out of her Will, Louise Monnier instead bequeathed sums of money to several other non-related beneficiaries. As she had done during her lifetime, once dead, she continued to treat her son with hatred and contempt. Her carefully-worded Will meant that Marcel Monnier, although a lawyer, was removed from the guardianship of his sister and from the administration of her property, in favour of people that Louise Monnier deemed, as she no doubt wanted her son to realize, far more competent to fulfil that responsibility.

Equally significant were the clauses for the family plot purchased at the Cimetière de Chilvert. Madame Monnier reserved a place in her grave plot for her daughter, then forbade the construction of another vault, thus preventing her son, her daughter-in-law or her granddaughter from being buried at her side.

All these provisions and clauses in her Will expressed Louise Monnier's true feelings towards her children. She had nothing but contempt and loathing for them both. She disliked her son, believing him to be unintelligent and incompetent, so lacking in drive and ambition that he had been unable to achieve anything in life other than the position of a lowly clerk, which he had obtained solely due to his father's intervention on his behalf. Marcel Monnier enjoyed money, but had no skills with which to earn it, so his mother made him beg for an allowance, which she then reluctantly paid while constantly arguing with him about the amount, and often refusing to pay him on the agreed deadline.

She disliked her daughter because Blanche was a strong-willed and independent woman who had never recognised Louise Monnier's authority over her. Blanche Monnier enjoyed physical and emotional freedom, so Louise Monnier took those freedoms away from her.

In her Will, Louise Monnier clearly wanted to be seen making provision for her daughter by fulfilling her maternal duties and expressing her concern for Blanche's welfare. She also wanted her son to understand that she had left him nothing.

The Will was published in its entirety in *Le Courrier de la Vienne* and reproduced in extracts in the other newspapers.

In Paris, on Sunday, June 16th, the sellers of evening newspapers spread out on the boulevards and entered cafes shouting: *'The prisoner of Poitiers affair! Read Madame Monnier's Will!'*

Everywhere, people were discussing the document, which if anything, clouded the issue. People were surprised by what Louise Monnier had done. Many thought she'd leave nothing to her daughter and everything to her son, whom many considered to be Louise Monnier's co-conspirator and accomplice in the kidnapping, imprisonment and the starvation of Blanche. The fact that Louise Monnier had done almost the opposite of this surprised everyone and fuelled a great deal of debate and conversation.

Some thought that to read the Will was to understand nothing, but the truth was far starker: to read the Will was to understand everything there was to understand about Louise Monnier.

Part Four:
Justice

The Trial – Day 1
Monday 7th October 1901

The trial began on Monday 7th October, 1901.

It took place, as did most major trials in Poitiers, in the main courtroom of le Palais de Justice on Boulevard Maréchal de Lattre de Tassigny, which was a twenty-minute walk from Rue de la Visitation.

On August 31st 1901, there was a pre-trial meeting at which the investigating judge instructed the court that although Blanche had been imprisoned for twenty-five years by her mother, it could only judge Marcel Monnier's culpability for the last three years of her imprisonment, as that was the amount of time that coincided with Louise Monnier becoming ill, thereby making Marcel Monnier responsible (as next of kin) for his sister's welfare during that time.

The investigating judge addressed the court.

Judge de Fresnal: *It is our conclusion that there are sufficient charges against him (Marcel Monnier) for having imprisoned the young lady, Blanche Monnier, his sister, with the circumstance being that the kidnapping lasted for more than a month and that the said Blanche Monnier was subjected to corporal torture.*

This was simply a recitation of (and a timely re-minder of the contents of) articles 341 to 344 of the penal code. For such a crime, the perpetrator and his or her accomplice faced the death penalty.

In his closing argument, the Advocate General, Maitre Marquet, stated that it was his considered opinion that the death penalty, which was stipulated in law as the punishment for imprisonment, kidnapping and corporal torture was, in this case, excessive. He therefore proposed that the court prosecute the case under a correctional classification.

Marcel Monnier's defence lawyer, Maitre Barbier, then read from a ninety-six page document which he had carefully prepared, entitled: Observations on M. Marcel Monnier, in which the lawyer demonstrated that his client was innocent of the charge of criminal confinement with aggravating circumstances. It was the defence lawyer's intention to obtain a judgment dismissing the case. The defence lawyer, along with his colleague Maitre Mérine, made a request for provisional release.

Barbier: *In my client's defence, I feel I must point out that 21 Rue de la Visitation is neither Marcel Monnier's home nor his property, nor has it ever been. He was refused admittance to said property by his mother on numerous occasions, therefore, there is no legal reason to charge Marcel Monnier with the crime of forcible imprisonment of his sister.*

Judge: *The misery and the physical harm that Mademoiselle Blanche Monnier suffered fall within the scope of Articles 309 to 311 of the Criminal Code. The charges against Marcel Monnier are that he is guilty of violence or intentional assault, punishable by imprisonment of two to five years and a fine of fifty to five-hundred francs for assisting his mother in the execution of the offence.*

Barbier: *After such a lengthy and unjustified detention, Marcel Monnier has suffered greatly and as the investigation is now concluded, the request we are making is not unreasonable. In addition, reason and humanity, like the spirit of our legislation, require the release of any accused person whose incarceration has not been or is no longer necessary.*

At half past eleven in the morning on 7th October 1901, a carriage which had been ordered for the occasion entered the courtyard of the Prison de la Visitation through the large gate, which was immediately closed by two police officers. A few minutes later, the carriage, in which the defendant sat, a gendarme on either side of him, left the prison and made its way to the courthouse.

The thirty or so people who were waiting in front of the prison for Marcel Monnier to leave were unable to see into the carriage because the blinds had been lowered. The horses trotted towards the court building. There were already a few people lining Rue de Basses-Treilles and Rue de Boncenne, and the prison vehicle was being followed by a few young men who were trying their best to keep pace with the carriage. A few groups were already stationed along the Place du Palais, and a crowd was beginning to form in the square because people who worked in offices and workplaces were stopping work for their lunch breaks.

When Marcel Monnier got out of the carriage between two gendarmes, the onlookers crowded the steps of the stairs of the Palace and quickly surrounded him. The gendarmes pushed a path through the crowd into the court building. Several people in the crowd swore at him or yelled out insults and accusations. The defendant was wearing a black frock coat and a hat that was too large. His nose, red and quite long, stuck out from beneath the hat; he made his way through the jeering crowd without expression.

Monnier was escorted into the courtroom where he was instructed to sit on the defendants' bench between the two gendarmes. By mid-day, the witnesses, the representatives of the press and the privileged few with invitation cards entered the courtroom through the small door of the corridor. Several people came forward to shake hands with the defendant, very aware of the scrutiny that their expressions of support and sympathy elicited. Marcel Monnier's wife, Angèle Monnier, dressed in mourning and her face wet with tears, arrived in the company of the Comte de Clisson and was directed to sit on a chair, a little in front of her husband.

Half an hour after mid-day, the large door opened and about three hundred people crowded in through the entrance. The part of the room reserved for them was soon full as there was only enough space for about a third of them. The Presiding Judge of the court, Alexis Fontant, had taken several measures to deal with the curious crowds: in front of the witness stand and on the side of the public prosecutor he had two large tables set up for the press. In addition to the journalists from the local newspapers, there were also journalists present from the *Havas Agency*, the *Fournier Agency*, *Le Gaulois, Le Soleil, Le Figaro, Le Journal, L'Écho de Paris, Le Drapeau, L'Éclair, La Patrie, Le Temps, Le Matin, Le Petit Journal, Le Petit Parisien, La France, de Bordeaux*, and *La Petite Gironde*. A cartoonist from *L'Illustration* sat near the witness stand, sketchbook open, pencil poised.

In the courtroom, to the left of the witness stand were the exhibits, all from Blanche Monnier's room. The items included: the door, the shutters, a chain, a padlock, three jars containing specimens of vermin, and, carefully packed into crates, the sheets, the scarf and the rotten mattress. Rolled up in a length of paper was Blanche's hair.

The courtroom was crowded; chairs and armchairs had been crammed into every available space. It was so crammed that the lawyers, Maitres Barbier and Maitre Mérine found that there were only small, cramped spaces reserved for them.

The judges and lawyers made their entrance at twelve-forty. The tribunal was composed of Presiding Judge Fontant and his two assessors, Rivasseau and Carol. Maitre Férot occupied the seat of the Public Prosecutor's Office. After reading out the judgment of the Indictment Division, the bailiff proceeded to call the witnesses.

There were exactly one hundred and two of them: the public prosecutor had cited fifty-eight witnesses and the defence had cited forty-four. Almost all of the witnesses called answered when their names were read out. Judge Fontant recommended that the public observe the most absolute silence, then the witnesses present were asked to go out to the room reserved for them.

Pierre Bucheton, the Central Commissioner, was the first witness called to testify.

Bucheton: *On May 23, 1901, by order of the public prosecutor, Monsieur Leon Bulot, I went to number 21 Rue de la Visitation, to investigate an anonymous claim that Mademoiselle Blanche Monnier was being held in her room against her will.*

As Madame Monnier, Blanche's mother, could not receive me due to being bedridden, I then addressed her son Marcel, who immediately claimed that his mother was being denounced unfairly. He then tried his best, using a variety of tactics, to keep me from entering his mother's house, therefore making a very real attempt to thwart my investigation. Monsieur Marcel Monnier had said to me at the time: 'I'm a Doctor of Law and a former sub-prefect. I protest very strongly at this denunciation of my mother and I shall be referring your accusations to the Public Prosecutor.' He then said he would need to get his mother's permission for me to enter the house as she was the mistress of her own home.

Initially, Monsieur Monnier refused to take me to see his sister, claiming she had a serious medical condition. Here is what he said when I insisted he take me to his sister: 'I cannot let you see her without first calling the family doctor. My sister has been suffering from a pernicious fever for about ten years and is not supposed to receive any visitors. Only the doctor will be able to determine if you can enter her room without upset-

ting or distressing her.'

Marcel Monnier made a further attempt to delay my investigation by pretending he did not have a key to the locked door. Once I had informed it that we would, if necessary, break the door to gain access to the room, Marcel Monnier took a key from his pocket and then unlocked and pushed open the door. I then discovered that the unfortunate woman was indeed locked inside a dark, shuttered room. I saw that she was naked, dirty and starved to the point of emaciation, and so I went immediately to confer with the prosecutor, who himself came to the house and, after examining Mademoiselle Monnier, had her transported to the Hôtel-Dieu.

During my observations, I saw that the door of the room had been repaired and that the walls bore inscriptions suggesting imprisonment: 'Will I ever be free?' – 'Will I always be in a dungeon?' – 'Am I condemned to remain buried in this tomb?' – 'Alas! It's over for me!' I also noticed that rotting food scraps and faeces covered the victim's bed.

Barbier: *Didn't the witness notice a bed other than Mademoiselle Monnier's in the room?*

Bucheton: *There was indeed a small iron bed at the entrance to the room, to the right of the door. When questioned, the maid, Tabeau, replied that she sometimes slept in the room. The Dupuis maid, on the other hand, said she slept on the landing.*

Barbier: *Were you not instructed to go to the General Revenue to ask who received the pension to which Madame Monnier was entitled as the widow of a civil servant?*

Bucheton: *At the Treasury, I was told that it was Monsieur Bourliaud or Monsieur Picherault.*

Barbier: *It was certainly not Monsieur Monnier.*

At one-fifteen that afternoon, the hearing was briefly paused. During the short break, under the orders of the Central Commissioner, the police officers, with the help of the gendarmes, unpacked the exhibits. They took the sheets out of the crate and unwrapped the rotten mattress. Ushers tried to spread out Blanche's hair, but it was so tangled together and bonded by filth, excrement and food that it was impossible to do anything other than set it down. As soon as all of those objects were placed on the platform, a foul stench spread throughout the room.

Some of the ladies that were present pulled hand-kerchiefs from their sleeves and held them beneath their noses. Other took out bottles of perfume and breathed in their fragrances or dabbed a few drops on their wrists or hand-kerchiefs. One or two hurried out of the room, despite the risk of losing their place. The windows were opened. When the judges returned to the sitting, the Presiding Judge took one look at the exhibits and ordered that they be removed immediately. Everyone applauded this hygiene measure, but removing them was not easy. To take the mattress and the sheets out of the room, it was necessary to have some of the seated public to move, which many did with great reluctance and more than a few indignant protests.

Finally, the hearing was able to resume.

The next six witnesses were police officers or people who had participated in the initial discovery. All of them repeated what the Central Commissioner had said about the filthiness of the room and the mattress.

On May 24th, Benjamin Fourrier, a public health inspector gave instructions for the room to be disinfected.

Fourrier: *The stench was appalling; on the rotten mattress, the maggots writhed in the middle of food debris and faeces. When I moved the sheet, countless creatures swarmed out. I couldn't help but reprimand the two maids.*

Férot: *What did you say to them?*

Fourrier: *I said: 'What do you think you're doing, leaving this unfortunate woman in such a state, and why didn't you say anything about it?'*

Férot: *What was their response?*

Fourrier: *The maid named Juliette Dupuis replied: 'What do you expect! We have been here for two years; we are twenty years old, when we arrived here we were eighteen years old, and Madame Bourliaud who was in charge of us maids in the house, and who directed everything, told us: 'Above all, do not worry about what is happening here, and do not say any-thing to anyone else, as it has nothing to do with you. And if you ever repeat anything to anyone, then remember, Monsieur Monnier, a member of Poitiers high society, has a very long arm and could hurt you and prevent you from earning a living.'*

These remarks, although reported second-hand, aroused very strong emotions in the public. One of the com-missionaires reported Blanche's words when he helped re-move her from her bed and transport her to the Hôtel-Dieu.

Bucheton: *When she was lifted off the mattress naked, Mademoiselle Monnier said: 'Why are these men here? What are these men coming here to do?'*

Five people, who had been taken up to Blanche's room at the invitation of the two maids, since December 1900, testified as to what they had seen. They all mentioned Blanche's foul smell, her filthy state, her nakedness, and her frighteningly skeletal thinness.

However, Maitre Barbier tried to use their testimonies to show his client's innocence.

Barbier: *Since strangers had been able to enter the room simply by pushing the door open, it is proof that there was no imprisonment, no confinement, no sequestration, even if the shutters of the room were padlocked.*

Then the Presiding Judge of the court called to the stand the experts appointed by the investigating judge. Doctor Léger, director of the bacteriology laboratory at the medical school, took the stand first. He identified the vermin specimens that were in Blanche's room, which were in jars on the Presiding Judge's desk.

Dr. Léger: *The specimens of vermin that were in Blanche Monnier's room, which are in the jars on the judge's desk, are mealworms and insect larvae which grow and flourish in kitchen detritus.*

Férot: *Could you give us your conclusions regarding the bones that were found in the garden of the house in Rue de la Visitation?*

Dr. Léger: *I had been asked to examine various bones uncovered by a search of the garden. The question was whether these were not the bones of a new-born child. I have not found any trace of such bones. These bones were from a cat, chicken, or a sheep.*

Doctor Chrétien, a professor at the medical school, then took the stand to explain the results of his examination of Blanche Monnier.

Dr. Chrétien: *The physical examination of Mademoiselle Monnier revealed extreme thinness resulting from a lack of food. The doctors found no traces of beatings, violence, injuries or wounds. Mademoiselle Blanche was extremely weak and unable to stand. She defecated and urinated onto the bed beneath her without any notion of cleanliness. Although her height was about one meter fifty to one meter fifty-five (five feet and one inch), she weighed, when she arrived at the Hôtel-Dieu, only twenty-three kilograms (fifty-one pounds), which proves a decrease in muscles due to a lack of food. Moreover, as soon as she arrived at the hospital, she began to eat with a very good appetite. Mentally, Mademoiselle Monnier is retarded. It is impossible to get anything coherent out of her. She has childhood memories, but she is usually reluctant to talk about them. She never speaks spontaneously; her answers have to be coaxed out of her. In general, she is calm, but sometimes she becomes over-excited.*

Doctor Lagrange took the stand and confirmed this expert report and answered a few questions about his patient.

Barbier: *In conversations, did you ever hear Mademoiselle Monnier making any suggestion of going home to Rue de la Visitation?*

Dr. Lagrange: *She often talked about her cher fond house, her Malampia.*

Férot: *Did she give any explanation for these turns of phrase?*

Dr. Lagrange: *No.*

Férot: *Did she express any concern that she was in a hospital?*

Dr. Lagrange: *No. None at all.*

Fontant: *When you mentioned her family to her, what did she say?*

Dr. Lagrange: *She never consented to talk about it.*

The Abbé de Mondion was then called to the stand.

Mondion: *Before giving my testimony, I must point out that I am obliged to not reveal anything told me during confession as confessions are protected by their sacred and confidential nature. My testimony may only contain facts that are already known to everyone. I am at liberty to give my opinion on all subjects pertaining to this case.*

Fontant: *Is Mademoiselle Monnier making progress?*

Mondion: *Since her admission to the Hôtel-Dieu, Mademoiselle Monnier has made a lot of progress, both physically and intellectually, since she now weighs thirty-nine kilos and her state of health is satisfactory. Unlike the forensic doctors, I do not think she is crazy, because she remembers facts and events that date back to her youth. She has spoken of the priests who had assisted her during her first communion, of the pastry confectioner from whom her parents bought her cakes and sweets as a child, and of the convent of the Union of Christian Ladies where she was a student. I cannot say that Mademoiselle Monnier is an idiot, for idiocy has no such answers; this, of course, is not saying that I know more than the doctors. Mademoiselle Monnier, in any case, is not in the least bit dangerous, not to herself and not to others. Cared for by a nurse who is herself lame and whom a child could easily knock over, Mademoiselle Monnier is careful not to do anything that could cause harm to her.*

Férot: *Does Mademoiselle Blanche still like to expose herself?*

Mondion: *She is always extremely modest. When she gets up, everyone in her room has to go out, and if anyone wants to see the thinness of her legs, she vigorously refuses to allow them to do so.*

Férot: *Does she dislike air and light?*

Mondion: *Little by little she has lost the habit of hiding her head with her sheet. She is very happy every time we open the window and she never stops admiring the Hôtel-Dieu gardens.*

Fontant: *Is she given flowers?*

The Abbé de Mondion: *Yes. She loves flowers very much and she is very good at recognizing them.*

Férot: *And how is she with regards to her personal cleanliness?*

Mondion: *She is very clean and she also looks very carefully at the meals brought to her before eating them.*

Férot: *Does she regret leaving her room at Rue de la Visitation?*

Mondion: *Every time I have offered to drive her back, she has always said, 'No, no, later.' Her response is the same every time.*

Férot: *Do you talk to her about her family?*

Mondion: *We don't talk to her about it, because it has quite a powerful effect on her. 'Don't bring them here,' is her usual response.*

The chaplain's testimony was confirmed by the two interns of the Hôtel-Dieu, by Sister Saint-Wilfrid.

The nurse, Aurélie Raymond was called. She advanced painfully to the stand because of her infirmity.

Aurélie Raymond: *At first, the patient constantly covered her head, but today she has become very docile. It is*

179

true that initially she refused our help keeping her clean, so we appeased her whims. Why do the opposite since she is not evil? Now, when it comes to grooming, she sometimes refuses, but it doesn't last. We like to talk to her for a while and she always sees reason. And she always answers the questions we ask perfectly.

Férot: *Does she talk about the property in Migné?*

Aurélie Raymond: *Very often, especially about her cave.*

Férot: *Have you ever told her about her brother?*

Aurélie Raymond: *Yes, she loves him very much. She said she loves him more than a brother. We are careful not to tell her anything bad about him.*

The nurse's response made a strong impression on the public, because this revelation expressed, for the first time, Blanche Monnier's obvious affection for the accused.

The hearing was adjourned at five minutes to four and resumed at ten past four.

The next witness to be called was Théodore Touchard, a plasterer who lived in Rue de la Visitation.

Férot: *You are here because we wish to ask you about incidents that occurred twenty years previously, specifically to the time when the neighbours in Rue de la Visitation constantly heard shouts of protest and screams coming from number 21.*

Théodore Touchard: *I asked one of the maids about Mademoiselle Blanche and I also spoke to Madame Monnier herself. I was told that Blanche was suffering from the type of madness that is caused by grief.*

Férot: *When would that have been?*

Théodore Touchard: *In 1883. I know that because I carried out some work in Mademoiselle Blanche's room on the second floor, which was already extremely dirty. I noticed that there were inscriptions on the walls. The window was open a little, but the shutters were padlocked. I did not find this strange, because, as I said, I had been told that Mademoiselle Blanche was crazy. She was not in her room and I did not see her while I was in the house.*

At the request of the Presiding Judge, the witness recounted a scene between Madame Monnier and her son which he attended. He thought it was a matter of money.

Théodore Touchard: *The mother said to Marcel Monier: 'You have nothing here, you are nothing here, so go away.'*

Fontant: *Have you seen Mademoiselle Blanche since*

then?

Théodore Touchard: *Yes, at the Hôtel-Dieu. At first, she didn't seem to recognize me, but when I told her that I was her closest neighbour, she exclaimed: 'Oh, yes, Monsieur Touchard!'*

Fontant: *Did you know Mademoiselle Monnier when she was young?*

Théodore Touchard: *Yes, she was a lively child. She would often come to our house and talk to my wife.*

Fontant: *And you only learned that she was mentally ill from her mother?*

Théodore Touchard: *Yes, from her mother. Personally, I never noticed anything odd about her.*

The next two witnesses called to testify were the two sisters and the sister-in-law of Marie Fazy.

The first witness was Louise Picherault.

Louise Picherault: *I never noticed anything amiss. Although I have not visited the house on Rue de la Visitation for over twenty-five years, when I did, I never noticed anything unusual. My sister told me that she was Blanche Monnier's personal maid, but she had never mentioned anything about Blanche's madness.*

Barbier: *You didn't see Mademoiselle Blanche at the time of your sister's death?*

Louise Picherault: *No, I only went into the hallway. According to Olympe Pelletier, the wife of Alexandre Poinet, and the godson of Blanche, Marcel Monnier never gave any orders in his mother's house and never had authority over her. I know that he has severe myopia. One day, when I was in his mother's room, he shoved past me nearly knocked me over because he hadn't seen me. Marie Fazy told me that Mademoiselle Blanche had suffered from a fever which made her lose her mind, after which they had been forced to close the window with shutters because she liked to be naked all the time and kept standing at the window so people in the street could see her.*

Olympe Pelletier was then called to give her testimony.

Barbier: *Did Madame Monnier, speaking of her daughter, ever say to you: 'What will become of Blanche when I am no longer here?'*

Olympe Pelletier: *Yes, she often said that.*

Modeste Bourliaud was then called. She was a key witness, because unlike her sister and her sister-in-law she had been trusted implicitly by Madame Monnier and she knew the Monnier family well.

Barbier: *What can you tell me about the relationship between Monsieur Monnier and his sister?*

Modeste Bourliaud: *Marcel and Blanche loved each other very much.*

Barbier: *And yet he is on trial. Does that seem fair to you?*

Modeste Bourliaud: *No, because Mademoiselle Blanche was never imprisoned.*

There were shouts of indignation from the public section of the room. The Presiding Judge called for silence. Once the room was quiet, the defence lawyer continued with his questions.

Barbier: *Did your sister [Marie Fazy] ever tell you anything about Mademoiselle Blanche?*

Modeste Bourliaud: *Yes, she told me she was deranged.*

Barbier: *Have you ever entered Mademoiselle Blanche's room?*

Modeste Bourliaud: *Yes, twice last year. Both times I was accompanied by Monsieur Monnier.*

Barbier: *What did you find?*

Modeste Bourliaud: *Nothing.*

Barbier: *Did it smell bad?*

Modeste Bourliaud: *Yes, a little, because the landing door was closed.*

Barbier: *In your statement, you say that you had a conversation with a maid.*

Modeste Bourliaud: *That's true. I talked to the maid [Juliette Dupuis] who told me she was going to report the plight of Mademoiselle Monnier to the authorities.*

Barbier: *And on the day of his arrest, didn't Marcel Monnier call to see you?*

Modeste Bourliaud: *Marcel Monnier visited my home early in the morning on Friday, 24th May, and insisted that I bear witness on his behalf. I reassured him by promising to say that his sister, Blanche, was well cared for.*

The Presiding Judge intervened at that point.

Fontant: *I must point out that in your statement to the investigating judge you claim you said exactly the opposite to Marcel Monnier. Your words have been included in my report. Didn't you say that Monsieur Monnier cried out: 'I am lost'?*

Modeste Bourliaud: *Yes, Monsieur le Président.*

Fontant: *That answer is incompatible with the answer you just gave about his sister being well-cared for. What you are now saying varies greatly from what you said in your testimony. Which one of your answers is the truth?*

Modeste Bourliaud: *The truth is the truth that I have just told the court.*

Eight servants who had been in the service of the Monnier family were then heard. Their testimonies showed the evolution of Blanche's disease, her seclusion, and her repeated acts of screaming out of the window for justice and release.

Madame Gautreau was the first witness. She had been Louis Demarconnay's maid in 1875.

Madame Gautreau: *When I worked there, Blanche was twenty-six years old, was very well cared for. At times, she showed a few signs of mental weakness. She sometimes broke a few of the objects she had on hand. She often refused to leave her room and to eat at the family table. She usually walked around the house naked, or played the piano. Sometimes she seemed very confused; at other times she knew exactly what she was saying.*

The next witness was Virginie Maingault, a former maid of Louise Monnier's.

Virginie Maingault: *I was employed as a maid in the Monnier house. I started there in 1883. At that time, Mademoiselle Blanche hardly left her room and Madame Monnier did not bother to inform me that there was a crazy person in a room on the second floor. One day, after hearing several screams, I became frightened. Marie Fazy told me about Mademoiselle Blanche, and about how she had bouts of madness. I saw her one day, dressed in nothing but a gauze veil over her face, go down to the ground floor. She seemed to hate her mother and went into angry paroxysms every time she saw her. She was always well cared for, thanks to Marie Fazy. Her room, although sparsely furnished, was clean. The shutters were locked closed. I was also told by Marie Fazy about the causes of Blanche's madness; she had wanted to marry a lawyer named Calmeil, but Madame Monnier had objected to him on the grounds that as a lawyer he did not earn enough nor have a personal fortune. After her mother had forbidden the marriage, the young woman had started to act strangely, as though she had* contracted a cerebral fever that had left her nervous and exhausted. I've heard that things like that can give some people a fever and drive others crazy.

Virginie Neveux, a maid who worked for Louise Monnier's for two years from 1871, was next to testify.

Virginie Neveux: *Blanche Monnier ate the same food as her mother, but Madame Monnier only allowed Blanche to drink sugar water in which she had dissolved a tonic. If it happened, as it sometimes did, that Blanche refused to drink it, then her mother had instructed us to take the drink out of the room and then offer it to Blanche in a different glass or cup throughout the day, until Blanche drank it, which she always did.*

Celine Quinqueneau, a cook, testified next. She had been employed by Louise Monnier for eight months, between October 1898 and June 1899.

Celine Quinqueneau: *I was hired to prepare meals for Madame Monnier and for Mademoiselle Blanche, who, I was told, no longer got out of bed and that she objected to having her hair combed. If I went to her room, she would hide her face with a scarf that was like a rag. One of the maids said that Madame Monnier would not allow clothes or bed linen in the room because Mademoiselle Blanche would either tear it to shreds or try to use the items as a rope to escape as she had done before. I suppose that's why the shutter had to stay closed and locked. The room was tidy because there wasn't much in it, but I can't say it was clean.*

Her comment caused a few of the public to laugh, because, in reality, the room was very dirty, as other testimonies have shown. She continued.

Celine Quinqueneau: *Mademoiselle Blanche's mattress had begun to rot, but there were no insects or vermin on it. Madame Monnier, however, refused to allow the maids to change the mattress, and her daughter, who soiled her sheet every day, had only two sheets at her disposal.*

The hearing was adjourned at half past five to allow the court maintenance team to turn on the gas lamps. A few minutes later, the court resumed hearing the witnesses.

Ernest Jacob, a clerk from Remiremont (Vosges) was next to testify.

Ernest Jacob: *I was a clerk at Mathias, a clothing merchant at Pont-Neuf, 2, Rue des Cordeliers. I was ordered,* on 16th August 1892, to take a selection of men's overcoats to Madame Monnier, which were probably for her son. I was asked to go up to the first floor, after which, I was left alone for a moment in a room. I then heard the sound of someone knocking on the other side of the partition. Then I heard moans, and then these words reached my ears: 'What have I done to be locked up? I don't deserve this horrible ordeal. God does not exist if He allows His creatures to be treated in this way! And no one to come to my rescue!'

A woman (presumably Marie Fazy) then entered the room and told me to take my merchandise and leave. As I made my way down the stairs, I could hear a lady of a certain age and wearing a black cap declare loud and clear: 'I don't know what's holding me back from getting rid of this damned vermin; one day, she'll get us all hanged with her screams.'

Madame Reine Chardon, the wife of a former colleague of Émile Monnier in the Faculty, and who had remained the only friend of his widow, then came to the stand.

Madame Chardon: *Madame Monnier said to me that she had spent a good deal of her life sacrificing herself for her daughter! And I believe her sincerity. She was deceived by her maids after the death of the Fazy woman in 1896. I witnessed violent scenes between Madame Monnier and her son. I knew afterwards that he wanted to put his sister in a nursing home and Madame Monnier refused. As a result, she kicked her son out. Madame Monnier said another day, speaking of her son: 'I do not want him trying to lay down the law in my house and, if he continues, I shall take away his pension.'*

The next witness called to the stand was Yves Agier Senior, the successor of Louis Demarconnay in his office as stockbroker, and sometimes a financial advisor to Louise Monnier. He confirmed the contempt Louise Monnier had for her son.

Agier Sr: *Marcel Monnier was at loggerheads with his mother over questions of finance and responsibility. Madame Monnier did not want to entrust the management of her affairs to her son, whom she considered incapable of managing anything. Moreover, with regards to her daughter, she followed in extremis the instructions that her husband had given her.*

The next witness called was Maitre Louis Bodin Senior, a former notary of the Monnier family.

Bodin Sr: *Marcel Monnier was always very respectful of his mother, very fearful, and very submissive.*

Férot: *Was there a specific quarrel between mother and son?*

Bodin Sr: *Yes. It was with regard to Monsieur Émile Monnier's library, which he had bequeathed to his son and which Madame Monnier refused to let him have.*

Férot: *What can you tell us about Madame Monnier and her daughter?*

Bodin Sr: *Madame Monnier loved her daughter dearly. Her love for her daughter was truly extraordinary. It was so strong it was almost a form of adoration.*

This comment caused many members of the public to start booing and jeering. The witness struggled to make his final words heard.

Bodin Sr: *Yes, she sacrificed herself for her daughter, as did her husband!*

Férot: *Is it to be understood that they all sacrificed themselves for Mademoiselle Blanche, even her brother?*

Barbier: *Exactly! They all sacrificed themselves, at least from the point of view of intentions.*

Férot: *I hope you will not try and support this by ignoring the facts.*

After this incident, the hearing was adjourned. It was six-fifteen in the afternoon. At the exit, a considerable crowd had gathered; there were people on the Palace stairs and in the square. To avoid any regrettable demonstrations, Marcel Monnier was taken out through the door in the right wing of the court building; a door reserved for use by the court judges.

A few of the more observant onlookers saw that the carriage was heading towards that particular door and so rushed over to it. When the defendant came out, he was greeted with boos, whistles and threatening shouts of: '*Hang him!*' and '*To the death, to the death*', and '*Take him away*'.

The gendarmerie, reinforced by a few police officers, had great difficulty in protecting him against the angry crowd. He got into the carriage quickly, with a gendarme sitting on each side of him. Some of the crowd shook the carriage so that it tilted alarmingly on its springs. The coach driver gave a flick of the reins and the horse started to trot. Marcel Monnier was taken back to the prison, escorted by a handful of young men who raced alongside the carriage, booing him, swearing at him and threatening him as they ran.

The Trial – Day 2
October 8th, 1901

The following morning at eleven-thirty on the 8th October 1901, Marcel Monnier left the Prison de la Visitation and boarded the carriage that would convey him to the court building. To avoid the protests and conflicts of the previous day, the carriage was escorted by five gendarmes on horseback.

There were only a few people gathered in front of the prison, but when the carriage arrived in front of the court building, there were about five hundred people waiting for the defendant.

Le Journal de la Vienne reported the defendant's arrival at court.

> *'When Marcel Monnier made his way up the court building steps, the gendarmes and the policemen who surrounded him had great difficulty preventing the protesters from blocking his way. Marcel Monnier looked at them with obvious contempt. There was a tremendous amount of pushing by the raging crowd, some of whom shouted: 'Death! Death! Death!' and 'Hang him, hang him!' which quickly became a chant that continued even after Monnier was inside the building.'*

In the courtroom, Judge Fontant opened the second day of the hearing at twenty-five past mid-day. Immediately, a matter was brought to the attention of the defence by the public prosecutor, Maitre Férot, who asked that the witness Aurélie Raymond, the nurse at the Hôtel-Dieu, be recalled.

The Prosecutor then asked that Doctor Brossard be recalled to the stand and be heard again to clarify a doubtful point. The doctor took the stand.

Férot: *Do you remember that Aurélie Raymond, a nurse at the Hôtel-Dieu, told you about Blanche Monnier's feelings towards her brother?*

Dr. Brossard: *Yes, I do.*

Férot: *What did she tell you?*

Dr. Brossard: *Mademoiselle Aurélie told me that*

Mademoiselle Blanche loved her brother 'very much' and as 'more than a brother' and that staff were 'careful not tell her anything bad about him.'

Férot: *That is completely correct. The reason I ask is because I wish to clarify this statement which I believe to be inaccurate.*

Aurélie Raymond was recalled in order to take the stand again and have the same question asked once again.

The nurse dutifully returned to the stand to provide a further explanation of her words. She had had many long talks with Blanche and only she really knew what had been said by Blanche and how Blanche had said it. She had reported everything she considered important to Doctor Brossard and to the Abbé de Mondion. She was also fully aware that any hint of incest which, even if it dated back to adolescence, would have caused a scandal, and would most likely result in Marcel Monnier being hanged. The Abbé de Mondion had already lectured her on the subject and had urged her to answer cautiously when interrogated on the stand.

Férot: *Tell us again about how Blanche Monnier felt about her brother.*

Aurélie Raymond: *I can tell you that Mademoiselle Blanche loves her brother as she loves everything she hears about. She said she loved her brother more than a brother; she also said she loved roasted chicken more than boiled chicken. It is how she said things. If anyone ever mentions her brother, she always says: 'Leave him where he is; he's fine where he is.' It is not right for those of us caring for her to say anything either good or bad about him; it is not really right for any of us at the hospital to talk about him at all.*

Férot: *But what about what you said yesterday? And the way you said it? You did not mention chicken yesterday, did you?*

Aurélie Raymond: *What I said yesterday was wrong. I did not mean to say that Blanche loved her brother more than a brother. I meant she loved him very much. I admit, I was troubled by the way I said it. I just meant that Mademoiselle Blanche, speaking of her brother, always said 'my dearest brother' or 'my very dear brother', but she uses the words 'very dear' about everything. I wish to withdraw what I said yesterday.*

Barbier: *The witness's statement yesterday was*

very formal and her testimony was very precise. In fact, Mademoiselle Aurélie stated: 'We are very careful not say in front of Mademoiselle Blanche anything bad about her brother.'

Aurélie Raymond: *Yes, I said that. And, like I say, I was very troubled by the way I said things.*

The Prosecutor, who wanted to redact the testimony of the previous day, insisted that the witness's retraction be noted, but the defence lawyer returned to his point.

Barbier: *The witness has just acknowledged that yesterday she did say the sentence I mentioned.*

Férot: *But...*

Barbier: *So, is Mademoiselle Aurélie as troubled today as she was yesterday? It is strange to see witnesses change their testimony in twenty-four hours.*

Férot: *There are others who have changed their testimony just as quickly.*

Barbier: *It is unfortunate for the prosecution that that is the case.*

Fontant: *The testimony we heard yesterday will remain on record, but it is to be noted that it has been retracted today.*

Férot: *I do not want there to be any ambiguity, so I would like to recall to the stand the Abbé de Mondion and Sister Saint-Wilfrid.*

The Abbé de Mondion took the stand first.

Fontant. *Do you want to tell us what Blanche's feelings were for her brother?'*

Mondion: *Everything I have said, written, and signed, I stand by. Whenever I or someone else, alone or in front of a witness, talked to Blanche about her brother, she always said, 'No! Don't bring him here!' Moreover, as every time she was told about her family she seemed to get very upset, we simply avoided the subject. I never noticed Mademoiselle Blanche express any interest in or sympathy for her family; if that had happened, my conscience as an honest man and as a priest would command me to speak of it.*

Despite this claim, it should be remembered that the chaplain of the Hôtel-Dieu had stated quite categorically that he would divulge nothing that had been told to him in his professional capacity, that is in confessional confidentiality. Therefore, he could not have been compelled to divulge what he had been told in confession, nor even in private outside the sacrament of penance.

Sister Saint-Wilfrid then took the stand. As might be expected, she confirmed the testimony of the Abbé de Mondion.

Fontant. *Would you be kind enough to tell us what answers Mademoiselle Blanche gave when she was asked about seeing her brother?'*

Sister Saint-Wilfrid: *She said: 'He's fine where he is, let him stay there!'*

Fontant. *Was she angry?*

Sister Saint-Wilfrid: *During her rare moments of impatience, she sometimes repeated the same thing.*

Le Courrier de la Vienne reported that it was likely that the nurse had been instructed to retract her testimony by the Abbé de Mondion, chaplain of the Hôtel-Dieu. Aurélie Raymond had naïvely pointed out Blanche's love for her brother, which she had spoken of in confidence to her nurse. However, the nurse's innocent testimony had inadvertently suggested something else, namely that there might have been an incestuous relationship between Marcel and Blanche Monnier. The incest had then been repressed to the point of each sibling turning excessively modest when in the presence of the other. This was borne out by the way Blanche hid her face but allowed her naked body to be seen in the presence of her brother. For his part, Marcel Monnier claimed he had never realized his sister's state of extreme thinness because he had never so much as looked in the direction of his sister, due to his strong feelings of decorum due to her being naked.

This particular claim of Monnier's was challenged by Juliette Dupuis's testimony in which she claimed Marcel Monnier stood and looked at his sister on more than one occasion while she was naked and on all fours on her mattress, facing away from him.

Incest is an absolute taboo; in 1901 it was unthinkable to mention it, or to even suggest it, even in a courtroom. So, for the public prosecutor, in the interests of a fair and impartial trial, it was necessary that Aurélie Raymond's retraction was stated and heard and reported as soon as possible to cut short any potential gossip.

The next few witnesses were several maids who more or less confirmed the statements made the day before by the various servants. They focused on the onset of Blanche's madness, her seclusion and the repulsive filth in which she lived, her lack of clothes and bed linen.

The court was waiting for the last two servants who worked for Louise Monnier, Eugénie Tabeau and Juliette Dupuis to take the stand. When they finally entered the courtroom, they caused a sensation, mostly because of the outfits they had chosen to wear for the occasion. While the maids who had presented themselves the day before at the stand wore a sober cut dress and the white cap characteristic of the profession, both were dressed in Parisian fashion and topped with a hat adorned with ribbons in rosette shapes. It looked like they were wearing their Sunday best clothes.

Fontant: *Were you in the service of Madame Monnier during the time Mademoiselle Blanche was a prisoner?*

Eugénie Tabeau: *Yes. I entered the service of Madame Monnier as a cook on 8th April 1899. After five or six days, when I entered Mademoiselle Blanche's room for the first time, I couldn't help but notice that the poor woman was lying on a rotten mattress with no proper bed covers. A few days later, I was told by Madame Monnier to sleep in Mademoiselle Blanche's room. She slept on a filthy mattress, but she was well fed. I took people into the room to look at her.*

Fontant: *Did you have permission to take people up to the room?*

Eugénie Tabeau: *We had no permission to do that, but we were never ordered not to.*

Fontant: *Why did you stay in that house?*

Eugénie Tabeau: *We weren't very well paid for what we did, but we stayed there all the same because it was not difficult work.*

Fontant: *How often did Monsieur Marcel Monnier come to see his sister?*

Eugénie Tabeau: *Every day.*

Fontant: *What was he doing in the room?*

Eugénie Tabeau: *He told us that he liked to sit in the room and read the newspaper; he usually stayed there with the door closed for about ten minutes and then he left. Sometimes he stayed for a quarter of an hour.*

Fontant: *While his mother was sick, did he give you any orders?*

Eugénie Tabeau: *No, but whenever Mademoiselle Blanche's door was left open, he would tell his mother.*

Férot: *Did Madame Monnier have a good supply of bed*

linen?

Eugénie Tabeau: *Yes, it was marked with her name.*

Barbier: *Did Monsieur Marcel Monnier have the keys to his mother's house?*

Eugénie Tabeau: *I didn't notice.*

Barbier: *Did you ever ask Monsieur Marcel Monnier for laundry?*

Eugénie Tabeau: *No.*

Barbier: *Did Madame Bourliaud often visit Madame Monnier?*

Eugénie Tabeau: *Yes. She often came to the house and entered Mademoiselle Blanche's room.*

Juliette Dupuis was called next. She had been a maid in the Monnier household since 1899, and she confirmed what was already known from previous testimonies.

Juliette Dupuis: *Blanche's mattress was rotten and dirty. She was never clean in her bed, but she was fed. We asked Madame Monnier for laundry, to change the bed sheet, but she refused us, saying that Blanche had worn everything out.*

Fontant: *Didn't you and your colleague bring people into the house to look at Blanche?*

Juliette Dupuis: *Yes. Blanche's condition was intolerable and we thought that in order to put a stop to it, we had to introduce people who would denounce Madame Monnier.*

Fontant: *Monsieur Monnier came to see his mother and his sister?*

Juliette Dupuis: *Yes, every day; he went to see his mother first.*

Fontant: *Did you sometimes remain in that room your-self, to care for Blanche? To sleep there?*

Juliette Dupuis: *Yes.*

Fontant: *But the judges found they could not stay in the room because of its overpowering smell.*

Juliette Dupuis: *We were used to the smell.*

Fontant: *Was Monsieur Monnier totally unaware of the state his sister was in?*

Juliette Dupuis: *Monsieur Monnier cannot say that he didn't see the filth in which his sister was left, because I swear that at least once in my presence and, on another day in front of Eugénie Tabeau, he [Marcel Monnier] watched, with his moth-er at his side, what we called 'putting Mademoiselle Blanche to bed', which consisted of the following: the young lady got up on all fours; the maid lifted up the sheet that the excrement from the last twenty-four hours was on; she folded it into quarters and removed it. She also removed a small straw-filled cushion that was absolutely filthy. The sheet was replaced with one that had been rinsed out, but which was still very dirty, but not as dirty as the one that had just been removed. The cushion was also replaced with another, also filthy. During this, Mademoiselle Blanche maintained her position on all fours. She kept her face covered even though she was facing away from us. I felt embarrassed for her. Once the bed was ready, she lowered herself back onto the bed and resumed her former position. Monsieur Marcel Monnier watched this scene more than once to my knowledge, so it would be very wrong of him to insist that he believed his sister was well taken care of. He couldn't have avoided seeing the state she was in.*

Fontant: *How often did he attend his sister's bedtime?*

Juliette Dupuis: *At least twice that I know of, possibly more.*

Fontant: *Did you change the sheets every night?*

Juliette Dupuis: *Yes, every night, between nine and half past nine. Mademoiselle Blanche got on all fours like I just explained and we removed the old sheet and put the other sheet beneath her.*

Fontant: *Did Mademoiselle Blanche talk to her brother?*

Juliette Dupuis: *Not often. She was usually looking away from anyone in the room. She was always naked. Sometimes she answered the questions he asked her.*

Fontant: *Did Monsieur Monnier give you orders?*

Juliette Dupuis: *He never gave orders in Madame Monnier's house.*

Fontant: *During Madame Monnier's illness, did you ask Monsieur Marcel Monnier for anything?*

Juliette Dupuis: *No, never.*

Barbier: *Did you ever ask Marcel Monnier for laundry?*

Juliette Dupuis: *Never.*

Barbier: *Did Marcel Monnier have the keys to his mother's house?*

Juliette Dupuis: *No, never.*

Barbier: *But you knew where the key to Madame Monnier's trunk was kept.*

Juliette Dupuis: *Yes. Madame had shown it to me because she had once needed take out a small amount of money during her illness.*

Barbier: *When you left the house, was it as disgusting as when you first arrived to work there?*

Juliette Dupuis: *Oh! It was the same.*

The last prosecution witness was Doctor Chédevergne, the director of the medical school. He had become the Monnier family doctor in late 1882, after the death of Doctor Guérineau, and he remained so until 1897. His predecessor had acknowledged that Blanche Monnier was suffering from a form of insanity, had prescribed a recognised tonic and instructed the family to care for her at home, therefore there was nothing more for the family doctor to do.

Dr. Chédevergne: *I continued to prescribe the tonic that had been prescribed by the previous family doctor for Blanche Monnier to take, as Madame Monnier told me how effective it was in helping her daughter have a few calm moments. Other than that, I did not prescribe any special treatment. I was content to go to see her from time to time. Eventually, Madame Monnier said to me: 'It's not worth visiting Blanche. She's always the same.'*

Férot: *When did you last see or examine Mademoiselle Monnier?*

Dr. Chédevergne: *It would have been about three years ago.*

Férot: *Are you sure, Doctor, that you saw her three years ago?*

Dr. Chédevergne: *No, I'm not sure. It could be longer. Besides, I did not go to the house to treat Blanche Monnier. I was there for her mother. As long as the Fazy woman was there, Mademoiselle Blanche was well cared for.*

Férot: *And since the death of the Fazy woman [on May 16th, 1896], have you seen Mademoiselle Blanche?*

Dr. Chédevergne: *No.*

Barbier: *What was the mother's relationship with her son?*

Dr. Chédevergne: *I've rarely seen them together. I think their relationship was cold. My impression was that Madame Monnier loved her daughter mostly.*

Barbier: *Was Marcel Monnier dominant or dominated?*

195

Dr. Chédevergne: *Oh, dominated. He was unable to dominate anyone; he didn't have enough strength of character.*

The hearing was adjourned at one thirty-five. At its resumption, a quarter of an hour later, the hearing of the witnesses for the defence began.

The first witness was Doctor Chiron, the Monnier family's physician since 1897.

Dr. Chiron: *I was Madame Monnier's doctor, and I had never heard of Mademoiselle Blanche until the day of Madame Monnier and her son's arrest.*

This was surprising news to some of the people in the courtroom, to say the least, since everyone who lived in the streets around the Monnier house knew that there was a mad woman on the second floor of 21 Rue de la Visitation.

Férot: *How did you hear of her?*

Dr. Chiron: *On the morning of his arrest, Monsieur Monnier called me to his house for a conversation.*

Férot: *What did he discuss with you?*

Dr. Chiron: *He informed me that he had a sister who was very ill. She was suffering from a form of madness caused by a fever. She had been taken to a hospital and he felt he would be in trouble for not caring for her adequately.*

Férot: *Can you recall his words?*

Dr. Chiron: *Yes, I can. I wrote what he said in my notes.*

The doctor opened a notebook and read from it.

Dr. Chiron: *He said: 'My sister has been taken to the hospital and they want to shift the blame for her poor state onto me. Now, you know that on several occasions when I have been looking for you to treat my mother, I had also been caring for my sister, since on the morning of the police raid (May 23rd), I pulled a firecracker with her...'*

Everyone present seemed to have forgotten Pierre Bucheton's statement detailing Marcel Monnier's attempt to stop him from entering Louise Monnier's house and seeing Blanche for himself by saying: *'I cannot let you see her without first calling the family doctor. My sister has been suffering from a pernicious fever for about ten years and is not supposed to receive any visitors. Only the doctor will be able to determine if you can enter her room without upsetting or distressing her.'*

Obviously, the doctor's testimony which revealed his lack of knowledge of Blanche Monnier's existence showed Marcel Monnier's lies for what they were, but before further questions about it could be asked, Maitre Barbier stood up and asked a question about Louise Monnier and her relationship with her son.

Barbier: *How would you describe the character of Madame Monnier?*

Dr. Chiron: *Very authoritarian. She intended to be mistress of her own home, to the extent that whatever she wanted had to be done.*

Barbier: *And in the last few weeks?*

Dr. Chiron: *She never lost her mind. Madame Monnier was still very much in command.*

Barbier: *And Marcel Monnier?*

Dr. Chiron: *He was not allowed to give orders in his mother's house.*

Subsequent witnesses confirmed the view that Marcel Monnier was a very weak character, unable to resist any imperious will, especially when that will was that of a person who had authority over him.

Edouard Broussard, the first Presiding Judge at the Court of Appeal of Agen, had known Monnier in high school and in law school.

Edouard Broussard: *He is very gentle, very easy-going, and intelligent, but with a few shortcomings. He sometimes showed no understanding of quite elementary things. He is not mean, but he lacks authority and is very easily influenced.*

The testimony of Arnault de la Ménardière, professor at the Faculty of Law and former President of the Bar Association, attracted particular attention because of his reputation.

Arnault de la Ménardière: *Having known the family for a long time, I am able to state three facts: first, it was common knowledge that for almost twenty-five years, Blanche Monnier has been in a deplorable mental state. Monsieur Monnier Senior was a clever man, but quite reserved and conventional. Eventually, fearing either a scandal or career repercussions, he did what he could to prevent his daughter from being seen naked at her bedroom window.*

Marcel Monnier was asked to explain what dowry his daughter might have upon getting married.

Monnier: *It was impossible for me to discuss the matter with my mother and so I went to Monsieur Yves Agier Senior and proposed that he be our mediator. The former stockbroker contacted my mother and reported back to me her intentions regarding my daughter's dowry.*

Yves Agier Senior was called to the stand to clarify the issue.

Agier Sr: *Madame Monnier told her son that if she did something for her granddaughter, it would not be without doing exactly the same thing for her daughter Blanche.*

Arnault de la Ménardière deduced that Louise Monnier had great affection for her daughter. With great self-righteousness, the law professor delivered his testimony, pointing out that the instruction had verified its three points.

Arnault de la Ménardière: *As for Marcel, he had no influence on his mother's decisions. He was a very weak man, with no will of his own, but as he was very honest, he could not be engaged in the responsibility of criminal acts that could be legally repressed.*

Two witnesses who had known Marcel Monnier when he was a prefecture councillor in Mont-de-Marsan were called.

The first, the musician Francis Planté, reported that the defendant was a veritable delight when he joined his entourage.

Francis Planté: *He is a gentle man, most of all, but very short-sighted, he also has a weak nature; devoid of a sense of smell, so much so that his friends often joke about him. I heard someone say very recently of him: 'Here he is, the man without a nose.' Because of his weakness of character, as well as his physical infirmities, he was often ridiculed in Mont-de-Marsan. I once lost a wager after Marcel Monnier was tricked into eating goat droppings sprinkled with sugar, believing they were strawberries. He is an excellent man, gentle, kind, and dedicated. I say this from the bottom of my heart: Monnier cannot be guilty, he is as innocent as I am myself.*

Some members of the public began to boo and hiss at the musician's last comment. The Presiding Judge threatened to clear the court unless there was silence during the proceedings. The crowd quietened down and the proceedings continued.

The second witness was Lassalle, the former chief of staff of the prefect of the Landes, who had also known the defendant well in Mont-de-Marsan.

Lassalle: *I have very fond memories of Marcel Monnier. However, he is very naïve, and often accepts the most implau-*

sible things as true or real. One incident comes to mind from a few years ago, when, one day, on a tour of the revision board, Monsieur Monnier noticed the black spots that were part of the wallpaper pattern in his room and asked me why there were so many insects on the walls.

Marcel Monnier's friends and relatives in Poitiers came in turn to testify on his behalf.

Maitre Louis Bodin Junior, the family's current notary, had known the defendant for a long time. He was called to the stand.

Férot: *Could you tell us about Monsieur Monnier's character, and any thoughts you may have on his relationship with his mother.*

Bodin Jr: *He is a good man, gentle and naïve; too naïve possibly. As for the relations that existed between Madame Monnier and her son, they were very tense.*

Barbier: *Could the witness tell us who was looking after Madame Monnier's pensions?*

Bodin Jr: *It was Monsieur Yves Agier who administered her fortune; Madame Monnier had her pension received by persons other than her son, notably François Bourliaud.*

Yves Agier Junior was called to the stand after the notary. The stockbroker was in charge of Madame Monnier's interests, which did not prevent him from having a good relationship with Marcel Monnier.

Agier Jr: *He was a good man, but quite naïve, He had a very troubled relationship with his mother, as she did not respect him at all and kept him away from her business.*

Captain de Lattre was the next witness.

Lattre: *I consider myself a close friend of the Monnier household. In all the years I have known him, Marcel Monnier has never hurt anyone. However, he's a man with his head in the clouds, unable to make any decision or resolution regarding anything.*

Barbier: *Are you aware of his myopia?*

Lattre: *He is so short-sighted that, on several occasions in his own living room, while my wife and I were visiting Marcel Monnier's wife, he sometimes did not recognize us at first. Whenever I passed in the street, I had to make myself known to him. He would not have recognized me otherwise. If I had ever wanted to avoid him, it would have been exceptionally easy to do so.*

The next witness, Paul Druet, was also very close friend of the defendant and his family.

Druet: *I don't know anything about the case itself. As for Marcel Monnier, I am one of his oldest friends. When I was a student, he was my classmate during my second year and my third; also, in the rhetoric class and during my law studies. I have stayed in contact with him since 1863. I have always considered him incapable of being abusive or of allowing anyone to exercise abuse.*

The hearing was adjourned at half past three for a short break and resumed ten minutes later.

The next witness was Doctor Jablonski, a prison doctor. He recounted the visit he had made to Madame Louise Monnier on the day of her death – a death he did not believe was so close.

Dr. Jablonski: *On the morning of June 8th, she died despite my care, without having been able to speak a word. I later learned from Marie Foulon, the inmate serving as a nurse, that around five o'clock in the morning Madame Monnier died shortly after having said: 'Ah! My poor Blanche!'*

Barbier: *In a report sent to the Prefect on 30th May, Monsieur Jablonski said that Madame Monnier could perfectly well live for several years. However, Madame Monnier died on 8th June after being questioned by the investigating judge. Is it permissible to conclude that she suffered a violent, unforeseen emotional shock that could have caused death?*

Dr. Jablonski: *It is obvious that Madame Monnier must have suffered, after being made aware of the grave situation in which she found herself, a violent emotional shock which possibly determined the final crisis.*

Since the inmate nurse who had treated Madame Monnier was unable to come to the hearing because of a rheumatism attack, Maitre Barbier had the bailiff who had given Marie Foulon the summons to appear as a witness read her statement to the court; a report in which she confirmed the accuracy of the words reported by Doctor Jablonski.

Marie Foulon (from her statement read by a court bailiff): *I could not say anything about Monsieur Monnier, but what I could affirm is that during her stay in prison Madame Monnier was constantly concerned about the condition of her daughter and she never mentioned her son.*

Auguste Joubert, the sharecropper, was the next

witness. He testified that the widow Monnier had forbidden her son to visit her property in Le Pilet, the care and maintenance of which she had entrusted to her gardeners, François Bourliaud and Pierre Picherault.

Maitre Barbier: *How long has it been since Madame Monnier and her daughter visited their property in Migné?*

Auguste Joubert: *They last visited fifteen years ago. The two women returned to Le Pilet two or three times in the two years following the deaths of Monsieur Émile Monnier and Monsieur Demarconnay, but their stays in the countryside ceased around 1885.*

From 1882 to 1891, Lady Perrin had Marcel Monnier's household as tenants on Rue du Moulin-à-Vent, and she lived on excellent terms with the accused. What Lady Perrin reported reinforced previous testimonies about Louise Monnier's marked indifference to her son.

Lady Perrin: *In nine years, Madame Monnier came only twice to see her son: the first when Dolorès, her granddaughter, was ill, the second time when Marcel Monnier was very seriously ill – and that last time, she only gave in and visited him because of Monsieur Perrin, who threatened to involve the police if she didn't do something to help her ill son.*

A locksmith, Pierre Ragueneau, was an important witness, because during the first day of the investigation, Pierre Bucheton had noticed, on the door of Blanche's room and on the frame, two small holes corresponding to each other which must have been made to receive pitons. These would have allowed a padlock to have been put through the pitons to lock the door from outside the room.

Ragueneau: *I fitted the pitons one day in January 1900, in order to prevent the door from remaining gaping for the few hours I needed to repair the damaged lock. I had to take the lock home to repair it.*

Fontant: *But why fit pitons? Why not simply tie the door closed?*

Ragueneau: *Madame Monnier said she did not want the room door to remain open, because it was cold, so I placed two pitons externally on the door and on the frame which allowed it to be held it closed from the outside with a length of string.*

Fontant: *You placed the pitons externally?*

Ragueneau: *That is what Madame Monnier asked for.*

She had contracted me for the work, so I did as she requested.

Fontant: *Is that usual? Fitting pitons externally?*

Ragueneau: *No.*

Fontant. *What condition was the room in?*

Ragueneau. *From the door, it seemed pretty clean, but it smelled a little strong.*

Fontant: *Did you undertake any other work for Madame Monnier?*

Ragueneau: *In February 1901, Madame Monnier asked me to place beading around the door of her daughter's room to avoid draughts. I made the doorway draught-proof. I believe that in the end, it was a maid named Modeste Bourliaud who put beading around the window.*

The next witness, Doctor Bessonnet, an oculist doctor, made an important statement about the defendant's eyesight.

Dr. Bessonnet: *I have examined Monsieur Marcel Monnier's eyes. He had already come to consult me once. Monsieur Monnier is very short-sighted; he has severe lesions of progressive myopia. He barely sees a tenth of what most of us can see. It is possible that he could not see the state his sister was in, given that the room was quite dark.*

Fontant: *In your professional capacity, would you state categorically that Marcel Monnier could not see his sister even though he sat next to her, spoke to her and gave her sweets?*

Dr. Bessonnet: *What is certain is that Monsieur Monnier has poor eyesight, but it is impossible for me to say that the defendant could not see his sister.*

The next witnesses, former servants in Marcel Monnier household confirmed the defendant's infirmities, adding details about his more bizarre behaviour.

The cook, Madame Gabriau, a widow, emphasised Monnier's short-sightedness and his lack of sense of smell.

Madame Gabriau: *At the table, he always put his nose on his plate and did not see what he was eating. In addition, he was devoid of smell. One day I had served him some sorrel soup and he found it delicious. [Sorrel soup is a dish left in the pan until it blackens. It has an unpleasant burnt taste.*

Several members of the public found this to be amusing and laughed very loudly. Once the laughter had finished, the proceedings continued.

The next witnesses, Madame Berger and Madame

Godard, had both been maids in Marcel Monnier's home. They testified, with great embarrassment as the details were repugnant, that their former employer liked indulging in filth.

Madame Berger: *He was very eccentric and had some filthy habits.*

Madame Godard: *When he defecated into the chamber pot, he would sometimes leave it for eight days without it being emptied.*

Madame Berger: *At other times, he would take it down into the kitchen at lunchtime or else deposit it in his wife's room, on the nightstand, taking care to close the windows so that she could smell it.*

Barbier: *Based on what the last two witnesses have just stated, it is not all that surprising, because of his myopia, his lack of hygiene and his coprophilic inclinations, that my client could have gone to his sister's room every day without seeing the vermin swarming on the bed, and without being inconvenienced by the excremental smells that permeated the room.*

There was great curiosity when Angèle Monnier, Marcel Monnier's wife, came to the stand. Her testimony, which was very short, had the sole purpose of showing the court on what terms she lived with her mother-in-law.

Angèle Monnier: *Madame Monnier was someone whom I saw only very rarely, and always and only on a day and at a time she decided.*

Barbier: *I would ask Madame Monnier to say what happened on the night of the Poitiers races.*

Angèle Monnier: *On the evening of May 19th, my mother-in-law was in pain. I went to see her. It was at a time when I would not usually enter her house. She got angry and exclaimed, 'Marcel will pay for this.' Then, in front of Juliette [Dupuis], she added: 'What will it take to sweep all of this away? I don't need all this fuss; can't I just be left alone?'*

Fontant: *Didn't the maids tell you something pertaining to Mademoiselle Blanche that day?*

Angèle Monnier: *Yes, they did. As they complained about my mother-in-law, they told me that there were creatures on Blanche's bed. I said, 'I'll tell my husband about it.' I did tell him immediately.*

Fontant: And what course of action did your husband

take upon being informed of this?

Angèle Monnier: *My husband said, 'I find that very surprising. I will inform my mother.'*

The defendant's wife had spoken all these words in an emotional voice and Judge Fontant decided that the entire situation was too painful for her to be detained in the court-room any longer.

Fontant: *I don't think it is necessary to prolong your presence here. If the defence does not mind, nor does the court, I authorize you, Madame, to withdraw.*

Angèle Monnier walked out of the courtroom through the hallway door, after shaking her husband's hand for a long time.

The next witnesses were hoteliers who had supplied Madame Monnier with prepared meals. The owners of the Hôtel de France and the Hôtel de l'Europe both said that for more than twenty years Madame Louise Monnier had ordered a variety of prepared dishes from them, including pâtés and chicken dishes – and those dishes had been delivered to 21 Rue de la Visitation.

A fishmonger claimed to have delivered oysters to the Monnier household almost every two or three days when they were in season.

A wine merchant testified that Louise Monnier bought an average of two hundred and twenty-five bottles of fine wine per year every year.

A lumber merchant received orders for logs, the length of which must have been quite large, because he was told the dimensions of the fireplace in the room occupied by Blanche Monnier.

All of the testimonies presented that day seemed to contradict the evidence of Blanche Monnier being found half-starved, filthy and naked, because they suggested that the unfortunate woman had been well fed and her room properly heated during the winter. The testimonies con-trasted starkly with the details of the report drawn up by the Central Commissioner, which detailed how Blanche had been discovered in a state that could best be described as resembling a living skeleton.

Not one single witness, on the other hand, mentioned that they had ever seen Blanche eating any of the meals that that the hoteliers claim they had prepared and had delivered.

No maid testified to ever having eaten a meal with Blanche in her room.

More ominously, due to the passing of the years, although everyone remembered the references to Blanche suffering from a pernicious fever brought about by immense grief, no one, with the exception of the woman who had been Louis Demarconnay's maid in 1875, remembered when that story had started, but even she was uncertain about who had started it.

The last witness of the day was a chimney sweep named Henri Château, who for ten years had been sweeping the Monnier house chimneys.

Henri Château: *For ten years I went into Mademoiselle Blanche's room three times a year, and it never smelled very good.*

The hearing was adjourned at five o'clock. No demonstration occurred against Marcel Monnier when he left the courthouse, but on Rue de la Visitation, at the entrance to the prison, some children booed the defendant and shouted a few profanities.

The Trial – Day 3
Wednesday, October 9th, 1901

At exactly half past eleven on Wednesday, October 9th, Marcel Monnier was conveyed by carriage from the Prison de la Visitation to the court building. Unlike the previous days, the blinds of the carriage were not lowered. A few gendarmes and police officers escorted the carriage as it made its way along Rue de la Visitation. Unlike the other two days, only five or six curious people followed it.

Outside the court room, the crowd was as large as it had been on previous days. Everyone was angrily awaiting the arrival of the defendant, but when he arrived at the bottom of the stairs the cab turned sharply to the left and stopped in front of a small door behind the courtroom. Monnier got out of the carriage and, guarded by gendarmes and police officers, made his way quickly into the building. The door was slammed shut behind him.

Realising they had missed their chance, the angry mob slowly dissipated, some vowing to return at the end of the day's hearing.

The courtroom was packed to capacity. There was considerable public interest in the Monnier case. More than two thirds of the crowd were women. The Presiding Judge, Judge Fontant, allowed a large number of those women to stand on the platform that dominated the room, to the left of the court.

Marcel Monnier, guarded by two gendarmes, contemplated the crowd with a vague, indifferent expression. He was wearing a black frock coat and black leather gloves, despite it being a sunny day.

After a few minutes, Maitre Barbier complained to the bailiff about the room's excessively high temperature. The Presiding Judge gave instructions for the windows to be opened. The bailiff hastened to carry out the instructions. Nevertheless, the heat was stifling.

At twelve-twenty, the court was in session. A witness who had been forgotten the day before was called by the defence and his statement heard. The witness was Joseph

Aulneau, a young trainee lawyer and member of the Society of Saint-Vincent-de-Paul.

Joseph Aulneau: *As a member of the Society of Saint-Vincent-de-Paul, I often went out and did what I could to assist the poor of Poitiers, usually in the company of Marcel Monnier. I soon came to realize, during those missions of mercy, that Marcel Monnier was very short-sighted and completely lacking a sense of smell.*

Marcel Monnier was then called to the stand.

After Monnier had stated his surname, first names and qualifications, the Presiding Judge, Judge Fontant, outlined in a few words the main dates of Marcel Monnier's life, then briefly summarized the case of Blanche Monnier. He then proceeded to question the accused.

Fontant: *When the Central Commissioner spoke to you on 23rd May, why did you try to make it difficult for him to enter your mother's home?*

Monnier: *I did not try to make it difficult; I simply said that it might be appropriate for him to consult a doctor before disturbing my sister, and I added that I was going to inform my mother.*

Fontant: *You said that your sister was suffering from a pernicious fever, and that you would need a doctor's permission to enter her room. The doctor testified that he was unaware of your sister's existence. You also very quickly informed the Central Commissioner of your former social positions and invoked your old titles. This is what you said: 'I am Marcel Monnier. I'm fifty-three years old. And let me inform you of something else; I'm a Doctor of Law and a former sub-prefect... and I shall be referring your accusations to the Public Prosecutor.*

Monnier: *I was shocked by the erroneous accusation made against my mother, but it was never my intention to prevent the Commissioner from entering my mother's house.*

Fontant: *Erroneous? Your sister was in a dark room, naked, filthy and starving. That was what you were told and that is what the Commissioner found. There is no error, only truth. So, tell me, how is it that a Doctor of Law believes a Police Commissioner is making erroneous accusations? Why did you not do everything in your power to aid the Commissioner's investigation? That would have been the correct and lawful thing to do, as you know.*

Monnier: *I was in shock at hearing the accusations aimed at my mother.*

Fontant: *I see. Accusations that turned out to be true. Tell us about your visit to the Bourliaud woman?*

Monnier: *The next day I went to the Bourliaud woman's house to ask her to come to see my mother, whose conscientious companion she was. I told her about the incidents of the day before and added, 'Besides, you know that my sister was receiving the most desirable care,' but I never said, 'I'm lost.' On the contrary, I left without showing the slightest emotion.*

Fontant: *What you say is the complete opposite of what the witness testified.*

Monnier: *I stand by what I say.*

Fontant: When the investigating judge arrived at your mother's house, *he immediately saw that he was in the presence of someone who had been treated horribly.* [Here he read out the details from the judge's report]. *Are you not ashamed?*

Monnier: *I was appalled by everything I was told. I had only ever seen my sister when she was lying on a sheet and, as I knew she was not wearing any clothes, I never wanted, due to a fraternal feeling I'm sure that you will understand, to look at her directly. That is how I saw, for the first time, the day before yesterday, her hair that was shown here in court. The room in which my sister lived was very dark and I could barely see anything in that room, and what I could only just make out was very confused.*

Fontant: *So, everything you have heard is news to you?*

Monnier: *Yes, it is. I never imagined that my sister was in such a frightful state.*

Fontant: *What can you tell us about the words and phrases written on the walls by Mademoiselle Monnier?*

Monnier: *The inscriptions that have been pointed out, written on the walls of the room my sister occupied before 1882... these inscriptions are mostly about the Sacred Heart, or about Jesus and Mary. I felt they were insignificant. However, I admit that they may indicate some religious thoughts in my sister's mind, which I ascribe to hallucinations. As far as I am aware, my sister never expressed any interest in taking her vows.*

Fontant: *I am referring to the inscriptions on the walls of a room she most definitely inhabited after 1882, inscriptions that include the following words and phrases: 'stolen freedom', 'solitude', as well as the sentence: 'One must live and die in a prison all one's life'.*

Monnier: *These are psychological phenomena that I will not try to explain. I admit, I accorded so little importance to these inscriptions that I did not bother to read them.*

Fontant: *It emerges from the testimonies of several witnesses that your sister was often heard screaming and pleading with someone. These witnesses reported her shouting very clearly the words: 'freedom', 'police', 'court' and 'prison'. On August 16th, 1892, Monsieur Jacob heard the following words: 'What have I done to be locked up? I don't deserve this torture! God does not exist if he lets his creatures suffer like this! Someone, please, help me!'*

Monnier: *All of those screams had no meaning. In my sister's mouth, those words had no value – she only said such things in times of madness and crisis. She never asked me for help or demanded her freedom in my presence. I did note that she used a lot of foul language during her frequent fits of anger, notably the word 'shit'. Sometimes she appeared to be talking to an imaginary person. I always found it difficult during those times to make her see reason. The more I tried to calm her, the more she screamed, raged and grew over-excited.*

Fontant: *How do you explain that this rage and over-excitement suddenly stopped as soon as your sister was admitted to hospital, and that it was replaced with a calmness and docility that has not wavered for a moment? Mademoiselle Monnier has showed great pleasure in breathing the pure air outside, or admiring the gardens outside her window, or the flowers that are presented to her. There is a very great and very worrying contrast here.*

Monnier: *I don't have the medical knowledge to explain this physiological change. It is possible that moving my sister caused her to feel emotions that delivered a beneficial shock to her troubled mind.*

Fontant: *In the presence of this sudden change, one is forced to recognize that it took very little effort to remove your sister from her filthy room.*

Monnier: *I never received a mandate to do that from my mother who, until the last moment, maintained absolute authority in her own home.*

Fontant: *We also see, at the Hôtel-Dieu, that your sister*

is very modest, that she is very calm and good-natured, and that she can be left alone near an open window.

Monnier: *Those protective measures date back to a very distant time. The shutters, for example, were installed according to my father's wishes. His actions were always guided by his love for his daughter and his concern for her safety.*

Fontant: *And what is your explanation of the disgusting state of your sister's room?*

Monnier: *Every time we wanted to clean it, my sister screamed, shouted and became violent. We wanted to avoid scenes like that.*

Fontant: *So, if she had acted in the same way at meal times, and had refused to eat, you wouldn't have made any arrangements for her to be fed?*

Monnier: *I had no authority over my mother and I thought my sister was being very well cared for by my mother's servants.*

Fontant: *It has indeed been said that your sister was well fed. Is it true that you forgot to check to see if she ate the food that was brought to her?*

Monnier: *The servants were trusted to do what was necessary.*

Fontant: *Did you go to see your sister often?*

Monnier: *Once a day, I went to my mother's house; I stayed about a quarter of an hour with my sister.*

Fontant: *You told the Commissioner that you visited your sister three times a day. You also mentioned that in your statement. You have just told me that you visited her once a day. Could you explain this contradiction?*

Monnier: *On some days, I saw her three times, on other days twice, and on other days only once. It very much depended on what my duties were elsewhere that day.*

Fontant: *According to the records, you are without employment, you live in a house owned by your mother and you receive a pension from her. What duties elsewhere are you referring to?*

Monnier: *I was a sub-prefect, I was a prefecture councillor, and I am a diligent husband and parent. I have, and have had, many duties throughout my life.*

Fontant: *Did you have conversations with your sister?*

Monnier: *I was always trying to distract her, but conversation was very difficult.*

Fontant: *She sometimes gave you sensible answers, however.*

Monnier: *But the insane sometimes do give sensible answers. Let me be clear, I often asked my mother to place my sister in a nursing home, which always gave rise to arguments between us. I didn't succeed, but my responsibility is covered.*

Fontant: *You didn't notice the very strong smell in the room?*

Monnier: *I never noticed anything. I simply read my newspaper and I was never inconvenienced by any odours.*

Fontant: *According to reports, your mother had been bedridden for several months prior to your arrest.*

Monnier: *In general, my mother stayed in bed in the morning, but she always got up in the afternoon. On May 24th, she was up when the police arrived.*

Fontant: *And she never instructed you to oversee the care of your sister during her illness?*

Monnier: *No, because I would have taken care of it.*

Fontant: *I read, however, in your statement that you had been instructed to supervise your sister.*

Monnier: *I just had to deal with the fire and make sure the room door was closed.*

Fontant: *You had taken on a certain responsibility, however, since you knew that your mother was no longer going to see your sister.*

Monnier: *I never felt that my sister's care was my responsibility.*

Fontant: *One fact absolutely demonstrates that your attention had been drawn to your sister's condition. On May 19th, the maids reported to your wife the presence of verminous creatures in Mademoiselle Blanche's bed. Your wife, Madame Monnier told you about this. What was it you said to her? Didn't you say: 'I find that very surprising. I will inform my mother'?*

Monnier: *I thought they were just bedbugs. If the police had not arrived when they did, it would have been taken care of. When I went to my sister's room, I always leaned against the wall, so if the insects had climbed on the bed, I would have seen them, but I did not see them.*

Fontant: *Instead of taking such measures as were appropriate, you just said you would talk to your mother. Whenever you requested anything regarding your sister to your mother, she refused. It is clear she would have, once again, done nothing about it. More to the point, neither did you. And meanwhile, your unfortunate sister remained on her vermin-infested bed.*

Monnier: *At that moment, I was so concerned for and troubled by my mother's dangerous state of health that I waited, promising myself that if my mother died, I would place my sister in care home immediately. At this point, I would like to add that I sincerely did not believe that my sister was in such a serious condition.*

Fontant: *You obviously knew how unwell your sister was, because you just said that you had proposed to your mother to place your sister in a nursing home. She refused to do so, and you obediently bowed to her decision. Was this because of your concern over money?*

Monnier: *I insisted so much that my mother ended up kicking me out of her house. On one occasion she threatened to disinherit me if I continued to insist on my sister being put in a care home. I remember that I even offered to transport my sister to my grandfather's apartment. My mother refused all of these suggestions and got very angry with me.*

Fontant: *Generally, what was your relationship with your mother like?*

Monnier: *I have always had feelings of the utmost filial respect for both of my parents and I have always had difficulties with my mother, either over matters of finance or about my sister.*

Fontant: *Your eyesight is weak and your sense of smell, you say, is not very sensitive?*

Monnier: *My eyesight is so weak that I have often been around my best friends without recognizing them. Finally, I repeat that I was never bothered by the smell that reigned in the room.*

Fontant: *You work a lot; you write newspaper articles.*

Monnier: *From time to time, a while ago, I wrote a few newspaper reports.*

Fontant: *You also paint.*

Monnier: *Watercolours.*

Fontant: *Watercolours from nature?*

Monnier: *Oh no! In my watercolours, my imagination plays a significant role.*

Fontant: *Do you ever go hunting?*

Monnier: *Never, because my eyesight is too bad.*

Fontant: *In short, you stand here today, accused of having done nothing to put an end to the terrible situation in which your sister found herself.*

Monnier: *If I didn't do anything, it's because I couldn't.*

Fontant: *You avoided taking responsibility. You could have done it and if you didn't do it, it's because you didn't want to.*

Monnier: *You clearly know very little about my feelings to use such words against me. I have never had anything but feelings of affection and devotion for my sister.*

The interrogation ended with that statement. The defendant had answered all of the questions in a very clear manner and in a very confident tone. As the journalist of *L'Avenir de la Vienne* wrote in his article: 'The credulous and easily-led fool that Marcel Monnier was, according to some of the witnesses, defended himself very well.'

During the investigation and since the beginning of the trial, it had become clear that Marcel Monnier knew the severity of his sister's situation. His attitude towards the Central Commissioner, his close relationship with the victim, his status as head of the family in the absence of his sick mother, all pointed to him as being as guilty as his mother.

Some of the witnesses had presented the defendant as a dim-witted fool, a victim of filial piety, incapable of wickedness or evil. It was possible that he was not scrupulous regarding his personal hygiene, but he was clearly not as stupid (nor as myopic) as many of his friends had stated. He had studied law with some distinction and his doctoral thesis had been praised. He had not been unintelligent when the government had employed him as a prefecture councillor, then a sub-prefect, both of which were jobs that required him to use his eyesight to read and write a large number of important documents. Since he had returned to Poitiers, the Red Cross had again retained him as its general secretary, and he was an active member of the Society of Saint Vincent de Paul.

On Wednesday, October 9th, at a quarter to one in the afternoon, the court convened and the floor was given to the Public Prosecutor's Office. The prosecutor, Maitre Férot began his indictment by recalling the emotion aroused by the discovery of the case.

Férot: *We have learned that selfishness and greed, the most depressing and shameful of the passions, has been the cause of the relentless persecution of a young woman deprived of her reason, so much so that the unfortunate victim was no longer treated as a real human being and was left to die on a filthy bed.*

As he concluded his remarks, the members of the public seated at the back of the room expressed their feelings of hostility towards Marcel Monnier with such angry shouts and violent gestures that the Presiding Judge halted the session in order to allow the police to evacuate the inner corridor.

The hearing resumed at five minutes after two o'clock and the representative of the Public Prosecutor's Office addressed the court, carefully setting out the evolution of Blanche's disease of the mind.

Férot: *In her youth, Blanche Monnier was a charming, distinguished, intelligent young girl, endowed with real musical talent, although not very original. Had she started suffering from a form of dementia, around her nineteenth year, as Doctor Lagrange attested? It is possible to doubt that, because witnesses, including the neighbour Touchard, who had often seen her up to the age of twenty-one had never noticed her displaying any signs of madness. She did not suddenly lose her mind; it was little by little that her intelligence atrophied and for a long time after that she had lucid moments. The first signs of this disease of the mind struck the young woman, according to some, in her early twenties. Sadly, she did not receive the proper care that her condition required; on the contrary, her mother had her put in her room, where she ended up remaining confined. After that, Blanche Monnier's condition worsened in successive stages, no doubt hastened by the death of her father in 1882 and the death of the maid, Marie Fazy in 1896. It is important to remember the endless parade of maids that followed Fazy's death, with many of those maids staying only one day, one night or a few months because they left as soon as they knew what services they were being asked to provide. I would ask the court to recall the testimony of each of the maids, who had all noted the uncleanliness of the room, well before the entry of Eugénie Tabeau and Juliette Dupuis in the service of*

Madame Monnier. This establishes the degree of guilt of each of those servants who are still alive. These maids should be here now being prosecuted, as they are the culprits, as the defence will no doubt say. The courts considered that, in view of their inferior situation, they could only be accused of an act that was immoral from the point of view of conscience, but not a criminal act. They were instruments in the hands of their employer? Why didn't they denounce her? Perhaps they had known about the previous incident involving the health inspector, when a denunciation had no discernible effect, or perhaps the words of the Bourliaud woman had frightened them.

Marcel Monnier, on the contrary, is a Doctor of Law and has written a thesis on complicity; as a former sub-prefect, he was aware of the law pertaining to the insane which he was called upon to apply; he realized the responsibilities he had pertaining to his sister; that is what he is being prosecuted for.

The Indictment Division has not found any characteristics of the crime of kidnapping in the facts that the investigation has brought to light, but the judgment referring the matter to the Criminal Court holds Marcel Monnier on a charge of an offence of violence, or at least complicity in violence, according to the terms defined by Article 311 of the Criminal Code.

While the 'assaults' that are mentioned in Article 311 refer to an act or acts of violence the word 'violence' has to be understood in a very broad sense. It refers to everything that could infringe on a person's freedom and security, such as serious omissions, lack of care, deprivation of air or light.

When the hearing was adjourned at three minutes past five o'clock, the intense heat in the room was bothering everyone.

Prosecutor Férot resumed his indictment at twenty-five past three by asking specific questions pertaining to the law and then developing the answers.

Férot: First of all, was Marcel Monnier responsible for the violence and the torture that was inflicted on his sister? According to the indictment chamber's judgment, Monnier's guilt started at the time of his mother's serious illness six weeks before his arrest. At that time, the defendant 'was master and commander of his mother's house', so he cannot escape his responsibilities. However, it has been proven that on other dates, although Monnier was instructed by his mother to watch over Mademoiselle Blanche, at that time he did nothing to remedy *his sister's condition.*

The Public Prosecutor's Office recalled that the order for reference had envisaged the defendant as the main perpetrator and as an accomplice, and then left it to the court to assess.

Férot: *I ask only this: what was the motive? What was the criminal intention that made Marcel Monnier act the way he did?*

A skilful defence will mention the kind and thoughtful letters, the testimonies of the many friends. The judges need to be careful not to be influenced by these testimonies; they have no bearing on the degree of responsibility of the accused. We will be told that this 'dear brother' is innocent of everything that was happening in front of him? Is there proof in any of his letters? In his mother's? But what value do either his letters, or the letters of his mother really have? She addressed him as 'dear Marcel', but she refused to allow him, along with his wife and his daughter, into her home for several weeks at a time on a number of occasions. And while the mother and son's exchanges ranged from polite conversations to heated exchanges, usually over money, let us not for one moment forget that Blanche Monnier was dying of neglect and starvation on a rotting straw mattress.

Does Marcel Monnier have his reason, yes or no? Is he responsible, this former civil servant, this Doctor of Law? If the defence had any concern for him at all, they would have asked for a psychological examination. We did not dare to go that far. He was not crazy and he was very aware of his sister's condition since, on more than one occasion, he advised his mother to have her put in a care home. He was obviously interested in her, often complaining about her situation. So why didn't he persevere in these feelings; why did he not continually fight his mother's fixed ideas; why, in the last few months, when his mother was ill and he was finally in charge of the house, did he not take it upon himself to deliver Blanche from her imprisonment, or at least to have her cleaned?

It's because Marcel Monnier was afraid of his mother. And why was he afraid? As I said, it's a matter of greed. A love of money. He was afraid that if he upset his mother over the care of his sister, Madame Monnier would disinherit him. And so, he let her control his life and his sister's life. Greed is the motive; it is what inspired Marcel Monnier's moral cowardice.

He feared that his mother would not only terminate his grandfather's pension, which she paid him without being obliged to do so, but that she would also disinherit him completely. So, if we accept greed as his motive, was Marcel Monnier a mere witness to his sister's imprisonment, or was he an accomplice?

The defence will say that there is no complicity without a main perpetrator. Then, they will try to demonstrate that Madame Monnier did nothing and that if she left her daughter in the state we now know of, it is due to an excess of maternal love. We will then be told about the Will, the infamous Will, about which so much noise has already been made, which gives Blanche Monnier the right to spend her income on her treatment, which merely continues to confine her to her room in the Rue de la Visitation house and which finally gives her a grave in the Cimetière de Chilvert. In reality, it was pure greed that made that unworthy mother act in the way she did. I refuse to canonize her in the same way that others have done.

The representative of the Public Prosecutor's Office then stood up to describe the odious scenes that had taken place at Madame Monnier's funeral and to blame the perpetrators. At the same time, he insisted on protesting against the perfidious insinuations made against the investigating judges who had fulfilled their duty.

Férot: *It was suggested that Madame Monnier was killed by the judges, and only yesterday we heard Doctor Jablonski ask this question: 'Don't you think that Madame Monnier suffered a violent, unforeseen emotional shock which could have caused her death?'*

Maitre Barbier immediately protested against the inference attributed to him by the Public Prosecutor's Office.

Férot: *I'm not wrong about this. I pay tribute to the great eloquence of my loyal and discreet opponent, but I know he will be unable to bring the slightest suspicion on the judges that we have on the bench of the defence. But the question put by that eminent practitioner was able to plant that thought in the minds of many, which is why he did it. The defence dared to state that the judges were villains and that they should be dismissed because of it. Well, no! They asked their questions because they wanted to know the truth and thereby ensure that justice prevailed. Is the defence really suggesting we should no longer attempt to obtain information from people suffering from heart disease?*

The hearing was then paused when the prosecutor asked for a short break. On its resumption, he recalled that if intention existed, the material element was not lacking either.

Férot: *It is established that the defendant often visited his sister. When he was asked to lead the way to his sister's room on 23rd May, he stated quite clearly to the Central Commissioner that he visited her at least three times a day. What was he doing in the imprisoned woman's room three times a day with the door closed? Apparently, he went there to read his newspaper and to keep warm in the winter. When entering his mother's house, he was always very careful to go immediately to report his arrival there and to take any orders from his mother she might care to give him, which he would then carry out immediately, due to his much-stated 'filial piety'. He himself acknowledged this several times; to the Central Commissioner, to the investigating judge and in the statement he made during his interrogation on 6th June.*

In April and May, when his mother was bedridden, Marcel Monnier was in charge of watching over his sister. When the Central Commissioner asked to see Monnier's sister, Monnier brought up several reasons why he could not do that when all he had to do was lead the Commissioner to his mother. He also tried using out-of-date job titles in an attempt to intimidate the Commissioner – in other words, he tried to use his authority. Despite the fact that Monnier had a key to his sister's locked room, as we heard when the Central Commissioner testified, a key which was obviously given to him by his mother, he now denies his responsibilities, although he has acknowledged them many times during the investigation. Monnier's participation in the imprisonment and the torture of Blanche Monnier is therefore criminal. Today, Monnier retracts and refutes his own confession and declares that he had no mandate, no responsibility for his sister at all. But didn't the obligation become a legal obligation when he accepted that key from his mother and agreed to visit his sister three times a day? If not, then why visit her three times a day? To read a newspaper! To enjoy a fire! On being discovered by the Commissioner to be the holder of the key to a locked door, perhaps it is Marcel Monnier who should be considered the main culprit, the perpetrator of this crime. Marcel Monnier carried out an act which was clearly one of responsibility and the court did not hesitate to consider that he had been given that mandate. The crime therefore exists and we hope we have now demonstrated it.

It will be said that Marcel Monnier could not do anything to help his sister because Mademoiselle Blanche refused and resisted any help and that her physical strength and her will. Monnier himself states that the strength and the will of a starved, naked, imprisoned woman were far stronger than his own. Those who would say this are quite simply inventors of stories for children, and it is enough to recall the statements made by the man who lifted, without any effort at all, Mademoiselle Monnier out of her room and carried her into the carriage outside, and the statements of all the staff of the Hôtel-Dieu.

We will also, no doubt, be told about the myopia of the accused. It is certain that Monnier has poor eyesight, but Doctor Bessonnet stated that it was impossible for him to say that the defendant could not see his sister. But Monnier said he noticed that his sister didn't show her face and that she had a scarf covering her face. I draw your attention to the fact that he noticed! The maid said that on more than one occasion he stood and watched as his sister knelt naked on her mattress while a sheet was changed. He claims he never looked at her nakedness out of a strong fraternal feeling we would understand. Then what was in his sister's room, in his sister's vicinity, demanding his full attention, at the exact same time that his sister's bed sheet was being changed; what was it that he was standing and looking at – but apparently not seeing, not able to see? Finally, he acknowledged that he often went to the prisoner's room to read his diary or a newspaper. It has been said that he insisted that the door remain closed so that he could read his newspaper in the dark – undisturbed! In all that time, it seems that Marcel Monnier forgot one thing – he forgot to approach the bed, and check his sister's health and well-being. He could see well enough to read tiny newspaper print in a dark room, but he could not see his sister! He stated he was afraid, out of what he says were feelings of modesty, to look at his naked sister. How did he know his sister was naked? And if he knew, why didn't he make any effort to cover her? And in order to verify her state of health for himself, why did he not simply ask his wife or a maid to do so?

So, yes, Marcel Monnier knew very well the state which Blanche Monnier was in. His wife herself had reported to him what the maids had said about cockroaches and maggots in his sister's bed, to which he stated he would inform his mother. Did he inform her? What did she do to alleviate her daughter's suffering? And when the defendant saw nothing had been done, what did he then do to end his sister's suffering? Nothing! So, in law, torture is established and it is comparable to the violence noted in Article 311 of the Penal Code.

We will also hear it said is that this drama was not real, that there was no imprisonment and that the whole thing was created in order to provide the public with a horror story. Unfortunately, the prosecution did not invent any of it! Neither Blanche Monnier, nor the locked and shuttered room, nor the door frame pitons, nor the rotten straw mattress are imaginary. Justice intervened just in time, because Blanche Monnier would certainly have died on her mattress in her own faeces. Hasn't this already been stated in this court by doctors as the inevitable result?

Justice then had to look for the culprit. It did precisely that. And contrary to what has been said, it can be seen that the investigation did not fail. Marcel Monnier is guilty and a conviction will soon reassure those who may have doubted that there will be justice. We claim against Marcel Monnier the whole severity of the law. I request that it please the court to apply Article 311 in its entirety.

The end of Maitre Férot's summary was greeted with applause and shouts of 'bravo!' by some of the members of the public from the back of the room.

The hearing was adjourned at six-twenty. The indictment session had therefore lasted nearly five hours. The public left the courtroom calmly, promising to return the next day to hear the argument of the Chief Advocate Barbier. Outside, one thousand, five hundred people, according to the press, surrounded the courthouse in the hope of seeing Monnier. When the defendant appeared through the concierge's door, the crowd started booing and hissing. Some shouted crude insults.

Surrounded by gendarmes and police officers, Marcel Monnier clambered into the carriage, the coachman whipped the horses to a gallop. The carriage was followed along Rue des Basses-Treilles by a mob of protesters, all shouting their hatred and swearing revenge.

The crowd blocked the street so that the carriage

had to slow to a halt. It then had great difficulty advancing. People tried to unhitch the horses, others talked about over-turning the carriage, or breaking the carriage windows and punching the face of the accused.

When the carriage finally reached the Prison de la Visitation, nearly two hundred individuals swarmed around it, ready to attack Marcel Monnier. The four or five gendarmes and police officers, although only few in number, tried to force the demonstrators back along Rue de la Visitation, but the crowd overwhelmed them, and two gendarmes were knocked to the ground.

It was with the greatest difficulty that the defendant was able to dart out of the carriage and enter the prison through the small street door.

The Trial – Day 4
Thursday, October 10th, 1901

On Thursday, October 10th, when he left the prison, Marcel Monnier was booed by more than a hundred people as they accompanied the carriage to the court building.

As on the previous days, a crowd was waiting on the courthouse steps and the same hostile denunciations and chants occurred when the defendant got out of the carriage. He hastily entered the building through the small door behind the court.

In the courtroom, the seats reserved for the public were already full and, as the day before, there was a very large number of women present. When the door was opened, there was a real battle for places. In an instant, there was no more room in the enclosure reserved for the public. This eagerness was easily understood.

Everyone was there to hear what Marcel Monnier's defence lawyer, Chief Advocate Barbier was going to say. He himself was very well prepared. He had his colleague and friend Maitre Mérine distribute to the representatives of the press a pamphlet entitled *The Truth About the Prisoner of Poitiers* in which he had reproduced his *Observations on M. Marcel Monnier.*

The hearing opened at fifteen minutes past noon and the floor was immediately given to Maitre Barbier who addressed the indictment chamber.

Barbier: *My client stands here today accused of criminal kidnapping with aggravating circumstances. Of this appalling and shameful accusation, there is nothing of any substance or merit left. A crime? In this respect, everything was invented by imagination, by passion and by lies, because, once I opened the file on this case, everything vanished into thin air.*

There were whispers of consternation from several members of the public.

Barbier: *Mademoiselle Blanche Monnier's misfortune deserves immense pity, although I see now that the anger that was once directed at the imaginary culprits has vanished. In the narrow heart of the mother, there was affection for her daugh-*

ter. She put that love far above any love she may have had for herself. Yes, she loved her daughter and devoted her life to her.

The defence lawyer's words elicited a huge outcry from the public. Some shouted in protest, some swore, and others laughed scornfully. The presiding judge called the court to order, but it was several minutes before Maitre Barbier could continue.

Barbier: *Which brings me to Marcel Monnier! For everyone who has listened to these long debates objectively, he deserves the same sympathy that is extended to his sister, for both of them are victims of their mother's psychological aberrations. Who would begrudge him sympathy? His weakness is what makes him strong today. From all sides, a great deal of harm has been done to this weak-willed man.*

Today, as on previous days, I have been looking for reasons for this trial. Why is he here? This man, it seems, agreed, in the last days, to report to his mother if the maids pushed – I do not say closed – a door. It is in this nothingness that all of the controversies will fade, because there is no other serious question in this trial.

Let us not forget that the Prosecutor disregarded the authority of res judicata drawn up by the judgment of the Indictment Division by rejecting the death sentence which is the usual punishment for the crime of kidnapping.

In law, there would be a punishable accomplice only if it was shown that there had indeed been a crime or misdemeanour committed by a principal perpetrator from the point of view of both the material element and the intentional element. However, this is not the case.

On what date would Marcel Monnier have participated in any direct and immediate act that would have caused him to be reproached by his mother? On what date and by what act would he have been complicit? The real questions before the court are therefore of two kinds. The first question is whether the accused was, six weeks before the arrest, the authority figure in his mother's house? The second is this: was he was responsible for what was done there?

In fact and in law, had there been a reluctant passing of authority from the mother to the son, how could the defendant be suspected of having had a guilty intention? These questions are closely related to the starting point of this case, which is to say to Mademoiselle Monnier's mental illness.

If you recall, the first symptoms of eccentricity and mental disturbance had manifested themselves in Blanche Monnier when she was a teenager. Then there was a significant worsening of her condition, especially after a pernicious fever that she had around 1873. That pernicious fever left its marks, both physically and mentally, so that Mademoiselle Monnier no longer took part in the family's life together and often confined herself to her room. For a few more years she went down, on rare occasions, to the ground floor of the house, but very soon she refused to leave her bed. The confinement was therefore voluntary and was consensual. It all started when her father had a chain with a padlock placed on the shutters of her room because Blanche Monnier did not want to wear clothes and repeatedly showed herself naked at her window. Her father, Monsieur Monnier, Senior, was the first to take steps to avoid the inevitable scandal and his widow merely continued with those steps he had taken. She was obviously wrong to keep her daughter at home, but she was carrying out her husband's last wishes to the letter.

Admittedly, the words 'Freedom!', 'Justice!', etcetera, that were found written on the walls of Blanche Monnier's room do suggest that the unfortunate woman was being held against her will. But any doctor of the insane will tell you that mad people constantly ask for justice to deliver them.

Insanity is not incurable, as we know today; but Marcel Monnier's father and mother were of a generation that believed such things could be treated in the family home. After her husband died, the widowed Madame Monnier only sought to stop as much as possible any scandal or notoriety from arising and tarnishing the family's good name and its honourable status. She firmly believed that it was a family duty to keep the mentally unstable young woman at home. The Monnier couple went to the trouble of employing a maid to care for their daughter; a maid who treated the woman in her care very well, a maid that the troubled young woman trusted.

We heard one witness say that Marie Fazy was always drunk. But other witnesses dispute this and praise Marie Fazy. Madame Monnier considered her to be an excellent personal maid. So where is the criminal intent in appointing a personal maid? There has been talk of dungeons and torture. The dungeon in question is simply a large bedroom in a well-appointed house, a room that has never been locked; no one *ever operated the key and if the door was pushed to, it was to prevent Blanche Monnier from getting cold. And how was the confined woman treated in her so-called dungeon? What sustenance was she given? Chocolates, brioches, chicken, chops, oysters, all washed down with flavoured water or vintage wine. Offering this food turned out to be pointless because Blanche Monnier refused to take advantage of it, but the fact is it refutes what the prosecutor also said: that Madame Monnier was mean and greedy. I do not deny she was thrifty; if she had realized that her daughter never ate the dishes brought at great expense from outside, she would most certainly have saved her money. On this question of food, the most decisive testimonies are those of the owners of the hotels of France and Europe, the oyster merchant and the wine merchant. Madame Monnier was inadvertently the cause of an immense catastrophe, but she never wanted to deprive her daughter of anything.*

The prosecutor also stated that Marcel Monnier was 'an underhand man', sneaky and hypocritical. His proof was that because things were strained between Marcel Monnier and his mother, the accused wrote her letters in which he took issue with some of her decisions, which meant he did not always show her the great respect she deserved. Since when do children, despite having had difficulties with their parents, no longer respect them, and does respect therefore never change nor waver? Well, let's see those letters! How do the two 'torturers', when they are not with each other, talk about their victim? They talk about her in the most affectionate terms. In all their correspondence, there is not a word, not a word, betraying the criminal thoughts of the two accomplices.

There was a great deal of consternation amongst the public at that pronouncement. Once the room was silent, Maitre Barbier continued.

Barbier: *But there is further proof of Madame Monnier's good intentions. The Will. I mention it because we have to talk about it. What provision is there in the Will for her son, the so-called 'accomplice'? None! He is not mentioned at all. There is no reward for the loyal accomplice. Oh no. He is in fact the only person not named as a beneficiary in the Will. He is in fact the only person that the Will ignores. Madame Monnier bequeathed fifty-five thousand francs of her fortune to people who had no familial claim to her estate. And why? It is because she had a grievance against her son because he constantly asked her to place his sister in a care home.*

And what does she do for her daughter in her Will? Isn't the purpose of the Will to provide Blanche, after Madame Monnier's death, with the care necessary for her condition? Madame Monnier designates a few trusted people to watch over her daughter, and she appoints nurses to care for her. She arranges her finances so that all of her daughter's inheritance is to be used on her care and well-being. Finally, she orders that her beloved daughter, on her death, be put to rest with her in the same cemetery plot. What she proclaims so clearly in her Will, her death states even more eloquently.

Finally, I wish to recall the arrest of Madame Louise Monnier, a widowed old lady, and her death in the Prison de la Visitation. The shocking idea that she could be considered guilty of harming her daughter is what killed her and it has just been stated by the prosecution that this woman did not like her daughter? Is there anyone who would be so low as to suspect her last moment? Hypocrisy in her final breath! What was her final utterance the moment before she stopped breathing: 'Ah! my poor Blanche!' And yet it is said she didn't like her daughter. Marcel Monnier therefore had the right, the obligation to believe that his mother's intentions were pure. There was no attempt at delay or obfuscation when he was asked about his sister on the day of his arrest. He knew his mother was doing all she could to provide care for Blanche Monnier. It will be necessary to take this into account when considering his actions.

Again, there were whispers of consternation amongst the public.

The hearing was adjourned at one-thirty. It resumed a few minutes later. Maitre Barbier continued.

Barbier: *My learned friend, the public prosecutor, is basing his case on a syllogism: Marcel Monnier is not deprived of reason, he was aware of a fact, a regrettable fact; he did nothing, so therefore he is guilty. But, of course, there are other explanations. The defendant was not crazy, but he lacked certain faculties. It was because he was deprived of the senses of sight and smell that he had neither smelled the overpowering smell of the room, nor seen the deplorable state of his sister who spent her time lying on a bed in the darkest corner of her shuttered room.*

The lawyer then read out a character study of the

defendant:

Barbier: *Marcel Monnier is not a fool; he proved this during his interrogation. But if he is not a fool in the true sense of the word, we can be sure the former sub-prefect is no intellectual giant. He is a simple, naïve man, who was often the butt of cruel jokes that made him a constant source of amusement to his uncharitable friends. The testimonies have abundantly demonstrated this, but, to make this point indisputably clear, all we need to do is remember that his father, Monsieur Émile Monnier, who was only too aware of his son's shortcomings and lack of employable skills, once wrote a letter to his former student, Edmond Ernoul, when he was appointed Keeper of the Seals, begging him to 'give my son a home in the judiciary'.*

The lawyer's comment provoked a burst of scornful laughter in the court.

Barbier: *To his eternal credit, Ernoul realized immediately that this requested appointment was far from ideal. However, as he wanted to oblige Émile Monnier, he arranged the interview and the appointment with his colleague from the Interior. And that is how Marcel Monnier began his administrative career as a prefecture councillor in Mont-de-Marsan.*

If Marcel Monnier is to be reproached for being unconcerned about the filthy state of his sister's bed, one must remember that filth not only did not bother him, but he seemed to indulge in it. We have heard several maids testify that he didn't want anyone to make his bed; that he liked to leave a full chamber pot in his room.

It is therefore quite logical to come to this conclusion: everything happened incrementally before his eyes without him noticing anything. Marcel Monnier's mother had kept him away from her house for a considerable length of time, and in the six weeks his mother was bedridden, he had received no instructions from her to accept responsibility for his sister, except for the recommendation that the door to Blanche's room remain closed. Madame Monnier retained her authority until the very last day.

In law, no son is the master of his parents' house, unless their authority has waned due to sickness or inability to wield that authority. But Madame Monnier never abdicated her intractable and absolute power, even during those six weeks. We have this information from the testimonies of several maids. They were asked: 'Did Monsieur Monnier give any orders?' – No. 'Did he have the keys?' – No. 'What was he doing?' – Nothing! Nothing! – So even though Madame Monnier was bedridden, Monsieur Marcel Monnier was not allowed to give the maids any instructions. Has there ever been a fifty-three-year-old man who has found himself in such a humiliating situation? His mother was extremely authoritarian, emotionless, vindictive. But she was not a criminal. We have heard more than forty maids testify; did a single one of them claim to have heard Madame Monnier utter any recriminations against her daughter? Not one. The Prosecutor should ask himself with some urgency why there is in this case no one who can provide such testimony.

There was a long moment of silence in the court. Ėdouard Barbier used it to his advantage.

Barbier: *I now turn my attention – and yours – to the last two maids, who seem to be the most guilty under the circumstances. The real accomplices are Eugénie Tabeau and Juliette Dupuis, and they are to blame for the lurid stories that have so alarmed the public and in truth brought so many here to this building, just as they took so many others into Madame Monnier's home and let them stare at the starved, unfortunate, unhinged woman in that room in that house. Those two accomplices wilfully betrayed the trust of their employer who had entrusted them with the care and the custody of her seriously mentally ill daughter.*

And besides, here is a thought that needs to be considered: If there has truly been twenty years of imprisonment; if for twenty years the unfortunate Blanche Monnier had the horrible tortures which the Prosecutor described to us inflicted upon her, how is it that not one of the many maids who were employed in that house thought of noting or reporting these horrors? Do we admit that they all witnessed the appalling spectacle they would have had to have seen? Do we have to believe that they were all accomplices, too?

Another thought to consider, which is something the Prosecutor has barely said a word about, is that there were, on the bed, around the bed, under the bed, bones, oyster shells, mouldy bread, food scraps and dirt of all kinds. But why didn't the maids remove it all? Who prevented them from sweeping the room, from clearing away that detritus, those oyster shells? Who, I ask you? Weren't they paid to do it? Didn't they have a maid's responsibility, a formal mandate from their employer to do so? But no! they did not sweep the room nor remove the rotten food scraps. Have they not, on the contrary, deliberately allowed all those horrors to accumulate as if they took pleasure from the discomfort of their employer's daughter?

The maids tolerated everything they saw for two years, yet they wanted to stay in that horrible house, and it appears from both of their statements, which we have on file, that they had only one fear: that of being kicked out of the house where they had wages, food, rooms, and a very easy, lazy life.

The hearing was adjourned at five o'clock and resumed at five-thirty. Maitre Barbier resumed.

Barbier: *In conclusion, I must mention the honour of Monsieur Monnier. The defendant had suffered numerous complaints from the prosecution, which I intend to refute. The prosecutor has reproached him for not looking closely at his naked sister, but the defendant is an honourable man and felt that such scrutiny by him would be morally wrong. We must also remember that Blanche Monnier refused to allow her face to be seen by her brother and she stubbornly resisted or started to scream and shout and grow violent every time anyone tried to remove the small piece of cloth that she used to hide her face. A man with more firmness of mind, more vigour, could perhaps have ignored her, but Marcel Monnier was much too shy, and much too complex to do so.*

In addition, there is no doubt about the defendant's short-sightedness, it is enough to refer to Doctor Bessonnet's testimony, which the public prosecutor has treated a little too disdainfully. The oculist said that Monnier has a tenth of normal vision and, moreover, Blanche Monnier's room was, as she preferred, dark and unlit. Certainly, Monnier read Le Journal de la Vienne in his sister's room and he painted watercolours. We all saw those aquarelles. Let the Prosecutor submit them to experts; he will be shown houses that will collapse because they were not painted accurately or in perspective. Monsieur Monnier therefore had a tenth of vision, in a tenth of light, with a tenth of his faculties. Without having any desire to appear scholarly, I would estimate that as being a thousandth. To his myopia is added his inattention to details and his gullibility. It was said that he found sorrel soup very tasty. The story of the sugared goat droppings made you smile. It seems far-fetched, I agree, but it is true.

There was a smattering of laughter from around the courtroom.

Barbier: *Although I had all of the evidence I needed in regard to that particular story, I requested a new testimony from the President of the Bar Association of Mont-de-Marsan. I have here a letter from him which verifies the authenticity of the practical joke. And that was just one of a thousand tricks that was played on the good and honourable Monsieur Monnier.*

There was more laughter from the public.

Barbier: *I sincerely hope that the Prosecutor will not try to suggest that the President of the Bar is a suspect.*

As for the defendant's sense of smell, the stench in Blanche Monnier's room was appalling and the defendant should have been as troubled by it as everyone else was. The repugnant details reported by two of his former maids about his coprophilic inclinations, however, should be enough to convince us that Monnier was used to smelling excremental odours to the point of not smelling anything unpleasant when he visited his sister. Other people, such as his mother's maids who slept regularly in the room, endured the terrible smell, not like Monnier, for only a quarter of an hour a day, but for the entire night for every day the last two years. What is there that remains to be said regarding the defendant's intentions?

Maitre Barbier paused dramatically, then continued.

Barbier: *I still feel it is necessary to point out the insistence with which Monsieur Monnier constantly and repeatedly asked his mother to place his sister in a nursing home. The defendant knew that by doing so he was going against his mother's feelings and express wishes. It was one of the few areas where he had dared to stand up, and his obstinacy ultimately earned him disinheritance. The Prosecution has suggested that Marcel Monnier could have arranged to have his sister abducted during the six weeks of his mother's illness, but let us examine this claim in more detail in order to show that such action by the defendant was simply not possible.*

Firstly he was neither the owner, the tenant, the resident, nor for that matter the guest, of 21 Rue de la Visitation. From a legal point of view, he had no right to do what he is accused of not having done. If he had wanted to abduct his sister for her own good, would he have seriously considered such a course of action? He was only too aware that the slightest shock would be fatal to his mother's health. Madame Monnier died in prison as a result of the immense shock she suffered at being arrested. Would she not have died from the same shock if her daughter had been forcibly taken away from her against her will; an iron will which was never denied, and against her express interdict? In short, Monsieur Prosecutor, what you have suggested my client should have done to save his sister is to kill his mother.

There was a moment of furiously-heated conversation and debate amongst the members of the public, and again the presiding judge called for order. After a few seconds, it was quiet enough for the defence lawyer to continue.

Barbier: *There were, of course, the unfortunate rumours provoked by the testimony of Mademoiselle Aurélie Raymond, Blanche Monnier's nurse at the Hôtel-Dieu. I feel that, in light of the opinion of the doctors themselves, who have stated that Mademoiselle Monnier is sadly unable to provide two sensible answers in a row to any serious questions about her family, it might be better to disregard Blanche Monnier's unfortunate wording and not attribute the slightest importance to what she said.*

The same disregard must also be applied to Monsieur Monnier's alleged remarks to Modeste Bourliaud on the morning of his arrest. I can assure you that the defendant never said: 'I am lost'. Madame Bourliaud originally said that Monsieur Monnier had uttered that phrase because she was concerned that she was also going to be charged for a crime of negligence, simply because she was regarded as the 'responsible person' in Madame Monnier's house and her husband had all the responsibility of Madame Monnier's properties. She first thought she heard him say it in order to make sure she was not held responsible. Later, on being recalled to the stand, she varied her statement to let the real conversation be known.

At that point, the court bailiff announced that it was five-thirty. If the court needed to continue, then the maintenance team would have to turn on the gas lamps.

Fontant: *How much longer do you intend to speak for?*

Barbier: *Half an hour, and I ask the court to allow me to finish.*

Fontant (addressing the prosecutor): *And how long will you need for your retort?*

Férot: *That will depend, but I'm willing to wait until*

tomorrow.

Fontant: *In the circumstances, the concluding state-ment by the defence and the prosecution's retort are hereby postponed until tomorrow at noon.*

The hearing was adjourned immediately; it was five-forty.

As he left the court building, Marcel Monnier was, as on previous days, booed and jeered at by a large and angry crowd.

The following morning, *Le Journal de la Vienne* reported the violence that erupted as the carriage carrying Marcel Monnier back to prison was attacked by a few angry citizens. Two men gain access to the carriage and one of them punched marcel Monnier in the face, causing him to cry out. The men were removed from the carriage by gendarmes.

> 'It is time, it is definitely time, for this trial to end. The violent demonstrations witnessed today were all the more regrettable because, among that screaming crowd, there were a few people who committed outrageous acts of vio-lence against an – until sentenced – innocent man. They did not just voice their displeasure at the carriage that was tak-ing Marcel Monnier back to prison, but they threw stones at the carriage and its escorts. One gendarme was even hit by a rock. Marcel Monnier himself was punched. It is very regrettable that some of the populace are eager to engage in such inhumane acts.'

The Trial – Day 5
Friday, October 11th, 1901

On Friday, October 11th, Marcel Monnier arrived at the courthouse at eleven-thirty and as he climbed from the carriage, he was greeted with jeers, hisses, boos, and crude insults. Someone had piled some wood at the entrance of the concierge's lodge, and several onlookers grabbed pieces and hurled them at Monnier as he dashed into the court building.

Inside the courtroom, Marcel Monnier looked slowly around the room. He seemed bored and disinterested. The section of the room reserved for the public was quickly filled. Some of the ladies sitting to the left of the tribunal chatted animatedly. Those present discussed the length of time the defence and the prosecution would need to conclude their cases. The general view was that the hearing, which everyone wanted to be brief, would continue until a late hour.

It seemed almost certain that the prosecutor, Maitre Férot, would take the floor to reply to Maitre Barbier as soon as he had finished his argument. If this corridor noise was confirmed, it was to be expected that this last hearing would not be lifted for a long time, because the judges had already been very late.

The clock indicated thirty-five minutes past noon when the bailiff announced that the court was in session.

Maitre Barbier took the floor and addressed the question of law.

Barbier: *For there to be guilt there must be a material fact and an intention. Is there intention? It should not be forgotten that it was Monsieur Monnier Senior and Madame Monnier who established the tradition of closing the door of the room. In this respect, there is no intention by Monsieur Marcel Monnier. But is there a material fact of violence? The Prosecution made a distinction between violence and assault, but could not, and did not even try to, define assault. Assault and violence are the same thing. It requires an act of brutality, an act of force, a physical constraint that does not exist in this case. The criminal law punishes only 'positive' acts: murder, theft which is analysed as a subtraction of the thing of others,* assault and battery, and insults. In all cases, there is a need for physical activity by the offender who has to have been actively involved through his or her actions, words, or writings. This is a crucial point of this trial from the point of view of the legality of offences and penalties.

The Criminal Code does not punish a breach of any so-called moral duty resulting from a simple abstention or omission, even if it has had the same consequences as a 'positive' action.

There is only one exception, which is the very recent law introduced on 19th April 1898, which penalizes the abandonment of a child, as well as the deprivation of food or care, harmful to the health of a minor under the age of fifteen. This is obviously not the case with Mademoiselle Monnier who, as the only adult daughter of a wealthy woman, had her own personal maids. Food and logs were delivered to her room for her comfort and her well-being.

Look for the act of violence allegedly committed by Marcel Monnier. There is none. Look again for the effects produced by that so-called violence. There are none. Yes, Mademoiselle Blanche was in a terrible state when she was 'found', but was it due to the effect of any alleged violence? No, it was not. The violence committed by Monsieur Monnier does not exist. The crime has vanished. This trial is over.

Maitre Barbier then addressed the representative of the public prosecutor's office.

Barbier: *I will not waste the court's time by detailing how this unfortunate man, who has been suffering in prison for more than four months, has become harassed and humiliated by undeserved opprobrium. Nor will I itemise the moral tortures suffered by Monsieur Monnier's wife and daughter, whose hearts are forever broken by the false claims made against this decent man. I want only for Marcel Monnier to leave here owing nothing, but for it to be acknowledged that he is in the right.*

As for public opinion: What is it? A few voices heard on the streets? Do you want to open the doors of this courtroom to it and then allow it to make legal decisions? Why not simply hand him over to it and allow it to become the reason of the state? After all, it is everything that is the opposite of justice? No! If misguided public opinion besieges this courtroom, then it shall be driven out! You will drive it out. And by doing so, you will prove to the nation that here in this building, we are only concerned with the law and the truth. I am confident of this because I still believe in justice.

Maitre Barbier finished his argument and promptly sat down. It had taken him an hour and a half to state his case.

The Prosecutor, Maitre Férot immediately stood up to reply to the defence.

Férot: *The honourable lawyer claimed that one word by him would be enough to destroy the prosecution, but he spoke throughout two hearings without eradicating any of the charges against Marcel Monnier. We now need to examine the intelligence of the accused. There is no question of anyone making him look like an idiot since he has lectured and written articles published in the newspapers. He is the author of an article on universal suffrage, an article which is very well-written and which denotes great intelligence. During the interrogations, we even found the beginning of an article written in his defence by Monnier himself, as though writing as someone else. It was found on the day before his arrest, when he had been ordered to be at the disposal of the police and this court. This article, which begins like this: 'One of our most compassionate fellow citizens has just been found to be the object of a regrettable situation...' could not have been the work of a fool.*

We are also accused of having listened to and been influenced by the public noises from outside; the screams of the crowd. You have heard those cries, those accusations, those opinions, gentlemen, resounding inside this Chamber; like you, we condemn them. We did not need them to substantiate our accusation. Everything that has been said during this trial, every document placed in the file, every deposition that has been given, supports our case irrefutably. Moral condemnation has long since preceded the hour of justice. When you speak, you will now speak the word of the law. You will wield justice. This man is an evil criminal who more than deserves punishment.

It was three o'clock when the representative of the Public Prosecutor's Office finished his reply. Maitre Barbier announced that he intended to respond.

The hearing was adjourned for half an hour but, as one of the judges, Monsieur Rivasseau, was feeling unwell, he was given some time to fully recover from his discomfort. The hearing resumed at four-fifteen in the afternoon.

Maitre Barbier took the stand to offer his rejoinder.

Barbier: *I have to admit I was surprised that the Public Prosecutor concluded that the Prosecution had a solid case based on the length of his plea. The Prosecutor forgets that the scaffold that takes the longest to dismantle is the one whose component parts are either the most fragile or the most worm-eaten.*

There was a ripple of laughter throughout the room.

After his lead-in, the lawyer then proceeded to dismantle, one after the other, the last objections of the public prosecutor.

Barbier: *I now wish to point out that the Public Prosecutor has made a number of false claims. For example, Maitre Férot has attributed to the defendant an article on universal suffrage, 'an article which is very well-written', he said, 'and which denotes great intelligence'. But this article was not written by Monsieur Monnier; it was written by the great sociologist Emmanuel de Curzon, a disciple of Frédéric Le Play, who published it in Le Études Sociales. And if my honourable opponent has got something that basic incorrect, it makes me wonder what else in his 'solid case' is erroneous or completely wrong.*

I will now return to the main issue of this case which is this: because there is no law in this country which equates abstention from action with positive criminal action, it is impossible for my client, simply by inaction, to have broken any law or to have committed a crime. That he is here on trial is a parody of justice.

He ended his address with a few carefully-chosen words.

Barbier: *I do not want to delay the acquittal of Marcel Monnier.*

He then took his seat.

The hearing was adjourned at four-twenty-five and the court withdrew to deliberate.

In the courtroom and in the corridors, conversations were heated. In general, despite Maitre Barbier's strong argument, people in the public were convinced that Monnier would be convicted. During this time, in the Palace Square, the crowd was constantly growing and the police had a hard time containing it.

The court deliberated for an hour.

They returned at five-thirty. The courtroom's gas lamps had been lit.

Judge Fontant then read out the judgment, in the midst of a profound silence.

Fontant: *While it has been established that, for a long time already, the young lady, Blanche Monnier, suffering with an unspecified form of insanity, was kept deprived of adequate care in a dark room, insufficiently ventilated, in her mother's dwelling in Poitiers; that in recent times especially she has been left in an appalling state of filth and deprivation; that on May 23rd, 1901, she was found in the same room, lying on a rotten mattress, in the midst of rotting food debris and filthy creatures, her body completely naked and lying on a dirty and torn sheet, her hair filled with food scraps, excrement and vermin, her toenails and hands disproportionately long;*

That the fact of putting or maintaining in a person's presumable condition, when he is unable to evade it, constitutes an attack against him by violence and assault, and falls within the scope of article 311, section 5 of the penal code;

Whereas the investigations reveal that the author of the criminal acts committed against the young lady, Blanche Monnier, is her own mother, now deceased, who has always kept her daughter's room closed, has always refused the objects necessary for her daughter's proper care and maintenance and has, under the pretext of not disturbing her against her will, rigorously prescribed to leave her where she was; but that the debates also reveal that Monnier was complicit in these same acts by aid and assistance;

That this complicity results from the fact that, he was able, whatever he says regarding having his sister given proper care, as evidenced by the attempts made to have his sister placed in an asylum, to ignore the horrible actions of his mother and the awful situation of his sister, and he accepted, in the end, the fait accompli and participated in it through his lack of intervention and his daily visits to the poor incarcerated woman;

That especially, during the five weeks preceding May 23rd, 1901, his bedridden mother gave him the task of watching over his sister, as he acknowledges in his interrogation statement of June 6th, 1901, in which he said: 'I did not go more than two or three times a day to my sister's room; often it was less or not at all. I did not give my mother's servants any orders, but I did make one or two simple recommendations. If, after seeing my sister, I went to my mother's room, it was simply so that she would know that I had fulfilled my tasks';

That having therefore the right and the duty to inquire about the condition and needs of his sister, he kept her in this state without inquiring about her needs, took no other care than to keep the door closed, as his mother prescribed;

That, alerted by his wife, who had been informed by the maids that there were cockroaches and maggots on Blanche Monnier's bed, he pretended not to know anything, was not moved to do anything, pretended he would inform his mother, and then allowed the vermin to invade the filthy mattress on which his exhausted and defenceless sister was made to lie;

Whereas, despite the gravity of the fact noted by the prosecution and also the gravity of the offence, it is necessary, for the application of the sentence, to take into account Monnier's personality and his state of mind which, according to many witnesses, is such as to mitigate his responsibility, his weakness of character, and the excessive domination exercised over him by his mother;

Finally, the attempts that he made to his mother to have his sister placed in a nursing home;

By these reasons, said Monnier is guilty of having been complicit in the offence of violence in Poitiers for less than three years, of the kind provided for and punished by article 311 of the penal code on the person of the young lady Blanche Monnier, by assisting and assisting, with knowledge, the author of the said violence in the acts which prepared and facilitated it or those who consumed it; the court orders him to be sentenced to be imprisoned for fifteen months and to pay the legal costs of all parties.

The statement of the judgment elicited applause throughout the room and Marcel Monnier turned to the gendarmes.

Monnier: *That is a very beautiful result.*

Someone sitting at the back of the public section opened a window and shouted to the huge crowd amassed and waiting expectantly in front of the court building.

Anonymous person: *Fifteen months in prison!*

A formidable roar immediately rose from the square. It sounded like a thunder storm. Over two thousand people were shouting: *'Long live Fontant!' 'Long live the Tribunal!'*

'Long live Justice!' 'To the death!' 'Execute him!' 'Kill him!' 'Give him to us!'

Meanwhile, the gendarmes quickly led their prisoner through the building and out through the tradesman's entrance which was behind the building. It opened on to the Rue du Marché, where the carriage was waiting to take him back to prison.

The carriage was guarded by a brigade of gendarmes on horseback and two brigades of gendarmes on foot. Monnier was therefore able to climb unhurriedly into the carriage, although many of the people who were being held back by the gendarmes were calling for his death or waving their fists at him.

With the gendarmes surrounding it, the carriage set off at a fast pace, the coachman forcing the horses to gallop. Despite the speed of the horses, about five hundred people kept up with the carriage as it raced towards the prison on Rue de la Visitation, where another angry crowd was waiting.

In front of the prison, the large crowd shouted insults and threats when the convicted man was escorted out of the carriage and in through the door. After a while, the crowd began to disperse.

Marcel Monnier, despite his optimistic words to the gendarmes, appeared to be dejected. He left his evening meal untouched and was unable to sleep that night; he spent most of the night pacing back and forth in his cell.

Legal Advice

On Monday, 13th October, 1901, Édouard Barbier visited his client, Marcel Monnier, in the Prison de la Visitation and the two men discussed the finer details on Monnier's appeal, which Maitre Barbier had lodged immediately after Marcel Monnier had been sentenced and led from the courtroom.

The appeal document had been completed and signed by both men on the day prior to the final day of the trial. Once Marcel Monnier had been taken from the courtroom, Maitre Barbier stated that his client wished to appeal the sentence. He dated the document and handed it to the court administrator, thereby starting the appeal process.

Following that first visit, Maitre Barbier visited his client almost daily, providing him with news and updates of the appeal.

Thanks to Maitre Barbier lodging the appeal on the same day as Marcel Monnier was sentenced, the appeal hearing was scheduled to take place on Thursday, November 14th, 1901.

So both men discussed the finer details, finally agreeing on a legally sound defence strategy.

The Appeal – Day 1
Thursday, November 14th, 1901

On Thursday, November 14th, Monnier left the prison at
five minutes to mid-day. He took his place in a carriage, still
escorted by four gendarmes on horseback, which followed
the same route as the day before. There were no incidents on
the courtyard, but when the carriage stopped at the bottom
of the Palace steps, a group of young men and children started shouting insults at Marcel Monnier. The police pushed
back the more belligerent members of the crowd, some of
whom began to advance, threateningly, towards the carriage.
The shouts increased when Marcel Monnier got out of the
carriage.

He was quickly escorted into the courtroom by four
gendarmes.

Inside the small courtroom, a handful of members of
the public occupied a few of the seats that had been reserved
for them. The court officials entered the room and took their
seats. Counsellor Gassan, presiding, called the defendant to
the stand in order to interrogate him.

Gassan: *I could dispense with this interrogation
because everything has been said about this case. You yourself
have provided both the investigation and the court with all
possible explanations. It is certain that I will shorten this
formality as much as possible; nevertheless, it will allow you to
present your defence before the court personally.*

Counsellor Gassan turned to face the court.

Gassan: *This interrogation will also make it possible for
certain important points to be highlighted and to measure more
precisely any degree of responsibility of the accused in this case.*

Counsellor Gassan turned back to face Marcel Monnier.

Gassan: *I now wish you to clarify the details of a
conversation you had with Doctor Chiron. What was your
reason for inviting Doctor Chiron to your home on May 24th?*

Monnier: *He was my mother's doctor; it was only
natural that I should inform him of the situation and the events
that had occurred.*

241

Gassan: *Doctor Chiron testified that you told him some-thing to this effect: 'My sister has been taken to the hospital and they want to shift the blame for her poor state onto me. Now, you know that on several occasions when I have been looking for you to treat my mother. I had also been caring for my sister, since on the morning of the police raid (May 23rd), I pulled a firecracker with her.' Would you like to clarify that? What is the meaning of your firecracker story, Monsieur Monnier?*

Monnier: *My sister really liked those sweets that are known as papillotes or firecrackers. I bought some for her at the Épicerie Parisienne.*

Gassan: *You explained that quite naïvely. Was it to show that you did not know what to invent to please your sis-ter? Your displays of fraternal affection seem peculiar because you must have been in close proximity to your sister to give her the sweet, but you did not notice her distress, nor the state she was in, nor did you help her.*

Monnier: *No. I pulled a firecracker to amuse her, but I could not see her because the room was very dark.*

Gassan: *I would ask the court not to forget this state-ment. Monnier pulled a firecracker with his sister. So he was able to see her. The court will make a note of his statement: 'I had also been caring for my sister, since on the morning of the police raid, I pulled a firecracker with her...'*

Monnier: *I did not see my sister.*

There were some whispered comments in the public section.

Monnier: *To see her, I would have had to have moved my head until it was right over her bed. I was not going to do that.*

The public prosecutor, always on the lookout for the slightest untimely or clumsy remark, took the opportunity to ask Marcel Monnier some related questions.

Gassan: *You were not going to do that. Were you going to do anything to improve her situation?*

Monnier: *I repeat. I did not know my sister's condition, because I never looked at her. You will understand the fraternal feeling of modesty that made me act in that way.*

Gassan: *You didn't need to exceed the bounds of your 'fraternal feelings of modesty' and study her nakedness in order to realize the state of repulsive filth that Mademoiselle Blanche was wallowing in. In order to be edified, it would have been enough for you to simply glance at the bed, or at the filth and the vermin on the floor around the bed.*

Monnier: *I could not really see the bed, because my view was blocked by three chairs.*

Gassan: *Well, couldn't you simply have moved a chair? Moreover, it is established that on two occasions you witnessed what is known as Blanche's bedtime.*

Monnier: *That particular procedure took place in the presence of my mother. As for me, I stood in the corner by the window; and from there it was impossible for me to distinguish the bed. Besides, I wasn't looking at my sister.*

Gassan: *What were you looking at?*

Monnier: *The wall.*

Gassan: *You were too short-sighted to see your sister, but you were able to see the wall beyond her. How so?*

Monnier: *I knew the wall was there, but I could not see it.*

Gassan: *Your sister often lay across the bed, so her thin legs would have been resting on the chairs you just mentioned. Does your sense of modesty forbid you from noticing thin legs?*

Monnier: *I didn't see my sister's legs, because they were hidden by bedclothes.*

Gassan: *Several maids have testified that your mother refused to allow any bed linen of any kind in your sister's room. When your sister was removed from the room and taken to the hospital, there were no bedclothes in her room and something to cover her nakedness had to be fetched from another room. What bedclothes are you referring to – those in another part of the house?*

Monnier: *I could see nothing in that room – the darkness of the room and my eyesight made seeing anything impossible.*

Gassan: *So you couldn't see your sister's painfully thin legs?*

Monnier: *No.*

Gassan: *Yet you knew she was naked?*

Monnier: *Yes.*

Gassan: *So why didn't you simply go into a nearby room and get a blanket or something to cover your poor sister with, thereby covering her nakedness – and of course preserving your 'fraternal feeling of modesty'?*

Monnier: *I couldn't see her in the darkness of the room.*

Gassan: *Really? Well, several people were able to see her. And they all saw your sister's thin legs. One woman even screamed when she saw these poor legs. She said there were only bones covered by skin; she was, said this woman, a living skeleton.*

Monnier: *I didn't see anything.*

There were significant exclamations of disbelief from the public section of the room.

Gassan: *When you spoke to the Central Commissioner, you stated that you went to see your sister two or three times a day, before your mother became sick.*

Monnier: *I didn't go there very regularly. In principle, I went there every night, after talking with my mother. I spent little more than ten minutes with Blanche.*

Gassan: *All the witnesses say – and on this point they are unanimous – that you would have had to be absolutely blind and have no sense of smell in order not to realise the odious and filthy state of the room and the appalling state of your poor sister.*

Monnier: *I never saw anything; I was never bothered by any smell. The proof is that I read my diary there.*

Gassan: *So your poor eyesight allowed you to see and to read?*

Monnier: *Yes, a little, although I had to go to the corner of the window in order to do so.*

Gassan: *You were able to read newspaper print and diary entries in utter darkness, but you were unable to see your sister on a rotting, vermin-infested mattress?*

Monnier: *The bed was in a far corner of the room and therefore plunged into semi-darkness, so it was almost totally invisible to me.*

Gassan: *So be it. With regards to your bedridden mother, what instructions did she give you?*

Monnier: *She has only ever instructed to me to ensure that the fire in Blanche's room did not go out in winter and that the door never remained open.*

Gassan: *Why would the door being open be problematic?*

Monnier: *My sister might have caught a cold from winter draughts. A closed door kept her warm.*

Gassan: *So has your mother been bedridden for longer than three months?*

Monnier: *She has been ill for a long time, but bedridden for three months.*

Gassan: *So please explain the winter draughts you mentioned? Do they now occur in March, or April or May?*

Monnier: *I kept the door closed out of my regard for my sister. She liked privacy. Also she was naked. I was doing my utmost to preserve her modesty.*

Gassan: *I see. To preserve her modesty. From whom? From the maids paid to care for her? From the doctor who never saw her?*

Monnier: *It is a fraternal feeling. I felt it was the right thing to do.*

Gassan: *Why leave her naked?*

Monnier: *My sister disliked clothing. I felt I had no right to try and impose my will on her.*

Gassan: *Didn't your mother say to you: 'It's impossible for me now to go up to Blanche's room, so go and see if your sister needs anything'?*

Monnier: *No, she did not.*

Gassan: *I thought you recognized that there was some responsibility in the instructions you were given. You said that your mother gave you tasks related to your sister's care.*

Monnier: *Perhaps my meaning is unclear. I never received any instructions...*

Gassan: *It appears that your line of defence can be summed up as follows: 'I didn't see anything, so therefore I couldn't have done anything reprehensible.' However, if you had seen anything that needed you to take action, would you have done anything?*

Monnier: *I don't know, because my intervention would have provoked my mother to a violent pitch of anger and most probably delivered a shock that would have killed her. I refused to accept any such responsibility.*

Gassan: *I would ask the Clerk of the Court to note this statement: 'I refused to accept any such responsibility.'*

Monnier: *That is not what I meant.*

Gassan: *Yes, yes, it is understood that once again, your words have exceeded your thought...*

The interrogation ended at three minutes to ten o'clock and a short recess was called. When the hearing resumed, twenty minutes later, Counsellor Gassan, presiding, gave the floor to Maitre Barbier.

Barbier: *The essential question in this case is, in my view, as always, whether, at a specific moment, my client had been given the task of looking after his sister and providing her with the necessary care.*

According to the report we heard from Counsellor Volf, it appears that Monsieur Monnier would only have needed to have looked at the door of his sister's room to know if it was closed, and if not, then pulled it closed, not to imprison the one that is now called the prisoner of Poitiers, but to prevent cold air from entering the room.

Where is the criminal act that was performed by the mother? What is the criminal act performed by the mother? She probably lacked the intelligence to make an accurate assessment of her daughter's deteriorated state of mind, and she had clearly not been able to give Mademoiselle Blanche the required and proper medical care she needed, but to say that she had wanted to make her daughter suffer is an aberration. Madame Monnier wanted to hurt her daughter! Hurt her, for whom and for what reason? So let's look for Madame Monnier's motive. Let's see what has been suggested. Avarice was one theory put forward. Greed. So let us recall the expenses made by the mother for her daughter, in relation to the food requested from the best hotels, in relation to the Bordeaux wine bought at two and four francs a bottle, and in relation to the cords of logs bought for her fire. And yet maids testify that their employer refused to allow bed linen or clothing into the poor woman's room. Why would Madame Monnier spend so much money on those items if she wanted to save a little on clothes and linen?

The defence lawyer was about to address the accusations made against Marcel Monnier when the chairman adjourned the sitting for five minutes to allow the service staff to light the gas lamps. The hearing resumed at five o'clock.

Maitre Barbier continued his argument.

Barbier: *Regarding my client's alleged motives, it is not acceptable that the prosecution employs, without any supporting evidence, the hypothesis that Monsieur Monnier did not insist that his mother improve his sister's lot, because he was afraid of being deprived of the pension that his mother paid him. We want to establish that this is not the case and that Monnier was not thinking of this at all. Another argument that has been made against Monnier could be formulated as follows: 'You talked about having your sister put in a nursing* home, so you knew that she was poorly cared for; you did not have the courage to insist on your mother until she consented; that is why we accuse you of complicity with her.' But what everyone seems to have forgotten is that Monnier had spoken to his mother about this endeavour as early as 1883. However, at that time, his sister was not in the state in which we found her last May; this is established by the depositions of the doctors. If Monnier had insisted at the time that his mother do something (his intelligence still allowed him this), it was because he understood that there are facilities where the mentally unstable can receive the sort of care that one is unable to provide at home. So yes, he is guilty of not having insisted more forcefully and for a longer period of time, but no, he is not guilty since he had no duty of responsibility to his sister and, moreover, he believed her well cared for by his mother and the maids his mother employed.

I come to the last question of fact, the one that interests this court the most, in short, since it is no longer a question of discussing my client's intentions, but of noting the materiality of the facts. I maintain that at no time, particularly during the last days of his mother's illness, did Monsieur Monnier receive a mandate from Madame Monnier to act and, consequently, to make him responsible for his sister. The maids are not suspected of any malice towards the defendant, yet they said that Marcel Monnier did not give them any orders and that they did not ask him for anything, neither laundry nor anything else. Marcel Monnier had no idea as to where the keys were kept. He had zero authority in the house as always. He was not granted any authority when he was allowed to visit and therefore could not have had any legal responsibility to anything or anyone in that house.

It was six o'clock.

Gassan: *The court will not sit for any longer today. Maitre Barbier, how much longer do you require?*

Barbier: *Monsieur le President, I have come to the question of law, which I believe the Court intends to postpone until tomorrow.*

Gassan: *Yes, it is now a question of whether we can conclude tomorrow.*

Barbier: *I hope so. I shall speak for three quarters of an hour, confining myself to laying down the principles of law and reserving to apply them to the facts when I have heard the*

Advocate General.

Gassan: *Very well. I declare that this hearing is now adjourned and postponed until tomorrow at half past one o'clock.*

The public left the room calmly, some of them discussing Maitre Barbier's points.

Marcel Monnier was escorted out of the Palais de Justice by the gendarmes. He was taken via the same route he had followed during his trial in October. He was taken through la Salle des Pas Perdus and out through the door that was reserved for the court judges, located in the right wing of the building.

About two hundred people were gathered in the Palais Square, but when the carriage and the four mounted gendarmes set off at a gallop towards the prison, only three individuals mustered the effort to shout insults at Marcel Monnier.

The Appeal – Day 2
Friday, November 15th, 1901

Marcel Monnier left the prison on Friday, November 15th, at one o'clock in the afternoon. As had been the case the day before, he was escorted by a troop of mounted gendarmes. The coachman, following instructions, made the horses gallop all the way to the Palace of Justice along the Rue du Marché. Unlike other times Monnier had been taken to court, there were hardly any people lining the streets.

There were only a few members of the public attending the trial, hoping to see justice done. The trial was taking place in the second, smaller courtroom, reserved for appeals. At one-twenty, the lawyers and judges entered the courtroom. After everyone was seated, the floor was given to Maitre Barbier who resumed his argument. The defence lawyer presented a summary of the arguments he was going to develop:

Barbier: *Defence for Monsieur Marcel Monnier, accused, appellant. We intend, if it pleases the court:*

To say and judge that it has in no way been proved that Monsieur Marcel Monnier acted with criminal intent in the facts attributed to him, either as a co-perpetrator or as an accomplice, and that his lack of wrong-doing is evident from a cursory glance at the documents of the case;

To say and judge that, in order to constitute the offence of violence or assault under Articles 309 and 311 of the Criminal Code, it is necessary, apart from the guilty intention, to prove:

1. That there has been an act of material violence;

2. That this act was committed directly against the body of a person;

3. That the act actually caused that person, either by the effect of direct contact or by the effect of a violent impression, suffering or physical harm (the attempt is not punishable);

4. That because of the degree of violence and the seriousness of the physical harm caused by it, this act falls outside the category of light violence;

To say and judge that Monsieur Marcel Monnier did not by himself commit against his sister any violence or assault that could make him as the main author or co-author incur the penalties of articles 309 and 311 of the penal code.

To say and judge that the lack of care heard, of which Mademoiselle Blanche Monnier would have been a victim, cannot be legally attributed to Monsieur Marcel Monnier who never had any authority in his mother's house, even in the last weeks before his arrest;

To say and judge, in all cases, that the lack of care cannot constitute the offence of Articles 309 and 311 of the Criminal Code;

To say and judge that it has not been proved, either from the point of view of the material element or from the point of view of the intentional element, that Mademoiselle Monnier's mother, Madame Monnier (or any other principal author) voluntarily committed violence or assault against Mademoiselle Blanche Monnier, in particular during the last six weeks preceding the information and during which would take place, according to the order for reference, the acts of complicity attributed to Monsieur Marcel Monnier by the judgment;

To say and judge that Mademoiselle Blanche Monnier would have been only the victim of a lack of care on the part of Madame Monnier mother;

To say and judge that Monsieur Marcel Monnier did not participate in the alleged offence allegedly committed by Mademoiselle Monnier mother (or by any other principal perpetrator) by any act falling within one of the three cases of complicity exhaustively provided for in Article 60 of the Criminal Code;

To say and judge that it is not proved that the only acts or negligence in which Marcel Monnier would have part-icipated, by pure hypothesis, as author or co-author or as an accomplice, in the period to which the indictment chamber limited its possible liability, caused Mademoiselle Blanche Monnier, either by the effect of direct contact, either by the effect of a violent impression or otherwise, the evil necessary for the existence of the offence provided for in Articles 309 and 311 of the Criminal Code;

Consequently, to overturn the judgment rendered by the correctional tribunal of Poitiers, October 11th, 1901. Remove the accused from the prosecution without costs. In the alternative, order for such a hearing as the court may please, the re-hearing of all or part of the witnesses already heard and such persons other than the Public Prosecutor's Office or the defence shall believe that it is necessary to have summoned.

All rights, means and costs in this case reserved.

Gassan: *Your points are duly noted.*

Barbier: *In conclusion, I will now outline my criticism regarding the judgment of the criminal court, which I find to be cruel, barbaric and unreasonable. If only for this lack of reason, the judgment should not be upheld by the court.*

According to the articles of the Criminal Code, at no time has Monsieur Monnier committed a violent act, that is to say an external or aggressive act; one that is essential for the articles to be applied. The offence of violence or assault does not exist. Under no circumstances can Marcel Monnier be held to be complicit in what can be blamed on his mother. There is an obvious solution. I appeal to the reason and conscience of each judge in this court, and I implore you to base your judgment on the true intention of the accused.

I will not speak of what Marcel Monnier and his family has suffered, nor of the pain inflicted on them by the public; a crowd which acted in anger at the way they believed an innocent person had been treated. As we now know, it was a crowd which had been led astray by a great deal of false information, so that that very crowd's overexcited passions ultimately led to this man, another innocent, being treated badly. Now, in asking you to restore this man's freedom and good name to him, I would also be tempted above all to say to you: Apologise to him, this most unfortunate of men.'

Maitre Barbier took his seat.

There was suddenly a lot of heated talk in the public section of the room.

It was three o'clock. The hearing was adjourned for five minutes, and the lawyers filed out in silence. Those five minutes stretched to ten minutes, then to twenty minutes, then to half an hour, then to forty minutes. Eventually, the court hearing resumed at a quarter to four.

Gassan: *I am about to give the floor to Advocate General Marquet. It may seem surprising that the representative of the Public Prosecutor's Office should be allowed to speak after the defence today, but that is the order of things as proposed by Article 190 of the Criminal Investigation Code, even if this order is not always observed. Simply put, the defence always has to be able to reply and, therefore, have the last word.*

Advocate General Marquet stood up and faced the room.

Marquet: *Here we are, gentlemen, at the end of this lamentable affair, on which everything has been said and everything has been written. When I say that everything has been written, I mean it to include the vivid descriptions of the violent attacks, driven by exaggerated feelings, that the public launched against the accused. I also mean the excesses to which the newspapers ran, before, during and after the trial, using their pages to label as murderers the judges who were merely doing their duty and nothing but their duty. So, all I ask is that all of that distracting noise is stopped at the door of this courtroom and that you simply examine, in good conscience, the facts that have just been submitted to your jurisdiction.*

I wish to make it clear to everyone here exactly who it is that bears the responsibility for the near-death, yes, that is what the doctors claim, the near-death of Mademoiselle Blanche Monnier. It is, as has already been decided by this court that those responsible are Madame Louise Monnier and Marcel Monnier.

As for the accused, he demonstrated, by repeating statements we all heard at the hearing, that he was neither the minus habens, the half-wit, nor the 'naïve fool' that his friends, so hastily and so self-righteously, presented him as. They made a concerted effort to create a myth of inability and incapability around the very honourable Marcel Monnier.

Which brings us to matters of personal cleanliness. Was the defendant, as has been claimed, ignorant or unmindful of hygiene? There are several letters from Marcel Monnier to his parents, in one of which he provides them with methods for getting rid of bedbugs. His sister lived in disgusting filth, but in another letter, Monnier writes at length on the essential rules of cleanliness he was teaching his daughter, Dolores. There is a particularly suggestive discrepancy there.

It is also said repeatedly that he is deprived of sight to the extent he cannot identify friends standing in front of him in the street; that his eyesight is so weak that he bumps into servants, unaware that they are there. Yet we find, in letters to friends he mentions that when he was on the Basque Coast, he had travelled to San Sebastian for the day in order to see the King of Spain pass through the town. He also painted many watercolours and, in another letter, he recounts how while painting, nature unfolds before his amazed eyes. In another letter, he even goes so far as to state the following words: 'There are lots of very pretty Spanish women here who impress me and who dazzle my eyes with their beauty.'

No, do not try to make me underestimate the ocular power of a man who is able to read his diary or a newspaper in his sister's room where the closed and sealed shutters permanently block out the daylight! The truth is so glaringly obvious. He almost gave it away when he stated that he was unable to see his sister's thin arm as he was pulling that firecracker that was talked about yesterday. But won't we, like he has done, insult the judges of this court, if we believe that they believe such things?

I wish to counter the testimonies of some of those people who came to the stand to defend the accused. Everything they had said about Monnier's sense of smell was imbued with exaggeration. Marcel Monnier's friends have protected him too much, that's the truth! Moreover, Marcel Monnier was always very well aware of his guilt, because on the day before his arrest, he hastily tried to get witnesses to support his assertions that he had cared deeply for his sister. One person he tried to do this to was Modeste Bourliaud, from whom Monnier try to obtain a testimony that would have presented him in a positive light; in short, as a responsible and caring person.

I now turn to the question of whether Madame Louise Monnier, on the day she fell ill, had given her son instructions regarding the care of Mademoiselle Blanche Monnier. Undoubtedly, it is not a power of attorney as is given in the recognised legal form; but from the statement made by the defendant himself, it is clear that Marcel Monnier, when his mother was bedridden, was given a set of tasks pertaining to the care of his sister – and that he in turn gave certain orders to the servants. This is how the defendant who, just yesterday, exclaimed at the hearing (when the presiding judge asked him if he would have been able to intervene, in the event that he had realized the situation of Blanche). He said: 'I refused to accept any such responsibility.' Of course, one cannot refuse to accept something unless it has been given. Therefore, the mandate from his mother is a certainty, not probably unlimited, *because it did not extend to an absolute power, but it was a clear instruction to watch over his sister, because during his mother's illness the son became the head of the house. What were his duties? What should Marcel Monnier have done? At the very least he should have ensured the cleanliness of his sister? He knew that cockroaches swarmed over his sister's bed and onto her body, and yet despite the maid informing his wife, and his wife informing him, he proclaimed disbelief. Surely if his wife informed him of such a thing, with his poor eyesight, he would have been unable to verify it for himself, and therefore have believed what his wife told him and acted quickly to alleviate his sister's suffering.*

And what of the food? We were told that the suppliers brought meals into Louise Monnier's home, but where did these meals go? They did not find their way to the unfortunate Blanche Monnier, ever; her state of appalling emaciation is the clear proof of that. Why didn't anyone watch Mademoiselle Blanche during meals, to make sure she ate properly? Why didn't Marcel Monnier act responsibly when he was with his sister? Why did he close the room door no matter what time of year it was? Didn't he need the extra light an open door provides to read by? Did he believe that the maids hired to care for Blanche had no right to see her naked?

Finally, we must examine the question of law and be aware of the distinction between acts of commission and acts of omission. The definition of assault punishable by Article 311 of the Criminal Code is that they are 'acts likely to endanger the security or liberty of a person'.

Here is an example to illustrate my point: A driver starts driving along the road in a car. He is in a race and he wants to win. In order not to waste time, he drives over and crushes someone standing in his way in the road. He did not intend to kill when he started the race, but he was aware that he was killing as he drove. Isn't he therefore reprehensible? The same is true of Marcel Monnier. We know he is guilty, because this man said to a witness (Modeste Bourliaud): 'If you are asked, could you say that you know that I did everything for my sister and that I cared for her very well?' Isn't he the same man who threatened to file a complaint with the Public Prosecutor if the Central Commissioner attempted to search his mother's house to find his imprisoned sister? I am well aware that Marcel Monnier admits and denies both of these crimes – yes, they are both crimes – simultaneously, thereby making fools of us all, but if we have to choose between the words of Monnier and those of the Central Commissioner, the court will have to decide who seems the more honest. Judge him, gentlemen. For me the court's duty is the dispensing of justice, so your decision will be just, for you will uphold the law and dispense justice.

It was five-thirty. Maitre Barbier stood up in readiness to make his retort, but the Presiding Judge, after consulting the court, postponed the continuation of the proceedings until the next day. At the end of the hearing, the public was somehow sequestered in the salle des pas perdus because the doors had been closed to prevent any exit before the defendant was taken away.

Acquittal - Day 1
Saturday, November 16th, 1901

On Saturday, November 16th, between twelve-thirty and twelve-forty-five, a large crowd of the curious, as on the previous days, made their way along Rue du Marché to the foot of the steps of the Palais de Justice, hoping to witness Marcel Monnier's arrival at the court building.

At about five past one, the carriage carrying the defendant stopped, contrary to its usual practise, at the bottom of the grand staircase leading to the main entrance of the Palace, where there was almost no one waiting because the door of the courtroom had been opened to the public slightly earlier than usual. Members of the public had eagerly filed in and taken their seats, thereby missing Marcel Monnier's arrival until the gendarmes escorted him into the room and sat either side of him.

The hearing commenced at one-twenty and Counsellor Gassan, presiding, immediately gave the floor to Marcel Monnier's defence lawyer, Maitre Barbier, whose retort turned out to be, due to its scope, a second plea.

Barbier: *Gentlemen, if I was not afraid to see the words of a judge whose person and talent I admire interpreted as criticism, I would say that I was astonished to see how far the Advocate General has been prepared to go in the art of dodging responsibilities and not responding to the objections that have been presented to him. He took from the file only the testimonies or rather, the parts of testimonies that could serve his thesis a little and he completely ignored everything else. However, it is unacceptable that all of the facts and every statement should not be taken into account. We must take the whole and base our conclusions on that whole. That's what I have done.*

When we compare the witnesses retained by the public prosecutor and the witnesses I called to the stand, you will see there is a marked difference. Among the first he called was Jacob, whose testimony is the only one to attribute words of anger that Madame Monnier used against her daughter. The witness was able to recall these words, which he would have heard in 1892 and repeat them verbatim; that is without forgetting a single word. Unfortunately, because Jacob was driven to avenge himself against Madame Monnier for her treatment of her daughter, whom he liked, he simply got confused.

The Public Prosecutor also relied on the testimony of the two maids, Eugénie Tabeau and Juliette Dupuis, whose morality no one has dared to defend. The Advocate General simply forgot that not only did they not take care of Blanche, but they took soldiers into her room to stare at the naked woman and perhaps to humiliate her.

The Public Prosecutor also made a number of derogatory comments about some of the expert witnesses called by the defence: the prosecution said that the witnesses had told implausible stories about Monnier, specifically about his poor eyesight, his lack of a sense of smell and his pronounced penchant for uncleanliness. These witnesses are experts in their medical fields, and enjoy good reputations that are above suspicion and there was simply no reason to question their word.

With regard to the casual use of the word 'avarice', used as a spurious claim concerning my client's motivation, let me say quite clearly that my client's conduct was not dictated by greed. Importantly, he never received a mandate or a set of instructions from his mother.

The crime of violence presupposes a positive act. I cannot abuse the benevolence of the court any more, since I no longer have an opponent. For too long in this case, it is emotions that have spoken; your calm and rational judgment, gentlemen, rather than unchecked emotions, will allow the citizens of our country to see what truth is, and to know that justice has been meted out.

Gassan (addressing the accused): *Do you have anything to say?*

Monnier: *No, I have nothing to add to the words of my defence lawyer.*

Gassan: *The court will now deliberate.*

The counsellors retreated to the back of the podium to discuss their decision. Two minutes later, they resumed their seats.

Gassan: *This case is under advisement. The judgment will be delivered next Wednesday. This hearing is now adjourned.*

It was two-thirty-five.

Acquittal – Day 2
Wednesday, November 20th, 1901

Four days later, on Wednesday, November 20th, 1901, at one o'clock in the afternoon, a very large crowd gathered in the smaller courtroom to hear the judgment. The court officials entered at twenty minutes past one, and the hearing commenced.

Counsellor Gassan, presiding, stepped up to the stand to make an announcement.

Gassan: *I regret to inform you that this court has to consider another case first, which means that the judgment in the Monnier case will be delivered only after the conclusion of that other hearing.*

There were a few groans. Most of the public were disappointed. Many opted to leave the building, unsure of how long the other case would go on for. Outside the room, the conversations were very lively and quite a few people pondered the reason for the delay. Someone pointed out that two counsellors who had sat at the trial were absent from the hearing and so it was likely that the drafting of the text of the judgment had not yet been completed.

The hearing was called at just after four o'clock. At four-fifteen, Counsellor Gassan, presiding, read out the judgment to a totally silent room.

Gassan: *It is our judgement which follows from the investigation and the testimonies that the internment or sequestration of the young lady named Blanche Monnier was likely necessary because of her deteriorated and deteriorating mental state;*

That, during the first years of this internment or sequestration, she did not lack the necessary care, but that after the death of her father (and although some documents and especially the Will of the widowed Louise Monnier testify that she had affection for her daughter; affection that was intermittent and not always obvious as affection) Blanche Monnier was left, for many years, in a room without air and without light, on a filthy and vermin-infested mattress and in a state of uncleanliness impossible to describe;

That, if an abundant and even expensive diet seems never to have been lacking, the complete absence of supervision and care rendered such care useless, and that, without the timely intervention of the police and the judges of this court, the barbaric way she was being treated would not have taken long to have a fatal outcome for her;

Whereas these facts have precisely aroused public disapproval and impose on the memory of the widowed Madame Louise Monnier a moral responsibility whose gravity cannot be exaggerated;

But whereas, more particularly, as far as Marcel Monnier is concerned, the facts of the case cannot fall within the scope of a penal provision;

That it is not possible to understand an offence of violence or assault without violence;

That no such act is established against Monnier and even against his mother, apart from the acts of confinement, the principle of which has been rejected by the Indictment Chamber, and that, if some jurors think that an offence of omission may sometimes replace it, it is only as far as this omission relates to a duty legally incumbent on its author.

Whereas it does not appear that Monnier ever had any authority vis-à-vis his sister;

That, no more in the last weeks of her life than before, Madame Louise Monnier would not stand for any assault on her absolute authority, especially from her son, who did not live with her, whom she did not love and whom she disinherited;

That the tasks which she had entrusted to him, during her period of illness, namely, to watch over his sister, does not imply any abandonment of this authority; it is not, moreover, established that any such authority was given;

That Monnier has always denied it and that the formal testimonies, both the acts of the servants who should have been used for his execution are clearly exclusive of it;

That in any case, it is in no way demonstrated that it was with a conscious and deliberate will that the accused would have participated, either as a co-perpetrator or as an accomplice, and by supposing them legally criminal or criminal, acts for which his mother appears to have been solely responsible;

That Monnier never exercised any direct violence against his sister. There were simply omissions of care and supervision, and a lack of cleanliness and hygiene. Negative facts cannot be regarded as constituent elements of the offence. In other words, violence, as provided for in Article 311 of the Criminal Code, must always be an act of commission and cannot be the result of an omission;

That, no doubt, despite his infirmities, which are also partial, it is not possible to believe that Monnier ignored the lamentable state in which his sister found herself, and that the purely passive role to which he thought he had to resign himself and his cold impassibility, which did not inspire any effective approach, deserve the most severe reprimand; that his conduct, not falling, nevertheless, within the scope of the criminal law to which the judges cannot substitute, it is necessary for the court to pronounce his acquittal.

By these reasons, we have considered the judgment rendered, on 11th October 1901, by the Criminal Court of Poitiers, and find that he was misjudged, and according to the said judgment and doing what the first judges should have done, and without there being any need to do otherwise to uphold the submissions filed, we dismiss Marcel Monnier of the facts of the case, without costs.

After the acquittal order had been pronounced by the court, the public left the courtroom peacefully. There were some whispers, but there was no shouting of threats or insults.

Marcel Monnier was returned by carriage to the prison, in order to collect his possessions.

As a free man, he left the Prison de la Visitation via the main gate at five o'clock in the afternoon in the company of his defence lawyer, Chief Advocate Édouard Barbier.

What the Newspapers Said (2)

The press reported Marcel Monnier's acquittal without bothering with the legalistic principle. The question of Monnier's responsibility became a non-subject, as it was too difficult, due to the many legal subtleties, to truly know whether or not he was guilty. However, his acquittal at least allowed the newspapers to criticizing the attitude of the judges, and by analogy, the judicial system of France.

A journalist for *Le Gaul* wrote: *'I am very pleased for him. The trial judges were led by their emotions; the appeal judges were led by a sense of justice and are to be congratulated; for, in these times in which we live, the judge who shows independence compromises his future and, more often than not, ruins his career.'*

Le Soleil said: *'This result provides the best proof that the sentencing judgment passed by the criminal court of Poitiers was only a lamentable backlash from local political pressure.'*

In an article published on November 21st, *Le Courrier de la Vienne* said: *'We feel great joy at finally witnessing the revenge of law and truth; joy especially to note that there are still judges in France who make sure that the overwrought emotions and hot-headed treachery do not cross the court's threshold. They judge according to reason, according to the principles enshrined in law. They remain deaf to the sounds of the public and listen only to their conscience.'*

In an article entitled 'A Judicial Infamy', *La Libre Parole* criticized the judges: *'They contrived to keep an innocent person in prison for six months. If there was no law broken, how then can the judges have prosecuted him? In fact, how did they find judges in the chamber of indictments willing to refer him to the criminal court? And how did these correctional judges convict a man they had no right to judge?'*

Le Figaro wrote: *'The court of Poitiers – no more than those who protested against the prosecution – did not intend to excuse the incredibly weak, the sadly indifferent, brother of the 'sequestered of Poitiers'. However reprehensible the acts of the defendant may have been, he can only be punished for the offences that are specified and punishable by law.'*

In 'Distributive Justice', published in *La Lanterne*, a journalist wrote: *'Public opinion which applauded the conviction will now rage in fury at the appeal judges. No doubt we will hear that, once again, occult influences have triumphed over justice; that a judiciary that is only concerned with class interests, and one capable of being guided by worldly or political considerations, and one causing a scandal by delivering a judgment such as this, is decidedly an institution of another age, condemned to disappear the day when democracy is fully liberated from the past...'*

La Dépêche du Centre, published in Tours, said: *'We heard that the majority of the counsellors at the court of Poitiers were clerical and reactionary. But it had not occurred to us that clericalism could be master and lord of the judge's conscience to the point of making him overcome the columns of Hercules of the most outrageous iniquity.'*

Le Réveil du Centre, a newspaper that circulated in Limoges, said: *'Marcel Monnier is acquitted. We will not investigate the degree of responsibility of Blanche Monnier's brother in the sad affair that has fascinated the country. Nevertheless, we must make one observation: it is that French justice is increasingly failing and, like the other outdated institutions of the old bourgeois society, feels the contempt the public have for it. Thus, here is an innocent man; a man who was arrested, thrown in prison by the prosecutor's office, tried, convicted, imprisoned by the trial judges and acquitted by the appeal judges. There is no excuse, no matter what anyone says, for similar misdeeds of injustice.'*

La Libre Parole said: *'Shame on those small-minded judges who allowed themselves to be influenced by the prosecutor's office and those of the criminal court who have just been refuted by the appeal court.'*

In an article published on November 23rd, *Le Courrier de*

la Vienne itemised the many incorrect news items about the Monnier case published by *L'Avenir de la Vienne*: 'We remember every horror, every cruelty reported at the time by *L'Avenir de la Vienne*, first of the discovery of the poor sequestered woman, and then other related news items. Above all, we would remind our readers that all of those abominable stories were based on misinformation and erroneous facts. To make matters clear, we report the following: There is no Prisoner of Poitiers. Blanche Monnier was never locked up to prevent her marrying a young man with no fortune. Nor did she lose her mind as a result of kidnapping and years of incarceration in a shuttered room. It is equally false to say or write that the unfortunate woman had been left abandoned and starved to death, so that an unscrupulous old woman could inherit her legacies. All of these so-called 'facts' have been found to be false, first by the judgment of the Indictment Division and then by the judgment of the Criminal Appeals Chamber.'*

Generally, the newspapers reported the case in one of two quite distinct ways: either Marcel Monnier was innocent and those who had imprisoned him deserved all the rigours of the law that they themselves did not know how to apply, or else the Court of Appeal judges had obeyed corrupt considerations that were unworthy of their office.

For most people, the Monnier affair was over. The former sub-prefect, by letting his sister languish on a filthy, vermin-infested mattress, did not elicit sympathy, but the principle of legality, the law of offences and penalties that was the fundamental condition of individual freedom and security, had been respected.

No matter what lies, threats and delaying tactics Marcel Monnier had tried to use on Pierre Bucheton, no matter what he had admitted to the investigating judge, no matter what several maids had testified he had done, in law, Marcel Monnier was innocent.

Aftermath – Marcel Monnier

When he was released from prison, Marcel Monnier was a diminished man; the six months he had spent in prison had worn him out. The trial and the prison sentence had left indelible marks on him and he struggled to get back into his habits. Although he was acquitted, Marcel Monnier was considered morally suspect in the eyes of the vast majority of the population.

The formidable journalist, Granier de Cassagnac, summed up this opinion in the concluding sentence in his article in the newspaper, L'Autorité: 'Assuming that he is not guilty, he remains absolutely repugnant.'

During his first day as a free man, Thursday, November 21st, Marcel Monnier received some close friends who came to share with him the satisfaction they felt with the judgment of the court of Poitiers. He continually refused to meet the press.

It was only in the evening that his wife agreed to receive a few journalists in her living room for half an hour.

Journalist: *Will Monsieur Monnier continue living in Poitiers or does he plan to leave the house that is located so closely to the prison from which he has just been released?*

Angèle Monnier: *In a few hours, my husband will leave Poitiers, but you will understand why I cannot at this time tell you the place of retreat he has chosen for himself.*

Journalist: *What are your plans regarding your sister-in-law?*

Angèle Monnier: *We will immediately ask for Blanche's ban [the legal action that deprives an adult of the free disposition and administration of their own property], the formalities of which will not take very long since everyone knows what state the unfortunate woman is in. As soon as that judgment is rendered, we will have her put in a nursing home.*

Journalist: *There is a clause in Madame Louise Monnier's Will which reserves for her daughter a suite of rooms on the second floor of her house, and which provides her with the care of one or two nuns.*

Angèle Monnier: *It was once thought that it would be*

possible to put Blanche in her mother's house under the super-vision of one or two devoted people. Unfortunately, this is not possible, as my husband has been subjected to such serious ac-cusations that we feel we no longer want to take responsibility for the treatment and care the poor deranged woman; if any misfortune were to befall her, we would be blamed again and that is something we want to avoid.

The next day, Marcel Monnier, accompanied by his wife and daughter, took the train to Saint-Jean-de-Luz, to his ocean-front villa in Ciboure.

The invigorating air of the Basque Coast soon restored his vitality and enthusiasm. He resumed his long walks and began painting watercolours again, seemingly untroubled by myopia.

He remembered to send his defence lawyer, Chief Advocate Barbier, greetings cards on every national holiday and, at the time of the end-of-year gifts, sent him a present accompanied by a letter with a black border, because he was still in mourning for his mother:

Ciboure by Saint-Jean-de-Luz,
December 31, 1901

My dear friend, I wanted to present you with a small memento that might sometimes remind you of the most un-fortunate client, perhaps, that you have had to defend in your career, and who, with God's help, you were able to extract from the most appalling situation.
No doubt, all I can do and everything I can say will be a very weak expression of my immense feelings of gratitude; therefore allow me to offer you, in my name and on behalf of my wife, an Empire lamp, in bronze, which may serve at the same time as a vase; the object itself has little value, but I hope you will attach some value to it, if, as I dare to hope, you see in it the mark of a deeply touched and grateful soul. I cordially shake your hand.

Marcel Monnier.

P.S. – The lamp in question is shipped to you by a boutique in Biarritz.

The Civil Court met on 6th May 1902, with the same judges as before. The court ordered the liquidation of Louise Monnier's estate; the court valuer fixed the price of the various buildings, then Maitre Bodin, notary of the family, was instructed to proceed with their auction.

With the exception of the Le Pilet property, which was immediately bought by Marcel Monnier, each of Louise Monnier's properties was sold.

It is worth noting at this point that according to French law, Le Pilet, the property that Louis and Louise Demarconnay had bequeathed to Blanche Monnier, was, in 1902, legally available for Marcel Monnier to buy. The man who had pleaded poverty for most of his life, and who had, during his trial, repeatedly made a case that his personal lack of money was what caused him to have problems with his mother (therefore providing some of the mitigating circumstances to the crimes he was accused of), was suddenly able to find the very large sum of money needed to purchase a sizable country estate at the moment it became available to buy. This sudden availability of funds by a man with no income and no savings was never questioned by anyone and was only mentioned in passing in one newspaper.

Marie Fazy's sisters and brother were paid their allocated bequests. The share of money allocated to cover the costs of Blanche's permanent hospitalisation was deposited with her court-appointed guardian.

The sum that remained from the proceeds of the auction of Louise Monnier's properties, as well as the trunkful of money saved by Louise Monnier and stored in her room, the contents of which totalled ninety-eight thousand francs (eighty-six thousand pounds), went directly to Marcel Monnier.

To give an indication of its actual value, one thousand pounds in 1902 would be the equivalent to £157,000 today, thereby providing the former sub-prefect with a personal fortune that was the 1902 equivalent of what would be thirteen million pounds today.

Finally, in the last twelve years of his life, Marcel Monnier had the means to live a quiet and unassuming life.

A few years later, when his daughter, Lola, married a lawyer from Poitiers, Marcel Monnier was able to provide her with a very substantial dowry.

For the next few years, Marcel Monnier and his wife divided their time between the villa in Ciboure, where they stayed in the summer, and Le Pilet, where they lived for the rest of the year.

Marcel Monnier died on June 23rd, 1913, at Le Pilet, at the age of sixty-five. He was buried in the old cemetery of Migné. In his Will, he left all his money and property to his wife.

His wife died in Paris on October 15th, 1915, at the age of sixty-three; her grave is next to her husband's. In her Will, she left all her money to her daughter.

Aftermath – Blanche Monnier

Blanche Monnier remained at the Hôtel-Dieu for another year, during which time doctors completed the necessary formalities to commit her to a psychiatric hospital that could provide her the specialist care she needed.

On June 10th, 1902, Blanche was admitted to the Hospice Dessaignes, a public asylum in the city of Blois. Her administrative file included, in accordance with the provisions of the law of 30th June, 1838 on hospitalised insane persons, an application for admission from her guardian, Maitre Molant; a medical certificate issued by Doctor Faivre, from Poitiers, stated that:

> *'Blanche Monnier is suffering from childhood dementiawithattacksofaffectivelypemania[melancholy]and photophobic monomania [obsessive delirium)', requiring her to be sent to a specialist hospital.'*

An entry certificate was issued, for legal purposes, by the Prefect of Loir-et-Cher.

A former priory of Saint-Lazare, where lepers were treated in the Middle Ages, was the Hospice Dessaignes, in Blois. Since the Revolution, the priory had belonged to a succession of owners, until 1861, when it was redesigned as an asylum for the insane.

The buildings were then considerably enlarged thanks to the donations of Philibert Dessaignes, former deputy of Loir-et-Cher. The whole building was a regular, symmetrical and quite austere structure, although representative of hospital architecture of the second half of the nineteenth century.

When it was created in 1861, the director appointed to run the asylum was Doctor Lunier (1822-1885), who arranged the interior of the main building specifically for the care and treatment of patients of both sexes with mental illnesses and nervous disorders.

In 1880, the management of the establishment was entrusted to Doctor Lunier's nephew, Gabriel Doutrebente (1844-1911), a Doctor of Medicine from the faculty of Paris and member of the Medico-Psychological Society. Doctor Doutrebente directed the asylum until he retired in 1906. He was an eminent psychiatrist and during his time there he made the Hospice Dessaignes a model asylum.

Doctor Doutrebente advocated rapid hospitalization of the sick so as to treat them while there was still time. The chances of recovery were dependent on the patient having treatment from the beginning of the disease, in the acute period, before the transition to the chronic state, where unfortunately there was nothing more to be done. The healing virtues of the placement and isolation of the insane were well established. These were considered the most useful ways to combat mental illness.

Following the innovations of his uncle, Doctor Doutrebente multiplied the wards and their subdivisions at the Hospice. Patients were grouped into categories, which allowed doctors to get to know them better and give them the appropriate treatment. The creation of wards with a small number of patients also prevented the spread of contagious diseases, especially tuberculosis.

Blanche Monnier was a residential patient whose expenses were paid by her guardian, so she had her own room in the Villa Lunier where the paying patients were admitted. The cost was 2,400 francs per year, plus 1,000 francs for the service of a nun. The sum was large, but the income generated from the capital managed by Maitre Jules Molant was more than enough to cover Blanche's hospital costs.

Doctor Doutrebente examined Blanche two days after her admission, as provided for by law in 1838. In his notes, the doctor recorded what he saw as the signs of incurable madness:

> 'Suffering from chronic mania with inconsistency in words – loquacity and childish acts – deteriorated physical health – considerable weight loss.'

Fifteen days later, he issued a new medical certificate still in accordance with the law, where he confirmed his first impression: 'Suffering from chronic disease with inconsistency in words, and in deeds – to be maintained.' Blanche lived eleven and a half years at the Villa Lunier, without her mental state having improved. The register on which are mentioned, under her name, the monthly observations of the doctor, shows that she had visual and auditory hallucinations. In July-August 1906, she claimed she saw small goldfish on all the furniture; next to this observation the doctor noted: *'Mental debility close to imbecility.'*

During her time at the asylum, Blanche was a quiet and calm patient. There were no outbursts of violence or anger. She stayed mostly silent and seemed melancholy. Sometimes she would laugh aloud for no obvious reason. Blanche sat all day in an armchair playing with a doll. Despite the care provided by the doctors and the nuns, Blanche remained passive and silent.

From February 1910, Blanche began to exhibit signs of aggression. The doctor noted her behaviour:

> *'Sometimes excitable and rude. Her mental state is steadily deteriorating. She has become precocious, has started talking to herself, laughs uncontrollably, and her occasional hallucinations are manifesting themselves more and more frequently.'*

Very occasionally, Blanche would sit at the piano and pick out a tune, but from the middle of 1911 until the last quarter of 1912, she was mostly listless and unfocussed. She often just stopped playing and sat on the piano stool motionless until a nurse led her back to her room. By the end of 1912, she no longer showed any interest in the piano. She had once had a modicum of talent and some ability. Music had once had a soothing effect on her and it had captured her attention. Now it seemed to mean nothing to her.

Blanche Monnier died at Villa Lunier of acute pneumonia on 13th October 1913, four months after her brother's death. She was sixty-four years old.

Maitre Claude Archambault, who took over as Blanche's legal guardian when Maitre Jules Molant retired, made the arrangements, using some of the money from Blanche's entitlement.

Blanche's place of burial was in direct opposition to her mother's instructions which she had stipulated in her Will. She had stated:

'In the plot that I had built in Cimetière de Chilvert… upon her death, my daughter Blanche is to be buried there.'

It may have been a lack of awareness of the stipulations in Louise Monnier's Will that Blanche be buried in Poitiers, or a simple case of laziness or oversight on the part of a hospice administrator. It may have been that Claude Archambault chose the cemetery nearest to the Hospice Dessaignes for Blanche's burial out of simple expedience, or because it was a less expensive option than having Blanche's body transported one hundred and sixty-six kilometres (one hundred and three miles) to the Cimetière de Chilvert in Poitiers.

Whatever the reason, Blanche Monnier's grave is in the Cimetière Blois-Ville, Rue Pierre de Ronsard, Blois: Section G, plot number 187.

The End

Acknowledgements

I wish to express my heartfelt thanks to Paul Childers for the comprehensive and invaluable information that he provided me with regarding the properties and the effects of Potassium Bromide.

And I cannot thank Lauren Dent enough for her careful proofreading of this manuscript during its early draft stages – and for helping me get it into publishable shape.

Bibliography

Newspapers and Journals:

Chicago Tribune, Sunday, 14th July, 1901.
L'Avenir de la Vienne, 25th-31st May, 22nd June 1901, 27th
       September 1901, 6th-14th October 1901, 11th-17th
       November 1901, 21st-23rd November 1901, 4th
       January 1902.
L'Écho de Paris, 8th June, 1901.
La Vie illustrée, 7th June 1901, 21st June 1901.
Le Courrier de la Vienne, 25th-31st May 1901, 1st-23rd June
       1901, 22nd-23rd September 1901, 26th-28th
       September 1901, 6th-13th October 1901, 15th-17th
       November 1901, 21st-22nd November 1901.
L'Illustration, 1st June 1901, 12th October 1901.
Le Journal de l'Ouest, 9th October 1901.
Le Journal de la Vienne, 25th-31st May 1901, 1st-20th June
       1901, 22nd September 1901, 25th September 1901,
       27th September 1901, 6th-15th October 1901,
       14th-19th November 1901, 21st-22nd November
       1901, 4th January 1902.
Le Petit Journal, 16th June 1901.
Le Petit Parisien, 9th October, 1901.
Le Temps, 26th-27th May 1901, 11th-12th June 1901, 14th-
       15th June 1901, 17th June 1901, 19th June 1901,
       8th-14th October 1901, 15th November 1901, 17th
       November 1901, 22nd November 1901.
The New York Times, 9th June, 1901.

Books:

Augustin, Jean-Marie. *L'histoire veridique la Séquestrée de
       Poitiers*. Fayard, 2001.
Barbier, Édouard. *Observations pour M. Marcel Monnier
       addressées à la chambre des mises en accusation de la
       cour d'appel de Poitiers.* Poitiers, 1901.
Barbier, Édouard. *La Vérité sur la Séquestrée de Poitiers.*
       Poitiers, 1901.
Gide, Andre. *La Séquestrée de Poitiers*. Folio, 1997.

Janouin-Benanti, Viviane. *La Séquestrée de Poitiers: Une affaire judiciare sans precedent*. 3E Editions, 2015.

Labchir, Lara. *Lieben Verboten!* Körber, 2021.

Monnier, Marcel. *De la complicite en droit romain et en droit francaise*. Poitiers, 1872.

Simmat, Gérard. *La séquestrée de Poitiers, regards croisés: psychiatrique, médiatique, judiciaire*. Centre Presse, 2019.

Websites and blogs:

https://www.thevintagenews.com/2018/01/05/blanche-monnier/?chrome=1

https://www.nytimes.com/1901/06/09/archives/she-imprisoned-daughter-girl-kept-in-a-dungeon-twentyfive-years.html

https://m.daily-bangladesh.com/english/Blanche-Monnier-spent-25-yrs-locked-up-just-for-love/28332

https://drvitelli.typepad.com/providentia/2016/10/the-case-of-blanche-monnier.html

https://www.retronews.fr/journal/le-petit-parisien/9-octobre-1901/2/86872/1?from=%2Fsearch%23allTerms%3D%2522blanche%2520monnier%2522%26sort%3Dscore%26page%3D1%26searchIn%3Dall%26total%3D845&index=1

https://casocriminal.org/en/brutal-cases/blanche-monnier-held-captive-for-25-years-by-her-own-mother/

https://soapboxie.com/government/The-Disturbing-Tale-of-Blanche-Monnier-Locked-Away-for-25-Years

http://sequestreedepoitiers.free.fr/Famille.htm

https://www.retronews.fr/journal/l-echo-de-paris-1884-1938/8-juin-1901/120/601821/1?from=%2Fsearch%23allTerms%3Dblanche%2520monnier%26sort%3Dscore%26publishedBounds%3Dfrom%26indexedBounds%3Dfrom%26page%3D1%-

26searchIn%3Dall%26total%3D138721&index=14

https://the-line-up.com/blanche-monnier

https://daydaynews.cc/en/international/the-price-of-love-french-girl-blanche-was-imprisoned-by-her.html

http://welovewords.com/documents/blanche-5

https://gw.geneanet.org/gntstarmonnier-blan?lang=en&n=monnier&oc=0&p=marie+leonide+-pauline+blanche&on_register_success=1

https://www-lanouvellerepublique-fr.translate.goog/poitiers/un-nouveau-regard-sur-la-sequestree-de-poitiers?_x_tr_sl=fr&_x_tr_tl=en&_x_tr_hl=en&_x_tr_pto=sc

https://www.retronews.fr/journal/le-jour-nal-de-l-ouest/9-octobre-1901/2161/4796982/2?-from=%2Fsearch%23allTerms%3D-blanche%2520monnier%26sort%3Dscore%26pub-lishedBounds%3Dfrom%26indexedBounds%3D-from%26page%3D1%26searchIn%3Dall%26to-tal%3D138729&index=0

https://www.unilim.fr/trahs/3578
https://readcastle.com/blanche-monnier-the-woman-who-was-locked-in-an-attic-for-25-years-for-falling-in-love/

https://www.newspapers.com/newspage/350266105/

https://www.watson.ch/wissen/history/742994765-blanche-monnier-25-jahre-lang-von-der-mutter-eingesperrt

Printed in Great Britain
by Amazon

57566751R00155